i'm with *Stupid*

elaine szewczyk

NEW YORK   BOSTON

5 Spot
Hachette Book Group USA
237 Park Avenue
New York, NY 10017

Visit our Web site at www.5-spot.com.

5 Spot is an imprint of Grand Central Publishing.
The 5 Spot name and logo are trademarks of Hachette Book Group USA, Inc.

Book design by Stratford Publishing Services, a TexTech Company

Printed in the United States of America

First Edition: July 2008
10 9 8 7 6 5 4 3 2 1

Library of Congress Cataloging-in-Publication Data
Szewczyk, Elaine.
   I'm with stupid / Elaine Szewczyk. — 1st ed.
      p. cm.
   Summary: "A hilarious tale of girl meets boy, girl falls in lust, girl discovers boy is dumber than a box of hammers"—Provided by publisher.
      ISBN-13: 978-0-446-58247-6
      ISBN-10: 0-446-58247-6
      1. Man-woman relationships—Fiction.   I. Title.
   PS3619.Z49I4 2008
   813'.6—dc22
                                    2007039793

i'm with *Stupid*

Dla moich kochanych rodziców

acknowledgments

Thank you to my loving parents, Maria and Stanisław, and my brother, Robert; my grandparents Aniela and Stanisław Szewczyk and Anna and Jan Nieckula; my cousin Peter, who encouraged me when I needed him most (I can't confirm it, but I think he puts laugh pills in my potatoes—there's no other explanation for why I have so much fun when he's in the room); my cousin Bob, who always thinks there's time for Jack and Coke, and his family, Janka, Jacob, Thomas— and counting; my goddaughters Gabriella and Klaudia; and the rest of the family, including Andrzej, Maria, Jacek, Jasiek, Zbyszek, Zosia, Hania, and Krzysiek Szewczyk; Anna and Franek Szewczyk; Maria, Brigida, and Wiesiek Kraj; Helena, Jan, Ela, Grzesiek, and Piotrek Hodorowicz; Aniela, Józef, Dorothy, and Bernadette Luberda; Gienia, Józef, Daniel, Andrzej, and Ania Szewczyk; Gail, Wally, and Alex Szewczyk; Tadeusz, Maria, Robert, and Emily Nieckula; Józef, Czesława, Adam, Ewa, Sylwia, and Hania Nieckula; Wojciech, Teresa, Piotrek, and Paweł Nieckula; Ela and Staszek Dawiec; and dear family friends Teresa, Jan, and Tomek Piskorz. Thank you to my wonderful editor Caryn Karmatz Rudy and the 5 Spot staff, and to my agent, Jeff Kellogg. Finally, thank you to Renee Orvino and Danny Sciortino (our friendship inspired the energy of this book); Amarula Cream and the staff of Brown-Forman, especially Rick Bubenhofer; Maxime Cescau (known in at least one French village as "Le Sugar Shorts") and his gracious parents, Patrick and Ursula; Colleen Corrigan; former baby model Ryan Darrah; Elizabeth Einstein; Matt Englund; Katie Hasty; Charlie Hrebic; *Kirkus* colleagues, past and present, Andy Bilbao, Karen Breen, Molly Brown, Tracey Davies, John Kilcullen, Eric Liebetrau, and Chuck Shelton; Ryan Kniewel; Jerome Kramer; Walter Lamacki; Patty Lamberti (for getting me to SA) and Dan Swan (for getting Patty); Adam Langer; John Lerner; Kristin LoVerde; Pete Nawara; Susie Nevin (this woman needs a talk show, seriously) and her partners in crime, Andy, Lily, and Marytherese; Chris Orvino (how dare you, sir?) and little Johnny, who has one hot mama; Elizabeth Passarella; Project Jenny Project Jan; Mark Sadegi; Nikki Tait; Ted Waitt (!); Eric Wetzel; Teresa Wisniewski; Josh Yaffa; and to Mordecai Corbin, who explained without words. I'm glad you made that long journey to Beirut.

I want to live and I want to love.
I want to catch something that I might be ashamed of.

—"Frankly, Mr. Shankly," the Smiths

Chastity is as great a perversion as libidinousness . . .

—Manuel Narciso Lorenzo Hernandez y Sanchez,
addressing a disinterested passenger in a safari truck

part **One**

The flight to South Africa is scheduled to depart in approximately two hours. I am at the airport, waiting at the end of a long check-in line, when I see him from across the terminal: a lone police officer, pushing four enormous designer suitcases stacked on a rickety metal luggage cart. The cart's loose front wheels dart from side to side like the eyes of the village crazy. The cop is wearing a dark blue uniform and matching hat. There is a nightstick hanging from his belt and a shiny badge over his heart. His polished shoes are standard-issue black. When our eyes lock he removes the nightstick from its holster and begins rapidly swinging it in the air in a circular motion. A mother grabs the back of her young son's red suspenders and pulls the boy toward her. "Get out of the way, Jimmy!" she screams and shields his head.

I squint at the police officer then glance at my friend Libby, who is sitting beside me. She is perched on her suitcase, wearing sunglasses, her head tilted back like she's relaxing on a beach of fluorescent lighting. She turns over her piece of watermelon bubble gum, pops a pink bubble, then holds out the pack. "You want some, babe?" she asks in her lulling voice, the auditory equivalent of two NyQuil doses. "I bought a bunch of packs so our ears won't hurt from the cabin pressure." I tell her not yet and with my foot absently push her an inch closer to the counter. Just then someone taps me on the shoulder. I turn and flinch. It's the cop. "How goes it?" he asks. "Ready for our safari?" I do a double take. It's my friend Max. Um, he's a personal trainer, not a cop. Libby pulls her sunglasses to midnose. "Why are you dressed like that?" she asks. He frowns at her: "I don't know, Fonzie. Why are you wearing sunglasses in an airport? You need a job." It's true. Libby does need a job. She was laid off a few months ago and hasn't made progress in finding a new one. I have unemployment check envy. But now's not the time to discuss that.

Max twirls his nightstick like he's a Keystone Kop then gently pokes me in the stomach with it. "The reason I'm dressed this way is because I just came from Richard's apartment building," he explains.

Revulsion slowly spreads across my face like a blot of black ink on paper. Richard Stein is the guy I dated for two months. He made a fool of me this past Valentine's Day, which was just three days ago. I haven't fully recovered.

"I knocked on all his neighbors' doors," Max coolly continues. "I told some of them that Richard is under investigation for organ trafficking, I told a few others that he is a convicted flasher and that, if he is seen around the building in a coat, neighbors should under no circumstances make eye contact, although it would not hurt to say 'We know about you' under their breath as he passes. My crowning moment occurred at apartment Nine-C, where I told a sweet granny that Richard is running a retirement home scam. She was taking notes." He tips his hat. "He's not going to be popular there. You're welcome."

I put out my hands. My mouth falls open. Wait, what? Max puts the nightstick under my chin and manually closes my mouth. "I must have forgotten to tell you," he says. "Did I forget to tell you? Yeah, I'm getting revenge on Richard. I'm not going to physically injure him, just really, really annoy, confuse, and inconvenience him." He begins stripping off his uniform, underneath which he is wearing civilian clothes better suited for a sixteen-hour plane ride. "The plan is to loosen the screws in his brain just enough so that pieces start falling out and it hurts to think straight." He stuffs the uniform in a suitcase then removes two stacks of papers. He places one on each arm. Suddenly he looks like Moses via Charlton Heston holding up a pair of Ten Commandments tablets. "Okay, I have no time for you two right now," he says. "I have to pass out these flyers. On my right I have five hundred with Richard's name and phone number advertising cheap laptops for sale, fifty dollars or best offer, and on my left I have five hundred advertising Richard's male escort service. Yes, he has one. He just doesn't know it yet. And as long as you're asking I should mention that this morning I put up flyers on street lamps all over town advertising an open house at Richard's place and about fifty advertising sheepdogs and greyhounds for sale. I'd love to be there when people start calling him up." He tilts his head and lets out a burp, thoroughly pleased with himself.

"Gesundheit," Libby offers. I turn to her and ask if she knew about this. She crosses her legs and nods. "Kind of," she admits. "But not about the police thing. The other day I walked in on him while he was on the phone making doctors' appointments in Richard's name for oozing blisters or something."

Max corrects her: "It was bunions, not oozing blisters, although that's not bad, Lib." She blows a bubble. He points at her mouth. "You got gum?" he quickly asks.

She hands him the open pack she'd been holding. "You can have the rest," she tells him. "I bought a bunch for the plane."

He takes it and stuffs it in his pocket. "Thanks. I'll need this when we get back from South Africa," he says. "I can smear it on Richard's doorknob." He pauses. "Come to think of it, I'm also going to need Vaseline so I can grease the handlebars of Richard's bicycle and some itching powder so I can send it to him inside a greeting card."

I fold my arms over my chest. "What the fuck is going on here?" I ask. "Who are you all of a sudden, Red Buttons? Harpo Marx? You're going to send Richard *itching powder* inside a *card*?"

Max eyes me disinterestedly. "Uh-huh, sure am."

When I ask the obvious question—Shouldn't I be the one exacting revenge? I'm the one who dated Richard—Max responds that I would never properly exact revenge because I'm by nature too nervous of a person (this is true), and that, furthermore, I lack the creative vision for what he has in mind, something I do not doubt. He gives me a serious look. "Richard is . . . ," he starts to say.

Max is momentarily distracted by a cute guy dragging a compact navy suitcase. The guy stops in front of a monitor displaying departure times. He studies his ticket, then studies the monitor. Max addresses Libby. "Libbers," he says, "I need your help." She stands up. He pulls her closer. "Is that cool drink of water straight or is he—" He whistles instead of speaking the word. Libby fixes on the cute guy. She takes off her sunglasses. She puts her hands on her hips, raises a manicured eyebrow, and pushes out her chest. Max stares at her expectantly. For a gay man, he has a shocking lack of gaydar, whereas Libby's gaydar may as well be approved by NASA. She never misses. "He's one of mine," she quickly concludes and sits back down.

Max sighs with disappointment. I again try to get his attention. "Richard is what?" I ask.

He looks over at the cute guy one last time. "Richard," he

says, "is not an upstanding guy. He's a douche bag. He needs a valuable lesson, and I want to personally deliver it to him. He messed with your head, and now I'll mess with his." He tells us to watch his bags and walks off whistling with the flyers.

Well, Max is right about one thing: Richard is not an upstanding guy. It was shameful what I put myself through waiting on his call. Bear with me for a moment as I explain how it went down, and then it's off to Africa.

* * *

So there I am, on Valentine's Day, in quite a mood . . .

I am lying on my lumpy deathbed in my studio apartment staring up at the huge piece of poster board that I duct-taped to the ceiling, with the words DON'T CALL RICHARD (AGAIN), YOU BIG EMBARRASSMENT scrawled in black Magic Marker, when the phone rings. Music to my ears! I jump up to answer, praying that it's Richard. I check the caller ID. It's not Richard, it's my mother. Fucking Richard, useless noisy phone making all that noise. I get back in bed.

"Hello, Kas?" my mother calls out from somewhere inside the answering machine. "Do you light mood candles in the apartment? It's dangerous." Kas. My name rhymes with ass. I've always resented that. I cover my face with a pillow. I'm twenty-eight years old. If I want to fire up a mood candle, whatever that is, I'll fire up a mood candle. "I was watching the news. A woman left one of those scented mood candles unattended in her apartment and burned down the building. I'll call later. I love you."

I throw off the pillow. Valentine's Day is today, and I have not heard from Richard in fifteen days. They always get you just as you're letting down your guard. Fifteen days ago he's telling me he's never met anyone like me and the very next he's gone. Poof. If he doesn't call today then it's official—I've been rejected. Thank God we didn't sleep together because that would make this moment really painful. Okay, we slept together, you got me, but no one tell my mother because I'm still a virgin. Besides, it only happened once. Fine, three times, we slept together three times. But the third time was a misunderstanding, if only because I thought there'd be a fourth and fifth time. I'm glad we didn't have three misunderstandings because that would have meant sleeping with him four times, which would have amounted to multiple mistakes, not to mention a lot of confusing math. I just don't get how he could stop caring about me so fast. I should call him. I'm calling. I need an answer. No, I said I wouldn't call. I promised myself I wouldn't call. I put up notes all over my studio apartment telling myself not to call (again) ((I already called three times, once for each of the nights we had sex)) (((I figured that was reasonable))) ((((by the way, I don't roll around like a sweaty pig with just anyone. I really liked this guy—he was smart, we had chemistry)))). Anyway, after calling repeatedly and not hearing back I put notes on the toilet, on the TV remote, in the freezer . . . everywhere, to remind myself not to do it again—after all, I have dignity. I even got one sign custom-laminated for the shower. Cost me twenty bucks. I drained an entire Magic Marker on that sign. I should have put a sign near the phone, that would have made sense. Now I'll let him call me. That's what I'll do. He'll come around. He has to! I'm an attractive girl: light brown hair, light brown eyes. It's an interesting combo, even though it may not sound like much. I'm fairly slender, and I know how to dress for my body type—which is to say I know enough to wear pants to cover any cellulite. Not that I have . . . yes, I do, a little, more every day, to be fair. In any event, it's not like I'm shedding skin in clumps while my nose hairs grow wildly like octopus tentacles. My gums don't bleed; I have all my own fingernails—which I trim regularly, if that needs to be said. Other guys like me. They're always guys I don't want to like me but they're guys . . . Maybe he fell for me so hard he can't bring himself to call and tell me how hard for me he fell. He did mention that he loves kids. Maybe he wants to get married and have kids. I should call and tell him it's okay, people fall in love all the time (I don't, but people do). Unfortunately I'm not ready to get married but if we take it one decade at a time, maybe we can get married and have a child. I like kids. Well, that's an exaggeration. Not all kids. Are Haley Joel Osment, Dakota Fanning, and Lil' Bow Wow still kids? If they are then I hate kids. But I might eventually be talked into a kid if he takes care of it . . . Okay, gives birth to it. If that's not too much to ask . . .

I light a cigarette just as my apartment door flies open. In walks Max holding a DON'T CALL RICHARD sign. Max, that red bouncing ball in the otherwise static world. He thinks fast, he talks fast, he moves fast. "That cigarette smells," he informs me and fans his nose. "You might as well crap on yourself." I ash my cigarette. He gestures in my direction with the DON'T CALL RICHARD sign. "Why was this thing taped to your front door?" I shrug and sheepishly explain that sometimes I need a reminder not to call Richard before entering the house. Dignity! It's called dignity! I can't call a fourth time! He tears it in half and looks around the kitchen. I cringe. I hope he doesn't notice . . .

He points up at the light fixture. There's a sign tied to it instructing me not to call Richard (ever again) ((because I'm the asshole who already called three times)). "What's that up there for?" he asks with a frown. I give him a look. He slams the door and drops his gym bag on the floor. "Get up, fatty-back-fat," he says. "We're out of here in ten." Max, whose ass is so firm it could double as a regulation Olympic gymnastics mat for the Bulgarian team, has many flattering nicknames for me: triple XL, chunky chuck, muffin man, hog-gone-wild. I've heard them all. He claims that because I don't work out I should prepare myself for the verbal humiliation that will one day come with a soft midsection. I think he might be trying to motivate me and, you know what? It's not working. I'm a tremendous fan of banana crème pies. And you know what else I'm a fan of? The crispy skin on fried chicken. I want to find a restaurant that sells just that and then I want to live under the counter.

He drags a chair into the center of the kitchen, stands on it, and unties the DON'T CALL RICHARD sign. He tosses it on the table. "You have nine minutes to get up and get dressed, chop, chop," he orders. When I hesitate he impatiently runs a hand through closely cropped brown hair (Max has had the same military haircut since college; it suits him, and he knows it), then walks over to the bed. He widens his green eyes, which are framed by his best feature, long curly lashes (I think he has twice as many as anyone else), and leans in until our noses bump: "It's Valentine's Day. I have tickets to a concert. You're not staying in, we're going, it's not an option." It's never an option with Max. The man wears confidence like a tuxedo. The fact that he's short, that his nose is a bit too pointy (don't tell him I said that), that he has a crooked smile, doesn't prevent him from hooking better-looking men than anyone I know. Because with Max, you'll never be sure where the day will take you, and everyone wants to be around that kind of promise.

When I don't move he pulls something out of his back pocket and sticks it in my face. I lean back. What the hell? It's the brochure for South Africa he's been flashing at me at every opportunity, on the front of which is a lion frolicking in tall grass. "Are you packed yet?" he asks. I take the brochure and open it. Three park rangers wave at me from a safari truck; one of them is exceptionally good looking. I gaze at the ranger for a moment then hand back the brochure. I've never been on a South African vacation, much less one I didn't have to pay for. Max got the trip—three days on safari inside Kruger National Park, three more sightseeing in Cape Town—for free from his father. Max's father originally planned to take the trip with business partners. When scheduling conflicts intervened, he simply gave Max the tickets, the way I might pass someone a Kleenex. I guess rich people can do that.

As I reluctantly get up, Max plops down on the couch, which emits a long groan, followed by a longer yawn. "Babe, get off me," says Libby. "You're sitting on me." Ah, Libby. She's Max's cousin on his mother's side. They are both only children and bicker like siblings. Max introduced us during our sophomore year of college, and she's just been around ever since.

Libby has been on that couch all day, lying facedown on the cushions, arms and legs splayed like a skydiver whose chute never opened. She came by this morning to offer moral support in the form of baked goods and never left, which is just as well. Libby lives directly across the hall. "Babe, get off," she again pleads. Max doesn't budge. She begins struggling under him, contorting her body this way and that as if she were being electrocuted. He looks over his shoulder: "Oh, you again," he says, pretending to be surprised. "I thought you died last November in a tragic car accident."

"You saw me last night," Libby reminds him. Her mouth is pressed against the cushions. The words are slightly muffled. Max starts bouncing up and down on her like he's test-driving a mattress. "I thought that was your ghost," he informs her as she groans.

When he finally gets off she lifts her head and peers around the arm of the couch at me. Libby always looks good, even just after waking. She has pale, flawless skin, red rosy cheeks, long black curly hair wound like coils, and green eyes (like Max's but a little brighter). She's petite but curvy and has huge boobs. Huge. She likes to dress up in skirts and heels and won't leave the house without makeup. She's a girly girl, and the boys like her. In fact, guys often completely lose it around her. Last week, for example, she went on a date—bowling— and her date rolled the bowling balls for her so she wouldn't strain herself. Pretty funny, I think, particularly considering that she won the game.

"I had the weirdest dream just now." She pauses, then puts her head back down. "I dreamed that I swallowed a bar of soap and started flying around." A yawn. "What day is it today, Thursday or Friday? I forget."

Max grabs her by the wrists and pulls her off the couch. She begins to sway back and forth on three-inch red heels. "Get to your apartment and change," he commands her. "Eight minutes and counting. We're all getting laid tonight." At the sound of this Libby's eyelids begin to flutter like those of a patient emerging from a coma. Laid? Max gives her a nod as she shuffles toward the door: "By the way, it's not Thursday or Friday, it's Saturday." Libby crosses the threshold and turns around. "What is, babe?" she dreamily asks. "Never mind," he responds and slams the door. He walks back into the living room and heads toward the closet. "You know what?" he says to me, reaching for the closet door handle, "last time I was

here I think I left my Puma sweatshirt. Did you happen to—"
As soon as he opens the closet door ten DON'T CALL RICHARD
signs fall from the top shelf onto him—ones I didn't put up
because I ran out of space. He looks down at the floor then
back up at me. He puts his finger to his lips like he's thinking hard about something and furrows his brow. "Um"—he
points at my face—"get a life."

We arrive at the club's entrance an hour later. Libby, who
always takes a long time to get dolled up, had to try on a
dozen pairs of heels and a dozen outfits to go with them,
not to mention give herself a facial and tie up her locks with
a flowing pink ribbon. I take a pull off my cigarette and tell
them I'll meet them inside after I finish smoking. (I would
never discard an unfinished cigarette. Unheard of!) They nod.
Max opens the glass door. Libby turns to him. "So you really
think I should lie on my résumé?" she asks in wonderment.
"Of course!" he cheerily responds as the door closes behind
them. I move several feet from the entrance, lean against the
graffiti-covered brick wall, next to a pay phone, and take a
long drag. While watching the crowds walk by I recall the pep
talk Max gave me on the way over: It's stupid to get hung up;
there are plenty of men in this city; it's not rejection if I don't
look at it as rejection. Max is happy to remind anyone who
will listen that it's a do-it-yourself world: No one thinks highly
of a person who doesn't think highly of himself. Be confident
and fabulous no matter what. And he's right, which is why
I'm going to stop looking at my feet when I walk; I'm going to
raise my head and make eye contact the way Max has always
told me to do; I'm going to be more open-minded; I'm going
to smile at every man that passes—oh God, not that one.
Sorry, sir. Ouch, he was ugly, looked like some kind of serial
killer with that greased-back black hair and pockmarked face.

I hope he didn't think I was flirting with him. Anyway, whatever! Maybe it's better that I not be too open-minded. Still, life is okay. I have supportive friends, I have a dangerous yet satisfying smoking habit, I have sultry, smoky eyes—that's what I was told by Richard. And just because he doesn't want to see them anymore doesn't make them less smoky and sultry. Hell, my eyes are so smoky and sultry there's practically a blazing fire between my ears. And there are definitely cute guys to spy with my sultry—

Are my sultry eyes fucking with me right now?

What do I see? I'll tell you what I see. I see Richard, walking past me, lovingly holding some ugly girl's hand. I don't blink. What-the-fuck? He hasn't called in fifteen days. I can't believe him. And why did someone hit his date with the ugly stick? Geez, on closer inspection it looks like she got crushed by the whole forest. I'm better looking than her! This is too much—and she's too much. Look at that makeup job! And that short messy hair! And there he is. Richard, fucking Richard, wearing a gray coat and gray wool cap, looking all matchy matchy. It takes me a moment to recover. That no-good son of a . . . Hey! He never tried to hold my hand when we walked the streets.

Richard and Ms. Ghoul America walk past. They don't see me. When they get to the door of the club they begin giggling like idiots about something. What's so fucking funny? You want funny? I'll give you funny. I'll give you a laugh attack, just give me a second to toss this cigarette. I sneak up behind Richard as the ghoul opens the door. Richard, fucking Richard. I tap him on the shoulder. He turns and immediately goes pale. I give him my most convincing smile even though my entire body is starting to shake.

"Oh, hi," he says tentatively as the ghoul turns to see what's happening behind her. Richard looks back at her and then pushes, and I'm not exaggerating here, pushes her into the club, closes the door behind her, and just stands there, looking at me, while the ghoul stands inside the club, industrial-strength glass separating her from the philanderer of my dreams. "What are you doing here?" he casually asks.

"I'm going in," I say, still smiling stiffly. "My friends are inside."

"You're going to this concert?" he asks. I answer with a nod: this very one. "Who are you going to see?" he asks, as if he might catch me not knowing who is playing, as if I might realize my mistake, turn around, and leave. I look at him: "I'm going to this concert. Same as you."

"Weird," he says.

"It's not that weird," I point out.

I follow Richard into the club. He has no choice but to let me. The three of us, one big, loving family, are together at last. I don't give the girl a second look. I get my ID checked, hand over my ticket with trembling fingers, and move past them.

The club is divided into two sections: the bar on the first floor, the music venue on the second. I march upstairs to look for Libby and Max. I don't see them. There are people milling about, all conspiring to block my view. There's a stage loaded with instruments and musicians scrambling to tune them. I need a drink. Badly. I walk back downstairs to the bar. I stand at the very end, near the staircase. "A double whiskey on the rocks," I hear myself say. I've never ordered a double whiskey on the rocks, but there's a first time for everything. And I'm only hoping that rocks mean ice.

The bartender pours and hands me my drink. I down the

thing. "I'll have another," I say, wiping my mouth. "Keep those rocks this time. They're getting in my way."

"Should I bring the bottle?" he says with a hearty laugh. I think he means to be friendly, but now's not the time.

"Don't smirk, just serve," I warn him.

"Coming up," he says with a nod. He pours again and cautiously slides the drink toward me like a zookeeper unloading raw meat at feeding time. I take a sip of my second drink. Feels good. I entertain the idea of going back upstairs. But Max and Libby can wait. Richard can't. Something has come over me. "Hey, don't look so down," the bartender says. "Let me tell you a joke. Why did the lettuce blush?" I look at the other end of the bar and spot Richard. I don't care about lettuce.

I make my way past the long line of occupied stools. Everyone has their backs to me. I need a cigarette. Richard is sitting at the front of the bar, near the door, nervously cradling a drink. The ghoul has vanished. I bet she does that on occasion so she can rob graves. I take the opportunity to reintroduce myself. Remember me, fathead? Because I remember you. Come here often?

"Wow, this is really weird," he says. When I remind him that he already said that he apologizes for not calling me. I don't take my eyes off him when I lie that it's quite all right and that it's clear to me now why he didn't. Richard is silent.

"So where is she?" I ask, looking around for the sheriff of ghoul township.

"Oh, she's just a woman I recently met," he dismissively says.

I push hot air through my nostrils. This is getting old. If my competition were attractive I might be more interested. I clarify: "I didn't ask you who she is, I don't care who she is. I have some idea who she is. I was asking where she is. I don't want to make a scene. Wouldn't want to spoil your night." (Like you spoiled mine.)

Richard informs me that she's in the bathroom. "The bathroom," I repeat. I picture the ghoul desperately trying to make herself more attractive. She'd need a team of technicians slaving day and night with chisels and paint thinner but whatever. Not my problem. It's not like I'm sleeping with her. "So Richard"—I put my hand on the bar—"I wish you had told me you were dating someone new." Richard stares at me as if I were a wall. I continue: "I mean not that it matters anymore, because obviously it doesn't, but you fed me some serious lines, Richard. You told me you've never met anyone like me. And I—fuck, man, I'm a little embarrassed now—I think I believed you."

"It's complicated," he says, "and this is not the best time to discuss it." Oh, really? It isn't? This comment strikes me as especially annoying. Who is he to dictate when the best time is? "I don't know about you," he continues a bit uncomfortably, "but for me this was a casual thing."

Casual. Now it's casual? It wasn't casual before. Regardless, and I make sure to emphasize this next point loudly: "It's kind of odd when you tell someone 'I'll call you tomorrow' as you are leaving their apartment *right after having sex with them* and then *never call them again.* I mean what the fuck is wrong with you? How casual are you?"

Richard thinks about this, or at least pretends to. "Well," he says, looking behind him at the bathroom door, "I think we're better off as friends. I realized it wasn't going to work out, don't take it the wrong way." I shift my weight from one foot to the other. Richard seems a tad distracted by that bathroom door. He continues: ". . . It's just hard to have serious conversations with you. It's always about some joke with you. Don't take it the wrong way . . ."

Where is this even coming from? I stomp my foot, then start rambling to save face: "Slow down, Richard. What, you think everything is a joke to me? You never had a problem before. What do you want to talk about: Armageddon, nuclear waste, Bulgarian orphanages? Why would I want to talk about that shit? Am I campaigning? . . ."

Richard rubs his forehead. "See, there it is again," he curtly observes.

"What is 'it'?" I ask, incredulous. "*It's' how my mind works—* 'it's' called personality. How do I change who I am? Everything is a joke to me? Do I look like I'm laughing now? Because I'm not." My chest starts to heave and at this point the words are just coming out, I have no control over them. "I'll tell you what the biggest one-liner of them all is, man, it's you and your clown-faced girlfriend who puts on lipstick with a paint roller during an earthquake in front of a fun-house mirror."

Richard again glances at the bathroom door. "You—" he starts to say.

I cut him off. "What? I what? Please enlighten me. Because that last bit you delivered was news to me." I take a drink of whiskey. My hand is shaking. I urge him to go on. I'm listening. "Perhaps it's a problem of garrulity," he says. I stare at him. Grrrrrrr what? "You talk too much," he says in a whiny voice. "Everything is about you. I don't feel like I'm being heard."

I lower my cup. Who talks too much? I talk too much? I talk too much! What am I talking too much about? "Richard," I say, "let me ask you a question. What's the name of the company I work for?" Richard just stares at me and shrugs. "Uh-huh," I continue. "Good answer. But I, I know the name of the company you work for. And do you know how I know that?" He again shrugs disinterestedly. "Because the last time we went out you talked about your job *for three hours straight!*"

Richard makes a face and again rubs his forehead. I've always hated that big forehead. The forehead talks too much. All of a sudden I realize that Richard is not at all attractive—it's like someone flipped a switch. His hairline looks like it's receding, his brown eyes are too close together.

I look beyond his shoulder and see the ghoul. She's coming toward us. I look back at Richard. I consider pouring my drink over his head but don't. I'm better than this; I'm out of here.

I start to turn around but can't get out of there fast enough. The ghoul is now upon us and seems intent on a chat. She demands to know what is going on. I try ignoring her. Obviously she feels threatened because, unlike some people, I actually combed my hair before showing up to the club. "Nothing," I mumble in her direction, "I was finishing up with your boyfriend, I'll be on my way."

"He's not my boyfriend," the ghoul abruptly states. I look at her. Man, does she have too much makeup on. I can see the right angles of foundation. The ghoul thrusts out her cat-woman nails in my direction. I take a step back. Easy, my dear, I'm not here to fight you. My eyes trail upward, in the direction of her thick wrist. I am staring at a colored glass bead. What is it, a memento from Cancún spring break? You know, people will buy anything after consuming a tray of Jell-O shots . . .

"I'm his fiancée, Noreen," she clarifies. "Richard and me are getting married next month. Who are you?" I hear Richard grumble that the grammatically correct way of saying it is *Richard and I*, not *Richard and me*.

Fiancée? I look from the ghoul to Richard and try to process what just happened. I point out that Richard just got through telling me that they had only recently met. Is that not true?

Upon hearing that she just met her fiancé the ghoul drops her left hand to her side. I'd get that ring appraised if I were her. She gives him a hard look: "We've been engaged for two years," she says.

My mouth drops open. Is she actually reminding him that he's engaged? I've been dating him for two months. Richard points to me: "She's a woman I recently met," he tells her, which is when my head jerks back involuntarily. I am? Where did we meet, in my bed? I hiss that he needs to stick that finger up his asshole. Richard drops the finger. Good idea. He tells the ghoul that this is all a misunderstanding. He wants to leave. As he starts to get up from the stool I push him back down. Not so fast, cheapskate, you and me ain't through.

The ghoul responds by pushing me. "Don't you push my fiancé!" she orders. I shout that she needs to get her hands off me and go join the navy if she's such a muscleman because this part doesn't concern her. I look down at my drink before taking a swallow. I'm not appreciating Richard right about now. "You lying piece of shit," I say with a nod, as if understanding what those words mean for the first time. "You tried to make a fool of me." Before I can curb the impulse I raise my plastic cup over his head and turn it upside down. I'm waiting to see the look on his face as liquor runs down his cheeks, hopefully into his eyes. Only problem: My cup is empty. I shake the cup over his head. Not one drop. I shake it again, just to be sure. I lower the cup. Ah, hell, how thirsty was I? I'm a fucking camel.

The ghoul pushes me again. I can't believe she's pushing me. I'm not the one she needs to be attacking here. I extend my free arm like a linebacker to keep her at bay. "Let's switch gears," I announce, trying to accomplish two tasks at once. I turn to the ghoul. I now have the palm of my hand pressed against her collarbone. "First of all," I say to her, "your dream-boat here slept with me not three weeks ago. He's a filthy pig. I would advise against an expensive wedding." The ghoul gasps. It's like staring at Munch's *The Scream*. I turn to Rich-ard: "As for you . . ." Richard tries to defend himself but it's too late. Before he can stop me I smash the plastic cup against his gigantic forehead. I crush it like an aluminum can, fraternity-style, then throw the cup in his face. "Don't fuck with me," I warn as a big red circle forms on his forehead. "There's your scarlet letter, dickhead. Eat it."

I let go of the ghoul and stumble off to find my friends. My mind is reeling. As I make my way across the bar I look over at the bartender. He smiles at me. I start thinking of all the times Richard stood me up at the last minute because he was "busy at work"; of all the errands I ran with him; of the time he told me that he hates condoms because sex doesn't feel as good—I was this close to letting him not wear one! I lean over the bar. "You want to know why?" I ask. The bartender looks at me expectantly and nods. I lean in closer: "Because he saw the salad dressing. That's why. It's an old joke, and it's not even funny."

Max, Libby, and I abandon the club in favor of a dive bar around the corner. I cry like a baby out of humiliation, even showing them the card, still in its envelope, that Richard sent to say how much he likes me (like a loser I've been carrying it in my purse). Max points out that there are flecks of Wite-Out visible by my name. Libby rubs my back to comfort me. "I can't stand people like him," Max says, quickly growing impatient. "He is the sort of human being who makes people afraid to trust. He is a liar and a cheater, and don't think he hasn't done this before. The difference is that now he got caught." He picks up the envelope. "Is this his address?" he asks, pointing to the left-hand corner. I nod absently. He leans back in his chair and puts his hands behind his head. "It's on," he says with a nod, "and he begged for it."

"What's on?" I hopelessly ask. "It's off."

He puts the envelope in his pocket and orders a round of drinks.

* * *

. . . And that's how it happened. But today is February 17, and for now I am leaving Richard behind—albeit slowly.

Max returns sans flyers. We inch our way forward in the check-in line for another twenty minutes. He notices that the lace of Libby's left gym shoe is untied (she's usually in heels; the gym shoes were bought especially for the trip) and tells her to tie her shoe. "I don't feel like it," Libby responds. "You tie it."

"Next!" the ticketing agent finally calls. Max maneuvers past us with his cart. "Hello, lover," he says to the man behind the counter from a distance. "I'm on Flight Twenty-nine Thirty to South Africa. First name Max. That's *M* as in malaria, *A* as in Arlington Cemetery . . ."

As soon as we board the plane Max begins looking around nervously. I can read his mind: He's trying to locate the children. He already mentioned that he doesn't want to be stuck next to any screaming toddlers. There's some irony in this, considering his highly evolved personality; right before we boarded he entered a magazine kiosk and pulled subscription cards out of thirty-some magazines—*Cat Fancy, Dog Fancy, Car Enthusiast*, et cetera—so he could fill them out in Richard's name and drop them in the airport mailbox. "Tie your shoe," he again says to Libby, whose shoelace trails behind her like a dying but still-faithful dog. We are walking down the narrow aisle, trying to find our seats. Libby abruptly stops. I run into her, Max runs into me. "Don't tie it now! Get with the program," he says. "Tie it when we sit down." She turns around. "I'm not tying it. We're a few seats back," she explains, holding up her ticket. "I misread." I turn around. A line is starting to form behind us. Oh well. We push back against the current. I hear Libby behind me saying sorry to everyone as we pass. She is holding her carry-on in her arms like it's a newborn. She accidentally hits a few passengers in the stomach. I know this because I can hear people moaning when they pass her. Followed by a "You hit me in the stomach. Watch it!" and an "I am so sorry, babe."

When we finally take our seats I immediately wrap a blanket around me. But I have Max and Libby on either side and they won't stop arguing about the shoelace.

"Tie it!" Max orders. "Pick up your leg already. You're sitting down."

"Forget it," she responds, digging through her purse. "I'd rather leave it untied. We'll talk about it later."

"What's there to talk about later?" he says. "You're two inches from the lace. Move your fingers, you robot." Max tries to pick up her leg.

She tries to pull it away. "What are you doing?" she yells. "It doesn't bend that way! That hurts!"

He tells her that it doesn't hurt and does it again. Libby makes a fist and swings repeatedly. A young girl in braids, about seven or eight years old, sitting across the aisle, glances over. If this keeps up we're going to get kicked off the plane.

Why do I have to be mature? I don't like it. Maturity doesn't suit me. Expensive clothing suits me. A monogamous rich husband who's away 99 percent of the time suits me. "That's it," I say. I throw off the blanket, get out of my seat, and tie Libby's shoe. I sit back down and rewrap myself. "You didn't have to do that," Libby says to me. "I don't know what he's on about. It's just a shoelace."

"It was annoying," Max retorts. "Keep your shoes tied or wear Velcro."

Libby slips a sleeping mask over her head. Max calms down and starts doing some kind of stretching exercise in his seat. By the end of the flight he'll be using a NordicTrack. I bet there's one in his carry-on. When his cell phone rings he jumps to answer it. "Hey, Peter!" he says. "Can you score those pigeons for me? Because I checked again and I think it's possible." Pigeons? He pauses, waiting for the answer. "Excellent news! You're a stylish man, Peter. Very nice!" he says. "And listen, do me a favor, while I'm gone order Chinese food to this address every day." He rattles off Richard's address. "Order the craziest shit on the menu, lots of lo mien . . ."

The flight attendant walks by and sternly reminds him that we are about to take off. He ends the call—in his own good time, much to the flight attendant's annoyance—and shuts off his phone. As the plane speeds down the runway he asks if we know what time it is. Libby slowly turns her head toward me. "Tell him it's none of his business what time it is," she says from behind her blindfold. "And tell him that he hurt my leg."

"I'm sorry!" Max calls to her. "I just don't get how you can leave a shoe untied. You wouldn't leave your pants unzipped, would you?"

"Maybe I would, babe," she says with a chuckle.

Many hours later, after a plane change in Johannesburg, we arrive in Hoedspruit, South Africa.

Af-reeeee-ka.

* * *

We are standing outside the airport, which is basically a shack next to a long strip of dust that serves as the runway. In the distance a single-engine plane is parked near a tree. Off to my right is a small parking lot with about ten cars. A group of drivers is chatting in a circle, presumably awaiting orders. One of them, a short black man in a white button-down dress shirt and black pants, takes the initiative and approaches. I smooth the gravel underfoot with my gym shoe: nice gravel, nice gravel. Max addresses him: "Hi-there. We-need-to-go-to-the-Ak-uji-Game-Re-serve." He's speaking slowly and incorporating a bit of pantomime, not being sure if the man understands English. The driver's lips barely move: "Five hundred rand," he says.

If it's one thing a New Yorker is always suspicious of, it's a stranger quoting a figure. "Five hundred!" Max challenges. "That's way too expensive." He turns to us. Not in a million years would it occur to him to buy a guidebook. It's one of the things I like most about him, this insistence that life will lay itself out smoothly, somehow, someway, without the use of a guidebook. "Isn't it? How much is five hundred rand?" he asks. "I can't do this kind of math."

Like I can. I thumb through my guidebook—of course I brought one. I drop my bag and squat down. I begin frantically turning pages. Where is it? Max takes the opportunity to push me. Good one, bud. I put out my hand to stop from tipping over. I stand back up—now my palm has gravel indentations—and announce that there are seven rand to the dollar.

"Seven rand to the dollar," Max repeats to himself, then glances at Libby.

"I'm terrible at math," she says. "Don't look at me." I remind Max that I'm not good at math, either. The only reason I passed calculus was because he stole the final exam for me.

Max turns to the driver and holds up a finger: This will just take a minute. But this will take longer than a minute. This will take a correspondence course. My Barbie doll never did arithmetic. She was too pretty. I venture that we need to divide, multiply, add, or subtract something and then do something else.

Max takes the guidebook from me. "That's helpful," he says with an eye roll. I hesitate: "It's like one over seven times five hundred over x," I continue, "or is it one over seven times x over five hundred?" Libby is puzzled. She demands to know what this x business is. I explain that x is the number we are trying to find. That's how you solve these kinds of problems. You need an equation.

She puts her hands to her hips. "Look at you," she says with admiration. I quickly add that that's all I know and that I didn't even follow what I just said. I'd rather be popular.

Max squeezes his eyes shut and begins mouthing something; I start moving my finger over an imaginary chalkboard like a savant; Libby repeats over and over the equation "One over seven times x over five hundred" while applying sunblock.

After a painful moment I put my hand to my cheek as if nursing a toothache. "I'm totally confused," I admit before reaching for Libby's sunblock. "The numbers are all jumbled up in my head." Libby informs me that that's a sign of genius. I'm sure it is. It feels like it. I squirt a drop of her sunblock onto my index finger and dab it underneath my eyes. I throw the tube back at her. She doesn't catch it. It hits her left boob and falls to the ground. Uuuuhhh, someone has to pick that up. I stare at the tube, which will probably still be lying here in three thousand years, when they begin excavating the site, looking for evidence of former civilizations. When it's finally unearthed, every news source throughout what's left of the world will run a story announcing that Coppertone SPF 45 was invented in Africa. For that they'll have Libby to thank.

Max smiles at the driver, who's standing with his arms folded over his chest, watching us. "Excuse me," Max says. "Do you happen to have a pen and paper we could borrow?"

Libby finally picks up the tube of sunblock. "Or one of those things," she suggests. "Those things where you move the beads from one side to the other."

I look at her. What is she talking about?

"It's like an ancient calculator," she explains, "and it's got these circle things you move around every which way." I lift the guidebook over my head like a visor to block the sun. I know what she's talking about. It starts with an *a*. Libby adamantly shakes her head: No, it doesn't. I tell her that I think it does. It's an ab, ab something. Max lifts up his shirt and points to his stomach: Perhaps it's abs. He does have very nice abs, but, no, not abs.

The driver looks at him with a blank expression. Every one of his stereotypes about American tourists has been confirmed. He's probably nailed down a few new ones in the past two minutes. He nods at Libby. "You're thinking of an abacus," the driver finally says, "and, no, I do not have one. The ride to the game reserve will cost each of you approximately twenty-four dollars."

Max is relieved. "Why didn't you say so?"—he offers a smile—"that's nothing. Libby here thought you were ripping us off. She was raised by wolves." He turns to us. "Ready?" he asks, already moving.

We're ready. Lead us into South Africa so we can damage its natural resources.

* * *

We are barely out of the parking lot when Libby shouts that she just saw an elephant. "Where?" Max and I scream in tandem, craning our necks. Libby taps her finger against the dusty window. We begin picking up speed down a two-lane road. If there was an elephant Max and I didn't see it. "Over there," she continues more softly. "Now it's gone but it looked like it might be an elephant." We all press our faces against the glass. She pipes up a second time. She thinks she saw something again. It's hard to tell, she admits. It looked like some sort of brown animal but it could have just been a rock. I turn away. I bet it was a rock. Max concludes that it was definitely a rock. "What is that?" she shouts, pointing again. "That big brown thing, there, there, there, hurry up!" She points to something on the left side of the road. The driver slows and looks over. He reveals that it's nothing more exotic than a termite hill. "Oh," Libby says. "That looks like what I saw earlier. Forget I mentioned it."

I continue gazing out the window. The landscape is not what I imagined it would be. When they talk about being in the bush they mean that literally. These are really bushes, low-to-the-ground tangled bundles of dry twig. I tell Max that I was expecting something more cinematic. He accuses me of complaining and threatens to slap me one. Is he kidding? I'm not complaining. I'm excited to be here. I'm merely observing. I'm ordered to observe in silence because he happens to like the bush. He takes out his camera, snaps a picture, and continues looking through the viewfinder. "I just said I like bush," he marvels.

Libby rummages through her purse for her sunglasses. When she takes them out Max snatches them from her and tries them on. Before she can protest he tosses them in her lap—his are better—and goes to take my picture. I cover my face with my hand. "Come on and smile," he urges. "I want to steal your soul."

"Get away from me," I order, keeping my face covered, "pictures of me never look good."

"Is that the fault of the pictures?" he asks as the flash goes off.

Libby, sunglasses resting on the tip of her nose, asks if I want a cigarette. I nod. Libby is one of those mystery people who has been smoking on and off for years but has not gotten addicted. She can go for weeks without. She leans forward and asks the driver if we can smoke in the car. To Max's great dismay, he gives permission. "For you," the driver says to her with a smile. "Okay." Ah, the benefits of being Libby. She smiles at him warmly. "Thanks!" she says. "I like your shirt," she adds for no reason and pulls out two cigarettes. Max gives me a dirty look and pinches his nose before we even have a chance to light up. "Smells like roadkill," he offers.

After struggling for a while to light her cigarette (she pulls it out, stares at it to see if it's lit, then tries again when she sees it is not), Libby finally hits gold. "I'm so happy we're here," she says, blowing a gust of smoke at the closed window. It bounces off the glass and hits Max in the face, or so he claims. "We'll be able to see the stars at night," she continues unfazed. "Do you realize that?" I rest my head against the back of the seat and mention that we'll soon be able to hear birds chirping. I forgot what that sounds like. Max rolls down the window all the way, creating a tornado effect. "It sounds like a car alarm with wings," he tells me as my hair blows around wildly, whipping me in the face, "now put out your pipe." When I refuse to cooperate he leans over me so that he can roll down the other window. He jerks the handle so hard that it comes off in his hand. Broken. He stares at it. I look up at the rearview mirror to see if the driver noticed. His eyes appear to be focused on the road. Max stuffs the handle between the seats. That's a much better place for it.

* * *

It's late afternoon when we pull up to the lodge. Max jumps out first and lifts his shirt to his nose. "I stink like smoke," he complains. "You two have a serious problem." Well, at least I didn't rip off a piece of the vehicle with my man grip.

After climbing out of the van we pay the driver (the tip comes out of Max's pocket and I think we all know why). He removes our luggage from the trunk and offers a quick good-bye. "See you soon, babe!" Libby says and waves. A group of uniformed staffers are already waiting to greet us at the entrance of the lodge, under an ornate arch that reads AKUJI GAME RESERVE in gold script. Everyone is smiling like it's their job. "This is going to be fancy," Libby comments. Max tells her it better be for the money it cost: The rooms are six hundred dollars per night. We need to get ready for the royal treatment.

A businesslike woman in white shorts and a starched white blouse marches over, checking her watch. Her movements are as sharp as knives, creating perfect geometric angles. "Late arrival," I hear her say from a distance. I throw my purse over my shoulder. "My name is Helga, the director of the lodge," she says in what sounds, at least to me, like an accent from

some really mean country full of really mean and jealous
light-skinned people who want to conquer Europe, or at least
blow up Warsaw, Poland, rendering it unrecognizable. She
squeezes my hand. "I trust you will have a pleasurable stay,"
she threatens. "We will soon be taking you to your individ-
ual chalets. Please follow me." Libby asks what a chalet is. I
explain that it's a six-hundred-dollar-per-night room.

We are following the officious Helga over to the group of
staffers for what we are told will be a brief introduction
when Max gasps. I ask what's the matter while keeping my
eyes trained on Helga, whose spiky haircut reminds me of a
hedgehog. "Well, well, what do we have here?" Max adds. I
turn to him. "What?" I repeat. "Look in front of you," he says
loudly. I look in front of me. There are about ten uniformed
individuals standing in line, yet I know immediately which
one Max is referring to. Tall, I'm guessing about six foot four,
lean, tanned, light brown hair, blue eyes, dazzling—there is
no other word—white smile. It's the ranger, a vision in khaki
short shorts. I recognize him from the South Africa brochure.
Holy shit, hotter in person. I have two thoughts; they come
in rapid succession. One—he must be a playboy. I want nothing to do with him. Two—he's the most beautiful humanoid
I have honestly ever seen. The brochure picture was cute but
it didn't do him justice. Libby sees him, too. It's not like you
could miss him. "Wow," she marvels in a discreet whisper.
When Max asks her if the ranger is gay or straight she flips
open her compact. "Straight as an arrow," she says, staring at
her reflection. As she applies blush to her cheeks Max again
points a finger. "I need to lie down," he loudly says. "With
him. I'm trying anyway." I elbow him to shut up; he's so inappropriate. I try to distract myself from what's in front of me.
I try casually looking at everything but the ranger's face. But

it's so hard and, well, the lookin' is pretty fucking good. We're all undressing him already. How's my hair?

Helga, who is not wearing a whistle around her neck but should be, introduces us to the people whose job for the next three days, at least according to her, is to make our stay as relaxing and enjoyable as possible. Helga is very adamant on this point. We are there to have a great time, like it or not. I briefly wonder if she has ever dropped sniffling employees through a trapdoor that leads to a cold basement. The introductions begin and I go down the line like a politician. I shake the first hand, I shake the second hand, I shake the third hand—I think of Max and start chuckling. I wonder what kind of tip he'd have to leave if he ripped someone's arm off right now—the fourth, the fifth, the six . . . "William," he says, extending his arm. I take his hand and tell him my name. "Pleasure," he says with a smile. You wish, I find myself thinking. Wipe that smug expression off your beautiful face right now, player. I can see that you're trouble and I'm not falling for it.

Following the introductions we gather around Helga, who will be escorting us to our respective chalets. When William picks up one of Max's suitcases she steps forward and, if I'm not mistaken, reprimands him. He nods and walks off. Damn! A group of porters take his place. They carry our bags while Helga describes some of what we will be seeing in the next few days. There will be loping giraffes, tamboti trees, and various other things that will relax us into a stupor. Libby points out a monkey jumping in the grass as Helga reiterates that our stay will be pleasurable (I think we get it). She stresses that the professional staff—porters, rangers, cooks—must cater to every whim. We are strongly encouraged to immediately

report any concerns regarding their performance. One of the
porters carrying Max's bag of dumbbells begins sweating pro-
fusely while trying to keep smiling. I don't blame him, though
I could. According to Helga it's within my rights as an asshole
on an expensive vacation.

As we approach the row of chalets I notice that each has a
veranda. This discovery nearly brings tears to my eyes. This is
so much nicer than my fire escape and the creepy neighbors
Max spies on while standing out on it with binoculars. Our
chalets are the last three in a row of ten. Max and I are next-
door neighbors. Fun! Max puts out his hand to Helga. "Where
are the keys to my kingdom, Helgie?" he says. "I want to get
in there." Helga shakes her head no. There are no keys. The
chalets are left unlocked. The theme of this experience is "no
worries." Keys would just remind us of our everyday lives and
that is not the intention here.

"Oh good," Libby says, relieved. "I always lose my keys."

Helga, whom I'm pretty sure has never lost her keys, gives us
a final handshake (she has the grip of a maniac) and tells us
to meet in the garden for an orientation in one hour. Okay,
Helga, no problem. Now march off and do some more geom-
etry and architecture with your weird stiff legs that make me
nervous and concerned. PS I hate you. Quit being mean to
the staff members, because one of them is super-foxy. I'd like
to keep admiring him from a safe distance if it's all the same.

The porter carrying my suitcase motions for me to follow.
When he leads me through the door of my very own chalet—
chalet being a fancy word for very fancy hut, it turns out—I
let out a whistle. The space, which consists of a sitting area/
bedroom combo and a bath, is adorned with rich fabrics and

mahogany furnishings. White mosquito netting has been draped over a bed that's bigger than my studio apartment. To the right is a big window and beneath that a sleek table on which a silver tray holding a crystal decanter of brandy has been placed. It's all very posh. If I were rich I might take the setup for granted, or at least at face value. But I am not. And while the chalet's interior is beautiful, I wonder what sort of mood the designers were trying to capture or reproduce. Clearly someone (Helga?) was feeling nostalgic for those good old days of colonialism. Put it this way: I would never pay for the privilege of staying here, if only out of guilt. Not that I'm complaining. I promise I'm not, and neither is my libido. William is so much fun to look at. Seriously, people, how's the hair?

While considering my grand surroundings—the marble bath, the artwork on the walls, that pretentious crystal decanter—I begin to think of how different this vacation is from any I have previously taken. For Max, a place like this is no big deal. His family travels the globe in style on a semi-annual basis. He doesn't set foot in anything less than a five-star hotel. My last vacation was a road trip with my family—my parents and seventeen-year-old brother, Henryk—to Missouri last year. We drove over sixteen hours in a Ford Focus, making only three stops, to pee and refuel on gas, and stayed for a week (for free) in an unheated log cabin on a dirty lake that belongs to some family friend. The vacation had a theme: "the ten-dollar-per-day Sienkiewicz challenge." Collectively we could not spend more than ten bucks a day on food and entertainment. The mastermind behind The Challenge was my father, Bronek Sienkiewicz. He's cheap, and something of a con man. Born in Poland during communism—he immigrated to the United States at twenty—he's a wee bit obsessed with sticking it to the man. Basically, he condones minor acts of thievery in theory and practice and has been known to purchase one bag of mulch for the much-beloved garden he maintains, with occasional help from my mother, in the backyard of their Brooklyn brownstone (free beets late August through September, by the way), and put three bags in the trunk of his car. No one would suspect an older, quiet man with thinning black hair, a potbelly, and reading glasses that he wears on a multicolored braided string around his neck like a librarian to be capable of much dishonesty. But he is. Sort of. Like a lot of folks who grew up during communism, he's been socialized to skirt the system. In some ways he would find it dishonest to pay face value for everything. Negotiations, bribes, hustles—it's the communist way.

My father met my mother, Estie, soon after he came to America. She's Polish, too, but was born in Brooklyn. My mother is in her fifties and looks good for her age, but it's a wonder she does with all the worrying she manages to accomplish. She has just a few wrinkles around her blue eyes (they are merciful or deceptively merciful depending on the day), no more than ten gray hairs. She has a cute short haircut, wears sweater sets and white tennis shoes. She looks young, even though she doesn't act young. Unlike my father, she is rather unappreciative of wrongdoing. Put it this way: When my father is putting three bags of mulch into the trunk of the car but has paid for only one, she's in the passenger's seat, acting like she has no idea what he's up to, then lecturing him when they get home while reminding my brother that stealing is wrong. I'm not sure Henryk thinks too much about stealing. Or thinks about anything, for that matter. Henryk is a teenage mute. He opens his mouth so infrequently I worry that bats will fly out when he does. He typically keeps to himself, and it doesn't help that he's always wearing a baseball cap pulled low over his eyes (this drives my mother crazy). When look-ing at him I usually see just a lanky frame, the frayed brim of a hat, a slightly flattened nose, and unusually large lips that look like they belong to some distant male relative of Ange-lina Jolie. There are days my mother will call me and talk for two hours about the fact that Henryk does not clean his room or make his bed. She says he's either "gallivanting" or "staring at the computer screen playing those video games with the door locked." I don't have the stomach to point out that what he's staring at on the computer screen is probably not video games. He's seventeen. He's a boy. You do the math. Gross.

No, "the ten-dollar-per-day Sienkiewicz challenge" was nothing like this South Africa trip. During the ride up to Mis-souri my father forced us to sing the Polish national anthem and practice Polish vocabulary words. We ate fattening deli meats and rye bread (my father doled out rations) and passed enough gas to run a semi-truck. My parents own a Polish deli called Polonia in Greenpoint, Brooklyn, and meat is some-thing we're never short on: ham, bacon, pigs' feet, pigs' knuck-les, garlic sausage, smoked sausage, liverwurst. They've had the deli, a neighborhood institution, for twenty-five years; it's even been written up in a couple of New York magazines.

When we were approximately one hour from Missouri the unmistakable sound of a wrapper being opened somewhere in the car could be heard. My father's ears perked up. He stopped singing. "What was that?" he asked. Everyone was silent. I leaned over the front seat. My mother had her purse in her lap and her hand buried underneath it. She guiltily pulled out a bag of mini Snickers bars. "They were on sale," she said in her defense. "You know I like something sweet after a meal. What?"

My father shook his head in disapproval. "You're not being a team player." He glanced into the backseat. "Kids," he said, "your mother is not a team player."

"The kids want something sweet, too," my mother said with a shrug, even though neither one of us had expressed any desire for sweets.

"The kids do?" he challenged. "Blame yourself, not them." She handed a mini Snickers each to my brother and me and told my brother to take off the hat. Henryk stuffed the Snickers in his pocket and put on headphones. Some rap song came on. She turned to my father and asked if he wanted a candy.

"How much did that bag of contraband cost you?" he asked. "We'll have to incorporate it into the budget. This is an important week. I want to teach the value of a dollar. This is what puts Americans in debt, mini snack cakes. When I was their age"—he looked at Henryk and me through the rearview mirror—"I had already saved thirty thousand bucks. Thirty thousand."

"Oh just eat," my mother said. She unwrapped one and shoved it into his hand. "They were on sale."

He put the whole thing into his mouth. "Next time bring Polish candy," he said. "The fudge ones, Krówki." He swallowed and licked his lips. "These are good, let me try another."

And that's how my family vacations. But today I am not vacationing with my family. I am vacationing with Max and Libby, and presently I am standing in my very own chalet. Did I mention that I have my very own chalet? Just checking.

* * *

When Max, Libby, and I arrive for the orientation in the garden, which is sprayed with colorful exotic flowers, several other guests of the lodge are already seated in front of an easel holding a map of the grounds. We take seats in the last row; I light a cigarette. Out of the corner of my eye I see William. He walks past a group of pampered faces and hands me an ashtray. I look up. It's like looking into the face of Jesus Christ himself. I'm in some kind of Gentile dream sequence. He has a glow, he actually has a glow! It's good that I'm already sitting down—it helps with the fainting, which I'm about to do. I have never seen a pair of bluer eyes. I don't think they make bluer eyes. These are the bluest eyes ever invented. I'm not kidding. What an extraordinary-looking man.

I take the ashtray and say thank you.

"Pleasure," he smilingly responds.

What's with this pleasure business, I think as William walks to the front of the group and stands beside the easel. How pleased could he possibly be? Libby raises a pair of binoculars for a better view. She confides that had she known he'd be making the presentation, she'd have sat in the front row. Max whispers that he would have sat in his lap. "Tell me you've ever seen anything like this," he marvels. I shake my head. I wish I could, for all our sakes. I can't believe how attractive he is. He's a total model. A magnet.

William begins: "The Kruger National Park is the largest wildlife sanctuary in South Africa. It encompasses two million hectares, approximately twenty thousand square kilometers . . ." I stare at him as he continues talking about something and something then something else. I'll be honest, I have no clue what he's saying. I'm too busy looking at him as he's saying it. He's saying it so well! It's a full-time job, consuming all my senses. William looks in my direction: "The Timbavati riverbed winds west to east through our fourteen-thousand-seven-hundred-hectare giraffe reserve—sorry, I mean game reserve . . ." I nod. Sure, sure.

Max starts to say that he realizes he hasn't met all the men in the world but . . . I finish the thought: They can't get better than that. Impossible. He's almost disturbingly good looking. This guy is a revelation, a modern miracle of engineering.

Libby and Max just stare. They've never encountered anyone like him, either. He's like a figment of the imagination. He's— I close my eyes—my . . . hero . . .

When I reopen my eyes William is wagging a finger: ". . . in conclusion," he says, "if you get home after this trip and start feeling sick—even if it's a common cold that won't go away— visit your doctor immediately." Everyone seated in front of me nods. Wait, what did I miss? I might have that cold. What is it, AIDS? I'll have to look into this later.

After the orientation we follow William (like rats behind the piper) and another ranger, poor guy looks like a dehydrated troll in comparison, back to the entrance of the lodge, where two open safari trucks are waiting to take us on the sunset drive. William and the other ranger lean against their respective trucks and begin a conversation. We hesitate briefly under the arch as other guests walk past, toward the trucks. Max does the math because, all of a sudden, he's better at math than Einstein. He tells us to make sure we get into William's truck. Libby nods.

William's truck has four rows of seats and we pile into the first row. Very subtle. William is oblivious; he continues exchanging pleasantries with the other ranger. We sit, fidgety hands in our laps, and wait. I'm unaware that there are other passengers in the vehicle until one of them taps Libby on the shoulder. She reluctantly takes her eyes off William and turns around. I do, too. The person in question—a boy, about fourteen years old, it looks like—is seated directly behind us, between two very tanned individuals—I assume they're his parents—wearing sunglasses and heavy gold chains. He is impeccably dressed in an expensive navy-blue suit and cream silk tie. As I give him the once-over, I see that he is sitting on a thick purple velvet pillow. His posture is perfect; princes on their way to coronations never looked this good.

He plays with the orchid peeking out of his breast pocket then runs a hand through locks of black shaggy hair. This is some kid. "My name is Manuel Narciso Lorenzo Hernandez y Sanchez," he confidently states, offering Libby his hand. "I am delighted."

Delighted to be doing what? Delighted in general? Libby smiles politely, quickly glances at William, then extends her hand to Manuel. He takes it and kisses it. For an uncomfortably long time. Crickets chirp. Clocks stand still. "Nice to see you," she says and pulls her hand away by force. She turns, sighs deeply with longing, and stares again at William. Manuel's hand is momentarily frozen in midair. I take a peek at William. You are too good to be true. Who made you?

Before long Libby is tapped again. Manuel is not done introducing himself. She turns around. "Allow me to introduce my parents," Manuel says.

"Oh," Libby tentatively responds. She nods at the parents: "Pleasure to meet you both, enjoy your stay." She turns back around, crosses her legs, and stares at William. She is, we all are, basking in his holy light. But Manuel Narciso Lorenzo Hernandez y Sanchez will not be ignored. He taps her a third time. She turns around. "Yes?" she hurriedly says. "Are you enjoying your stay?" young Rico Suave asks. Libby nods in confusion: "Sure. Fine." She again fixes on William. "Delightful," Manuel says mostly to himself.

Max leans over and asks me to speculate as to what might be wrong with our little friend. I advise him to ignore it. It's the kid's first family vacation and the excitement will wear off with the sugar rush. But when Manuel taps Libby a fourth time we all turn around. Max groans. "Yes?" she asks Manuel in a tone that, for Libby, approaches frustration. The delighted kid has successfully tap-danced on her last nerve.

"When you gaze at me I am reminded of a rose bending involuntarily toward the sun," Manuel gushes. Maybe it's her sexy yellow tube top that's causing all this commotion. Perhaps this child has never seen big boobs—he's staring at them with zero discretion. I study Manuel's face, then glance at Libby. It's funny because they actually look alike. Both have the same curly black hair . . . "Are you married?" he inquires.

This time Libby reacts as if Manuel had accused her of shitting her pants: "Am I married?" she responds. "No." She looks over at William to make sure he heard that she is not married. No need to worry: William is still immersed in a separate conversation with the other ranger.

"I am delighted to hear you say it," Manuel reveals. Libby doesn't speak a word. Manuel tries to account for the silence. "Are you delighted that I am delighted to hear it?" he asks hopefully.

Libby looks exasperated: "Huh?"

"It is not important," he quickly concludes. "We have all the time in the world. How long will you be staying at the lodge?" When I answer on Libby's behalf—two nights, two very short nights—Manuel won't acknowledge me. It seems I'm annoying him as much as he's annoying the three of us. I glance over at his parents. They are looking in opposite directions, neither one paying attention to the boy. Maybe they're contemplating putting him up for adoption. Best to leave them alone. It's a big decision.

"Two nights can be an eternity," Manuel continues. "So many felicitous and serendipitous moments may be had over the course of two nights." He touches her on the shoulder. She flinches. "Are you a virgin?" he asks, taking away his hand.

When she makes no effort to respond he continues: "Ignorance is born of circular trepidation, my darling, and chastity is as great a perversion as libidinousness. Dare to take risks with both body and mind."

Libby rubs her eyes, evidently hoping this will make the wordsmith spontaneously combust. "Who are you?" she finally asks.

"Manuel Narciso Lorenzo Hernandez y Sanchez," he tells her with pride. "But please call me Man—"

"Listen, babe," she says, cutting him off. She explains that she had a long flight and that her neck is sore. If he wants to keep talking he can, but she's not going to keep straining it. As soon as she turns around Manuel's lips come within a breath of the nape of her neck. Good morning. "I would be honored to rub it," he softly whispers. "You have a firebrand's spirit."

She doesn't turn around: "I'd rather you didn't."

"But you would not mind if I did?" he presses. "I have an excellent aromatic balm that my Vietnamese apothecary brought back from Ho Chi Minh City." Out of his pant pocket he pulls a small red tin with a picture of a cat.

"Yes, I would mind!" she says with genuine frustration, not really sure what is happening and why. "Please do not rub me!"

Max loudly asks if she's sure. She's never refused a rubdown from anyone, so what's wrong with getting the treatment from the world's youngest registered sex offender? This seems like it would be right up her alley. Manuel hears this and pounces. "Is this man your husband?" he asks in the tone of a jealous lover. Libby does what she said she wouldn't do, she turns around, then asks Manuel if he's still talking to her. "Of course," he says. "I asked if this man is your husband." Libby rehashes the info: She's not married, her neck is sore, she doesn't want to be rubbed. "Are you his intended?" Manuel wants to know.

Max turns around and rolls his eyes. "Hardly," he says. "Now get a grip before you start beating your breast with your fists like a gorilla."

Manuel can't be bothered to make eye contact with Max, either. Max turns back around and looks at William, who's still conversing with the other ranger. Let's go, William. Talk to him another time.

"I am relieved to hear it," Manuel says to Libby. "A radiant maiden such as yourself must attract legions of suitors—your anomalous charms are beguiling. You have quickly become as precious to me as the Bible with the false bottom given to me by a baron in honor of my first holy communion. This acquaintance—this sedentary barnacle—is neither clever, distinguished, nor handsome enough for you."

Uhhhh, Max is not going to like that. He doesn't even bother pointing out that he and Libby are cousins. He whips around, his agenda clear: "Did you just tell me I wasn't good looking?" he snaps.

Now Manuel is annoyed. He must think he's inside a discotheque instead of a four-by-four with his folks. "I am not interested in qualifying your physical limitations, sir," he says. "That is surely something you must contend with alone." And then to Libby: "What is your favorite color? Pink, I imagine. Mine is green, the color of money." He pauses, then adds: "I own a renowned seamstress capable of designing delicate muslin frocks and negligees as thin as gossamer." No response. Libby would rather be getting a Pap smear. Manuel is not worried. In fact, he seems eager to offer the complimentary breast examination. "I feel compelled to confess that your generous bosom—an emblem of fecundity—gives—" He is cut off.

"It gives you a hard-on, we get it," Max cracks.

Before Manuel can defend his motives William climbs into

the truck. Damn, does he have nice legs—muscular, long, tanned, not a lot of hair. He smiles and asks if everyone is ready to see some animals. The three of us nod, as if in a trance. Yes, please. And we're off.

The two-hour game drive is magnificent, the views are spectacular—and the truth is that we don't care. We could be driving through a minefield or New Jersey and it would be just as inspiring. Unicorns could be gliding through the evening sky and it wouldn't change a thing. We are being driven around by William, it's really all that matters. Where has he been all our lives, in a test tube? I can't imagine he was birthed by a mere mortal.

The orange sun is setting as we drive through an open field of tall faded grass and pull up alongside a pack of lions feasting on the remains of a water buffalo. William cuts the engine; the lions go about their business. Some have had their fill and are lying on their backs, moaning out of satisfaction. Others, meanwhile, are tearing at what's left of the carcass. I notice a sad pair of enormous black horns protruding from the thick blades of grass. "You're lucky," William explains in hushed tones, "we don't come across this every day." I study his profile. Don't I know it, toots.

La Familia Sanchez begins snapping enough photos for all of us—it's like they're working the place with submachine guns. Pop! Pop! Pop! I pull out my disposable camera and wonder if there's any subtle way of taking William's picture when he addresses me directly. "Where are you from?" he asks, a beautiful smile spreading across his beautiful face. I'd be smiling, too, if I looked that good.

"New York," I say, trying to control myself. The last thing I need is for this guy to think I like him. I don't chase men, not anymore. I'm going to try to keep quiet—for once. Besides, William's handsomeness is intimidating.

Manuel takes a break from snapping photos to address Libby: "Do you hail from the Liberty State as well?" he asks her.

"No," Max says without taking his eyes off William. "She's from Uranus."

Undeterred, Manuel continues: "I have an uncle who resides in Brooklyn, New York. He is a failed entertainer specializing in stand-up comedy who now works at a restaurant catering to the lower classes. He does not know the difference between a burgundy and a merlot. We view him as an outcast."

Libby ignores this. When Manuel resumes his picture taking, William tells me that he's always wanted to go to America—New York especially. Many of the lodge's guests come from the United States, and from them he has learned many American phrases. "I don't even say loo anymore," he reveals. "I say bathroom."

As another lion rolls onto its back, Libby, who's practically waving a sign in front of William's face to get his attention, tells him to visit New York because it's a great place. William acknowledges that that would be a lot of fun and looks at me again. Stop! I can't handle those blue eyes. I feel like I'm being hypnotized.

"It would," Max enthusiastically decides, trying to get William to notice him. "We could go dirty dancing. The clubs are great. I'll take you around, it's the least I can do. You've done so much for me already."

Dirty dancing. I crack a smile and look at William to see if he got the joke. "I love to dance," William says with excitement. Libby informs him that she, too, likes to dance.

"She has two left feet," Max says to William, "but I'm good.

If you're ever in New York I'll take you out. We can go to the Manhole. Great music. And if it's slow dancing you want we can do that afterward—or before. I'm flexible."

I picture William walking into the Manhole. He would need a security team or police escort. Walkie-talkies and helicopters would have to be involved. He'd be black and blue from the ass pinching if he ever made it out alive. "I don't think he'd be safe at the Manhole," I say under my breath. Max informs me that he'll watch over William. I bet he will . . . and when he's not watching over him he'll be watching him from underneath . . . or from the side . . . or some such thing.

"So how old are you, William?" Max asks. William tells him that he's twenty-three.

"And do you have a girlfriend?" Libby asks. I look over and shake my head. Their victim blushes. He doesn't have a girlfriend.

"Interesting," Max says. "Is there any chance you have a boyfr—"

Libby interrupts to ask William how long he's been working at the game reserve. Two years, he tells her. She nods: "Since you were twenty, then."

"Twenty-one," William corrects her.

The math whiz nods. She asks if William lives on the grounds. He does. He works for five weeks and gets one week off. Max asks what he does during his week off. Nothing much. He stays with his parents on their farm. "You're a family man." Max nods. "How inspiring." William affirms that he loves his parents and glances over at the lions. I hope they're not his parents. Libby notices his preoccupation and leans in. "William," she asks, "in your time here at the lodge have you ever been involved in any dangerous situations with the wildlife?"

"Yeah, I have," William starts to say. "This one time—"

Manuel leans over: "I have been involved in many danger-ous predicaments," he offers to Libby. "Once, while on a tour of Easter Island, I was accosted by a scrofulous native. He was a scrimshander by trade, at least that is what he claimed. Eager to purchase whalebone carvings, I followed this imposter to his hut. I did not notice the knife until it was too late . . ."

Max turns around. "No one's talking to you, beaver fever," he says to Manuel. "Your life has no meaning, I just got the telegram." Max apologizes sweetly to William for the rude interruption and encourages him to continue with the story.

"It's not much of a story," William says, "but there was a time, oh, about a year ago, when a guest stood up in the truck to take a picture of an elephant and the elephant got mad and charged at us. I had to make a fast getaway."

Libby's eyes widen with concern. "But you got away?" she asks. Obviously. We're not in Heaven. Or are we? William assures her that they made a clean getaway. "You tell a great story," she marvels.

Max seems to agree. He begins behaving as if William just got done recalling his experiences fighting in the Civil War. He breathlessly asks William if he was scared when the elephant attacked. "A little," William admits. "I didn't want the man to fall out when I was pulling away. I would be responsible."

"So you really gunned it then?" Max asks. William nods. He really gunned it. "How many miles per hour?" Max wants to know. I correct him: How many kilometers per hour. He glances at me. I think he forgot I exist. "How fast were you going?" he demands of William.

"The truck doesn't go that fast," William admits. "About twenty kilometers per hour."

"That sounds really fast," Libby says. "And dangerous," Max adds.

William looks at the lions. Manuel grows impatient in the back: "My own predicament was much more complicated," he starts to say, "it eventually involved a hot-air balloon and an engorged . . ."

"Keep it to yourself," Max says over his shoulder.

William takes his eyes off the lions to address me again. He asks what I do in New York. "For a living, you mean?" I ask. William nods. Even his long neck is awesome. And that skin. My goodness gracious.

Before I can answer Libby assures him that what I do in New York is not nearly as dangerous as what he does here. I give her a look: *Come on, kiss his ass a little more.* "What?" she says innocently and points at the lions. "It's not. Those are lions."

I explain that I work at a literary agency and that it's uneventful. Max nudges me. "Tell him about Jennifer Leon," he says like some stage mother. "You discovered her." (By the way, I did not discover Jennifer Leon. Jennifer Leon is a writer whom my boss signed two years ago. Her book fetched a lot of dough, which is not surprising considering that she's a moron. End of story.) I remind everyone that I didn't discover Jennifer Leon. I'm pretty sure she discovered herself.

Max slaps me hard on the back. I cough. "Oh, don't be modest," he says, then turns to William. "She discovered Jennifer Leon and the agency got her a four-hundred-thousand-dollar advance on her first novel."

William's eyes light up. "Four hundred thousand dollars!" he gushes. "I didn't know you could make that much money as a writer."

Usually you can't, not by a long shot. Example: One of the agency's clients recently got screwed with a twenty-five-hundred-dollar advance on her first book. She could barely upgrade her laptop with that. A pity, too, because she's good.

I offer that most people don't make four hundred thousand per book. It's not exactly a flat rate.

"Unless they have you on their side, babe," Libby says.

Who am I, Johnnie Cochran? I seriously don't know what Libby and Max are talking about right now. I know they don't, either. All they are doing is putting me on the spot, which I'm not appreciating. "They're exaggerating," I say to William, rather embarrassed.

"We never exaggerate," Max says. Yes, and my mother smokes.

William asks how I got the writer four hundred thousand dollars. He concludes that I must be really smart. Libby announces that I'm a genius. Not to be outdone, Max tells William that he's a genius, too. I shake my head at William. "I didn't get anybody four hundred thousand dollars," I clarify. "I just happened to be the first person at the agency to read her manuscript. I passed it on to my boss; he's the one who negotiates deals with publishers. I opened the mail. It's my job." I pause, trying to deflect attention from myself. "My job is to open mail. That's all." And I can't even do that right. We have not signed a good author in ages. Lately most of the work I've passed on for consideration is crap.

"Don't get down on yourself," Max says, offended by my supposed modesty. And then to William: "She's always getting down on herself."

I inform William, who continues smiling at me, that I am not always getting down on myself. I look at Max. I want to tell him to go down on William already but am afraid he might. A series of flashes go off in the back row as William asks how much money Tom Clancy makes per book. I tell him that Tom Clancy makes millions of dollars. He's in a whole separate category. I don't even think people consider him to be—

William cuts me off to ask if I'm friends with Tom Clancy. I think about the role of Tom Clancy in my life. I offer that my boss met him years ago. Is that even right?

"Wow, that's fantastic," William says. "I would be honored to meet Tom Clancy! He's a great writer."

Libby adjusts her tube top. "Come to New York and she'll introduce you," she offers.

I remind her that I've never met Tom Clancy.

"But you could," Max says, sensing that this is one topic William is eager to discuss. "He lives in New York, doesn't he?"

"I have no clue, I don't think so," I say to Max. I'm done talking about Tom Clancy. I've never talked about Tom Clancy this much in my life. I feel like his stalker. Max assures William that we'll introduce him to Tom Clancy when William visits New York. William looks down at his lap—I've been doing that, too!—and shyly mentions that he'd like to write a book someday. Max jumps in. "Oh, what about?" he asks William. "Your adventures fighting lions and tigers and bears? I'm sure it would be wonderful."

William grows pensive: "I would like to write a book about the political situation in Monaco." Max grabs his arm and asks him to explain. "Well," William begins, "I think the world should know how people in Mo have been treated. There are a lot of bad things happening there."

Max agrees, it sounds complicated: "People across the world should know about the struggle, whatever it is," he says. "But you probably shouldn't call it Mo. That could mean more than one thing, especially in New York."

Libby turns to me: "What's Mo?" she absently asks. "Like homo, right?" I nod—in New York, yes—then explain that William means Monaco. "Oh," she says, losing interest. She pulls a cigarette from her purse. William regretfully informs her that there is no smoking in the vehicle. As soon as Max hears this he takes the cigarette from her and throws it out the side of the truck. I follow its graceless trajectory into the grass. He starts nodding like a bobble head in William's direction. "And will your book be an action-suspense novel?" he wants to know. "A mystery, a thriller, perhaps a romance? What do you have in mind? You could make four hundred grand like Jennifer Leon. You could be the next Tom Clancy. Have you begun the work yet?"

William smiles at me. I nod. I love you. Max snaps his fingers at him as if to say, *Over here!* (Like Manuel, he's obviously not done introducing himself.) William continues: "I was thinking it would be a nonfiction book."

Max is still nodding. "That'll work, too," he is quick to add. "Okay. Yeah. I can see it now, splashed in neon, *Monaco* by William—" He asks William for his last name.

"Johnson," William answers.

Max hesitates after hearing the word *Johnson*. "If you insist," he says. "Okay. It'll be called *Monaco* by William Johnson or *Johnson's Monaco* or *Mo's Johnson*, even, but I think that would definitely have to be a romance with an interesting cover, not necessarily PG, but your photo would certainly be involved. How could it not?"

William smiles. "It would be great to see my picture on a book," he admits, amused.

Libby asks if he has started writing and he shakes his head no. Max shares his philosophy on writing. I never knew he had one. "Well you should start!" he tells William, who's no longer sure which of my friends he should focus on. "No time like the present. Seize the moment. Writing is a powerful tool and so is a johnson, if I'm imagining it correctly."

"Go for it," Libby adds.

"Please do." Max nods playfully. "Please go for it right now." He really is shameless. Completely self-amused.

"Maybe I will," William says, warming up to the idea. He smiles at me: "Maybe someday I can come to New York." I nod. Hello, gorgeous. I'd like to swing naked from your eyelashes if you don't mind. Let me just get undressed real quick. Hold my bra?

"That's the spirit," Max says to William. "Believe in your dreams passionately." He pauses for dramatic effect and puts his hand over his heart as if preparing to recite the Pledge of Allegiance. Manuel leans over, taking advantage of the opportunity to speak: "My dream is to one day own a diamond mine in Zimbabwe and employ many workers," he offers to Libby.

Everyone ignores this. William looks over at the lions. He really loves those lions. One of them bites into something hard. A bone, I imagine. The crack is audible. Max notices the lions, seemingly for the first time. "Oh!" he exclaims and gets up from his seat to take a picture. "Would you look at that! I can't believe how close you got!"

William grabs him by the arm and commands him to sit. "That's dangerous," he adds disapprovingly. Max calmly snaps a few pictures of the lions. He sweeps imaginary crumbs off his seat and sits back down. "You may have just saved my life," he says to William and snaps a picture of him. "I'll send you the negative so we can both remember this day until death do us part."

The lions continue eating as if nothing out of the ordinary has happened.

* * *

"We should be getting back," William says after the lions finish their meal. He looks at his wrist. I notice that he isn't wearing a watch. So does he. "I forgot my watch," he says to himself.

Manuel offers his services: "Allow me to consult my Rolex." The word *Rolex* reverberates through the bush like a growl. "According to my Rolex it is time for us to return to the lodge and enjoy a sumptuous meal together." He wraps his arm around Libby's neck so she can see the watch. "This time-piece is a work of art," he brags, keeping her in a headlock. Libby looks away but William seems interested. He asks if the Rolex is real. "Of course it is," Manuel informs him. William admits that he's never seen a real Rolex up close; no guest has ever pointed one out. He asks if he could try it on. Manuel lets out a laugh, his first. "I'm afraid that would be impossible"—he pulls away his arm—"but be assured that it is made of the highest-caliber platinum. It is flawless, like everything I own."

William nods, turns back around, and restarts the engine. About the same time, Libby restarts hers: "Tell us that story again about how the elephant charged your truck and you got away," she coaxes. "That was a great story." I look out the side of the truck for the cigarette that Max chucked into the grass. May you grow and prosper, wherever you are.

"It isn't much of a story . . . ," William begins.

My friends bombard William with a thousand more questions on the ride back, about anything they can think of, it seems. They just want an excuse to keep looking at him. I find that I'm not terribly interested in putting my two cents in. It's kind of amusing to see them working—especially Max, who excels at this kind of thing. Besides, this is two nights and three days we are talking about. In three days William will just be an amusing and very, very delicious memory. I'm proud to say I already have the experience in perspective. The truth is that this guy is way too hot for his own good. And unless he's a complete moron, he knows it. He probably gets laid left, right, and center. He's probably done it in the truck, right where I'm sitting. Besides, I need a break from men, even men who look like he does. Not that I've seen men who look like him. I'm not convinced others exist. That would just throw off the whole universe.

* * *

We return to the lodge after nightfall. Helga is waiting under the arch with a clipboard. We are informed that dinner starts in one hour, which, according to the freak monitoring our eating and hygiene habits, if not our blood pressure, leaves just enough time to shower. By getting into William's truck for that first game drive we unwittingly secured him as our designated all-purpose guide for the remainder of the stay. In addition to taking us out on safari, he will accompany us on nature walks and—big bonus here—share our table each evening at dinner, giving us an opportunity to ask any questions we might have about South Africa. Helga is quick to stress that just because William will be sharing our table it does not mean that he is one of us. The food is for guests only. In essence: Don't feed the wildlife, rangers included.

When I get back to my room I kick off my shoes and leisurely start to unpack my suitcase. I don't feel like showering. I hope this decision does not get me executed in front of Helga's firing squad. I am stuffing underwear into a drawer when I hear a series of loud knocks on the door of my very own chalet. I walk over and swing it open. It's Helga, looking stern. She hands me a piece of paper. My parents' telephone number is written across it, and underneath that, one word: EMERGENCY. I look up in confusion. "Come with me," Helga commands. "The office has just received a telephone call from your family. There's a problem. You must phone home straightaway."

In a panic, I ask what is wrong. She repeats that it is an emergency, then turns and begins marching down the path. I grab my shoes off the floor and race after her. I only manage to put on one shoe before she shouts for me to hurry.

Helga leads me back to the entrance of the lodge. Just inside the arched entrance, to our left, is a small building, which we enter. It houses a gift shop and several offices. Helga unlocks one of the doors, marked PRIVATE. Inside is a desk and a phone. The walls are bare. She takes the piece of paper from me and dials my parents' number. She shoves the phone against my ear as it starts to ring. She mentions that guests are not normally allowed to make free international calls but since this is an emergency an exception has been made. She moves to the open door and stands there, scrutinizing me.

The phone rings and rings. My muscles tighten. My mother finally answers. "Hello?"

"Mom! It's me!" I scream into the phone. "What happened?"

"Oh God, it's you!" she exclaims. She is shouting, too. There is a knot in my stomach. I hope no one is dead. I brace myself. "I was at the store this afternoon and they're having a sale on canned soup," she says. "I'm going to buy you some. You like cheese and potato?"

I quickly glance at Helga. "What's the emergency?" I say into the phone.

"What?" my mother asks. I tell her that I received a note saying there was a family emergency. "I don't think I said emergency," my mother corrects me. "I may have. What kind of soup should I buy? Minestrone or cheese and potato?"

I clumsily put on my other shoe. I cup my hand over my mouth and try to look casual. "Cheese and potato," I whisper in horror.

"What?" she screams. "I can't hear you!"

"Cheeeshnpotato," I repeat, trying to stiffen my lips. I want to scramble the communication so that Helga doesn't know what we are discussing. She continues staring.

"Cheese and potato. That's what I was thinking," my mother says. "I'll buy it tomorrow."

"I love you," I say, signaling that I need to hang up. (My parents, brother, and I end every call with "I love you," whether we're feeling loving or not.) But she keeps talking, now about South Africa.

My mother panicked when I told her I was going on the trip. She put together a "first-aid travel kit" for me to take along. When she gave it to me I thought, What am I doing, serving overseas? But I knew better than to argue. After the New York Blackout of 2003 I was actually surprised when she didn't offer to build a fallout shelter next to my bathroom with her bare hands. So it didn't come as a surprise when she handed me a pair of underwear that had a little change purse sewn to the waistband. Keep your money in there, she explained, and added that if I need to buy a soda or pretzels I should go to the bathroom and take the money out in there so no one sees me doing it.

As I stand in the middle of Helga's office in a pair of untied shoes, my dear mother, who hates to leave her Brooklyn neighborhood, begins lecturing me on how to behave in a foreign country. "Speak as little as possible and keep your head down. Everyone hates Americans," she advises. I pull out the chair and take a seat as she explains that I shouldn't wear any "flashy clothes" that might attract unwanted attention, and that I probably shouldn't iron my pants—better to look poor—and that I definitely shouldn't wear any necklaces because they might get torn off me. I shake my head.

She's always telling me to dress like a lady, like Libby. Now, because I'm in a foreign country . . . She continues: As for my passport, I'm told to put it in a legal-size envelope and hide it under the mattress. And don't take the camera out to take pictures! she adds. It might get stolen!

After my mother is done lecturing she puts both my father and brother on the phone to say hello. My convo with dad (who excitedly asks how my "free vacation" is going) and the teenage mute (who merely listens as I talk) is much more brief. Thankfully. When I finally hang up, Helga asks what the problem is. "Our dog died," I blurt. We don't have a dog. Helga scares me. I don't want to pay for the international call.

* * *

Max and Libby are waiting for me in front of my chalet when I return from Helga's office. Almost immediately I can smell her perfume and his cologne. Oh brother. "You guys are over-sexed," I observe. I let myself in and take a seat on the bed. They do not follow me inside. Instead, they continue to stand on the threshold. "Is all that room deodorizer for the benefit of a certain ranger we know and love?" I ask.

"You betcha," says Max, rattling the door handle. "Now let's move." He rattles the door handle a second time. I ask what the rush is. I just need a five-minute catnap. We have time before dinner.

"No, we don't, babe!" says a revved-up Libby. "We can't sleep now! Did you see how cute that ranger William was?" She remains standing at Max's side. I give her a look. Good Lord, is she sweating like a crack addict? These people have lost their damn minds. She of all people can't take a nap? She sleeps standing up.

When I finally get up Libby gives me a standing ovation and recommends that I put on a "cute dress." I look down at my T-shirt and jeans. I'm certainly not going to be hyperventilating over William. At least I'm not going to show him that I'm hyperventilating. He already knows he's attractive. I guarantee he's a big-time player. He probably owns the whole team. No guy who looks as good as that could be anything but. When I express this sentiment aloud Max pleads with me not to say the word *butt*. I tell him to get over it and, while he's at it, tone down the flattery. He's delivering more bullshit to William than a teahouse geisha. I'm surprised the guy hasn't caught on and seen through it. Max tells me to relax. He's just having fun— where's the harm in that? "There's a chance he's gay," he adds.

Libby looks at him in disbelief. "No," she says, pushing out her chest, harnessing her gaydar powers, "he's definitely straight."

Max makes a fist. "Quiet, you," he tells her.

We stroll to the courtyard for an African feast near the boma fire. I don't know what *boma* means. I wasn't paying attention when Helga explained it. Sorry. Libby and Max, who have been plucked, tucked, and polished, reminding me of the king and queen of some high school prom, certainly don't know what *boma* means, either. I go in the T-shirt. I know what T-shirt means. It means I'm done trying to impress. Nothing has changed, at least that's what I tell myself.

The long dining table at which we will be taking evening meals is perfectly appointed, laden with an array of dishes whose names I will never remember. Flash cards would be useful. I can already envision the three of us arguing over who gets what first, but they have something else on their minds. William. He's already sitting down. Who needs me at a time like this? There's a vacant seat next to him and they race to claim it. I'm afraid one or both will be injured. Max gets there first. I guess it pays to work out. Libby and I have no choice but to claim the seats across from William and Max. As we pull out our chairs, William stands and tells us not to sit just yet—he should pull out our chairs. At the sound of this, we laugh in amazement. Pull out our chairs? There's no need for that, really. What kind of asshole would need a chair pulled out? William sits back down and smiles. He's really going to have to stop that smile of his.

As soon as we sit down Manuel arrives to claim the vacant spot next to Libby. "Good evening," he offers. He is carrying an oblong-shaped wooden box, as well as a gallon-size jug of alcohol, which he sets in front of her. An offering. He stares at his chair, clears his throat, and looks over at William expectantly. William jumps up, walks to the other side of the table, and pulls out Manuel's chair for him. Manuel nods approvingly before sitting down. He opens the wooden box using a tiny gold key. Inside there is a long-stemmed wineglass and a gold knife-and-fork set with matching porcelain handles onto which flowers have been hand-painted. He brought his own gilded cutlery? He brought his own gilded cutlery. "Did you enjoy the game drive?" he asks his reluctant love interest while returning the gold key to his breast pocket (the orchid that was there earlier has been replaced with a white lily). When she tells him it was "all right" he points to the bottle. "I brought this for you," he says. Libby looks away. She doesn't want William to think she's interested in Manuel. "Aren't you going to ask what it is?" Libby answers no. This does not faze Manuel, who tells her what it is anyway. "This," he explains, "is a native blend called Winta. It is renowned as an aphrodisiac. The African name means"—he pauses for emphasis—"desire."

Max spits his wine. William looks concerned. I ask Manuel if he's old enough to drink. Boy wonder looks at me for the first time. He declares that he is a man. He is seventeen.

Max puts down his glass. "Libby here is knocking on death's door," he says. "She's not even young enough to be your babysitter's great-aunt." Libby tells him to keep it to himself and looks nervously in William's direction (oh no! has he figured out that she's not twenty-three?). Max assures her he's only trying to help. I know what he's trying to help himself to. Manuel quickly decides that "age is a state of mind." I tap my knife against my palm and remind him that so is insanity. William smiles at me and I smile back at him because I am very funny. Boy, this vacation is fun! I look around the table. No one else looks amused, certainly not Manuel, who turns his full attention to the woman of his dreams.

"Libby, do you know how to prepare authentic Latin cuisine?" he asks after mentioning that he's always been attracted to older women. He goes on to explain that when he is not studying the classics with his tutor, he is eating and nibbling and savoring—he's a regular gourmand, whatever that means. Latin cuisine is his favorite but he's tried it all: snake, eel, rat, even panda, which he claims tastes like koala when seasoned with saffron, shallot, and a teaspoon of Himalayan goat's milk (a slice of chayote garnish is optional, as is the glass of vintage claret).

William suppresses a gasp upon hearing that Manuel eats koala. Libby just stares into space. Her eyes are crossing. "It does not matter," Manuel finally says. "We have servants to do that. I was merely curious to know how you enjoy keeping life's supreme blessing—time." Max, who's still annoyed with Manuel for suggesting that he's not attractive, blurts that she doesn't want to spend it eating pandas. "Shouldn't you be with your parents?" he adds. "I'm sure they're worried about you."

I pile food onto my plate. I'm going to eat enough (of the meatless dishes) for everyone.

"My parents are not worried about me," Manuel answers. "I am a grown man. They entrust me with everything."

Max tears a piece of bread in two and sticks the larger piece in his mouth. "Is that right?" he says, turning the food over slowly like a bored cow.

"That is correct," Manuel stiffly says, then turns to Libby: "I am the heir to my father's fortune. I will be a rich man in two months' time." I ask Manuel what will happen in two months' time. "In two months I will take control of the tube sock factory," he says. This gets everyone's attention, including Libby's. She asks what he's talking about. Manuel treats the question as foreplay. It's time for desire, perhaps premature ejaculation. He elaborates: "We own the largest and most profitable tube sock factory in Mexico City. It is a very lucrative business."

"Tube socks?" I ask. I can hear Max laughing. "Tube socks," Manuel confirms. "I wear them every day but never the same pair twice." I take a peek under the table. Between Manuel's pant cuff and his beautiful (I can only imagine Italian leather) shoe, I see the fashion mistake of the century—a white gym sock.

William seems intrigued: "You never wear the same pair of tube socks twice?"

"Never." Manuel shakes his head. "I wear a pair once and immediately dispose of it. Socks are nothing to me, like toilet paper." I take a moment to consider this. Fascinating. Manuel agrees. He turns to Libby: "I want to know everything about you, starting with your birth."

"I don't remember my birth," she says.

"Tell me, then, what is your first memory," he presses.

"Babe, I don't remember my first memory," she responds.

"Then what is your favorite memory?" he asks. She shrugs: She's not sure. Manuel looks around the table before pushing away his still-empty plate: "My first memory is indelible—"

"Good for you," Max interrupts. "We'll call you collect if we ever feel the need to hear it."

Manuel continues: "I was sitting on my father's shoulders when—" Max asks when this was? Last week? Manuel pauses and closes his eyes. "I will not dignify that with an answer," he says and reopens them. I look over at Libby. She closes her eyes and keeps them closed. She has no dignity. "My first memory is most cherished," Manuel continues. "I was sitting on my father's shoulders . . ." Max raises his hand to signal that he has a question. Fat chance. ". . . when I heard my father speak the words that would go on to change the rest of my life. My father said, 'Manuel Narciso Lorenzo Hernandez y Sanchez, my namesake, my precious only son, all of this will one day be yours.'" Libby's head is now on the table. She weakly asks if we're talking about the tube sock factory again. Pretty soon there will be a pool of drool to wipe. Manuel nods: "We were in a field adjacent to the tube sock factory. He said, 'Manuel, all of this will one day be you—'"

"We heard you the first time," Max assures him with a sneer.

Manuel nods again, as if someone asked a question: "It is a risky business, more dangerous than that of a beekeeper. I travel in a customized Rolls-Royce with bulletproof windows. I have my own chauffeur."

William looks enraptured: "You have your own chauffeur?" he asks. I can't tell if he's just being polite. It is his job, after all. I should remind him that Manuel has to have a chauffeur because he can't reach the pedals.

"I have my own chauffeur, of course," Manuel says. "He is a humble man. A simpleton with a heart of gold . . ."

Manuel is too busy yapping to notice his mother, who

approaches him from behind and says something in harsh-sounding Spanish. Manuel flinches at the sound of her voice. Before he can get up she pulls him up by the ear. "A pressing matter demands my attention," he says to Libby with a pained look as his mother squeezes his earlobe between two fingers, draining it of color. I notice that when Manuel's mother is upset with him his whole countenance changes to that of a weepy child. He begs his mother to let go of the ear. When she finally does, he gathers up his belongings and bows dramatically. "Please excuse me," he offers, regaining a measure of nobility. The bow is quite impressive, actually. Manuel's knees are touching his face at one point. He should become a personal trainer. "I will see you at dawn for the game drive," he assures Libby before turning on his heel. I rest the bottle on its side and slide it toward her. I advise her to drink the aphrodisiac: She's gonna need all the help she can get. William smiles at me. Did I mention how much I loooove my free vacation?

* * *

My eyes open at four o'clock the next morning. Jet lag, nice to meet you. I push the mosquito netting aside and get out of bed. I wash my face and throw on the usual T-shirt and jeans. I look out the window. Black. I take my pack of cigarettes off the nightstand and step onto the porch barefoot. Barefoot. When's the last time I went outside without shoes? After lighting my cigarette, I take a seat and stare into the night. An hour or so later, when the sun begins to come up and the world reappears, I stand and stretch. Maybe I'll go wake Libby and Max—or just Max. Libby will want to sleep till sundown. But when I look in the direction of their chalets I find that they are already quietly sitting on their respective porches.

At 6 a.m. we climb into William's safari truck. As Manuel's parents snap pictures of zebras, giraffes, hippos, and rhinos, and leopards lying on tree branches, he force-feeds Libby more information about the family business while looking down her shirt. I'm surprised he isn't carrying his checkbook or a flowchart illustrating his mounting earnings. When he's not bragging to Libby's boobs about his financial situation, he's bragging about the life his financial situation affords:

"Libby, have you ever attempted the beguine?" he asks. "It is a favorite dance on the island of Saint Lucia, where I spent my fifteenth birthday . . . Libby, have you ever sung traditional Neapolitan songs comparing love to the cruel force of the Tyrrhenian Sea? I would like to introduce you to Naples, where we own a villa . . . Libby, have you ever confided your earthly torments to a sultan counting ingots near a riverbed in Turkey? I have, and we shared so much. I would like to buy you a diamond ring to match the one worn by the sultan's fifth wife . . ."

Libby, Max, and I do our best to ignore him. We have a day and a half of William ogling left and don't intend to squander it. Every time William smiles, we smile wider—whether he's getting out of the truck to examine tracks in the dirt so he can assess in which direction some animal is moving or pointing at the trees while saying things like, "Look! Lilac-breasted rollers! This must mean there are elephants nearby!"

After the morning game drive William announces that he will be taking guests on a noon nature walk. He asks if anyone from our group is interested. Manuel's parents decline the offer. Another argument erupts; Manuel sulks. They hurry off; Libby breathes a sigh of relief. Of course we agree to participate in the nature walk. We don't even have to look at one another—we're ready to walk all the livelong day. This is William we're talking about. He could throw me into the mouth of a rhino and, as long as he was doing it himself, hopefully feeling me up in the process, I probably wouldn't put up a fight. We agree to meet at the entrance in two hours.

* * *

William is already waiting with a group of six guests when we arrive. He is holding a rifle and wearing a belt of bullets around his waist. Love that cute little waist. What are the bullets for, teddy bear? He arranges us around him and stands with his legs slightly apart. The rifle is like a second penis. Oh my. William informs us that we are going to be walking in a restricted area. He has to carry the gun in case we see any animals.

"To protect us from danger?" Max asks.

Exactly right.

"I feel safe," Libby irrationally blurts.

That's the point.

Max smirks: "Is it loaded, the gun I mean?"

William tells him that there is one bullet in the barrel. Max wonders aloud if this is enough. He suggests that William bring a few more rifles and offers to go with him. Maybe they're kept in his bed. As he wastes everyone's time posing a number of less-than-plausible scenarios—I mean what if the gun accidentally misfires and then, when we are out of bullet, we see a dragon? Would William have to beat it over the head with the rifle?—the guests look on quizzically. Max is oblivious. He points to the belt of rifle bullets around William's waist. "You know what I mean?" he asks. "Because I see that you have the bullets attached to you somehow"—he makes a looping motion with his finger—"and I was just wondering if you would need to . . ."

Take off your pants?

". . . take out the bullets one by one to load the gun in case of an emergency. That might take some time. Our lives are precious." Only I know that by "our lives" he means his life and William's. He points to Libby and adds that he hardly knows her.

I tilt my head back. The sun is bright and I'm not much of a sun worshipper. I can't lie on a beach for more than half an hour without getting a splitting headache. After a while I start losing my grip on reality . . . I should have brought a hat. I tell Max to wrap up the Q and A. I assure him that I can throw the bullets myself if it comes to that. Upon hearing this Max thrusts his thumb in my direction: "She sure is something, isn't she?" he says to William. "Doesn't give a damn about public safety."

William squeezes the rifle's handle (he must be so sick of us) and addresses the group, most of whom we have not seen before. They look confused and hot. One guy, with his hanging, pasty flesh and double chin, resembles an ice cream cone that's been left on a windowsill in the sun. William leans against his second penis—careful!—and says that he'll need all of us to walk in a single-file line behind him.

"I'll be first," Libby says.

"No you won't," Max shouts. "I already volunteered."

"No you didn't," she protests in frustration.

I wipe sweat from my forehead. Why is Libby not complaining? She's usually my inspiration. "You must have not heard him," I say to Libby. I really need that hat.

"Thank you," Max says to me, then turns to Libby: "See? She heard me."

Libby gives me a look; I shrug.

William begins talking directly to me: "Now, if you see me give the signal . . ." I impulsively give William the middle finger. Okay, so I'm flirting a little, too, albeit in my own delicate way. He raises an eyebrow. "Not that kind of signal," he says with what seems a mixture of amusement and embarrassment. A woman in a Hawaiian shirt, meanwhile, begins taking his picture. I know, lady, I know, just one for the fridge. Her annoyed husband takes the camera out of her hand when she starts behaving like a *Playboy* photographer, bending at the knee to snap him from every angle. "When I give this signal"—William throws up the universal gang sign for *stop*— "you must stop. That means I've seen something."

"I'll be sure to stop on command," Max says.

"I'll stop first," Libby tells him.

"You won't."

"Oh yes I will!"

William asks if everyone is ready for the nature walk. As a very old man inexplicably wearing a polo shirt with a popped collar grumbles to his friend that they better not be walking far, Libby and Max shout that they are ready. William turns around and throws the rifle over his shoulder. It's pointing directly at the old man and his friend. I move slightly to the left, having little interest in staring down the barrel just yet. Libby pushes Max and gets directly behind William. She's first . . . to die. The rifle is now pointing at her. "I'm first," she announces.

Max pushes her: "Get out the way, jelly bag!"

Before long we are walking three abreast, ignoring William's rules in an effort to get a better view of his behind. William has no idea what we are up to; absorbed in his work, he begins talking over his shoulder, delivering a history of the different kinds of plant life found on the reserve in his ridiculously sexy accent, a cross between a British and an Australian accent, but better, I suspect, than anything found in either place. Max picks up a rock and throws it. "God, he is so fine," he grieves. "I just want to have SEX—" As luck would have it, William stops the lecture immediately after the word *have*. Everyone turns their attention to Max, who basically just randomly screamed the word *sex*. He gives the guests a defiant look: "Sex," he repeats a bit more softly. "Yeah, I do it."

The object of Max's passionate outburst seems to be the only person who didn't hear. With a tranquil smile, he silently bends down, picks a little white flower, examines it briefly, and puts it in his pocket. This, aside from William himself, is the only nature-related thing we collectively notice.

"What was I saying then?" William asks.

Libby stops him before he can continue the lecture. "You're picking flowers," she observes gushingly.

Just then a red-and-green-striped grasshopper jumps across my path. I consider telling William to shoot it with the rifle. It scared me; I need protection. Libby takes a step forward. "Why were you staring at that flower like that?" she asks him.

William takes the flower out of his pocket and holds it up for everyone to see. "I don't know what kind of flower this is," he explains to the group. "I'm going to bring it back to my room and look it up in a book. It's our job to learn what everything is, and when I see a flower or plant I don't recognize I take it with me and look it up." I picture Helga whipping the staff because they can't identify a tulip in two seconds or less.

"That is so nice," Max says.

"That really is nice," Libby agrees.

That is so ridiculously adorable, I think to myself. I envision William on his bed in the ranger uniform, a leather-bound book about flowers open before him. William, trying to focus attention back on nature, picks another type of flower, this one yellow and significantly bigger. He informs us that anyone can make honey using it. It's simple. He explains: "Just pick two hundred of these flowers and lay them out on paper for a few minutes, then put them in a pot, add one and a half glasses of water, and boil—" One of the guests, a woman whose sunburned arms look like they've been dipped in goat's blood, complains that William is going too fast. She wants to write it all down. William apologizes and starts again. "Just pick two hundred of these flowers and lay them out on paper for a few minutes, then put them in a pot, add one and a half glasses of water, and boil. Set that aside and let the concoction—" The woman asks William if he has a pen and paper. What's the matter with her, she didn't have these crucial materials when she interrupted him the first time? It's hot out here! William, accommodating as always, pulls a notepad and pen out of his breast pocket and hands them to her. When she takes them he says, "Pleasure." Max mumbles something I can't make out.

William tries again: "Just pick two hundred of these flowers and lay them out on paper for a few minutes, then put them in a pot, add one and a half glasses of water, and boil. Set it aside and let the concoction marinate overnight. The next day, drain the flowers and add half a kilogram of sugar and one to two teaspoons of lemon. Cook this mixture without a lid until it's thick and syrupy and there you are, it's honey!"

After reciting the recipe, which he explains he had to learn by heart when he became a ranger, William unexpectedly hands the yellow flower to me. He gives me a little smile as he does so. Thanks, honey! I examine the petals. Libby pipes up that she wants a flower, too. An older gentleman with a walker, whose son stands next to him, voices a request for one as well. William picks more flowers and passes them out. When he resumes the walk, Max grabs Libby's flower out of her hand. "He meant to give this to me," he tells her. Libby is furious.

They play tug-of-war with the flower until all the petals fall off. This doesn't take long. It's not the kind of flower you can chew and spit out without consequence. Libby cries out: "Look what you did!" Max keeps walking and tells her to pick them up. She retaliates as best she knows how. She stomps her foot. "You pick them up!" she shouts, looking back at the petals.

Max tells Libby that he despises her. William turns around and asks what's going on. Max hides the mangled stem behind his back. "I think we just saw a condor," he says and points to the sky with his free hand.

William looks up. "A what?"

"It's gone now," Max explains with utmost sincerity. "It was beautiful. Carry on."

* * *

After the nature walk we relax by the pool, which is empty save for a perfect leaf floating in the center. "It hurts me to say this," Max announces while rubbing sunblock on the ridge of his nose, "but Lib and I concede: Tarzan has a major crush on you."

Libby and I are sitting on towels, dipping our feet in blue chlorine. I look up and see a monkey watching us from a tree. I wonder if he's ever peed in the pool. I bet he has, which is why he's watching so intently. I ask Libby what they are talking about. "William," she answers while unscrewing the top of a nail polish bottle, "we call him Tarzan." William! William does not have a crush on me. I can't believe what they are saying, though I want to, damn it. I take my feet out of the pool and start rambling. I tell them that he's smitten with everyone; He's always smiling; It's his job; Helga would beat him otherwise; He's running in circles trying to please everyone like some glorified servant; It's actually kind of sad; He seems like a nice guy; I've never even heard him swear.

"Babe, he picked a flower for you," Libby observes. "He didn't pick one for me or for the guy with the walker until we asked"—she signs—"he likes you. I've given up flirting with him." She applies red nail polish to her right thumb and blows on it.

Max frowns. "Too bad," he tells her. "It was going so well." They exchange dirty looks.

William has a crush? She's imagining things and I tell her so. He looks at the lions more than he looks at me. Besides, I point out, what am I going to do with a guy I'll never see again after tomorrow?

"I can think of a few things," Max says.

Out of fairness, so can I. I shake my head—I don't think I want to discuss this—then begin to nod emphatically: I need to know everyone's thoughts on the subject immediately. Max unrolls his blue yoga mat: "He has a crush on you," he says. "I was watching him and he kept stealing these glances at you. It was obvious. There's nothing more to say." I look at the monkey, then put my feet back in the water.

Max starts doing yoga, contorting his body in ways that look outrageously painful. "How do you stand it?" Libby asks while watching him. Max does a headstand. "It relaxes me," he says. "And I'm better in the sack for it." Does he do headstands in the sack? That seems troublesome. Oh well. I light a cigarette and take a deep breath. The air smells so fresh here. It really is relaxing. I can't believe the cute ranger likes me! I honestly didn't think he did. Okay, maybe I had my suspicions but he's just so cute. Not that I would admit this to anyone but, well, he's completely out of my league.

After an hour of yoga Max gets up. He's going back to his room to lift weights and asks if anyone wants to come. Libby just stares at her nails: She's staying put while they dry. Besides, she's tired. He reminds her that earlier she had boundless energy. She was lifting submarines. She in turn reminds him that she only has energy when William is near. Without him, there is nothing. Max looks at me next. What's he looking at me for? What am I going to do, lift weights with him? Since when? He urges me to come and keep him company: talk to him, tell him my hopes and dreams. I shake my head. I don't want to. I talk to him enough as it is. He sighs: "You guys are no fun. I miss Richard." I crack a little smile. "No, I do," he says with mock sincerity. "I really do. Which is why"—he rolls up his yoga mat—"I'm going to crank-call him right now. My dad gave me one of his cell phones and I can make international calls." I'm glad my mother doesn't have the number.

He starts walking away. "I just want to hear Richard's voice. I have so many great things planned for the little guy . . ."

Almost immediately after Max leaves I get really hot sitting in the sun. Whatever distraction he was providing is no longer at my disposal, and I am starting to feel like my organs are boiling. I pick up my towel, frantically wipe sweat from my brow, and hop across the cement to a deck chair under an umbrella. I take a long drink from a bottle of water as Libby carefully rolls herself over. I don't understand how she can look so relaxed when her body resembles a stick of butter on a frying pan. All I know is that my chest hurts, and I think I just figured out what sweat is: It's the body crying.

I spend the next few minutes idly thinking of William. Was he really stealing glances? I can't believe we leave for Cape Town tomorrow. Our time here is going by so fast. As I slowly get up from the deck chair—if I don't go back to the chalet and take a cold shower I might explode—Libby opens her eyes and asks what language people in South

Africa speak. I tell her that the official language is Afrikaans (I read it in my guidebook). "That's so weird," she mumbles and starts snoring.

＊ ＊ ＊

I wear a skirt to dinner that evening and hope my friends don't notice. I rarely wear skirts. It's not that I don't like them, I do, it's that when I wear one I immediately feel more girly and, by extension, somehow more vulnerable. I'm sure it's all in my head but then, what isn't, right? Before leaving my room I check my reflection no less than twenty times.

"You're dressed up," Libby teasingly points out when we take our seats for the last supper. I dismissively tell her that I am not dressed up. Dressed up. What would I be dressed up for? I've had this skirt forever. She tells me that my hair looks cute, too (I'm wearing it down, which I rarely do), but that I needn't worry, she didn't notice that, either. I want to defend myself but can't find the words. Libby just caught me trying to impress William, something I said I would not do, under any circumstances. There is no reason to embarrass myself by having this conversation. "Never mind, Libby," I say.

"You look very nice, babe," she says approvingly as I look up to see William standing before me. I tuck a strand of hair behind my ear. Hi, handsome ranger. His eyes are as big as saucers. He blushes. "You got some color today," he observes, taking a seat. I explain that we went to the pool after the nature walk. William asks if it was nice. I offer that it was. What's not to like? Max tells him that we are planning to hit the pool for a late-night swim later if William would like to come. William looks down at his linen napkin and says he can't. "It's for guests only," he explains. "I'm not allowed."

"You can't eat or swim!" Max exclaims in disbelief.

William shakes his head no as plates of food are passed

around. He looks sad and we are sad for him. Max studies William's face and cocks his head. When Max tilts his head like that it usually means there's going to be mischief. The last time he tilted his head like that he was informing me of his plan to put a wad of bubblegum on Richard's doorknob. I pour myself a glass of wine. "I'll sneak you into the pool," Max slowly says to William, as if already working out the strategy.

Libby objects: "But he's not allowed," she says with concern before taking the bottle of wine from me.

Max, who is very good at making people feel guilty about having morals and fear, looks in her direction. *Not allowed* is not in his vocabulary. "What?" he challenges. "I can sneak William into the pool if I want. It's my vacation."

William seems reluctant. "Thanks for the gesture but I don't want to get in trouble or worse—sacked," he says. "This job means a great deal to me. I love animals."

"Sacked," Libby repeats. "How cute."

"I mean fired," William clarifies.

Libby nods and smiles. I look at Max but think of Helga. I don't want to do anything to get William in trouble. "I'll figure this out," Max insists, annoyed at our lack of creativity. "It's my last night." His last night? What, am I staying behind or something? "Everything is so regimented here," Max complains. "I'm starting to feel suffocated." He starts bouncing in his chair. "No offense, William, but we go on walks, take the same safari rides. I want to see what else this place has to offer. I want to go off the beaten path—or at least see you in a pool."

William nods to himself. "I'll tell you what," he says. "After dinner I will take you on a private ride in the truck. It will be an adventure, I promise." Just then Manuel walks past the dinner table with this mother, who is holding him by the arm.

She will not let him stop. He waves to Libby anyway and blows her a kiss, which causes his mother to pull with more force. William looks over at Manuel. Max pats William on the knee to get his attention. "What were you saying?" Max asks. "Like, can we go do peyote with some natives somewhere?"

"Some what?" William asks. Max waves his hand dismissively: Nothing. "I was thinking," William continues, "that so far you have only seen three of the Big Five." Libby asks what the Big Five is. "The Big Five game!" he tells her excitedly. "You've seen the lion, leopard, and rhino, but you have yet to see an elephant or buffalo, or at least a live buffalo. You saw a dead one being eaten by lions." We nod, we vaguely remember that, yes. "It is said that a successful safari entails seeing all five. Tonight we'll go on a nocturnal hunt, and if we're lucky you'll see the remaining animals. But we have to keep this just between us. Supervisor Helga would not be happy."

"Cool," Max says, patting William's shoulder. "I'm in. If that's the best you got, good enough." Anything that involves making an authority figure unhappy is sanctioned by Max.

* * *

That night, as promised, William whisks us away from the lodge, and he takes the truck off road. We drive in the dark over tall grasses, under glimmering stars. Gentle breezes blow through the trees. For a time there is silence, there is magic. He drives us to an open field, to the edge of a lake, and stops the truck. The moonlight reflects off the gentle ripples. I stare at the back of his neck until he again drives off. As we approach an area of low, bare trees, thick branches, really, poking out of the ground, he spots a pack of scrappy, white-and-brown-spotted wild dogs fleeing from the headlights. He excitedly tells us that wild dogs are his favorite among the animals on the reserve. They are, he adds, some of the more elusive. "Give them a chase!" Max urges. "Let's see how fast this baby can move!" For a time, William tries following the pack so as to give us a closer look. In this South African middle of nowhere we hoot and holler as he plows through the bush, defiantly mowing down branches in the process. "Faster!" we scream in encouragement. "Faster!" Only when the dogs disperse among taller trees do our heart rates return to normal. William checks his watch. It's something I notice him doing often.

We get back on one of the main dirt roads, still giddy from the wild-dog adventure, when William stops the truck and tells us to close our eyes. Of course we don't close our eyes. We are babies. We want to see right now whatever it is we are supposed to close our eyes for. I look down the dirt road but don't see anything other than a dirt road illuminated by headlights. William urges us again to close our eyes. He tells us he has a surprise. We reluctantly agree to obey our master. "Fine," I say, closing my eyes. "I've closed my eyes." Libby giggles. "This feels so good," she says, "it's been a long day." Maybe William is kissing her. I open one eye to check. Nope, that's not it. She's just happy to have her eyes closed. I put my hand over my eyes—it's the only thing I can think to do to stop from peeking.

"I'm peeking," Max announces. William tells him not to peek. Max assures him that he's no longer peeking. We are again asked if our eyes are closed. They are. We mean it this time.

William gently puts his foot on the gas pedal. The truck lurches forward. "I just peeked again," Max whispers. "I can't help it. When I close my eyes I can't see William, which is a problem, at least for me personally."

William slams on the brakes. I open my eyes just in time

to get lots of dust in them. My eyeballs are burning. I glance at Libby—her head is all the way back and her mouth is wide open. Is she asleep?

I squeeze my eyes shut and advise Max to do the same. He reluctantly cooperates. William again puts his foot on the gas pedal. I feel the car moving. Not five seconds later Libby screams that she thinks she just swallowed a bug. "Oh shoot!" she howls in disgust.

"Just swal-low," Max sings.

I hear Libby spit. "I don't swallow," she coolly corrects him.

"Guys like it when ya do," Max sings. "It turns 'em on. Get with the prooo-graaam." If only Manuel were here.

Max leans over and whispers in my ear: "I hope he's pulling down his shorts. Wouldn't that be a nice surprise?" he says. "And I hope he slaps his dick against my cheek." I start laughing as the truck inches along the path.

Moments later William stops the truck and tells us to open our eyes. I open my eyes and nudge Libby, whose head is now against her chin. When she doesn't move, I nudge her again, harder this time. She jerks away, then lifts her head. "I think I have jet lag," she says with a yawn.

"You were born with jet lag," Max points out.

William puts his finger to his lips to signal that we should be quiet. Good idea. "What are we looking at?" Max says in a loud stage whisper. "I knew there was dirt here before I closed my eyes." William points to a cluster of trees to the left of the truck. "There," he whispers and shines a long beam of light. I look over. In the center of the light is an elephant, its ivory tusks much bigger than my cranium. "How'd you know it was there?" Libby asks. "Wow!"

William shrugs: It's his job to know. Max leans into William. "Can we ride it or teach it to paint for money?" he asks. William turns around. His mouth is open. "I'm just goofing around," Max explains. "What I meant to ask is if we can poach it." William is bewildered. "I'm just teasing," Max assures him. "I just wanted to know if we could murder it and boil the bones—"

I hit him so he'll shut up.

None of us has ever seen an elephant around which there weren't at least ten barbed-wire fences. It's thrilling and very intimidating. This thing could charge. It's right in front of us. William looks at me. Oh, beautiful blue eyes. Oceans, two of them. Skinny-dipping, anyone? "What do you think?" he eagerly asks. I nod. About what? "This time of year the elephants eat fruit from the marula tree," he begins, his voice set on autopilot. "The fruit has a soft, yellow skin that . . ."

"Absolutely wonderful," I whisper, forgetting about the elephant and his fruit.

Only when William resumes the drive do I return to consciousness. As we travel along yet another dirt road William periodically looks left and right in an effort to spot more game. But after another half an hour it is evident that there is nothing more to be found. Four out of five ain't so bad. The elephant was cool. William again checks his watch and tells us he has to be up early tomorrow. His day starts when the sun comes up.

We agree that it was fun while it lasted. William puts pedal to metal. The lodge's ornate arch is visible in the distance when I feel the truck slow down. I look at William, thinking he's probably spotted an animal. Shall I close my eyes? "Oh no," William groans as the truck's engine sputters and we come to a standstill. William shifts gears. He examines the gadgets on the dashboard. He tries starting the truck. "Oh no," he repeats.

"What's going on?" Max asks, jumping up in his seat.

William orders him to sit back down and looks around. "We're out of fuel," he reveals. "I should have checked that before we left. That's rule number one."

Max makes a face. "Oooo-uuuu," comes out of his mouth. He turns to Libby and teasingly tells her to get out and push. We're close now.

"Yeah right," Libby says in disbelief. William again tries to start the truck, to no avail. "We should walk back, huh?" Libby finally asks. Shit, he wasn't supposed to have this truck out in the first place. Can we just leave it here? Libby pulls her compact out of her purse and flips it open. The mirror's border, encrusted with specks of (I'm betting cubic zirconium) crystal, is illuminated by light. She checks her makeup.

"That thing is wild," a now curious and distracted Max says, before snatching the compact. "Does it have a battery in it or what? How's it stay lit, mama?"

"Yeah, babe, I think. It's Chanel," she says, trying to get it back from him. "Give me." Max playfully throws back the hand in which he is holding the compact so as to keep it away from Libby's fingers. The compact slips from his grip. It falls out of the truck. "Max!" Libby pouts. "That thing is expensive, watch it!" She abruptly gets out of the truck and picks it up off the ground. As soon as William notices that Libby has exited the truck, he stands straight up. He orders Libby to get back in. I turn to Libby. She's staring straight ahead, her mouth open. She presses her tongue to her upper lip, makes a face, and points a finger. "William," she says in a soft voice. William turns around to see what Libby is pointing at. Max and I look, too. "William," she repeats, "is that a—"

"BUFFALO!" William screams. "STAY CALM!"

But there's nothing calming in William's voice. Libby swiftly spins around and begins running toward the golden arch, flailing her arms. "Help!" she shouts. Max bolts out of the truck and follows suit. "Mother fucker!" he yells. William told us on day one that whatever we do we should never get out of the safari truck. When we are inside the truck the animals think we are the truck. When we are outside the truck, we are just tiny prey.

The buffalo begins to toss its horned head up and down and side to side. It flares its nostrils. I am frozen in my seat. William jumps out of the truck and drags me out by the waist. I bump my knees against the door. He throws me over his shoulder, caveman-style, and starts to run. I begin to slide off and tightly grip his neck and wrap my legs around his torso like a child in a BabyBjörn. My upper and lower teeth bang against each other as we cover ground. I turn my head and see the buffalo moving toward us. William shouts to Libby and Max to keep moving left. "Left! Left! Left! Go! Hurry! The buffalo can reach speeds of forty-four kilometers per hour!" I momentarily squeeze my eyes shut. William finally catches up to Max and Libby, gets between them, and grabs them both by the waist as I hold on to his neck and press my heels into his ass. I feel myself being raised into the air as Libby screams. We are airborne.

✳ ✳ ✳

The four of us simultaneously crash into a body of water and sink. My skin stings from the impact. We untangle limbs, kick at one another wildly, and return to the surface with our hair attractively plastered to our skulls. Only then do I realize we're in the swimming pool. Libby's compact floats by on a wave. I cough and attempt to catch my breath. "We're safe now," William says and spits. "The buffalo won't come into the pool." I look up and see a black buffalo with imposing gray horns, the ends of which curl as if in a smile, standing at the edge of the pool, looking down at us.

"It's gi-normous," Max marvels. "Look at its hooves." *Ginormous* is a combination of *gigantic* and *enormous*. Usually when he uses the word he's referring to . . . never mind, get your head out of the gutter.

We all tilt our heads back. It's like staring up at a building. The deep layers of skin under the buffalo's moist eyes sag heavily. He, she, it, whatever, blinks. I try not to make any sudden movements.

"What is this commotion?" someone behind me says. I recognize the accent and ever-so-carefully turn my head. It's Manuel, at the other end of the pool. Max points at the buffalo. Manuel notices Libby and swims over from the deep end. The buffalo turns and slowly walks away. It flicks its tail once, then disappears. William tells Manuel what just transpired: that we ran out of gas, that Libby got out of the truck . . .

"You saved us," Libby says to William. "You saved our lives." Manuel studies Libby as she compliments William, who swells with pride. I cough again and wipe mucus from my nose. Max moves to the edge of the pool. "How you like me now?" he says, leaning out of the water. I presume the question is meant for the departed buffalo.

"It's wonderful to see you, Libby," Manuel says. He admires her white dress, which is soaked. Luckily, her polka-dot bikini top is all that's visible underneath; thinking we would go to the pool after our Big Five hunt, Max, Libby, and I wore bathing suits under our clothes.

Manuel volunteers to Libby that he was enjoying an evening reciting Shakespeare's most famous soliloquies under the stars when he heard the commotion. He rattles off the names of a few plays—*A Midsummer's Night Dream, The Taming of the Shrew, Henry IV Part 2, Love's Labour Lost, Troilus and Cressida, Romeo and Juliet*—and mumbles something about killing the envious moon because Libby is so pretty.

"Thanks for saving me," Libby says to William.

"Pleasure," William responds.

Manuel interjects that William hardly saved Libby if the truck ran out of gas. In fact what he did was put our lives in grave danger. He turns to William and reminds him that he should not be in the pool. "Go on now," he adds. He looks at Libby. "I'll take over."

Max returns to the group. "What are you talking about?" he asks, annoyed. He peers into William's baby blues and tells him to stay put.

Manuel grabs William's left arm. "This is an employee," he reminds Max. "He is forbidden to enjoy the swimming pool." Max in turn grabs William's right arm. William resembles a *t* that's just been crossed.

Max takes a step toward Manuel. Sensing that Max means to inflict bodily harm, Manuel, still gripping William's arm, hides behind his back. William starts to say something but is drowned out.

"Take a walk," Max tells Manuel.

Manuel lets go of William and shakes his head no. "If the park ranger is staying in the swimming pool," he retorts, "then I have no choice but to stay as well. It is my duty as a gentleman to ensure the ladies' safety." He bows dramatically.

Max carefully pushes back Manuel's head with his open palm. "You'll drown," he tells him.

Manuel straightens his back and pats his hair. "I certainly will not. I am an accomplished swimmer," he begins, the volume of his voice steadily rising. "I have a medal in the field. I was the envy of my peer group. I AM—"

"We should lower our voices," William interjects.

"Shhhhh!" Libby commands in a panic and looks around, evidently hoping not to wake Helga from the dead. Not likely; I mean if the buffalo didn't do it, I'm guessing we're fine.

Manuel catches himself. He begins to whisper to Libby: "My apologies for raising my voice. It was my attempt to convey that I am trained in an array of fields, including pole vaulting, marksmanship, and ventriloquism," he tells her. Libby looks at William. "Ventriloquism is the art of voice projection," Manuel adds without moving his lips. My head jerks back. Did anyone else notice that? That was spooky it was so good. His lips did not move. I thought one of the trees was talking.

Manuel repeats that he will report this incident to William's supervisors. Libby's mouth drops open in disbelief. "Like heck you will," she says in a huff. Manuel can't believe his ears: "Do you mean to say that you would permit a staff member to swim alongside you?" he asks. She nods. Yes, she would. "Think of your reputation," Manuel pleads as Libby smiles at William. "You could be mistaken for a tart, a Jezebel!" Manuel repeats his warning. "I am going to report this," he threatens. "This is against lodge rules. It is a gross violation of etiquette . . ."

Max takes another step toward him. "You're the gross violation!" he counters. Libby tries to shush Max but it's no use. "If you even think about reporting this," Max continues, pushing his finger into Manuel's chest, "I swear to God I will—"

Libby tells everyone to calm down; we can all just stay in the pool. Max throws up his arms. "Why me," he moans. Manuel's eyes widen. "I knew it," he says excitedly to Libby, who peels off her white dress, revealing her polka-dot bikini and mounds of cleavage. "I knew you had feelings for me." Max gives Libby a sour look. "Do me a favor and cover up those tits," he says, pointing at her bikini top. "I can't deal with this shit much longer."

Manuel begins doing laps around the pool to show Libby how fast he can move; Max and I follow Libby's lead and peel off wet clothes. I'm in a black bikini and Max is in red trunks. William takes off his khaki uniform shirt but leaves on his khaki shorts.

We congregate around William's hairless chest, which, according to Max, would make a wonderful dessert tray. When Manuel realizes that Libby is not paying attention to him, he gets out of the pool to retrieve a bottle of Winta and a glass that he left on a deck chair. As he exits the water I notice something gravely unfortunate. Manuel is wearing an orange Speedo that glows in the dark. Libby gasps: Manuel has an erection. And unlike every penis I've ever seen, Manuel's is not pointing up, toward the chin, if you will. No, Manuel's penis is pointed straight ahead. Let's say this: If Libby backed into him right now, she'd immediately be having anal sex. Not good. He holds up the bottle of Winta and waves it at her, leaving me to wonder if he has a factory that makes that, too.

He takes a running start and does a swan dive into the pool, bottle and glass still in hand. Libby covers her eyes. Earlier in the day Max mentioned wanting to see William in a Speedo. Well, there's the Speedo, it's just on the wrong guy. At least he's not wearing the socks.

Manuel and his penis and his bottle and his glass begin swimming underwater toward Libby. They stop at her feet but show no sign of coming up for air. Libby wonders aloud what Manuel could possibly be doing under there and, when a few bubbles break on the surface of the water, I joke that perhaps he knocked himself out, knowing full well that he's doing nothing more than checking out her thighs. A look of concern spreads across William's face. He reaches underwater, pulls Manuel out by the back of his Speedo, and asks if he's okay. Manuel throws him off and leans into Libby. When he puckers his lips for a kiss she leans all the way back. The conversation again turns to Winta. Would Libby like some? Her answer comes quickly: No, she would not. He promises that she will not regret indulging. "Winta is a very sensual drink," Manuel says. He shakes his wet head, spraying fat drops of pool water into Max's eyes. Gracias señor! "It is made from the extract of a rare flower coveted by tribal chiefs and shamans of the hinterlands," he continues. "It enraptures and titillates the senses. I drink it at elite social gatherings, not to mention the occasional vernissage."

Max flicks water in Manuel's direction. "What's a vernissage, sock puppet?" Max mumbles. "What are you even saying?"

Manuel is quick to explain: "A vernissage is a private showing of an art exhibition that has not yet been opened to the masses. A vernissage is certainly not something you would ever be asked to attend." Max gets right up in Manuel's face. He speaks slowly, carefully pronouncing each syllable: "I-do-not-un-der-stand-a-word-you-just-said," he concludes. "Speak-Eng-lish-next-time."

I look over at Libby. Vernissage. Man, oh man. As far as she's concerned vernissage is something you put in a bun and eat with mustard. Vernissage. She couldn't give a flying fuck. The other day she asked me if Art Deco was a painter.

Manuel holds out the bottle and she shakes her head no. She doesn't want any of what she calls his "Spanish fly." Manuel jumps to his own defense: Oh, no, no, it is not like that at all. (This from the kid who asked if she was a virgin the second they met.) Max impatiently grabs the bottle from him, unscrews the top, and takes an impressive swig. He informs us that it tastes like cold Irish coffee. Not bad at all. Manuel takes the bottle from him and wipes down the opening with his palm. "This is a product to be savored," he says under his breath. "Not wolfed down in the manner of a savage, you *bête sauvage*." After thoroughly disinfecting the bottle he asks Libby if she's sure she doesn't want to try some. He explains that it's like a piece of velvet on the tongue.

"I don't want a piece of velvet on my tongue," she answers.

Max turns to me. He's had enough: "Come on, let's go to the deep end. Don't be afraid, mother, I'll take your arm." I hesitate and William notices. He asks what I'm afraid of. I explain that I don't know how to swim and that Max just enjoys making fun of me. William turns his back toward me: "Hop on," he says. "I'll take you around the pool." I contemplate William's muscular back while considering the graphic thoughts that are likely swirling in Max's head. I don't embarrass easily, not with a friend like Max always at my side, but here I'm momentarily overcome by shyness. I hope it doesn't show. I shake my head and answer no: I'm just going to stay in the shallow end.

Libby hears our exchange. "I don't know how to swim, either," she lies. "Take me around, William. I'll get on your back." Upon hearing this, Manuel forcibly shoves the liquor bottle and glass against Max's chest. "Don't mind if I do," Max says, scooping up Manuel's tools of seduction.

Manuel grabs Libby by the arm. He begins to shout: "Why, you did not tell me you were unable to swim! I am a glorious swimmer! You will be my pupil!" Before Libby can stop Manuel, he has her by the waist. He begins to move her around the pool. Libby makes no effort to cooperate; Manuel looks like he's dragging a corpse. Max, for his part, takes a second drink from the bottle, then points to a deck chair. "I'm going to be over there if anyone needs me," he explains. "You know, this stuff really isn't that bad," he adds, more to himself this time. "It's like a spiked milk shake. Kinda tropical." He gets out of the pool and I'm left standing in the shallow end with William. He's adorable. What else is new? After an awkward pause William tells me that he's sad I am leaving. I admit that I am sad, too, and that it was very nice meeting him.

"You're very easy to look at," I add. I don't know what possesses me to say the last part. It just comes out. He answers without hesitation: "I think you're beautiful." It may be dark but I can see that his ears are red. I can't believe he blushes. I let out a laugh; William looks petrified. I think he thinks I'm laughing at him. He blurts that he has a hard time explaining how he feels. I encourage him to give it a shot. I definitely want this man to do the talking. After all, it's not every day that a heartthrob with a sexy accent confesses his feelings for me in South Africa. A week ago I wouldn't have been able to identify his country in a lineup.

"You're so quiet, like me," he starts. Quiet? Yes, exactly right. I am quiet. We know each other so well! "But you're also fun," he adds. "You're . . . unique." William cups his hand around the blue water and lifts it out of the pool. He looks up at me as liquid slowly drips through his long fingers. "I like that," he says. Fuuuuuuck me. That one I felt.

I look over at Max, who seems to have fallen under the spell of Winta. He's staring at the bottle, turning it around like a hippie grappling the meaning of his lava lamp. "We're all amusing," I blab, trying to distract William from what he likes. "The three of us."

"But you're so smart and accomplished," he continues as a bead of water rolls down the center of his chest. "You're . . . ."

"What?" I ask, fishing for more compliments.

"You're like no one I've ever met."

William says this last part with such sincerity that I almost believe him. He's lucky I've heard every line ever used, including that very one. Fucking Richard. Before William can say another word, Manuel drags Libby back to the shallow end and releases her from his clutches. She smacks her ear to get the water out and declares that she's had enough of the pool for a lifetime. "I think he fractured my hip out there. I need a drink," she adds, panting. Manuel lunges forward in the water. "I will get the Winta!" he says. "It will warm your delicate bones."

"Don't bother!" Max shouts from his deck chair and turns the bottle on its head. "I just drained it!"

Manuel lets out a moan but quickly recovers. "I have more," he promises and keeps moving.

"No!" Libby screams in terror. "I'm going to bed. Good night."

Manuel follows her out of the pool. He adjusts his orange Speedo and stares directly at her breasts, which for him are at eye level. If he got a little closer he'd have his cheeks between them. "May I escort you to your boudoir?" he asks her breasts.

"No, babe," she says while drying herself with a towel. "You're seventeen."

Manuel pulls the Speedo out of his crack. "Almost eighteen," he corrects her. "This reminds me of a story. Once, when my family yacht was approaching the shores of Corsica, I said to—"

"Manuel!" I hear a woman shout. It's Manuel's mother, the perpetually enraged señora. She walks determinately across the deck, past a row of reclining white chairs, wagging her finger and screaming in Spanish, her high heels banging against the concrete, her gold bangle bracelets clinking. A uniformed ranger, her escort, stands off to the side. Manuel swaddles himself in a terry-cloth robe that has the words CARNIVAL CRUISE LINES 2000 stitched on the pocket as William dives underwater, afraid he'll be turned in for associating with the wealthy. Manuel's mother stops at the edge of the pool to

confront her son. William looks up at me from beneath the
water. He is pinching his nostrils, his hair swaying like seaweed. After some heated words from Señora Sanchez, during
which Manuel keeps his head down, she abruptly walks back
up the path, past that same row of reclining white chairs, her
high heels banging against the concrete once more. She howls
a one-syllable command in Spanish. Disobedient Manuel turns
to Libby and translates: "I must leave you now," he explains.
"My mother suspects that you are a gold digger after our family treasure. I am in the process of convincing her otherwise."

She said all that in one word?

With his chin against his chest, Manuel follows his mother.
Max can't stop laughing when she grabs her son by the ear
and begins dragging him like a mule. The ranger-escort follows behind with a rifle.

William and I get out of the pool once the coast is clear. His
glistening body glows in the moonlight. Now that the hardest
part of her day is over, Libby invites us to have a drink on her
fancy wraparound porch. Max throws me a towel and a look.
"Offer good for one night only." He smiles.

Libby nods: "Yeah, and I'm wide awake." The comment
surprises even her.

We agree to have a drink on Libby's porch; the idea of calling it a night is painful. William seems eager. He walks us to
Libby's then tells me he's going to put on some dry clothes
and get gas for the safari truck, and that he will be back.

We wait for William. Our hostess comes out of her chalet with
a decanter of brandy. "I took a sip of this and it's very sweet,"
she marvels, setting it down on the table. I pull out one of the
wicker chairs. As soon as my ass touches the seat Max is on

me like a vulture. He grabs the arms of my chair, pulls me toward him, and asks if I'm going to sleep with the ranger. What? Is he totally crazy? I'm not sleeping with him. That honestly never crossed my mind as a legit possibility. I've just been fantasizing is all. I can talk a badass game but deep down I'm an innocent. I don't just sleep with people. I don't even know William. I waited a long time before sleeping with Richard.

I remind Max that William and I have exchanged a total of ten words. "Who cares," he retorts, pouring out the brandy into crystal glasses, "it's not words you need to be exchanging." He fixes me with his eyes and points out that never again in my lifetime or his will there be a better-looking man than William. He is unbelievable. He is beautiful. Do I even know how beautiful he is?

I frown at him. He wants to know if I know how beautiful William is? Yeah, I think I felt how beautiful he is in the pool. I had to cross my legs, that's how beautiful he is.

Max proclaims that people would kill to sleep with William. I believe that he would, yes, and assure him that I know how beautiful William is. "I can't take my eyes off him," I answer. "Stop reminding me how—" Max jumps in: "Please sleep with him. Do it for us. Do it for me. We would sleep with him if we could but he only has eyes for you." I mildly protest that this is not the case, though it's nice to think it might be. Libby nods: William only has eyes for me.

"What was he saying to you in the pool?" Max asks. "I was trying to eavesdrop but you two started whispering."

I let out a squeal before revealing that William told me I was beautiful. Libby puts her hand to her heart. "Babe! He said that?" she asks in awe. That's all she needed to hear. Now she, too, wants me to hook up with the ranger. I continue, reveling in the attention: "He said he's never met anyone like me. It was such a line but a part of me wanted to believe him."

Max rolls his eyes. "Why wouldn't you believe him?" he asks. "You're so jaded. You can't afford to be jaded."

"No, you can't," adds Libby, hand still at her heart. "Just kiss him once. It would be a fairy tale, babe. He saved us from a buffalo." She momentarily closes her eyes and puckers her lips. "That face, that uniform," she gushes. "Those shorts. I wonder what kind of clothes he wears in his off time."

"Who cares," Max says, "as long as he's willing to take them off."

We down a few brandies and I immediately start to feel light-headed. Max continues: "The truth is that he hasn't met anyone like you. You heard him admit it, girl. You're gorgeous and you're the light of his life."

Libby takes my hand: "Invite him back to your room for a kiss," she says. "It's our last night and he really adores you. And don't listen to Max, you don't have to sleep with hi—"

Max cuts her off: "Do it! Sleep with him!" He hits my shoulder. "It'll put Richard in total perspective!"

Libby pauses and crosses her legs. "You know," she adds, a twinkle in her eye, "this could be like that movie *How Stella Got Her Groove Back*." I lift an eyebrow. "Well, it could," she says, giggling. "She got together with a hot guy on vacation after getting dumped or something. I've been meaning to rent it for like four years. It looks cute."

Max tells me I'll regret it if I don't maximize this opportunity—people who have never met me will regret it. Life is too short not to find out how long William's penis actually is. I consider the advice. The thought of walking back to my room and never seeing William again is in fact tragic. I light a cigarette. "You guys really think I should invite him back to the room?" I ask, not quite believing that I'm even talking seriously about this. "Isn't that cheesy?"

"Yes, do it! Yes!" Max shouts. He's like a town crier having an orgasm. "You're cheesy, so have a cheap thrill already! What's the harm? Loosen up. I will not let you go through life regretting this. This and the buffalo will make such a great vacation story. I could tell it for years! This is not the time to think. It's the time to act!"

I hear a noise and put out my cigarette. "Keep your voice down, trumpeter," I say, looking behind me. "Here comes William."

* * *

William walks onto the porch, back in uniform. Maybe he doesn't own regular clothes. He takes a seat next to me. I smell the air and my eyes widen. He put on cologne. It's subtle but I can smell it. It smells great. He put on cologne to impress me! That is so adorable. He is so adorable. Max sniffs the air and yawns loudly. "Wow! I'm exhausted," he lies. "I'm so off to bed. Can't keep my eyes open. I'm out of it." When Libby just sits there, staring at William, he hits her shoulder, which is when she begins yawning, too. Take it easy, I think to myself.

William is puzzled by this sudden change. "I thought you said you were wide awake," he says to her. "Didn't you say you want to have a drink?" Max shakes his head no, then again slaps her shoulder. "Mosquito," he says to William when she begins rubbing the spot where he hit her. He takes the empty brandy decanter from the table and places it under his chair. He gets up, wishes us a good night, then reaches into his pocket and tosses something at me. "There's your chewing gum," he explains as I catch it, "you left it by the pool." I look down at what's in my hand. A condom. A condom! Oh Jesus! I tighten my fist around it and smile weakly at William.

"I left my gum by the pool," I blankly repeat, squeezing the crunchy wrapper. William nods and asks if he can have a piece.

Max clears his throat. "You can have a big piece in just a little while, William," he says with a serious face. "Hold your horses." He taps Libby on the back of the head. "You're tired now, go to bed," he flatly reminds her before stepping off her porch. He races to his chalet before William can get up to walk him. "Ye-aaaah, tired," Libby says tentatively, trying to keep up with the pace. She attempts another fake yawn. Before I know it she's inside her chalet, door closed. William and I are alone for the first time.

I look at the ashtray on the table. My cigarette is smoldering. I tell William that I'm going back to my chalet. He hesitates. I begin to ramble that he can join me if he'd like but of course he doesn't have to because it's no big deal because we can just stay here on Libby's porch and have a platonic talk because we need to sit down because sitting is good. I squeeze the condom wrapper like a stress ball. It doesn't have to be more than—

He cuts me off and says thank you.

I start to get up, my cheeks flushed from too much brandy, when I hear a scream coming from Libby's room. William immediately jumps to his feet and puts out his arm to stop me from getting any closer to her door. "It could be a wild animal!" he exclaims. Libby's door flies open before he can save the day. Out runs Manuel. "I misinterpreted your advances!" Manuel shouts over his shoulder and keeps running. "You must remember that love and hate are equiponderant!"

Libby reemerges. I watch Manuel's slight figure disappear among the trees. He'd better hope that buffalo isn't still out there. "He was hiding under my bed," she sourly explains before slamming the door. Bang—the only bang Manuel will get tonight.

* * *

William seems a little overwhelmed when I bring him back to my chalet. Convinced he needs assurance, I ramble that he should make himself comfortable. I'm just going to change—it's no big deal.

I go into the bathroom and close the door. He smells so good, I think, leaning up against it. I take a look in the mirror. I run a brush through my hair, pat my cheeks, check my teeth for spinach. Everything looks as good as it's going to. I change into a white T-shirt and gray cotton shorts. Innocuous enough. Before opening the door I visualize Max's face and recall his carefree words, offered with a *what's the big deal* wave of the hand: "What's the harm? Loosen up."

When I step out of the bathroom William is lying on my bed in a pair of tighty whities. His khaki uniform has been folded neatly on a chair. He definitely made himself comfortable. He smiles, I smile. We are mirror images of each other. I lie down, he lies down. I stare into his eyes, he stares into mine. What's the harm in this?

"Hi," he says.

"Hi yourself."

William takes my hand and studies it. I recall the white flower he plucked and considered so earnestly while out on our nature walk. "Your skin is soft," he whispers. It is? It is. I look at his lips as he looks at my hand. Maybe just one kiss . . . "Look at my hand," he says, sliding it toward me, palm-side up. "It's calloused."

I run my finger across his palm. "I think you have a nice hand," I offer, then awkwardly add: "You saved us with this hand."

He looks at me, looks at me, looks at me, then tells me he

would like to kiss me but isn't sure if it would be okay. I look even deeper into his eyes: I think it would be okay. William leans in and kisses me. He kisses me the way I've always wanted to be kissed. The way every woman, I can only imagine, deserves to be kissed. Perfectly. He kisses me perfectly. And then he pulls away, for just a moment, and says, in the meekest voice I will ever hear: "Where did you learn to kiss like that?"

I can't believe this. What the hell would you do? "I'm just doing what you're doing, William."

He kisses me again. He's really good at this! Shoulder, earlobe, neck—William is touching them as if my female form is the first he's known. Maybe it's the brandy but out of nowhere I find myself confessing that I want to have sex but that I'm afraid: We just met. William puts his arm around my waist and tells me we don't have to have sex. I look at the clock. It's late. "I love this part of your body," he whispers, putting his hand against the small of my back. I arch it as he touches me.

As we continue touching each other like we have all the time in the world it occurs to me that we have no time at all. In the morning I will be gone. I will get in a car and never see this person again. This person who has made me forget, for just one second longer than anyone else, all about the dishonesty that passes for courtship. Will he call, won't he? Who cares anyway? Let's hope he doesn't. He's usually doing you a favor by not calling. And now, here in South Africa, with William, a man with the honest-to-goodness innocence and curiosity of a child, none of that matters. None of it matters and I, for one, am grateful. William is making me forget, and for that I will always remember him. How romantic . . .

Wait, though, did William say we don't have to have sex? Don't have to have sex! Of course we have to have sex. We need to be having it right now! This instant! There is no time to lose!

Hurry! Sex for everybody, I'm buying! Sex, sex, banging sex . . . one door closes as another opens. How fortuitous! (Sorry, Manuel.) "Maybe we can try having sex for just one minute," I say. "I just want to see what it will feel like. Just for a minute."

"Are you sure?"

"I am. Just for a second."

William gently rests my head on the pillow and looks deep into my eyes: "I want you to know that I've never m—" I put my finger to his lips. I don't need to be reminded that he's never met anyone like me. If he says it again I'll get suspicious. It sounds too much like what Richard said. I kiss him as he presses himself against me . . .

Wow, this is nice. This is real nice. What a kisser. It's like licking honey . . . which William knows how to make, by the way. Kiss me again, William. Kiss all you want. Kiss me until . . . but where are you going? Don't leave. Is it over already? I need you to kiss me once more . . . oh, that's where you went. Hello. Well, that isn't bad, either. Not at all. Wow. Did I already say wow? This time I mean it. Okay, you're definitely a good kisser. Sure are. Oh. Uh. Yes, sir. I like this. I do like this. This I like so very . . . ooh, yeah. What a wonderful vacation. Spectacular. South Africa is a magical place, just like Helga said. And come to think of it, she isn't so bad. She's wonderful, actually. I mean she's just doing her job. Everyone's wonderful. Helga, Manuel, my mailman. I love people! All kinds, every nationality. Uh. I love them, I do. Oh. And the trees and the flowers and my toaster. Even mice and snakes. What's wrong with snakes? And speaking of snakes, I'm just going to ask William to rejoin me up here so I can see something. Just for a second. I'm curious . . . I'm going to reach down . . . Hal-le-lu-jah! Hal-le-lu-jah! HallelujahHallelujahHallelujah, Hal-le-lu-jaaaaaaaaaaaaaaaah!!

Holy
Toledo,
what
a
fucking
torpedo.

* * *

William is dressed before the sun comes up. He can't take the chance of getting caught but assures me that he will be there later in the day with the rest of the staff to see me off. I'm not sure how this happened but I have a tear in my eye. Just one, but there it is. I wipe it with the back of my hand. I'm going to miss this guy. He gave me quite an orgasm. And damn is he hot!

William reaches into his breast pocket. "I don't have much experience with women," he confesses, "I've only had two girlfriends, but I know that I at least want to stay in touch." He hands me a card. Two girlfriends? They must have taught him a lot of moves. I look down at the card. It's an official Akuji Game Reserve business card with William's e-mail address typed at the bottom. The thought that he does this all the time speeds through my mind like a fire truck. I look up. "I hope you will write to me. We have a computer room here at the lodge," he explains. "I've been carrying the card around wondering if I would ever give it to you." Well, you gave it to me all right, I think, breathing a sigh of relief.

I open my arms. One hug for the road? William returns my affection. "See you later," I say when he finally pulls away, "I love you." William gives me a startled look. I cover my mouth. Okay, that totally slipped out. I bite my lip. Why am I always blurting crap? I'm just used to saying that. I say it to my parents all the time. I say it to Max and Libby. It's a figure of speech. "Sorry," I offer. "That was embarrassing. I didn't—" William silently looks at his watch. Now he really must go. Damn! That was absolutely the by-product of fatigue. He looked at me like I was nuts, and who could blame him?

As soon as he leaves I fall back into bed and close my eyes. So sleepy—and yet so satisfied! Sorry I ruined it for him by declaring my love. Oops. At least it happened on the last day. God, what a loser I am.

* * *

Later that morning Libby and Max race into the chalet. "Did you do the deed?" Max shouts. I open one eye. He begins pulling my shoulder out of the socket as if he were opening a car window while Libby aggressively jumps around my legs with all her might. My mattress is her trampoline—and it's the closest she'll ever come to getting on one. She must be drawing from a tremendous stockpile of fossil fuel for this delirious effort. It's like the power surge before the blackout. "Walk me through it!" Max begins to shout. "No, I take that back, walk me through it slowly! Very slowly! I need a Power-Point presentation, I need diagrams and video stills! I need every groan and measurement! I'll pretend I'm you"—he lies down next to me—"and you ravage me! Just ravage me! Do it before I change my mind!" I open the other eye. Max frowns at me disappointedly. Not sultry enough for him? "I changed my mind," he says. "Don't bother ravaging me. But I still need you to get up and do all the other stuff. I put a glass to your door last night but it didn't help. I need to know everything right now. Now! I can't wait. Don't make me pull your hair."

Libby takes one more ambitious jump and thunders down on top of the bed. Someone help her. She moans and rubs her forehead. It's quite possible she's losing consciousness and entering a parallel universe.

I sit up, feeling like the high school quarterback who just sexed up the varsity cheerleader. Max pulls my hair. So that's how it's going to be? "Fine, have it your way," I tell him, relishing the attention. "The truth is as plain as the big nose on your face . . ." Max pulls my hair again. "He has, if you really must know, the most . . ." Max pulls my hair a third time. ". . . fabulous . . ." Max pulls my hair a fourth time. I pinch his nostrils and tell him to stop pulling my hair. "He has the most fabulous"—I pull Max's hair as he pinches my nostrils—"dick I have ever seen."

"I knew it!" he yells, almost tearing off my face. "I knew you couldn't resist him!"

He turns to Libby and sticks out his hand. "Pay up. Told you she'd lay him." Libby reaches into her pocket and pulls out a five-dollar bill.

I give up the details, as requested: uncircumcised, briefs not boxers, long, smooth . . .

"How wide?" Libby asks.

I demonstrate how wide.

"Wow," she says.

"Good one," he says approvingly. "Packing a little heat there."

Libby laments the fact that the last two guys she slept with had penises the size of gherkins. I pat her on the back. Size doesn't matter. Who's the jerk that told her it does? That was silly.

Max spots William's business card on the side table next to my bed. He reaches for it as I describe the smooth texture of William's skin to an enraptured Libby. "What's this?" Max asks, holding it up. I explain that it's William's card, which he gave me before leaving this morning. Max chuckles. "He gave you his card?" he asks with a grin. I nod and ask what's so funny. "Well you have to admit it is funny," he says, "that's a total pro move." He shakes his head. "A card."

I jump to William's defense—or to my own defense. "He doesn't do it all the time," I say. "He told me he's only had two girlfriends."

Max, still amused, nods: "Maybe he slept with them at the same time. That shows emotional maturity."

"He did not," Libby objects, offended by the very idea.

He climbs off the bed. "So what else happened?" he asks. "Who made the first move to have sex?"

I give a little smile. I explain how sweetly it happened, that he said we don't have to have sex, that he would have been fine just holding me. Max covers his grin with his hand.

"What's the matter with you?" I ask.

He shakes his head: "I have to give it to the guy, he made some good moves on you, whether he meant to or not."

"Like?" Libby asks.

"Well," Max says, walking toward the door, "like the part about how you don't have to have sex. It's the oldest trick in the book. It gets women to have sex every time. It plays on their insecurities." Libby asks how in the world he would know that. "I might be gay," he answers, "but I'm still a man."

Libby pats my shoulder: "Don't listen to him, babe," she says.

Of course I won't listen. "You think he's a pro?" I reluctantly ask Max.

"Noooooo," he answers and chuckles again. "I'm just teasing you. Though he did agree to come back to your room fast. Maybe he's used to fucking the customers. Could be part of the gig."

"Max!" Libby protests.

"I'm kidding," he says. "And besides, who really cares? You're not going to see him again. Now get up and get dressed. I need to take my sexual frustration out on break-fast. What are the chances they're serving a genetically modified cucumber with a pair of plump, vine-ripened tomatoes placed on either side?"

* * *

We sit around a table overlooking the pool, sipping mimosas. I am relishing my newfound fame, listening to Max inform me that I am the wind beneath everyone's wings and that I will forever be considered an icon in both the straight and gay communities for bagging a supermodel. A memorial paying tribute to the event will be erected when I die—unless, of course, the act of sleeping with William gave me immortality, in which case a medium-size unframed painting, to be hung in a university library, will suffice. Max offers to stab me with his butter knife to see if I bleed. I look beyond his shoulder and grab the knife. Here comes Manuel. Manuel straightens his silk tie while standing over Libby. He plucks a pink flower peeking out from his breast pocket and rests it near her plate. "I have been looking for you," he says. "I leave this afternoon for Mexico. There is a great deal of work to be done at the tube sock factory. I am overseeing the installation of a state-of-the-art sprinkler system. One can never be too careful. I am relieved that you have not yet departed; I worried that I would be denied an opportunity to say good-bye."

"You won't see her again," says Max. "Buenas noches."

"I will initiate a correspondence," Manuel continues. "I will compose sensual poetry in an impeccable hand. It could very well result in a volume—a book of poetry for my lady. Tell me your home address. I have a photographic memory." Max blurts that we're all homeless. "I am not surprised that you are," Manuel says to Max. He hands Libby a sheet of stationery filled with writing. "Here are my addresses in Mexico City and around the world. We have a number of residences. One

home is made almost exclusively of mother-of-pearl. Send letters to all the addresses, especially this one"—he points to
one of the addresses on the list—"I am there quite often soaking in the Jacuzzi while reading top secret documents. Phone
as often as you like. My butler will likely answer. He is paid to
do my bidding." Lucky guy. He's probably planning to hang
himself before Manuel crosses the border. "It is important that
we never lose touch," he adds.

Libby takes a sip of her mimosa and examines the papers.
"Nice knowing you," Max says dismissively as Manuel pulls
out his wallet, which he claims is made from dyed boa con-
strictor skins. He takes out some laminated photographs and
waves them in front of Libby's expressionless face: "Allow
me one last indulgence before we part," he says. "Here are
several photographs of my thoroughbreds. They were taken
by a famous Mexican artist whom I paid handsomely for the
service." Max informs him that Libby is allergic to donkeys.
Keeping with tradition, Manuel ignores the comment: "Yesterday, in the safari truck, I could not help but overhear that
you are next traveling to Cape Town. You must visit Boulders
Beach while you are there. You can swim with the penguins
while thinking of me."

"Penguins on a beach?" I repeat in disbelief.

"Yes, of course, the beach is teeming with them," he says,
nodding. "They adore the sun." What a sack of crap; Manuel is
so full of it. "Meeting you was one of the great pleasures of my
life," he says to Libby. "Although we live far apart I cannot help
but think we shall meet again. I am confident of it. My father
often travels to New York on business. Perhaps I will accompany him on his next trip." Max begins to say something but
Manuel cuts him off: "As for you, laggard, good luck finding
shelter. You are equal parts undignified and unseemly."

"Oh yeah?" Max answers. "You really think so? Why don't you challenge me to a duel then, ye royal highness?" Manuel calmly kisses Libby's hand, then nods in Max's direction: "Good day," he says under his breath and begins walking away. Max gets up from his seat: "Make me," he calls after him, "I'd like to see you try!" Easy does it. Don't go so hard on him. Max snatches the pieces of paper: "I wouldn't dry my ass with these," he declares and crumbles them up.

We all lean back in our chairs. Libby asks if I'm going to stay in touch with William. I tell her I didn't give him my address and don't plan to. "Why wouldn't you, babe?" she asks in disbelief.

"What's the use?" I answer. "Are we going to have a love affair through the mail?" Libby thinks a love affair through the mail sounds sweet. I scoop up a forkful of her omelet and pop it into my mouth. I encourage her to be a bit more realistic. My chances of maintaining a love affair with William are as good as her chances of swimming with a bunch of penguins on an eighty-five-degree beach in Cape Town, South Africa. I pull out my chair. We need to get back to our rooms and pack.

Helga accosts us on the way to our rooms. She informs us that we must return to our rooms and pack. Is there an echo in here? A car has been arranged to take us to the airport; it will arrive momentarily and we cannot keep it waiting. I go back to my room and pack. Quickly. I don't dare keep the car waiting. Helga might put my head in a vise or check my tonsils with a stun gun. I throw everything into my suitcase, take a final look around, and walk out.

✳ ✳ ✳

Libby and Max are already waiting at the entrance of the lodge, arguing about something, when I get there. The staff, William included, have been lined up like a package of plastic toy soldiers. Helga tells us to shake everyone's hand for the last time. What if we don't want to? I shake everyone's hand and thank them. When it's my turn to shake William's hand he gives me a sad smile.

We are ushered into the waiting van. I take a window seat and look at William. He must pretend, as I must pretend, that nothing happened between us last night. It's like the ending of some melodramatic B-movie. And since when did romance become so unromantic that even a scene such as this gets dismissed—in my own mind—as a scripted TV moment, as sincere as a soap opera? Am I too pessimistic? I can't even give him a parting hug. His skin will never touch my skin again. The driver loads our bags and gets behind the wheel. I want him to race off so we can get this part of my life over with. I look at William again. This is good-bye, you were wonderful.

Before the driver can pull away William risks Helga's wrath and walks over to the open window. I catch my breath. He doesn't say anything, just puts out his hand, palm-side up. I touch the center with two fingers. It's not calloused. I have an irrational urge to jump out. I take in William the way newlyweds take in the setting sun on the last night of their Jamaican honeymoon. I am trying to memorize his face.

As we start to pull away I glimpse four porters standing off to the side, near a cluster of trees, smiling broadly. They look more relaxed than I've seen them since we arrived. As I stare at the group, one of the men glances my way, points—or does he wave? I can't tell—then looks at the porter to his left and starts talking and laughing. Then someone in a white uniform identical to Helga's—one of her minions looks like— runs out of the office waving a piece of paper. He says something to Helga, who looks at me and yells for the van to stop. She marches over and hands me a yellow Post-it note: "Call mother, emergency," it reads. My parents' number is written underneath it. Helga explains that she was just informed that my mother called. It is an emergency. I cringe; how embarrassing. Max and Libby appear worried; Max offers to let me use his phone. I fold the paper in half: That will not be necessary. I thank Helga and tell her I'll take care of it. When she walks off I tell Max and Libby that my mother already called here once, about soup.

"She's a character," Libby says with a laugh.

Yeah, she is. "Well, I'm not calling back so we can discuss what kind of soup is better: minestrone or cheese and potato," I tell them. "Everyone knows the superior choice is—"

"Minestrone," Max and Libby say in unison. I told my mother cheese and potato. That's too bad.

I tell the driver he can go now. I don't need to make a call. He takes off. Just then, Max reaches over me and throws something out the window. It all happens so fast that I don't have time to process it, much less react. The van is rounding a corner when I notice William bending down to pick up a scrap of paper. His ass is the last thing I see. Just like that a little world evaporates. Poof. I turn to Max: "What was that?" I ask. "What did you just throw?"

"Your e-mail address," he reveals. "Made more sense than throwing mine. That, and I wanted to see him bend over one last time."

* * *

We spend the rest of our vacation exploring Cape Town, a bustling city surrounded by lapping white waves. In the evenings, as we drink at bars, eat at restaurants, dance badly at clubs, Libby talks about William. "Did you see how he touched your hand?" she says about fifty times per hour. "What a gentleman," she repeatedly sighs. Max recalls William, too, albeit in a slightly different way. During those next three days, whenever the mood strikes, he flips open his cell phone to show me the picture he took of William bending down to pick up my e-mail address. "What an ass!" he routinely chimes in with a laugh. Each time he does this I can't help but chuckle—I can tell that Max is proud of me for letting loose and sleeping with William. I have to admit that it was one of the better decisions I've made, and from now on I'm going to defer to Max in all matters of love. While standing among the penguins at Boulders Beach on our last day in Cape Town— it turns out Manuel was not making that up—I find myself hoping that the world is hiding men who are just as sweet, if not nearly as good looking, as William. At least one of them will be the guy for me. All I have to do is open my heart.

When our plane finally touches down at New York's Kennedy International Airport, officially signaling the end of our romp, Libby turns to me. "You should go back to visit him this summer," she suggests. I lean across her for a look out the window. There are traces of snow on the ground. Libby tugs at my arm when I don't answer. "Did you hear me, babe?" she asks. I nod without turning away from the window. I do wish I were still on vacation. Perhaps someday I will go back to South Africa. Optimism! And what would William think if I showed up for an unannounced visit, just to check in and say hi? He'd be thrilled to see me again. Wouldn't he?

part Two

When we get off the plane Max calls his father's driver, who is picking us up. After pulling our bags off the luggage carousel we follow Max outside to a black Town Car and get into the leather-upholstered backseat. When we finally enter Manhattan I stare out the window thinking how weird it is to be back. I liked being abroad. True, 99 percent of the enjoyment came from the fact that we were staying in fabulous places I could never afford.

We are heading up Fifth Avenue, driving parallel to Central Park, when Max shouts to the driver. "Stop the car! Pull over to the curb!" The driver swerves to the curb without objection and parks. "Kas, duck down!" he orders. "I don't want him to see you!"

I duck down. "You don't want who to see me?" I ask startled. I have my hands around the sides of the driver's seat, my face pressed against the cold leather.

"Richard," he says in a whisper.

Richard! I slowly lift my head so just my eyes are visible through the car window, then duck back down. Max unzips his carry-on and removes binoculars. I peek again. That's him all right. Richard is sitting on a park bench across the street, at an entrance to Central Park, his arm around a girl. I tell Max that Richard has evidently moved on: that girl is not his fiancée Noreen. "That little asshole," Max marvels. "He's still at it. And after all I've done. This calls for Phase Two."

"What's Phase Two?" Libby asks in wonderment. She takes out her own binoculars. "I like that girl's shoes," she adds, peering through them. "Wonder where she shops."

Max orders her to focus. "Phase Two comes after Phase One," he explains, "and it's worse." He tells the driver to pull up a few yards to a row of hedges and drop us off, then wait for us on the next block. I take the opportunity to grab my binoculars. The driver nods and smiles. "Mr. Max, you are crazy," he says. Max pats him on the shoulder. "Thanks, George," he responds.

We jump out of the car and beeline it for a row of hedges as the Town Car pulls away. We do an army crawl through the dead grass and squat down behind the bare bushes. It's still technically winter and they have not yet turned green, but the branches are dense enough to provide cover. We pull them apart and stare at Richard through our binoculars as he continues flirting with the girl. It's kinda like being on safari. Maybe an elephant will walk by. "I want to give him a hotfoot," Max whispers. And then I hear a voice behind us. It's mousy. "Hey, aren't you that girl?" it says. I turn around. It's fucking Noreen, the crypt keeper, still wearing way too much makeup. Oh shit. She is moving toward me on all fours. I quickly stand up then squat back down. Max turns. "Hey! Get your own bushes," he says to her, annoyed. "We're busy here." I tell him to shut up and explain that this is Noreen, Richard's fiancée. She continues staring at me. "Are you the one who's been playing all those tricks on Richard?" she asks, pointing a Lee press-on finger.

My mouth falls open. Max comes to my defense. "We don't know anything about that," he dismissively answers.

She looks at Max then at me and finally at Libby, who gives Noreen her hand. "Hello, I'm Libby," she cheerily says.

Noreen has a confused look on her face. "Well, if you do have something to do with it, I want to thank you," she says to me. "I'm so glad I ran into you on Valentine's Day."

Noreen explains that, like me, she had no idea that Richard was cheating. She didn't believe it at first—and when they came home that Valentine's night Richard tried to convince her that I was just a crazy person, and that he didn't even know me. But when she couldn't shake her suspicions she started following him. And her suspicions were confirmed. She says he tries to hit on everything that moves. He's made a fool of not only me and her but a handful of other girls that he's been seeing on the side.

"So if you *are* the one behind the pranks I want to thank you," she says to me. "He deserves it."

Max interjects: "Why are you still here?" he asks in confusion and blows into his cupped hands to warm them. "Who are you?" He wasn't listening.

"Richard's fiancée," she repeats. "I've been following him, and now I'm ready to confront him. Richard and me are through. I want to get married but not to someone like that." She takes her engagement ring off her finger and puts it in her pocket. "I don't know why I'm still wearing this," she mumbles.

Max jumps in. "Oh, Noreen," he warmly says to her. "You are wearing too much makeup but I like you anyway. Don't confront him yet. Why do that? Let's work together instead. I'm sure I could put your knowledge of Richard to use." He offers her his hand. She takes it, then touches her face. "Do you really think I wear too much makeup?" she asks with genuine concern. Max smiles at her wistfully and nods: "Of course you do." He points to Libby. "But Libby here is an expert. She'll give you a little update." Libby moves over to Noreen and nods enthusiastically. "Totally," she says, lifting Noreen's chin to the sun with a manicured finger. She examines Noreen's blue eye shadow and too-dark foundation. "I know just the right shades for you."

Noreen turns to me: "Sorry I pushed you on Valentine's Day," she says sheepishly as Libby continues examining her face. I smile at Noreen. She's not my type of chick, not by a mile, but she's genuinely harmless—especially now that she's not trying to scratch me with fake nails. Max breaks up our love fest. He knows the neighborhood; there's a convenience store one block away. He's going to run over there to pick up a few supplies. He tells us to stay put and keep an eye on Richard.

We see Max again some ten minutes later. He is now across the street. He casually sits down on a park bench twenty feet from where Richard and the girl are sitting. Libby, meanwhile, opens her purse, removes some cosmetics, and begins redoing Noreen's makeup. When Richard and the girl finally get up, Max gets up, too, and begins jogging toward them, his head down. When he gets to Richard he bumps into him but doesn't stop running. "Sorry!" Max calls over his shoulder and keeps moving down the block. Richard and the girl turn to look at Max then continue walking in the opposite direction. I raise my binoculars. There is a sign taped to Richard's back: I WET THE BED. Mature. Completely. Just then Libby's cell phone rings. It's Max. He tells us to meet him and the driver on Madison Avenue, one block away. He adds that Noreen should leave her cell number with us. She does so, gladly. "Tell him to call if he needs anything," she says. "And let him know that I still have the keys to Richard's apartment." Her makeup, by the way, looks great.

* * *

George the driver drops off Libby and me in front of our apartment building. We air-kiss Max good-bye. Libby and I, as previously mentioned, live across the hall from each other. We have identical two-room studios consisting of a kitchen and living room—the living room also serves as the bedroom. If Libby opens her front door and I open mine we can see into each other's kitchens. The space between our doors is about four paces. Libby has lived in the building for years. I'm a more recent addition, having moved in one month ago, when Libby told me about the vacancy. I'm indebted to her. The place is rent-stabilized—which means the rent can only be increased a nominal percentage each year. It's a steal by New York standards. Most people I know have to move every couple of years because landlords raise their rents out of the blue by two or three hundred dollars. The market is evil.

As I reach into my jeans for the house keys the yellow Post-it note given to me by Helga falls out. EMERGENCY. I wrinkle it into a ball, unlock my door, and wave good-bye to Libby as she shuts hers. Home sweet home. I drop my suitcase and walk around to make sure nothing has been stolen, and nothing has. I begin sorting through my stack of mail. Okay, a few too many credit card bills here. Not ready for that just yet. Wish someone would steal those. I put the mail aside, press the play button on the answering machine, and collapse onto the couch. I-am-back. Let's see what we have . . .

The first message is from my mother:

"I know you're in South Africa right now but I have a question for you about canned soup. You like soup, I know you do. It's the good kind. But I don't know what flavors to buy. Okay, call me as soon as you get home. I love you. And remember we want to come see the new apartment. We need to set up a day. You know I'd rather have you home in Brooklyn but your father's been asking . . ."

The second message is from, oh, what do you know? My mother. Same with the third and the fourth and the fifth. I momentarily zone out, thinking of William. I press stop on the machine. I turn on my computer and get online. Before checking e-mail I look up flights to South Africa, just for fun. It's never too early to plan another vacation. Besides, seeing William again would be great. It would be amusing to rendezvous annually. Ha! I can't believe I had a one-night stand. It feels surprisingly liberating. I feel like a guy.

I type in two arbitrary dates during the month of July. I light a cigarette while waiting for the results. I begin to hum. What a memorable trip. The price pops up at last. I lean in for an oversize dose of reality . . . $2,230! Holy cow, that's expensive—and that's the cheapest fare? I check a few other dates—same price. Okay then, never mind. That sucks. Wow, why is it so much money? Crap, so much for that. I next open my e-mail to check messages. I scan the row of new messages but nothing catches my eye. Nothing from William.

I pour myself a tall glass of sink water. Here's to living dangerously! I again press play on the answering machine. It starts the messages from the beginning. I listen to the same messages about soup and start systematically pounding the delete key. This is why I don't have a cell phone. And then somewhere around message eight the tone of my mother's voice changes. I catch the first words in a message that begins, "Your poor dad . . ." but I accidentally press delete before it ends. It's my mother's voice but it's not her voice. It's broken. It sounds like she's been crying. I lean into the machine for the next message. "I can't get in touch with you. Where are you? Dad is in the hospital . . ."

Hospital. The water glass drops from my hand and crashes to the wood floor. It shatters, spraying shards across the room. I fumble with the phone and dial my parents' number. When my mother answers she is angry. "Where have you been?" she asks, her voice unraveling. "I've been trying to reach you for the last four days. I've left messages saying it's an emergency. Dad had an accident."

Within five minutes I'm in a taxicab, on my way to Brooklyn.

* * *

I let myself into my parents' house using the key I never relinquished after moving out years ago. I hear my parents talking upstairs. I race up the stairs two at a time to their bedroom. My father is lying in bed on a floral bedspread. His right leg, propped up on pillows, is in a cast from the knee down. His left thumb is completely bandaged up, too. He is holding a stack of papers, which he sets next to him when he sees me. "There you are," he says and smiles weakly. He takes off his reading glasses on a rope. They fall against his chest. I give him a hug and he kisses my cheek. My mother hugs me, too, but I can see she's ticked. She has her coat on and is holding her purse. I ask what happened. Start from the top. I only got part of the story on the phone.

"He fell off the roof," my mother says. "A man his age acting like a twenty-year-old. I told him not to go up there but does he listen to me?" I ask what in the world he was doing on the roof. My mother gives him a look.

"I was hooking up a satellite dish," he answers.

"He was hooking up an illegal satellite dish so he could get every Polish news program," she says. "I ask you, what does a man living in America need with that? What does he care what's happening in the village of so and so at this very moment? Even the people who live there don't care. But your father . . ."

I ask how he's feeling. "It hurts like a son of a bitch," he offers. "Your mother is right, maybe I shouldn't have gone up there." She throws up her hands: She knows she's right. "But I'll tell you," he says with a smirk, "that dish works."

"It works," my mother repeats sarcastically. She buttons up her coat. "I have to go to the deli. Your father can't do it."

My father is a fixture at the Greenpoint, Brooklyn, deli he and my mother own; he knows every customer by name. Apart from family vacations, he's never missed a day.

My mother removes gloves from her purse and puts them on. She tells me that Henryk is at the deli now helping out, and that she's going to check in on him. She adds that it would be nice if I pitched in, too. I nod.

My father calls to my mother as she leaves. "Tell Henryk to cut the Krakus ham thin," he orders. "People don't like it too thick. Mrs. Kurczynski will complain. She doesn't have all her own teeth."

"But she still has a mouth on her," my mother offers.

He next addresses me: "You want to watch the Polish news?" he asks.

"Yeah," I answer. I sit down next to him in bed and pat his hard cast. "You gave me a scare."

"Did I?" he asks with some pride. "You were worried about this old man?"

I look at him disbelievingly. "Of course," I say.

He looks off for a second and shakes his head. "Came right off that roof. When I landed I couldn't breathe." He picks up the remote and turns on the TV without speaking another word. For some reason I'm afraid to ask more questions. Despite what Richard thinks, everything is not a joke to me.

* * *

On Monday, beat from viewing so much Polish programming with my father, I return to my job at the literary agency, where I am an assistant, an assistant who daily considers staging a heart attack at lunch so she can go home early and rest. It's not that I don't like my job, I just prefer rest. See, I am at heart a slacker. I don't understand those who want to wring their jobs of status, power, and promotions, those who yearn for trophies and plaques announcing their valuable commitment as team players. I'm not going to lie: As far as I'm concerned all the team players in the world can take turns hitting each other on the spinal column with trophies while brainstorming. I'll hang with whoever is left.

I settle in at my desk and open the first manuscript in a pile of unsolicited manuscripts that will surely challenge my attention span. It's a memoir by some woman named Sandra May Hanson. I don't like the name and toss the manuscript aside. Unless Sandra May pulls up to my desk in a pink Cadillac I'll continue to assume no one by that name is good at anything. I take another manuscript from the pile and open it to page 134: "The moon crested over the dunes . . ." What's that supposed to mean? I look at the clock. I've been sitting at my desk for two minutes. Okaaaaay, time for a drink of water.

I walk to the watercooler. My boss's secretary, Barbara, whose job it is to be really loud on the phone, lumbers over. There's something unsettling about Barbara. She's really fidgety and nervous and can be sweet one minute and Beelzebub the next. She humiliates the mailman on a regular basis. And she's always crying—not to mention throwing office supplies when she's frustrated: paper clips, pens . . . they usually manage to strike me when I'm walking past her desk to use the copy machine.

"How was your trip?" Barbara asks while smoothing her brown hair, which reaches to the chin, where it swoops out dramatically, giving her the appearance of the Liberty Bell.

"It was good," I answer. "South Africa is—"

She cuts me off. "I've had a busy few days. The kids were acting up," she informs me while anxiously tugging at her New York Yankees jersey. I don't know what's going to happen if my boss ever enforces that dress code. I am about to make my exit when she starts telling me about her daughter's medical bills, which are skyrocketing. Unlike Barbara, I don't consider her daughter to be a human being. She's unique among "daughters" because, unlike most, she eats cat food. And she eats cat food because she's a cat, not a child. Barbara's two pets are her life. I know this because she talks about them all the time. There's Buddy the beagle and Tchotchke, the sickly, aforementioned cat. Around here they are often referred to, exclusively by her, as "the kids." (This is what happens when you don't have kids: You start calling animals kids. Someday I may be Barbara.)

Barbara yammers on while I consider what I can bring my father to help him pass the time while he's laid up at home. I nod my head at her for what seems like two hours until I hear the question: "Do you want to take a look?"

"What?"

"Do you want to take a look?" she repeats.

Yeaaaaaaaah, I heard that part. But that's all I heard. "Sure," I tentatively respond, hoping she doesn't want to show me a mole. She drags me back to her desk, which is crowded with framed photos of her pets as well as stuffed animals and inspirational and feel-good messages like THANK GOD IT'S FRIDAY! and the very confusing IF AT FIRST YOU DON'T SUCCEED, SHOP!!! She pulls a framed photograph from the desk and hands it to me. "Isn't it darling?" she gushes, standing too close to me.

I examine the picture. It's Tchotchke, wearing a baby bonnet and bunny slippers. She looks pissed. Plus she's ugly, a total garbage face. "Very charming," I tell an expectant Barbara, whose eyes are now watering.

"I know," she says, taking it back. She wipes tears with the back of her hand. "I'll get you a copy. I'm having wallets made."

I return to my desk and collapse into the chair. A manuscript laying next to the wastepaper basket catches my eye. I pick it up off the floor. In lieu of a cover letter the author attached a brief note, with just an e-mail address at the bottom:

To whom it may concern:
I wrote this novel to impress a girl.
Sincerely,
S. Konrad

S. Konrad, huh. I wonder what the *S* stands for? I open it and start reading: "On Sunday somebody said something. Somebody said something but it didn't sound like anything . . ."

I read a few more pages and get that feeling. The feeling that doesn't come that often, but when it does I sit up and take notice: This book is pretty great. I wonder what S. Konrad is like? I bet he is really funny (the book at least is). By page ten I'm wondering what the author looks like. And then I start to think of William. I have not heard from him. I thought he'd at least send one message . . .

My boss clears his throat. I look up from the manuscript with a start, like I just got caught doing something I shouldn't be doing. "Welcome back. How's it going?" he asks. He is wearing his standard outfit of brown pants and corduroy jacket with patches on the sleeves. The three remaining sad hairs on his otherwise bald head sway gently as he talks. I tell him everything is fine. Just reading a manuscript. He nods at me absently. "Keep me posted," he says and begins walking away. "We need a winner."

Do we ever. We have not had a "winner" (that's what he calls every manuscript whose author he eventually signs) in a long time. The dry spell has been painful; I can see it's making him nervous. The truth is I'm at least a little responsible for it. He doesn't know this but a few weeks ago we got a manuscript for consideration that I tossed back into the slush pile and then that same author signed with a rival agency. The rival agency sold the manuscript to a big publishing house—it was an eight-way bidding war—for half a million dollars. We could have had that contract. I may not be the most dedicated employee—far from it, in fact—but I have to be paid so that I can continue to eat. What happens to him trickles down to me. Even though I still insist the manuscript was cheesy, the oversight made me question my judgment. Yeah, we definitely need that "winner."

I am absorbed in S. Konrad's manuscript when Max calls. "What's shakin', bacon? Libby and I were thinking of getting smoothies. Wanna come?" Ah, the benefits of setting your own schedule, or, in Libby's case, being unemployed. I tell him I shouldn't. I should work. "It's lunchtime," he reminds me. "Come on." I finally say okay. "Good. But I need to run to the library first to get a few books. Call Libby and meet me there and then we'll go do something fun." He rattles off the cross streets of the library.

"Okay," I answer, "but, Max, I don't have all day, why do you need—" He hangs up. I put the manuscript aside.

* * *

Libby comes to my office and we head to the library together When we arrive Max is at the front desk, chatting with the silver-haired circulation clerk wearing Ben Franklin–style wire-rimmed glasses. "This is really going to be a big help for the research I'm doing," he says to the man. "It's amazing how many great books you found for me in this dilapidated joint." When Max sees us he grabs a big cardboard box off the counter and walks over. "Hi, girls!" he says with a smile. He lifts the box to his shoulder, then places it on his head.

"Need a hand?" Libby asks as we head for the door.

"No thanks," he answers. "I got it."

"Good," she says.

He kicks the door open with his foot. "Let's get a cab and go downtown."

I wave down a cab and Libby and I get into the back. Max decides to sit up front with the driver. He places the box on his lap. Libby then asks the natural question: How is he going to walk around downtown with a huge box of books? He starts to answer but his cell phone rings and he picks up instead. "Peter!" he shouts. "Did you take care of business?" He pauses. "You're a genius, I like it, I'm attracted to it. That is great news . . ." While he chats on the phone I fill Libby in on the morning's events. Max says something to the cabdriver then proceeds with his phone conversation. A few minutes later the cab stops. We're still on the Upper East Side of Manhattan, not far from where we started, near the mayor's official residence, Gracie Mansion, which is situated in a park that overlooks the East River, which separates Manhattan from the borough of Queens. Max ends his call, pays the driver, and we exit the cab. I ask why we are at Gracie Mansion. Do we have an audience with the mayor? He again lifts the box of books and balances it on his head. "I have to run one more errand," he says.

We walk down a path toward the East River and arrive at the guardrail. Max places the box of books on the ground beside him. I gaze across the East River at the factory chimneys billowing black smoke in Queens. A seagull flies by, then another. I look down at the box of books. The one on top is called *Houseboys in Ancient Greece*. Max takes it out of the box. He takes out the book under it as well. This one is called *History of Gay Porn*. He takes out three more books. He holds all five in his arms. And then he throws them, one by one by one, into the East River. "I met up with Noreen last night. She gave me Richard's library card," he says. He takes more books out and throws those in, too. "Looks like Richard will be paying fines on some pretty interesting titles."

He lifts the box off the ground and turns it upside down. The rest of the books fall out like body bags. Splash, Splash, Splash. He sets down the empty box and slaps his hands together a few times like he's cleaning them off. "Well," he says, "my work here is done. Let's go get smoothies."

Libby pulls out her nail file and shakes her head.

"Max," I ask, "don't you think you're taking this a bit far?"

"No," he answers. "It's not my fault he's careless." He taps his temple with an index finger. "Lesson one, when cheating on your fiancée, don't leave shit lying around that can be used to punish you later."

I take a final glance at the books, now receding into the great, polluted watery abyss, gray and white seagulls curiously circling above them. One of the seagulls aggressively swoops down toward the water and hits a book with its exaggerated beak, presuming, I imagine, that it has caught its prey.

* * *

I get home from work that evening around six thirty. I eat, wash some dishes, then find myself with nothing else to do. I drag the only chair in my possession over to the window. My apartment is in the back of the building and faces what only a New York real estate broker who gets paid to make straight faces could call a courtyard. Basically my view consists of a couple of dead trees and the apartment building beyond them. I take a seat, put a cigarette between my lips, and pull back the curtains. I wish I could look out my window in peace. Instead I'm immediately confronted with ten identical windows glowing with light. They're like TVs. I look up, I look ahead, and then down, into an apartment on the first floor. No curtains. I suppose the person living there has given up the delusional notion that there is such a thing as privacy. I have a direct view of the bottom half of a kitchen cabinet and a segment of the shiny hardwood floor (better than mine, by the way). Before long I see a pair of legs, a woman's, followed by another pair of legs, a man's. From the angle at which I am positioned I can only see the couple from the waist down, but, from the way their toes are pointing, I know they are facing each other. They are far enough apart to be talking and close enough to be kissing. Whatever it is, it looks intimate. I get up.

I turn on the computer and check e-mail. My eyes travel down the row of spam. I consider walking over to Libby's to ask if she wants to go get some dessert, when . . .

I focus on two words: *William Johnson.* An e-mail from William! Oh, how sweet. He didn't forget me after all! Self-esteem restored! I was beginning to wonder if I was bad in bed. I need to tell Max to send me some of his pictures of William so I can forward them to everyone in my college graduating class. He's right, I have the best vacation story—and some major bragging rights. People are going to be so impressed with my skills. I never thought I'd say this but a one-night stand can be a big confidence booster—well, if you have it with William. Goodie, goodie, goodie. An e-mail! He was a nice guy. And to think I deemed him a player. I have to be more positive.

I open the e-mail.

> Subject: Hey gorgeous!!!!!!
> wht a wondfull last nite!!!sory fro the weird sent-off bt helga
> wantching me like a hawk!!!!!!!!All I wanted t=o2 do ws kiss u.
> Imiss u. ill right again son!! Luvies☺ w

I read William's message twice. Wow, that is some e-mail. Looks like he lost control of his muscles. I open the rest of my e-mails and send a few, including one to William. He's so hot. And that was a really nice thing to say. I would have no problem kissing him again.

> Subject: Hi William!
> Thanks for the e-mail. I had a wonderful time with you in South
> Africa. You remain, without a doubt, the best-looking man I
> (and Max and Libby) have ever seen.
>   PS--New York anyone? Come on by, I miss you too!

I press send and immediately notice that there is something new in the inbox. Arrived while I was writing. Let's see. Four new messages . . . Four new messages from William. Four? I read the subject headers. They all say "hey gorgeous" but this time without the exclamation points. Maybe he woke up from whatever was preventing him from spelling words correctly. I open the first e-mail.

Subject: hey gorgeous
Helgas ontoo/us!!!!!%$^&#!!!! will

What's he saying now? Helgas ontoo . . . seriously, did he compose this while drunk driving? Hel-ga-is-on-to . . . Oh no, maybe she found out about the sex. I hope she doesn't fire him. That would be terrible. He was so worried about that.

I open the second e-mail:

Subject: hey gorgeous
Hlga just saked/fired me-he sakd mee as I ws righting te first emal. She went threw me drawerz&found te card u droped& I puked up!!! She red the back where u rote: "Thanks for last night. Your dick is HUGE!" shejust showed it 2 mee !!!!!!!!!!!!! I had 2 tell te truth. i broke the lodge rulz bysleeeping w/a guest. I hav 2b gone by end o f weak. i dont now what 2 do!!%^^& tis is terrible, willy

Tis is terible. Tis is willy, willy terible. He got saked/fired! I can't believe he got fired. I can't believe she fired him. Damn. I wonder what he's going to do now? Stupid Max, dropping that card—and writing thanks for last night on the back, not to mention YOUR DICK IS HUGE. Of all the dumb things to do. And William thinks I wrote that? Hope he doesn't blame me. I never would have left evidence like that behind—and I certainly would never have said that thing about his huge dick. He kept saying how nervous he was to lose that job. I stare at the message and reread it. Is this some kind of e-mail code he keeps using? It's like a bunch of gibberish. Why is he writing like that? It seems like he's typing with his nose.

I open the third e-mail:

Subject: hey gorgeous
I dn't want 2 eb a ranger anymre william.
im soo drepressed--soso depresssed

He don't want to eb a ranger anymre william? Why he don't want to do that? What else he gonna do, teach English? And speaking of English, what is the matter with his? Was he writing like this when I met him? This has to be a mistake. I'm pretty sure writing in English is a minimum requirement for me. Until now I didn't think he was capable of doing anything to turn me off. That is such awful news about his job, though. I feel bad.

I open the fourth e-mail:

Subject: hey gorgeous
I wnt 2 come 2 nyc & be sty with u [4 just a litel awhile] & wirte my 400.000$bok on monaco!!!!!!!!!!!!!!! U r a litery agnt. Plese help me///iam soso sad&represed. I ned help!!!!!! Ur a kind persn//I beileive that!!!!!!
I hav something 2 say--I am in love w/u2--I cn't bellive I just told u the truth!!! right buck--plese.i lov ur, willy

I read the e-mail and read it again. It doesn't get any easier. Great God, what is happening? If someone saw these e-mails I would seriously be embarrassed. As I again picture William's face, his beautiful features begin to run together like ink on a tearstained letter. I light a cigarette. I look at the message again . . . he just called me a litery agnt. Wait—does he think

I can get him a book deal? I'm going to kill Max. I don't even remember all the stuff he was saying. Max will say anything to amuse himself. I have to write William back to clear this up. I feel awful . . . I mean he got fired from his job . . . wow, I can't believe he said he loves me. He doesn't even know me—and come to think of it . . .

I take another drag off my cigarette and feel my face get hot as the short days I spent on the reserve flash before my eyes. Oh . . .

I look back at my own e-mail to William. The thing is galloping through cyberspace right now. That last line. "PS— New York anyone? I miss you too!" Is he going to think I was responding to his e-mail? He wouldn't think that, would he?

I look at the inbox. I have a new message.

Subject: Hey Gorgeous!!!!!!!!!!!!!!!!!!!!!!!!
Thnx 4 th fast respinse. Im coming to nyc-can u beleve iit!!!!
    Thnx so much 4 understdin. u saved my lif I cant wait 2 c u.
u-r- all I thnk about gorgeous!!!!!!!!! My reel dreams r comin
tru!!---ill write when I reserv the flight!---iam soso gled I
trustd u!!!!!!! sosoglad!!!!!!!!!!!!!!!!!!!!!!!!!!!!!!!!!!! luv, willy 😊😊

He's so glad he trusted me? I mean this is not a fucking joke. He talks like a normal person when you meet him face-to-face but what is happening inside his brain? And he just told me he loved me—*over e-mail* . . . but then . . . I told him I loved him, too. I didn't mean love as in love love but it sounds like he doesn't know that. Come to think of it, what does he know? What is he thinking right now? That I'm going to make his dreams come true. What can I do, help him learn to write? Was it his accent that threw me off? Did it make him seem smarter than he is? But he is smart, isn't he? He knew so much about nature. The more I stare at William's words the more I feel that maybe his writing is normal and I'm insane.

I open a blank e-mail. I start typing furiously:

Subject: big misunderstanding
dear william,
sorry for the misunderstanding. when I said "new york anyone?" i meant that in a rhetorica . . .

I look over at the inbox. I have a new message. I read the header. Subject: Hey Gorgeous!!!!!!!!!!!!!!! Im cumin!!!!!!!!!

Is he on crack rock right now? How is he doing this so fast? Maybe he knows magic. I can't even take a sip of water this fast. Im cumin? Im cumin? I'm glad someone's cumin because I'm not cumin. And how is it that he can spell *gorgeous* but nothing else? I open the e-mail. William is fading fast. I can scarcely make it out. What is wrong with him??????????????? He's blowing my mind right now.

I continue staring at the screen while trying to piece the clues together like a detective solving a crime. Maybe he has a learning disability. Someone should run a battery of tests . . . or at least one decent drug test. Don't they have compulsory education over there? He's acting like he's never seen the inside of a school. He's having a serious Koko the Chimp moment.

Subject: Hey Gorgeous!!!!!!!!!!!!!!!!!!!! Im cumin!!!!!!!!!!!!!
I bokd meflite ill be thre nxt weak. Hoop u can pike mee up at he aeorport!!!!!!!u-r-alll I thin abut. Iam in lov w/ur WILLY

I jump out of the chair. Good thing the walls in this building are as thin as the Olsen Twins. I start shouting Libby's name. "Get over here now," I bark. "Noooooow!"

Libby bursts through the door seconds later. She asks if I was robbed. I shake my head and explain what just happened. I let her read the e-mails. "What is this gibberish?" she asks, staring at the screen. She's crinkling her nose like she smells dogshit. My eyes widen: "That's what I called it, Libby. Gibberish! It's incomprehensible, right? I barely know what he's saying. Do you know what he's saying? What is he saying?"

"I don't know what he's saying," she admits. "I thought I couldn't spell but he can't spell at all. I think he's coming to New York." Libby turns to me. "Oh, that's nice."

Wrong.

That's not nice. He wants to live with me? I pick up the phone and call Max. He sounds rushed when he answers. I tell him to get over here right now. We have a situation.

"What's the matter, were you robbed?" he asks.

"I wish. It's worse than that. Just get over here."

"Can't," he says. I hear cooing. "I'm on Richard's fire escape with my buddy Peter"—he struggles with something—"we're releasing pigeons into his apartment." He laughs. "One of them just crapped on the couch . . ."

"Got over here now!" I tell him. "You have five seconds to get in a cab. Move it! I'm not kidding."

"What is the matter with you?" he asks, annoyed.

I squeeze the receiver like a lemon: "You want to know what is the matter with me. I'll tell you what is the matter with me. William is the matter with me. He just sent me fifty moronic e-mails in two seconds. He's like the fucking roadrunner. He's coming to New York—"

"Oh my God!" he squeals. There is more cooing in the background. "William is coming to New York! No wonder you're yelling. You need to go to the beauty parlor, chop off those dead ends. Is he going to bring the ranger's costume? It's a little too cold for short shorts but—"

"Max, I need you to focus," I tell him. "I need you here right now, in the moment." Max tries to convince me that he's always in the moment. I look at Libby, who's at the computer rereading William's e-mails. "No, you're not," I point out. "You're in South Africa with William and his rifle." I pause. "Just get over here," I add, my voice trailing off, "and you'll see for yourself. This guy is not right, Max."

* * *

Max comes over half an hour later. He sets down a monkey wrench, a thick piece of rope, the kind you might use to tie a boat to a dock, and a cage. I ask what took so long. "Gravity," he answers sourly. His shirt is smeared with dirt; he brushes off feathers. "Now what's going on?" I let him read the e-mails. He looks at the screen and squints. He has the same look Libby had. He looks like he smells dogshit. "This is a bunch of gibberish," he marvels. "I can barely make out what he's saying. He's a worse speller than Libby." Libby nods: He is. Max takes his eyes off the screen: "So why am I here?" he asks. "What's the trouble?"

"Look at the screen!" I plead. "Don't you see a problem?"

"So he can't spell," Max concludes. "Big hairy deal."

"Don't you get it?" I push. "Don't you see anything wrong with this situation?"

"Let's see," Max says. "There's a hot park ranger coming to have sex with you all the way from South Africa. He's over six feet, has blue eyes . . ."

I begin manically rubbing my forehead. "Stop, right now," I moan. "Max, he doesn't just want to sleep with me, he wants to stay with me and, to top it off, help him with his book on Monaco." I need to send another e-mail.

Max folds his arms. "I forgot about that book," he says as if recalling someone from high school who dropped out after getting pregnant. "Sounded boring. I wonder if he took my advice and started writing?"

"That's the problem!" I scream. "He can't write, he can't spell! Is no one seeing this?"

Libby reminds Max that he encouraged William to become the next Tom Clancy. She wonders aloud if William took him seriously. Max waves his hand dismissively: "Please," he says. "He did not. Who would take that seriously? I was just making conversation. Who would want to be the next Tom Clancy? He's fat."

I look Max in the eye. I'm ready to hit him over the head with the shovel I will use to dig his grave: "Do you want to know who would take such a thing seriously?" I scream. "William would take it seriously. William does take it seriously! He must have believed everything you said, do you understand the implications of that? He must have thought we were big city slickers, thanks to you. He grew up on a farm. He's delusional."

"You're delusional," Max says.

"No, I am not," I protest. I sit down in a chair and put my head between my legs.

"Relax already," Max advises. "I hate it when you get panicky like this. Tell him to cancel if you're going to get your shorts in a knot. You're not under any obligation."

I look up: "He already booked the flight. He's the fastest man alive. How am I supposed to tell him to cancel now? He told me I just saved his life by letting him come to New York. And do you know why he needs his life saved? I'll tell you why, because you got him *fired* when you threw that card with the charming little message, 'Thanks for last night! Your dick is HUGE!' Helga went through his stuff and found it. Apparently it was grounds for dismissal. You forced me to sleep with him. You confused me. This is your fault. If it wasn't for you

I never would have had a one-night stand. You never should have given him my e-mail address without permission."

"First of all," Max says, "this is not an after-school special, Tori Spelling. I didn't make you sleep with anybody. Second of all, you are absolutely blowing this way out of proportion. Stop screaming at me. You're being so loud, and this is so not a big deal."

As soon as Max tells me to stop screaming I start screaming again: "How am I blowing this out of proportion? What am I blowing out of proportion! Tell me, quick. What? Huh? Because I'm not blowing anything out of proportion. He told me I was the best thing that's ever happened to him. He told me he's in love with me. These are not small things. They're weird! I'm not in love with him. I don't know him. I met him *on vacation*. This was supposed to be a no-strings-attached fling. This was supposed to be a movie—*How Stella Got Her Groove Back*. I was trying to get my fucking groove back!"

Libby smiles warmly: "I can't believe he's in love with you. Didn't I say he was a sweet guy?"

Max turns from the computer screen and nods at her. "You did." Then he looks at me and holds up two fingers. Is he giving me the peace sign? It's not going to be that easy. I ask what he's doing. "Nothing," he responds, "I was just wondering why he wrote that he loves you too in his e-mail." He looks back at the computer screen. "You didn't happen to tell him you loved him in the throes of passion, did you? I could see you doing something like that."

I attempt a chuckle. "Yeah, like I would really do that," I uneasily respond. "No, of course not. It must be a typo like everything else."

"Just checking," he says before walking into the bathroom to take a leak. He doesn't bother shutting the door behind him. "Well I for one am looking forward to his coming, blubber buns," he calls over his shoulder. "Do you know how much fun we'll have parading him around town? It's going to be a blast. We're going to get free drinks everywhere we go. This is the best thing that could have happened."

"Somehow I doubt that," I tell him.

"I don't know, babe," says Libby. "He's just a bad speller. It's not that big a deal. I'm a terrible speller and look at me." I look and advise her to stop telling me to look at her.

"Oh let him come," Max calls out from the bathroom. "He can always stay with me."

The phone rings and I jump, praying it's not William. I check the caller ID. It's my mother. I pick up the phone without meaning to. She starts telling me something about more cans of soup she bought in bulk, then something about earmuffs, and then about setting up a couple of days to come work at the deli. I say yes a few times, to what I don't exactly know, while staring at the computer screen. Max flushes the toilet. More bad news. I have one new message.

Subject: Hey Gorgeous!!!!!!!!!!!!!!!!!!!!!!!!!!!-my flite itinerary.

I don't bother opening it. I knew this was way too good to be true. I hear my mother's voice through a fog: "So is that okay?" she asks.

"Sure," I say absently, "I love you."

I hang up and turn to my so-called friends: "Well, it's official," I announce. "He just sent his flight itinerary."

"I'm excited!" Max shouts. He opens my fridge and removes an apple. There is a piece of paper taped to it instructing me not to call Richard (again) because I'm the asshole who called three times. I have to get rid of those things. Max peels the note off the apple's skin.

"It'll all work out, babe," Libby concludes.

I look around. "He's going to stay with me in this two-room studio?" I disbelievingly ask.

"It'll be cozy," Max tells me. "We can all snuggle up in bed together and read stories."

"He's probably too tall to fit." Libby giggles.

Max walks over to the computer and peers at the screen one last time. He makes a face and turns to Libby. "Hey, Lib, so do you think he was serious about Salt-N-Pepa being his favorite group?" he asks.

I can see that Max, for once, isn't kidding. I lean in, stupefied: "He said that?" I ask. "When?"

Libby nods, explaining that William mentioned it in the safari truck on our first night. He did? Where the fuck was I? Obviously not paying attention to the red flags. Max heads for the door. He'd better run. "He's like Crocodile Dundee," he offers. "I think it's sexy."

"Shut up," I call after him.

"Oh loosen up," he responds and bites into the apple. "It's just William." He makes a face, sticks out his tongue, and scrapes it with his finger. "I just ate tape," he mumbles.

I consider Max's words: It's just William. And then I realize something extremely important for the first time, something that I had until now completely overlooked: I have no idea who William is.

I

don't

know

anything

about

him.

None of us does.

* * *

The next few days are a little hectic. For one thing, there's the mouse. Mouse, you say? Yeah. Allow me to share: I was sitting on the couch, minding my own business, when I saw it, moving across the floor like a lone shadow across a sun-drenched sidewalk. Except it was not that romantic. My toes curled involuntarily. I picked up a penny off my coffee table and threw it at the mouse, which began to run toward me. I performed some sort of tribal rhythm dance as it zigzagged between my legs. It bolted past me and escaped through a jagged crack underneath my door that I never noticed was there. Rent-stabilized buildings are great, but they are old as shit, and they have squatters. That night I picked up every couch cushion, every ashtray, every magazine in the apartment expecting to find it hiding underneath. Since then I've purchased two dozen glue traps and placed them around the apartment. I even put one on the spare pillow on my bed, like a hotel mint, because you never know. So there's the mouse, which continues to haunt me. And now, when I'm not wondering whether the mouse is going to crawl into my mouth while I sleep, I'm checking e-mail. I am spending way too much time online, deleting William's messages, which pile up like snow in my inbox. It's a blizzard of nonsense, basically. Apparently he is taking full advantage of his last days of Internet access. Having been sacked/fired, he has nothing better to do. I am now the proud owner of about thirty e-mails regarding his thoughts on the political situation in Monaco, which seems to be worsening (it getin wors!!). I don't even bother reading the e-mails, which are not exactly lucid. In addition to the Monaco e-mails I have received approximately forty or so forwarded mass e-mails—from everyone William has ever made contact with, it seems—on an array of topics including diet pills and horse tranquilizers. An e-mail about the benefits of Viagra was also sent. Twice. As was a link to a Web site where one can buy pocket-size remote-control blimps (Subject: i wan 1!!!!!). And right below the link, six characters: "I luv yu." I can't even count the number of e-mails received with links to various humanitarian organizations. Save the whales, save the trees, save the planet . . . I saved none of them. I pressed delete.

Max and Libby insist that William's visit is going to be great, but it's a little hard to ignore the fact that he can't compose a clear sentence. No one, least of all me, is pretending to be a genius, but William's recent displays of madness have made me wonder if I should. After all, no matter how shallow and superficial I am, no matter how many dumb things I do or say—and it happens all the time—I at least understand my place in life: I am here to make fun of the world. It's usually no more complicated than that. It is entirely weird to be confronted with someone who does not seem aware of his limitations—someone with career goals and dreams that, pardon me, seem beyond his reach. It is surreal to think that in a few days that person will be sharing my four hundred square feet of rental property. The reality of the situation is ever apparent: I'm screwed. How did I get myself into this?

"You are not screwed, babe," Libby tells me.

"You will get screwed soon enough, if you're lucky," Max laughs.

"I am screwed," I answer. "I don't need this in my life. I mean I feel sorry for him." Max reminds me that I need to relax. "Relax?" I repeat. "Yes, maybe I should go on vacation again. Maybe take your advice and sleep with another park ranger and let him follow me to New York so I can fulfill his dreams. It really worked out well the first time. Very relaxing. I mean is this guy trying to use me? He thinks I can hook him up with some kind of book deal?"

He waves me off: "Listen, no one put your hand on his gigantic penis. You keep trying to pin this on me. It's not my fault."

"Max, you were practically on your knees begging me to sleep with him!" I shout. I get on my knees and inch toward him to illustrate the point.

He takes in my pitiful display before helping me up. "He's not even here yet and look how you're acting," he says. "How can you possibly know what is going to happen? Get up already and enjoy the ride. If it's the book thing you're worried about, don't. It'll work itself out. I'm sure of it. He'll be gone in a day or two."

I shake a fist at him. I don't have the nerves for this. I'm a very anxious person when I don't have control over my environment.

"When is he coming?" Max asks.

"This Friday night," I flatly answer.

He claps his hands. He's excited.

I turn to Libby and point a finger: "As for you and your suggestion that I get my groove back like Stella?"

She looks up: "Yeah?"

"Well, I took in a screening of the movie last night—you know, the one you recommended I take a cue from but that you never actually saw—and guess what happens?"

"What?" she innocently asks.

"HE FOLLOWS HER TO THE UNITED STATES AND CRASHES A FAMILY PICNIC!"

Libby enthusiastically nods: "I think someone told me that," she says. "How cute. I can't wait to see William."

* * *

At work that Friday I finish (for the second time, just to be sure) S. Konrad's manuscript and compose a note to my boss highlighting its merits. I leave it on his office chair along with the manuscript. If this is not a "winner," I don't know what is. I think it's good, and I hope he does, too.

With half a day left to kill before I have to leave for Newark International Airport, I go through a fresh stack of manuscripts submitted for consideration earlier that week. If I could just find three decent books to pass to my boss. Three. Is that too much to ask? Even though I can't control the submissions we receive, I feel responsible for the lack of material we have to work with.

Not seeing anything suitable among the submissions, I begin sending rejection letters via e-mail. It's standard practice. Once a week I send generic letters to authors thanking them for their submissions and wishing them luck. In an effort to de-stress I also compose a fantasy letter that thanks an author who submitted a particularly bad book for being such a talentless loser. Feels good! Wish I could really send it! Toward the end of the day Libby calls to arrange a time to meet at the airport. As we talk I send several rejection letters, cutting and pasting the same bullshit about the agency being grateful for the submissions. All in a day's work.

* * *

"It'll be fiiiiiiiiiiiinne," Max assures me as we wait inside Newark International Airport for William to reenter my life. "You are way too high-strung." He checks the monitor and informs me that the flight, lucky number 13, has landed. I nod; it'll be good to see him again. He's absolutely gorgeous, for one thing. And he's certainly the sweetest guy I've ever known . . . or at least the sweetest guy I've known for . . . let's do the math . . . okay, like ten hours, that's how much total time I spent with him—it seemed like it was longer. But this is going to be fun. This is going to be an adventure, like Max said. So what if William has displayed some weird behavior? And so what if he can't write? I mean, who can? Honestly. Let's think this through. Who can? You tell me that. Who really and truly knows how to write an e-mail? Who really knows how to write, come to think of it? It's all a matter of opinion. Maybe he was so busy as a ranger that there was no time to write a complete sentence. Maybe he broke his arm when he picked up the piece of paper Max chucked out the window like a dipshit. Maybe his fingers were chewed off by a shark right after I left and he didn't want to upset me by saying something. Maybe he needs medical attention. Maybe he's been paralyzed. Maybe he accidentally tipped over a bottle of slow-acting poison and swallowed it, impairing both his vision and his ability to think like a human being. Maybe he's hallucinating. Maybe he's high on mushrooms. Maybe he's Jerry Garcia. Maybe he's dying and writing poorly is the only way he has of lashing out at society. Maybe he needs counseling. Maybe I do. Maybe we should go together. It could be any number of things, that's my point. How do I know? I'm not a fortune-teller, warlock, or oracle. And, besides, who am I to judge? I don't want to judge. I want to be open-minded. I want to open my heart. I've been told I'd be a better person for it. I don't remember who told me that but someone did. And here's a thought: Maybe his e-mails were some sort of code meant to throw Helga off his scent. He did tell me he loved me *over e-mail*—maybe he was trying to protect me so she wouldn't find out where I live and come speak to me with a threatening accent that invades my personal space. Maybe his e-mails weren't a bunch of mumbo-jumbo gibberish from another planet that took a team of people to translate. Maybe his e-mails to me were actually hieroglyphics. Maybe he's versed in the ancient art. Maybe the e-mails were dictated to someone else. Maybe a secretary is to blame. (We've all seen Barbara in action.) Or maybe it's a computer virus. Maybe he's a relentless practical joker like Max. April Fools' Day is almost here. Maybe it's that, and maybe something else. The world is a funny place after all. Just when you think you know a person after ten hours he mixes it up a bit to keep you guessing. So who knows? But this is going to be fiiiiiiiiiiiiiiiiiiiiiiiiiiiiiiiiiiii iiiiiiiiiiiiiiiiiiiiiiiiiiiine. I need to relax.

The heavy steel doors open and passengers begin to file out. I anxiously scan the crowd for William's face. And there he is, towering over the competition! Ahhh, he is so cute. He is cuter than I remember. Honestly. A calm comes over me. Man, is he cute. This is going to be okay. He may not be very bright but this is going to be okay. I'm not that bright myself. If I were bright I would not have slept with a person after knowing him only a handful of seconds. The side of practically every New York bus warns against sleeping with people you don't know. I had unsafe sex. This is what happens. I am a statistic. I must deal with it. But this is going to be just tremendous. It could be worse. It could have been herpes.

William moves a little closer. Come to mama, get your ass over here! The old couple in front of him gets out of the way. Shoo, seniors! Come on, hot stuff. Wow! He is so handsome . . . better than I remember.
   Wait a minute.
   Wait one minute.

What

the

hell

is

he

wearing?

"Would anyone mind telling me what he's wearing?" I ask through clenched teeth.

"Tinfoil?" Libby suggests, bewildered.

"Looks like aluminum siding," Max observes, "but where's the rest of the barn?"

William is walking toward me, an enormous smile splashed across his face. He is gorgeous from the neck up but after that it's like a boating accident. He is wearing a fitted silver tracksuit that rustles when he moves. He looks like a cross between an astronaut and an early 1990s rap star. He looks like MC Hammer by way of Vanilla Ice . . . by way of the Space Center. He looks like he dances to Salt-N-Pepa. Where's the uniform? Where is the uniform, William! I forgot he was a human being with feelings and his own clothes. And here he comes, here he is, to remind me—with a soundtrack no less. William rustles over.

"Hey gorgeous!" He picks me up and spins me around. I realize I'm afraid of heights and hold on for dear life. He kisses me as my legs dangle several inches off the ground. (In spite of everything, he's a great kisser.) I try regaining my composure when he puts me back down and tells me I look wonderful, just how he remembered me. I wish I could say the same. I can't. Instead I simply say thank you. Max and Libby give him a hug next. "Hey!" he says. "Great to see you guys again." They answer tentatively: "You, too." The four of us stand there and nod. One of us nods out of desperation. Max opens his mouth first. He suggests we go get William's luggage. Chop, chop. William slaps his hands together: "Let's do it," he says. I give him a look. Really? Because I don't want to do it. Next time I have an urge to do it I'll do it alone.

We begin walking through the terminal, past a row of windows, to baggage claim. "So this is New York," William says. "Great!" Max informs him that actually this is just an airport in New Jersey. He points arbitrarily at the wall. New York is right outside there somewhere, past an expensive tollbooth. William glances out the window. "Right. I'm excited," he says.

"We are, too, babe," Libby concurs with an assuring smile.

He nods again, taking in the airport shops on his right: "Yeah, this is great!"

I look into William's eyes and wonder what's behind them: A sausage casing? A footprint? He seems normal—but he isn't. His e-mails prove that. How does he process thought? Through a pasta machine? He says he's excited. It sounds like English but is it? How would the words *i'm excited* look if he wrote them? Bing, bang, bong, gong, ding, dong, ring—like that? It's shocking to imagine.

Max jumps in: "So, William, I'm noticing this ensemble—"

William cuts him off. He tells Max to call him Willy. Willy is what all his friends call him. I shake my head. Willy Johnson, I think to myself. Willy fucking Johnson. That is two dicks too many, man. Seriously.

Max gives him a look: "You know something? I'd rather not. I'm going to pass on calling you Willy Johnson. Anyway, it's very bright, your outfit. I can't say I've never seen anything like it, I've seen my share, but I can definitely say I never thought I'd see it on you. I almost want to tell you not to rub your legs together when you walk for fear that the material will ignite and blow you up."

We are back on home turf. Max, who can say the most

inappropriate things with a smile that makes you think he's complimenting you, has regained his composure, and his acid tongue. William looks down in admiration at his outfit and informs us that he's had it forever. "This is all I wear when I have time off," he adds.

Libby gets a pained look on her face. "This particular outfit, Willy?" she asks.

Please don't call him Willy. No one call him Willy.

William mentions that he has a bunch of them in an array of colors. Max sizes him up. "It's got a funky urban street feel to it, doesn't it?" he asks.

"I don't know," William answers. "It's just comfortable."

Max touches William's arm and rubs his hand back and forth across the shiny fabric like a DJ scratching a record. "Check one, check two," he looks up and says.

"What's that supposed to mean?" I ask annoyed.

"I have no idea," Max admits, "but that experience warranted some kind of comment. You should try it." Libby asks William if his ranger khakis were uncomfortable. "Good point," Max chimes in, "you should put the uniform back on and give it another shot. If you wait right here I'll run out and buy a Japanese changing screen so you have some privacy." William shakes his head. He doesn't have the uniform anymore. Helga took it all away. Max offers to sew him a new one and asks if anyone has needle and thread. William smiles. He says that now that he doesn't have to wear the park ranger uniform all the time he feels liberated. I wait for Max to tell him that liberty is overrated and that we'd all be more comfortable in a totalitarian regime but he doesn't. Instead the three of us nod in silence as William reveals that he is actively building his tracksuit collection: He has so many great colors, more than could fit in a box of Crayola crayons. The Crayola hues he mentions: Hot Magenta, Electric Lime, Magic Mint, Radical Red, Macaroni and Cheese, Wild Strawberry, Laser Lemon, Razzmatazz, Timber Wolf, Dandelion, Purple Mountains' Majesty, Purple Heart, Orchid, Shamrock, and Asparagus.

William puts his arm around my waist: "I didn't realize how great I'd feel when I got here. I feel great! I'm in love, I'm in a new city. It's a fresh start. I'm already happy."

He's in love.

"Good," says Libby cheerfully. "It's so nice to be happy."

"I am happy," William insists.

"We believe you," I flatly assure him as he pulls me closer.

Max can't get over the tracksuit. He asks if the material breathes. Does William have any rashes to report? "Oh no," William says. "This thing has treated me well!" Max nods. He was just wondering; it was a long flight. William laughs: "I'll check it out when I get home." Home. He means my home. I'm not laughing.

Libby looks down at William's shoes. "I like your hightops," she offers. "I think I had a pair of those exact ones in the fifth grade. Except mine weren't purple. I didn't know they still made those."

I loved those damn ranger boots!

William informs Libby that she was "already styling back then." I think of Terry McMillan, author of *How Stella Got Her Groove Back*, that godforsaken book on which the movie was based. If I ever see Terry McMillan on the street I'm going to trip her.

We pick up William's luggage from baggage claim and take a taxi back to my apartment. The ride home—to my very small home—involves a lot of gawking and explaining. Max and Libby interrogate William about his plans. This time I pay attention. He informs them that he is here to live out a dream and help Monaco in the process. He reminds me that I am the generous girl who made it all possible and assures me that he will not be staying with me forever. (He actually uses the word *forever.*) He is eager to point out that he can access his life's savings using any ATM machine and tells me that he will be helping to pay rent.

* * *

The first thing William does when he walks into the apartment is step on a glue trap. I peel it off the bottom of his high-top like a wad of gum. I feel like his mother. Not cool. He furrows his still-adorable brow: "What is that thing?" he asks. A part of me wants to tell him that my home is overrun with vermin and that I eat beans out of a tin can and don't brush my teeth. Anything to get him to change his mind about staying here. But I don't. I'm embarrassed to tell the stranger I slept with that I saw a mouse. I choose to lie. I begin to explain that it's a glue trap. I don't have mice, he needn't worry, it's a precautionary thing. "It's for mice!" William shouts. I take a step back. What's he shouting for? Maybe he thought it was a stick of gum. Eat it if you want. "That's so inhumane," he tells me, shaking his head. William looks startled and wounded. He's acting like he uncovered an electric chair and black hood in my kitchen. I try to explain the necessity of mousetraps. William informs me that mice are living creatures that deserve to be treated with respect. He collects the traps and puts them on the counter, next to the sink.

Max sighs: "This is New York, William," he tells him. "No one gets treated with respect. You'll be lucky if you don't get punched in the stomach when you go out for a bagel in the morning."

"What's a bagel?" William turns and asks.

Libby finds this question charming. "What's a bagel!" she says. "You never had one?"

I stare at the glue traps on the counter. "It's bread with a hole in it," I mumble.

William says he'd like to try a bagel. Max opens an imaginary book and turns its imaginary page. "Maybe you can write a novel about it," he suggests. He thinks he's being funny. He's not funny. There isn't enough funny in the world to make William's garments or his affection for rodents funny. Libby happily adds to the problem by asking how his book is coming. William takes the question very seriously, as I suspected he might.

William explains: "I wrote a chapter but I don't think it's very good. Writing is hard, you know? It's like you think you're going to say one thing and then on the page it looks like another. And sometimes when you reread what you wrote it can even be a little embarrassing. You thought it was better than it is, you know?"

I must confess that I completely understand. It hurts to admit how well. I tell him that I know what he means: You never get what you expected.

"Yeah, it's hard"—William screws up his face—"but I'll get there. I just have to keep doing it. I'm really proud just to be a writer—and to think I never attended university!" He asks if anyone would like to read the chapter he wrote: It's not that good but it's a start.

Max shakes his head: "That's okay, we've seen enough of your talents via e-mail. We'll just let you simmer for a while in your creative juices. Maybe you can jot down your best ideas in an invisible ink. Writing is a solitary activity. Let's keep it that way, shall we? In fact, it might be good not to let anyone read your work until you are completely done. Maybe next year or the year after that."

"Next year!" William says in disbelief. "I want to be done long before then. I have to be. I don't have any other prospects. I'm counting on this book. Maybe I'll get a big advance of four hundred thousand dollars, or even two hundred thousand. I'm willing to compromise for my dreams. Most of the proceeds will go to charity. I live modestly."

"Modestly?" Max asks. "Did you tell your tracksuits that?"

I look up at the ceiling. I hate you, you no-good fucking ceiling. Max pulls a piece of lint off my sweater. He examines it before letting it fall to the floor. "Maybe you will get an advance and maybe you won't," he tells William. "In the meantime, let's do up Manhattan right. What do you say?" William admits he'd like that and asks if he could unpack his luggage first—he doesn't want to leave a mess on the floor. No, God forbid there should be a mess on the floor. How about the mess in your brain? Clean up the broken bottles in there first. William looks at me expectantly. I hope I didn't just say that thing about his brain out loud.

"Can I unpack?" he asks.

I nod.

Max spreads out on the bed. "Don't worry about making a mess," he offers. "With Libby across the hall this apartment is usually a war zone. Concealer, hair extensions, and fake eyelashes flying like shrapnel. You're going to have to learn to duck." William points out that war zones are not a joking matter. Max ignores this comment and pats the mattress. "This thing is bouncy," he says. The observation seems to overwhelm the ranger, who is blushing as he begins to unpack. Max tucks a pillow under his chin. "So whatcha got in the bag of tricks?" he asks. William pulls a long swatch of fabric out of his raggedy suitcase, which has more holes than a golf course, and explains that he only brought the essentials. Libby takes a seat on the couch. I collapse next to her. William unfurls the fabric. It's as big as a tent, as tall as William himself. It rolls toward me. I lift my foot to stop it. "It's the flag of Monaco," he says, holding it out for us to see. The flag is red on top and white on the bottom. If you turned it around it would be the flag of Poland. Monaco sucks. They need a flag that isn't the Polish flag turned upside down. Libby lifts a corner of the flag off the floor. When she marvels at its size, Max turns on his side and props up his head with his hand. He wonders aloud if it's as big as . . . He hesitates and looks over at me. I shake my head no, then ask William what he plans to do with the flag, hoping he doesn't want to hang it up someplace.

"I was hoping you would let me hang it," he says. "I know I won't be living with you forever, I am planning to rent my own apartment, but for the time being I was hoping you would let me hang it. It would mean a lot to me."

Max calls out from his spot on the bed: "Oh, don't be silly, William, now why hang that thing up?" For the first time since we returned from South Africa I am grateful to Max. "Seriously," he continues and pats the mattress, "you shouldn't hang it. You should use it as the bedspread. I mean you might want to run it through a dryer with some fabric softener but after that I bet it'll be as soft as a kitten on a summer's day." He gets off the bed and snatches the flag before I can suggest a few more options, including using it as a carpet or pool cover. He drapes it across his back like a superhero and takes a few bold steps. He asks if he can borrow it for Halloween. I tell him to give it back. Now. He relinquishes the cape and lies back down on the bed. "Come on," he sulks. "I don't want to have to dress up as Agatha Christie two years in a row."

"Then go as a fool who offers bad advice," I tell him, "that way you won't need a costume."

William doesn't know what to make of this exchange and says nothing. Libby asks where he wants to hang the flag. He looks at me. What, you gonna hang it on me? Haven't I suffered enough? He answers that he was thinking of hanging it over the sofa. I glance behind me at the empty wall. I knew I should have put an eleven-by-fourteen of my family right there. Damn. I sadly answer that he can hang it if he's sure it's the right thing to do. "Thanks!" he shouts. "This makes me very happy. It's going to inspire me. I can look over at this flag while I write my book about the political situation in Monaco."

Max rolls onto his back. He stares at the ceiling. "Aren't you done writing that book yet?" he moans. "I feel like it's all we talk about anymore. It's driving us apart." William looks at me for help. I assure him that Max is just kidding. "No, I'm not," Max protests. A confused William shakes his head. He tells us that we are a lot of fun but that he's definitely going to have to get used to our sense of humor. Libby reminds him that there will be plenty of time for that. Yes, tremendous.

I help William hang the flag of Monaco on my wall. I can't believe it but there it is: I am helping a former park ranger/one-night stand hang his flag of Monaco, which is the Polish flag upside down, on my wall. Once the flag is up, Max offers his unprofessional opinion. "I'm not a huge fan of those colors in this apartment," he admits. "You should hang the flag of some other country on the wall instead. Do you have a French flag in that suitcase of yours?"

The flag looks terrible; it makes my place look like a college dorm. I say nothing; William continues to unpack. I give him a section of the closet to hang his tracksuits. By the grace of God, everything fits. "Done," he finally announces. Libby opens her eyes. Max sits up: "I'm really, really, really, really bored right now. I can't keep lying here or I'll get rigor mortis. Can we leave?" I tell him to get his ass up. He jumps off the bed. "Where to first?" he asks. William turns to me. He expresses interest in buying one of those T-shirts that say I LOVE NEW YORK and asks if I think he can find one in New York. I shift my weight from one foot to the other. I don't think it's appropriate to love New York that much. What would the neighbors say?

"No," Max lies. "They stopped making those because they're ugly. Sorry. Besides"—he points at a pair of apricot-colored nylon pants on the floor that William forgot to put away—"it looks to me like you have enough clothes." I nod. We are not buying any dumb clothes. We have an abundance of them already. William looks disappointed. Max sighs: "Tough break but they just made those I LOVE NEW YORK shirts illegal, William. It was on the news. You'd be arrested if you got caught with one. There are a lot of con artists in this city so if you see those shirts spread out on a folding table or dirty towel when we are walking around just resist the urge to approach the vendor. He could be an undercover cop." William wants to know why they are illegal. I jump in, explaining that they are not really illegal, Max was just kidding.

Max pats William on the back: "No, I'm not," he says. "They are illegal. It's the mayor's fault. We're trying to vote him out of office but we don't vote." The expression on William's face is blank. We have so much in common.

In an effort to speed the party along I ask William where he would like to go on his first night in New York: Soho, Chinatown, the East Village, the West . . . "Times Square," he says. "I want to see where they film MTV videos." Max bows his head as if in mourning. He explains that, unfortunately, that has been made illegal, too. So has the Empire State Building in case that was going to be William's next suggestion. "Let's go to the East Village instead," Max tells him. "It's a way more fun neighborhood. Less generic."

William nods. He walks to the door, which is when he notices the intercom and moves toward it. He wants to know what it is. It's a bagel, of course. When Max jokes that it's used for killing animals that don't deserve our respect and compassion William grabs it with both hands. I hurl myself at him before he can tear it off the wall. I explain the intercom's function. You press the talk button to talk and the door button to open the door. Now I know my ABCs next time won't you sing with me. Come on!

Libby is brave enough to ask William if he'd like to change before we leave. I hope she means into a tarp. That would be an improvement. Max takes a moment to squeeze William's bicep before grabbing him by the arm. "It's the Village," he casually offers. "As long as he's not wearing an I LOVE NEW YORK T-shirt he'll fit right in. He wouldn't stand out if he got electrocuted in the street, which I've actually seen happen." He rubs the tracksuit for the second time. "William," he says, "I bet your costume conducts some major electricity. We could probably get phone reception out of the zipper. You may not need a cell. These garments are saving us money already. The more I see them, the more I like them. Come along, I'll let you buy me a bottle of booze to celebrate."

William turns to me. "Is it true that New York is the city that never sleeps?" he asks out of nowhere. I put my hand on my hip and tilt my head to the right. I don't even know how to answer that. It strikes me as one of the most random things ever uttered. It's like waking someone from a sound sleep to ask if they like peppermint. I could tell him what a friend of mine once said, that New Yorkers never sleep because they are too busy trying to afford to live here. I could say this, but where would it get us?

Max answers for me: "Yes, it's true. New Yorkers never sleep. Always believe everything you read and hear."

William nods.

Now, see, here's the problem: There's no telling if William knows my friend is kidding, now or ever. Even when it's something as obvious as that, I can't be sure. Max, Libby, and I are just similar: We get one another. We're like girls who hang out so much our periods come at the same time. William does not get our humor. Even in South Africa our banter soared over his head like a great American eagle. At the time it didn't matter. I have to point this out to Max before he accidentally convinces William to throw himself off the Brooklyn Bridge.

* * *

We take the 6 local train to the East Village. William is mesmerized by the sights and smells of the New York subway system, the only place where you can mingle with a thousand nationalities simultaneously passing gas. Our ride is rather like the Noah's Ark of this scenario. I wish I had nose plugs— and maybe sunglasses to take the glare off William. Every time I look at his clothes I feel like I'm forcing my eyes open during a solar eclipse.

As soon as we get out of the subway William notices the little stores and booths lining St. Mark's Place. "What's all that?" he asks excitedly and veers left. I call after him: "It's just a bunch of junk! Your typical tourist trap." He turns around: "Looks cool. Can we see?" His face is amazing. I do not have the power to resist. I tell him to be my guest. "Great!" he says and bolts toward a display of hats, bracelets, and sunglasses. I turn to Max and shake my head disapprovingly. "What?" he responds. "Take it easy, let him look at the crap." I whisper that I don't want William to stay with me and that this is already incredibly stressful. He sees that I'm being dead seri-

ous. "Here's what will happen . . . ," he begins. He repeats
his earlier promise: William can stay with him; he has plenty
of room. He tells me that when—if—I am feeling truly overwhelmed, all I need to do is give him a signal. I should touch
my finger to my nose. When I do, he will jump in and invite
William to stay with him. I nod, then point my finger at his
chest and warn that I will take him up on this if need be.
He raises his hands over his head like he's the victim of a
stickup. "Fine, go ahead," he says. "I think it would be fun!"
He pauses. "But I have to admit, he feels like a whole different person to me now that he's in New York."

I stare at him. "Really?" I sarcastically ask. "You think?"

We stroll over to Libby and William, who is turning over the
useless loot like an enchanted magpie. Libby asks what he
likes. "Everything!" he exclaims while examining a knit cap
with the letters CIA printed on it. Max takes the CIA cap from
him and puts it back on the table. "You don't want that," he
says disapprovingly. "Let's keep it moving, hot pants." William
moves to the next bin and picks up a necklace of oversize
white stones with gold accents. I suspect it was stolen from
Elton John's 1973 garage sale. The only thing it would go well
with is a broken piano. Max touches one of the stones: "That
actually matches your outfit a little more," he says to William. "You'd be making a very bold statement. I'll write up
the press release tonight." William holds out the necklace for
me to see. What kind of idiot would be caught dead wearing
something like that? I wouldn't use that clunker to prop up
a door at the Little Rock, Arkansas, county jail. "I'm going to
buy this for you," he says.

My mouth drops open. "Oh, no, please don't," I plead. "I
don't need it. I have enough jewelry. I'm begging you not to
do this thing, William."

"No, I insist." He grins. "I want to buy my girlfriend a present."

Girlfriend?

"How romantic," Libby coos. I step on her foot. Shut it.

William pays for the necklace and makes me try it on. I put it around me and immediately get a headache, possibly whiplash. It's so heavy I wonder if my kneecaps will crack under the pressure. I take a look at myself in the little mirror near the display. I bear a strong resemblance to a sick dog who's been made to don one of those preventive plastic cones around its neck. It's completely humiliating.

"It looks beautiful on you!" William exclaims.

Max touches my cheek. "It's certainly a striking ornament," he says with mock sincerity. "It's like you're wearing a grand ruffled collar. You look like Shakespeare and Queen Elizabeth on their first and only date—right before they had a one-night stand."

I widen my eyes. I'm really going to kill Max, talking about one-night stands like that. Now he's stepping over the line. No more. I stare him down then touch my finger to my nose. I repeat the move five times. That's right, pal, he's all yours now. Bet you didn't think I'd take you up on it.

William doesn't seem concerned that I'm touching my nose. He throws his arms around me. "You remind me of a princess in that necklace," he says with pride. "I love you so much, and I'm so glad I gave up my virginity to you."

I begin to feel the blood draining from my face. I pull back. I'm sorry, what was what? He's a virgin? Or was a virgin? Max lets out a deep whistle. "No way," I hear him say.

I look at William to see if he is being serious. When he said he's only had two relationships I obviously assumed . . . oh sweet,

sweet and precious angels of mercy, what kind of shit have I stepped into here? I thought Salt-N-Pepa was bad but this. All eyes are now on William. "You've never had sex?" I finally ask.

William smiles: "I have now!" I respond that I had no idea he was a virgin. (My God, if I had known that I never would have slept with him.) "Yes, you did," he tells me. "I told you the same night that I lost my virginity." I shake my head. No, he did not. I'm positive I would not have missed that one. He continues: "We were in bed. I started to say that I had never made love before but you put your finger to my lips and said, 'I know.'" I smile weakly. I remember it now. I thought he was going to tell me he had never met anyone like me. I was trying to spare myself the line; it was the same bullshit Richard had fed me. William affectionately squeezes my hand. "What's a one-night stand?" he innocently asks. "Is that when people stay up all night drinking?"

Ohmygod.

Max covers his face with his hands. He slowly splays two fingers and peeks through. "Uh-huh," he confirms, still keeping his face covered. "That's exactly what a one-night stand is. You and I are going to have one tonight." William smiles. "New York is the city that never sleeps!" he says.

Oh-my-God.

Max brings down his hands. "William," he tentatively says, "how would you like to stay with . . ." I mouth the word *No* and bow my head. I can't pawn William off now. Consider the finger removed from the nose. This is a huge development.

William continues perusing the merchandise. He buys several Big Apple–themed knickknacks, including a Giants pendant that my colleague Barbara would adore and a shot glass with a picture of the Statue of Liberty. He informs me that he loves the Statue of Liberty and asks if it's made of wood. It isn't, but your head is, I want to suggest. How is it that he knew so much in South Africa? Now he's just an unsocialized mess. Damn! I had no idea that there were any twenty-three-year-old virgins anywhere. I really didn't. Yes, I've been using the *I'm a virgin* line on my mother since I turned eighteen, but I'm still surprised that she falls for it. Now I know why she does: It's not unfathomable.

Before long William is offering to buy me a shot glass or two of my own. Max intervenes, informing him that I don't need any because I already have a collection of shot glasses from my travels to Rio de Janeiro. I have never been to Rio de Janeiro and Max knows it. He's just saying this to torture me. Isn't the fact that my apartment will soon resemble a gift shop torture enough?

As we wait around for William to finish up his shopping spree I begin to notice the effect he is having on passersby. Every woman and many of the men are tripping over their shoes while giving him the eye. If you've never seen William, looking at him for the first time is like witnessing a miracle. It's not the hideous clothes you pay attention to, it's the face, which is flawless perfection. But William couldn't care less about these people. Even a pretty blonde bumping into him doesn't make an impact. William only has eyes for trinkets, and for me. He takes my hand: "You're wonderful. And I love that necklace!"

Yes, the necklace. I need someone to hold me upright when I have it around my throat. It's like wearing a candelabra or an inner tube.

* * *

Late that night, after William arranges NYC souvenirs on every available surface in my apartment, we have sex for the second time. Or, as William puts it, we make love for the second time. I enjoy being with William but I don't enjoy the feeling I have afterward. I can't separate my thoughts from the act itself.

William means well but this is not going to work. I am not in love with him. How could I be? But the thought of telling him breaks my heart. I robbed him of his virginity and he responded by professing his love and loyalty—if I dump him now he could be fucked up for the rest of his life. He could turn into a misogynist like Richard. Introducing another Richard into the world is not something I'm interested in doing. Damn, I feel like a heel, especially when William looks me in the eye and says things like: "I want to tell you again how happy I am that you are helping me. I was really confused after getting fired. I thought I was going to amount to nothing. But you really, really helped me. You are the nicest person I know. Someday I will return your generosity. Before my uncle Dale died he told me I could do anything if I tried hard enough—all I want to do is make the people I love so much proud of me. Thank you for the opportunity. You're not only my girlfriend, you're my best friend."

I put my clothes back on before returning to bed for the night. William is already asleep. Not a hint of jet lag on his sweet face, not a single care in the world. I'm going to have to learn to tolerate him for a little while. I have no choice.

* * *

I tiptoe out of bed the next morning and go into the bathroom to shower. I turn on the hot water and take a seat on the edge of the tub. I light a cigarette and watch the water run down the drain. Before long I hear what sounds like the buzzer and then, if I'm not mistaken, William saying something. I open the bathroom door to find out what's going on. He's supposed to be asleep. William is standing over the intercom, scratching his balls. "What are you doing?" I ask, walking toward him.

He turns around. "Good morning!"

I repeat my question.

"You have visitors," he says. "I just buzzed them in using this intercom, just like you taught me to do last night."

I open the door and peek into the hallway. "Who is it?" I ask suspiciously. "You can't just let strangers into the building."

"They're not strangers. She said . . ."

I hear my mother's voice. "This hallway is dirty," she says between deep breaths. I slam the door. Oh shit! I look at William in terror. "You let my mother in?"

"I think it's your whole family," he explains. "She said you were expecting them."

I take in William's appearance. He's practically naked in a pair of too-tight white briefs—it's like we're on the set of a porno. His dick is enormous.

It's important to understand something: This is a problem. My relationship with my mother is defined by the things I choose not to reveal. She is about to see a side of me that I have never exposed—that I never planned to expose. My mother is moral, she is strict, she is a traditionalist. She thinks women should marry, be wholesome, go to church, and not have illicit sex with strangers and then invite them into their homes. I don't talk about men with her. I would not dream of it.

I begin jumping in place, flailing my arms at William. "What are you standing there for? Hurry up!" I shout, my head spinning. Where can I hide him? A matchbox? He's too big. The stove, the fridge, behind the flag of Monaco? Maybe I should just jump out the window . . . "Go put some clothes on. My

mother is going to kill me when she sees you here." Maybe
I can stick him in the corner and put a lamp shade on his
head . . .

"You didn't tell her about me?" he asks, confused.

I open the closet. "Why would I tell her about you?" I
scream.

"I told my parents all about you," he responds, sounding
rather hurt. "They love you as much as I do."

I need a tracksuit. "It never came up," I shout. "My mother
is always the last person I tell anything. She can't handle the
truth." Holding the cigarette between my lips, I pull a canary-
yellow terry-cloth number off a hanger and toss it at William.
It hits him in the face like a bucket of ice water. Wake up!
"Get in the bathroom and put that on," I order, my hands
shaking. "Hurry up. Move it!" Before he can close the door I
run in after him and throw my cigarette into the toilet bowl.
Shit! She's definitely going to smell that. She's a fucking blood-
hound. Fuck. I don't smoke.

My mother walks in. Her long black coat is open, revealing
a preppy light blue sweater with pearl buttons. She is followed by my brother, whose baseball cap with the frayed bill
is pulled low over his eyes, and my father, on crutches. He
peers at me from behind his reading glasses. "Who was that
that let us in?" my mother asks and immediately wrinkles up
her nose. "It smells like a cigarette in here. Were you smoking cigarettes?" I remind her that I don't smoke. I ramble that
I had a party last night (lie). Some girl lit a cigarette before
I could stop her (lie again). I ask what they are doing here.
My mother answers for the group: "You knew we were coming today." No I did not. "No I didn't," I respond as if it mat-
tered at this point. "You did," she confirms. "Your dad, who
should be resting"—she gives him a look—"wanted to see the

new apartment. You've been here a month now." My mother reminds me that we spoke on the phone about this. She hands me a heavy plastic bag. Don't I remember talking about the cans of soup? As soon as she says soup I recall the day of the conversation. We were talking while I was getting the bad news about William's arrival. We made plans without my realizing it. I put away the bag and tell her that it must have slipped my mind. "So how is it living all alone?" she inquires and takes off her coat.

The bathroom door opens and William comes out wearing the yellow tracksuit. He's a banana. Everyone turns. He hands me my cigarette pack. "You left your cigarettes in the bathroom," he says. "Here you go." I gingerly hold the box between two fingers and glance at my mother. I quickly explain that the cigarettes are not mine. "Are you sure?" William asks. "They look like the ones you were smoking last night."

I shake my head wildly: "You got me mixed up with someone else, friend. I don't smoke. Everyone knows that." I shrug in my mother's direction. This is such a big misunderstanding! William is mystified. He's a mystified rotten banana. "They do?" he asks. I face my mother and start rambling out of nervousness. "It was a dark night," I offer. "He doesn't know what he's talking about. He had too much punch."

"What kind of a party did you host?" my mother asks. "You turned off all the lights?" She looks at William: "And who are you?"

William offers his hand. "I'm Willy Johnson, your daughter's boyfriend."

My mother's eyes widen. "Boyfriend?" she repeats and glances at me. "I had no idea."

I shake my head no. No, I don't have a boyfriend, not on your life.

My father looks to my brother. "Willy Johnson?" I hear him repeat. William approaches my father, offers his hand, and explains that all his friends call him Willy. My amused father accepts the challenge. "What do your enemies call you?" he asks.

William looks confused. He's about to say something else but my mother won't let him. She has her own agenda. "Did you sleep here last night?" she asks him after looking around the room. I try to get in there before it's too late. "I live here," William clarifies. Shit. It's too late. My mother looks appalled. I am a virgin after all. Besides, as mentioned, people in my family get married. They don't live together in sin. She takes me in with eyes so cold I begin to wonder if there are icicles on the tip of my nose. In fact, I'm almost positive I have freezer burn and need to be thrown out with the rotten banana to my right.

My brother chuckles under the hat: "I knew you smoked," he quietly says.

My mother moves into the living room. She confronts the unmade bed as if it were the defendant in a murder case. "He lives here?" she repeats. I need to step in—I'm the lead witness . . . a very chilly lead witness.

"No he doesn't live here," I start. "Not here. He lives, but not here. Why would he live here when he lives so far away? This is my friend from South Africa. When he said boyfriend he meant friend. Those words are synonymous in his home country. He came to visit for just a few days. He's on a whirlwind tour sponsored in part by a local college. It's a cultural exchange program. He's leaving on Saturday . . ." My father reminds me that today is Saturday. I nod, I can't stop myself. When I'm nervous (read: trying to avoid getting busted for something) I have a tendency to ramble. The words pour out like vomit as I free-associate like some bad beat poet. "He's leaving Sunday morning, bright and early," I explain, mostly for my mother's benefit. "He's off to stay with another platonic acquaintance to study his domestic habits." I look over at William, widen my eyes, then rapidly blink several times. I'm hoping he'll hop the hell aboard and work with me here. William looks at my mother and smiles. All is not lost. William's smile is irresistible.

"Where's he been sleeping then," my mother suspiciously challenges.

I point to the couch. Right there. Where else? "In the bathroom!" William announces at the top of his lungs.

"In the bathroom?" my dismayed mother repeats. I lean up against the kitchen table. I look at my father on crutches and blurt that William has a bad leg. He has more room to stretch out in the tub. William looks from my mother to me and back again. My mother just stares ahead. I start counting the veins in her neck. One, two, three, four . . . there sure are a lot of them. William notices her expression and begins to nod, like he finally understands. "I'm leaving tomorrow and I sleep in the bathroom," he awkwardly says. "And I have a bad leg." He walks over to me, faking a limp, and takes the pack of cigarettes out of my hand.

My father studies William. "Is he mocking me?" he asks Henryk.

"This is my pack"—William waves the box—"I just remembered all about that."

"You forgot you smoked?" my father challenges. I can tell he believes none of the crap we are shoveling. William makes a display of opening the pack and putting a cigarette between his lips. "Care for one?" he asks my father, holding it out tentatively. "They're delicious. I'm addicted to the richness."

"Maybe later," my father answers.

Henryk steps forward. He'll take one. My mother turns

around, slaps him on the head, and tells him his days are numbered. He straightens his hat and tells her he was just kidding. I take the opportunity to warn William not to light the cigarette, knowing he would choke if he did. William is grateful. He takes it out of his mouth. I wish he'd take his tongue out.

"Good idea," William mumbles.

My father slowly makes his way to the cabinets over the sink and opens one. Thank God I didn't hide William in there. "So this is the apartment," he says, beginning the inspection. One of my DON'T CALL RICHARD warnings falls out. I race over and pick it up off the floor. "How much did you say you're paying for this place?" he asks as I return the sign to the shelf piled with dishes. I know my father knows how much I'm paying and I remind him of this. He just wants the opportunity to tell me it costs too much. According to him, everything in America costs too much. He responds that I should have haggled over the price. *"Nie umiesz handlować?"* he asks in Polish. I tell him the price was fixed. He offers that I should know better and turns on the faucet full blast. Thank God I didn't stuff William in there. He proceeds to explain that he gets discounts all the time. Yeah, discounts of the five-finger variety.

My hot-blooded mother gestures in Henryk's direction: "Don't listen," she orders. She puts her hand to her cheek: "You should be ashamed of yourself, Bronek," she scolds. "I don't care what you do anymore," she dismissively concludes. "Do what you want. And have a seat instead of walking around."

My father continues doing what he wants, which in this case means peeking into corners and testing hinges. He looks down at the hardwood floor, points to a spot, and tells Henryk to jump up and down on it. He wants to see something about those floorboards. Henryk walks over and jumps. Thank God I didn't bury William under the floorboards. I still can, though. After they leave. The beating of his heart won't bother me a bit. I'll dance the rumba to it. As Henryk jumps my father concentrates on the sound. "They should fix that for you," he says once Henryk stops jumping. "It squeaks." I tell him it doesn't bother me. I don't spend evenings jumping up and down on the floorboards. "You should have them spend the money to fix it," he persists. I tell him I'll call to get it fixed even though I'll never do any such thing; he is momentarily appeased.

He next notices William's heap of New York City souvenirs, some of which, including the shot glasses and a beer mug with a red apple on it, have been displayed on the kitchen counter. He moves one of the glasses across the counter and asks why I have all these knickknacks. My mother glances over. "Oh, that's from the party," she confidently answers. I nod. Very good. William clarifies: Those are his keepsakes; he loves New York. My father picks up the beer mug and turns it over, probably looking for a price tag, as my mother dismissively tells William to buy himself one of those I LOVE NEW YORK T-shirts because they're trendy, everyone's got them. William looks at me; I shake my head no.

I proceed to apologize to my parents for the state of my apartment. I don't have any food, much less kitchen chairs (I have only one of those). It's just not a good time to be playing hostess.

An overeager William offers to get provisions. My mother refuses, saying they already ate. He hasn't won her over. Henryk takes a seat on the floor and reminds her that he hasn't eaten. My mother reminds him that he should have eaten when he was given food; instead he's always going off to McDonald's filling his body with junk. I catch William's eye. I ask if he'll run down to that store on the corner of the block and get a coffee cake or chips or something—anything.

"Of course," he says. "Pleasure."

I take out my wallet and hand him a ten-dollar bill and my keys. I tell him to just stroll down to the corner store, pick out something, and please, please take his time. "I'll hurry back," he says and leaves. Yes, hurry back. You read my mind, mind reader.

* * *

"This is quite a shock," my mother says as soon as he's gone. "This is the last thing I expected when I showed up here." She snatches the pack of cigarettes William left on the table and puts them in her purse. Damn! Cigarettes are expensive. I assure her it isn't what it looks like. (It's worse, for a slew of reasons. And here I am, a grown woman treated like a child by her mother, having to lie about all of them.) I promise her that I am not sleeping with William and that he certainly is not living at my place. My father lifts the cover off the stove. He's making sure the pilot light is on. He asks if I met William on the trip. I tell him that, yes, William and I met on the trip. I really hope he doesn't ask about the cultural exchange program. I'm out of strength.

"So he's South African?" my mother asks.

"He is," I nod nervously. "Hence the accent." My father replaces the stove cover, confident that I'm not dying of gas poisoning. "I'm surprised he's not black," she responds. I point out that there are both white and black people in South Africa. She folds her arms and observes that William is very tall. When she asks if everyone in South Africa is as tall I shake my head no. I don't think so. "Sure is a looker," she adds. He is that.

My father walks into the bathroom and begins banging on a pipe with one of his crutches. My mother takes the opportunity to ask what William's parents do for a living. I tell her I have no clue because I don't. I conveniently leave out the part about how, immediately after the first time we had sex, I forgot his first name for a good ten seconds. She offers some advice: "Put garbage bags down at the bottom of that tub as a precaution. Never know what kind of diseases people are carrying. He may have something, being from a foreign country." I roll my eyes. My father comes out of the bathroom. He's from a foreign country. I ask my father if he has any diseases. "Xenophobia," he jokes. "I contracted it from my wife."

My mother isn't in the mood for jokes. She reminds him that he once knew a guy who came back from some tropical destination with a disease. He nods—"It was sun poisoning," he tells me—then asks why my friend was wearing that bright yellow outfit. My mother answers for me: "That's how they all dress these days. It's the fashion. It's trendy." Yes, it's so trendy. I love New York. When Henryk volunteers that not everyone dresses like William, and that, in fact, he never has, my mother reminds him that he's unique. He protests: "No I'm not. I don't own any outfits that are as unique as what he had on."

She looks at him with annoyance: "Take that hat off your head now. You're in the house."

He makes no effort to do so.

I hear keys jingling and turn toward the door. William enters empty-handed, his beet-red face glistening with perspiration. Where's the coffee cake? Maybe he couldn't find the store.

"I was mugged," he announces in horror. "The ten dollars is gone." He begins to pant, like he's hyperventilating.

My mother gets to her feet: "Mugged! Are you okay?" she screams, her eyes darting from side to side as if muggers are taking over the apartment. I reclaim my keys and ask what happened. William explains: "I bought the coffee cake and was walking back to the apartment when a man came up, took it out of my hand, and walked away. I tried to convince him to give it back but he wouldn't. I followed him to the liquor store and that's when he took the change. He bought beer with it, I guess to wash down the coffee cake. I came home. Sorry."

My mother opens her arms and William bends at the knees to claim his hug. He's the tallest baby in the world. She assures him that everything is going to be okay and that he should have a seat with her on the sofa. He had a very traumatic experience. I throw my keys on the table. This is the worst thing that could have happened. Now my mother feels vindicated: Crime is rampant! I'm not safe. She'll be talking about this for years. Thanks, William. Pleasure.

My brother opens his mouth as William follows her to the couch. "What happened to your limp?" he asks him. I bite my tongue. Shut up, mute boy. This is no time to discover your vocal cords. William looks down at his own legs. "I forgot," he mumbles. My father clears his throat. "I've noticed that you're very forgetful, William," he observes. After a moment's hesitation, during which time my mother offers that he must be in shock, William continues toward the couch, limping like a bastard. He cozies up next to her as she comforts him. If only I had a fireplace in which they could roast chestnuts. When he begins to nostalgically discuss his peaceful life as a humble park ranger she gives me a disapproving look and says that I live in a terrible neighborhood. A person can't leave the house without getting mugged twice in broad daylight. I have to move back to Brooklyn. This is an unsafe area . . . especially for an unwed girl.

I tell her that I don't think it had anything to do with the neighborhood or my marital status. The neighborhood is perfectly safe. And my marital status, like my nonexistent kids, is not something I want to discuss.

"Then what did it have to do with?" she challenges.

I don't know. An idiot waving coffee cakes and change in the air, I want to say. I reason that it was just a bit of bad luck. My mother suspects this is more than bad luck. This is senseless violence. She recommends alerting the police. I protest: We are not calling the police. What would we call the police for?

William is following our conversation as if it were a tennis ball. Henryk, meanwhile, is at my bookshelf, examining the novels. He pulls down Kazuo Ishiguro's *The Unconsoled* and opens it to page one.

My father interjects that he hates the fuzz. He wouldn't call a cop even if we were being slaughtered right now. This comment only infuriates my mother. She turns to me: "There's been a mugging and a madman is on the loose. That's why we should call. The police would want to know about it. You don't keep this kind of thing to yourself. People like that can't be running through the streets high on drugs . . ."

Oblivious to the noise, Henryk flips to page two. Page two is even better than page one. I really should reread that book. I wish Kazuo Ishiguro would give me my groove back, and if not him then the guy who gave me the novel in the first place. What was that guy's name? He was cute. He should give me my groove back. He knew how to spell. I know that because I didn't sleep with him after two minutes.

I tell my mother that it was just a bum. It's not a big deal. She gets huffy: Now I'm rich all of a sudden? I can afford to lose ten dollars? I remind her that I'm not the one who lost it. She points at William: "Are you blaming him because you live in a bad neighborhood?" I throw up my arms and emphasize that I'm not blaming anyone. I just think we should forget about it. It's over now. "He's lucky he wasn't stabbed or gunned down," my mother continues. "He could have been seriously injured. These bums just wait for people to leave their homes. They work in groups." William smiles to signal that he's doing just fine. She turns and orders me to get the coffee cake: The bums know me, I'll pass without incident.

I grab my purse off the kitchen table. Amuse yourselves in my absence, I need to buy cigarettes. "Kasia!" she shouts as I turn the door handle to get out of there. Now what? I turn around. She points a finger: "Clutch that purse. Sometimes they use scissors or razor blades to cut off the handles when you're not paying attention." I frown. Doesn't she think I'd notice if someone was using a razor blade to cut my purse? It sounds like a long process during which I might need to pull up a rocking chair. She calls out again as I open the door. I turn around once more. "Where's your hat?" she asks. "You're going to get an ear infection!" I pat the pocket of my coat. Right here. "Put it on!" she says as I close the door. I don't even own a hat.

* * *

I walk to the corner store and buy two packs of cigarettes. I light a cigarette in front of the outdoor flower stand and inhale deeply. These things are the best . . . but they stink. I begin walking quickly down the street (it's almost a jog), toward nothing in particular, while puffing away. I move so fast that the cigarette smell can't possibly attach itself to me. After tossing the cigarette I make two more laps around the

block for good measure, then return to the store for an assort-
ment of coffee cakes and rolls. I'm happy to report that no
one mugs me. As I walk back up the stairs I reach into my
purse and pull out a tube of scented hand lotion, which I
slather generously. Before opening the apartment door I pat
my cheeks with my scented hands as if applying aftershave.
All pretty! And all this so as not to get caught smoking. By
now I'm used to it. I've been pulling this stunt for a decade.

* * *

I open the door to find that all of a sudden my mother is
William's biggest fan—or at least his biggest fan in the room.
I race into the bathroom to wash my hands and spray perfume. I hear him telling her how easy it is to make honey out
of flowers. (Been there, done that.) When I come out of the
bathroom she gives me a studied look. What? Can she smell
the cigarette from across the room? I wouldn't be surprised.
"You didn't tell me he was a writer," she says. She begins to
size him up like she's fitting him for a wedding tuxedo. William modestly informs her that he's just started. "You have
to start somewhere," she nods and promptly suggests that I
write a children's book. William chimes in that he adores children—they are so pure and good. My mother beams when
he says this. I give him a dirty look. I don't need him giving
her any ideas related to her favorite topic. William gets up and
finds the binder that contains his collected works—he's no
longer limping but thankfully no one comments, even though
both Henryk and my father are staring intently at his legs. He
asks my mother if she would be interested in seeing the first
chapter. She admits that this would be lovely then mentions
how important children are. This time I give her the dirty
look.

William opens the binder to the first page and hands it

to her. She tells him she's not wearing her reading glasses and asks that he pass the binder to my father, who would be happy to read it to us.

I ask if anyone wants cake, hoping to distract them. My mother puts out her hand like a crossing guard: "Not right now. We're having a book reading."

I pull the chair into the living room so my father can finally sit. He takes the binder and I take his crutches. I liked this day more when I was contemplating hiding William under a lamp shade. "Go on and read it," she urges my father, "let us hear all about the political situation in Monaco. I'm told it's terrible."

"Who told you that?" I ask.

"He did." My mother points to William.

William sits back down and points at the binder in my father's hand. "It's terrible," he earnestly says with a nod. He shakes his head and blows out some air. "Really, really awful."

My father puts on his glasses-on-a-rope and silently examines the page. He looks like he just smelled dogshit. After squinting at the page he inquires whether the thing is written in some sort of shorthand. He can't make it out. I need another cigarette. My brother closes *The Unconsoled* and stands up. He leans over, glances at the page, and announces that it looks like gibberish.

"I'm a fast typer," William explains.

My father gives him the hairy eyeball: "Then slow down," he says deliberately.

My mother pats William on the knee: "I know what you mean. I'm fast, too. I can type a hundred words per minute." William smiles. He's a fast typer. A fast, fast typer. She turns to my father. "So what's it say?" she asks him. "Read a paragraph."

My father frowns. Seems that all he can make out are the words *chapter one*. After that he's lost. Henryk leans in again. "It's definitely a foreign language," he concludes and sits back down. I take the binder from my father. "Who wants cake?" I try again. My brother agrees to cake. I set it next to him on the floor. Eat up. Good doggy.

My father breaks an uncomfortable moment of silence by announcing that there's going to be a family get-together. I ask what he has in mind. He explains that we are going out to dinner to commemorate two very special events. It's his mother's birthday (my grandmother, naturally) and it's the twenty-five-year anniversary of the deli. A big deal, he adds, on both counts. "I figured we'd do one big dinner instead of two, it will be more cost-effective." Ah, a two-for-one special, just his style. "We're getting your mother drunk to celebrate the day she helped me start our little business," he cracks. My mother, legendary partier that she is, makes a motion with her hand like she's swatting a fly in front of her face. She's not getting drunk, trust me. She's still recovering from the white wine spritzer incident of '94 when she kept telling everyone that she was going to fall and crack open her head because the drink was too strong (this thing was weaker than a teardrop of Children's Tylenol).

I ask when this event is taking place. Thursday, it turns out, at Leona's. My mother nods. "You remember Leona's," she offers. "It's that Italian restaurant where all the Catholics go." You would need to hit me upside the head with a brick to get me to forget Leona's. Of course I remember it. It's a Catholic-themed Italian restaurant for overeaters. Each table has its own lazy Susan at the center of which is a replica of a pope's head. Kill me if I'm lying. Patrons sit around and eat off plates as big as their heads while surrounded by religious iconography. I like to think it was Leona's that turned me into an atheist.

William addresses me: "Are you very Catholic?" he asks.

My father winks at me. "She's very Polish," he happily points out.

William considers my family tree. He's over it. He's a fast typer. "Why do all the Catholics go to Leona's?" he asks.

My father laughs: "To see the pope."

"The pope goes to this restaurant!" William exclaims. Yes, and so does Tom Clancy. I tell him not to get excited, he isn't there, and proceed to explain the conundrum that is Leona's.

"They have all the popes," my father enthuses, "including, of course, my favorite, Pope John Paul the Second, born Karol Wojtyła in Kraków, Poland, in 1920. He took over the Vatican in 1978. What a man! The first non-Italian pope in four hundred fifty years."

William asks my father if he knows a lot about the popes and their lives. I shake my head, fully aware of my father's passionate interest in popes—and Italian food for that matter. He wouldn't even be mentioning this if Pope John Paul II weren't Polish. My father loves anything Polish. Anything. He even likes nail polish. He just likes the word *Polish*.

"Yup," he says to William, as if reading my thoughts. "Poland is a great country." It is. Because South Africa and Monaco are not.

William thinks the restaurant sounds like a lot of fun. My mother pats him on the back and asks if he'll still be in America then. I tell you, getting mugged was the best thing that's ever happened to him. And it just gives my mother more fuel. Now she can remind us how important safety is and when I tell her to calm down she can cite the day that that nice South African boy I befriended was mercilessly robbed twice.

William grows uneasy: "I think so. Yes?" I just stare at him. As long as my mother is involved this is a runaway train. There's no need to agree or disagree. I just stare. Stare, stare, stare. Blankly. "Good," she decides. "You can come. Bring the novel. It'll give me something to do." William reminds her that it's not a novel. It's nonfiction. "Come anyway, the more the merrier," she offers.

"Since when?" my father asks. "Are you sure you haven't been drinking?"

"I'm in a good mood," she says cheerily in her defense. "The more the merrier."

"If you're planning to pick up the tab it will be," he points out.

I ask if I can bring Libby and Max. I beg. Please, please, please. (I mean if my mother gets to bring a friend I should be allowed, too.)

"Bring them," my father finally says. He looks at my brother. "Don't bring anyone," he tells him. Henryk looks up. The cake box next to him is now empty.

Having secured an invite for Thursday, William regains confidence and grins at me. Leona's here we come! I try to smile back. How could he be so dumb and so good looking? It's like getting a piece of candy and not being able to open the wrapper. He is certainly no S. Konrad.

My father points to the flag on the wall. I can't believe he didn't notice it sooner. It's not exactly small. What kind of apartment inspector is he? He asks why my Polish flag has been turned upside down. My mother looks behind her and flinches. "Oh, what is that ugly thing?" she asks. William informs her that it's his flag of Monaco. It inspires him to write. My father doesn't take his eyes off the flag. "Inspires you to write how?" he wants to know.

I have to keep my father away from the subject of William's book. I ask if he'd like something to drink. Water, milk, soda . . . "Uh-huh"—he turns to me—"beer."

My mother frowns. "Beer?" she asks. "In your condition?"

"I'm not pregnant," he responds. "I have a broken leg."

My mother points out that I don't have beer because I don't drink. My father tells me to hand him his crutches. He moves over to the fridge and takes out a beer. My mother is shocked all over again. Since when am I a drinker? How often am I drinking? *And why?* People who keep alcohol at home turn into alcoholics. This could be an indication of bigger problems. Pretty soon I'll be off in a ditch somewhere . . .

She goes on like this for a good five minutes longer.

When it's time for them to leave my mother digs through her purse. She almost forgot. She brought me something. "What's that?" I ask, knowing it's something I don't exactly need, like cheese and potato soup. I wish she'd buy herself a present with the money she wastes on stuff I feel too guilty not to accept. She pulls out a pair of red earmuffs and explains: "These are for you, I got them on sale. They're to keep your ears warm when you walk around. Wear them over your hat." I nod. Man, if she knew I didn't own a hat she would never leave this apartment. I look down at my new ear warmers. Oh great. What I don't need most, another demoralizing gift. This will go perfectly with my new necklace. All that's missing from my life is a cane and top hat—the crucial pieces I'll need to take part in the Vegas lounge act I've had my eye on all winter.

My father pats me on the shoulder before they file out. He asks if I can come to the deli tomorrow and work the afternoon shift. I tell him yes, anytime. "Come at noon," he tells me. William, meanwhile, gives my mother a long hug good-bye. When she's halfway down the stairs he calls after her. "See you at Leona's!" he screams. "I can't wait to have a one-night stand with you!" I push him out of the way and slam the door.

* * *

William spends the afternoon polishing his glassware. I read and smoke until dinnertime. When I ask if he's hungry he pats his stomach: "I'm starving!" Staaaving. The accent is cute, I'll give him that. Even though I don't want to see his binder for as long as I live the accent is something I can handle. I suppose it's one of the things I fell for. I thought it represented something loftier, like common sense. He's staaaving. I'm staaaaaving, too. William suggests that I let him cook the evening's meal. Is he going to set fire to himself and run around screaming? I'm not sure what he's capable of creating or destroying. Additionally, I don't own an extinguisher. "I'm a good cook," he confidently says. "I'll make burgers."

The trouble here is that burgers sound delicious. I haven't had a nice juicy burger for a long time. I nod: Burgers it shall be. William kisses me on the cheek and tells me it was nice of me to introduce him to my family. Okay, but I never introduced him. The only comment I make is that my mother took a shine to him, which is true. Cute people have the world fooled. And cute people with irresistible accents? Well, forget about it. The universe is doomed.

"Your mother is super," William informs me. "And your father is great, too." I tell him that my father is super-great: I take after my father. "I don't know about that," he says. "You're a lot like your mother." I light a cigarette and explain that I just look like my mother. The similarities end there. "No they don't," he persists. "I can't explain it but you talk alike, too." I offer that maybe our voices are similar. That must be it. "No, that's not all. You talk alike. You're similar. Your father is different. You're just like your mother. Like when she was saying she wants to inform the police. Remember that? It just seemed like the kind of thing you would say. I don't know how to explain it. It's something in the tone of . . ." All right, enough. La, la, la, I'm done listening. We're not similar. My mother is crazy. I'm just sensitive. And speaking of that I need some comfy garbage bags to line the tub. "She's great," he says and gives me another kiss, "just like you." Similar. We are so not similar. My mother is neurotic and hyper. Neurotic and hyper. Well, those aren't the best examples. We are very, very, very, very different. Very different. We are . . . "Two peas in a pod!" he says. "That's the American expression I was searching for."

Oh get lost, Johnson. What do you know about my mother? Nothing, which is just perfect considering that you're planning to have a one-night stand with her. He puts his arm around me: "But you know, you should be more honest with her. I covered for you, and I don't like to lie." I nod, I know he doesn't like to lie. The being-honest-with-my-mother part, however, is more complicated. She's not an understanding woman.

William gets up. "Okay," he says. "I'm going to walk to that corner store and get the ostrich meat, be right back." The what now? William is out the door before I can tell him that he has a better chance of getting a blow job from a transvestite with ostrich features in his/her hair than he does of finding a frozen ostrich patty at the corner store. Maybe he'll get mugged again. Better go follow him.

* * *

William and I walk to the grocery store to buy burgers made from a cow. I'm surprised William eats meat in the first place but don't raise the issue. Burgers are all we have in common and I don't want to ruin it. As we approach the grocery store's sliding doors I notice a poster taped to the glass. It's a black-and-white picture of Richard. Underneath the image is written: MY NAME IS RICHARD STEIN. I CHEAT ON WOMEN. IF YOU SEE ME, RUN. I HAVE MORE PENILE WARTS THAN PIMPLES ON MY ASS. Richard's number is printed at the bottom. Hello, Max, nice work. William stops and considers the poster. He shakes his head disapprovingly. "Americans have strange customs," he observes. "This is not something to be proud of." I don't say a word.

Turns out William loves the grocery store. It's much bigger than the one he's used to. He wanders through the aisles touching everything. He picks up tin cans and reads their labels the way another man might read the great American novel. Slowly, he reads slowly. He walks to the seafood counter and stares knowingly at the fish of the day. He goes to the produce department and smells the lemons and the cucumbers while employing pained expressions and full-on emotional range. He squeezes the grapes and the toilet paper with equal enthusiasm. After an hour of aimless circling and several suspicious looks from the derelict stock boy with a walkie-talkie, we get in the checkout line. Finally. In addition to the necessary ingredients William is buying several bottles of a new drink obviously marketed toward children called Tummy Shockers. I'd like to meet the adult who brainstormed that one. William drinks two sixteen-ounce bottles while we wait for the lady in front of us to hand over $21.76 in pennies. She is wearing a brunette wig that is slowly sliding to the back of her head, revealing gray hair underneath. I would move to another register but this is the only one that's open. Why overwork the staff?

"Eighteen fifty-five, eighteen fifty-six . . . ," she says. I stand behind her, impatiently, as she counts the money. I begin manically flipping through every magazine displayed near the register. William, meanwhile, is downing more Tummy Shockers. "This is the best!" he says, wiping his mouth.

"Nineteen ninety-nine, twenty . . ."

"Really?" I rhetorically say, only because I can't think of another response. He takes a bottle off the conveyor belt and asks if I want to try some. No, I don't. He insists that it's very good and twists off the top. He hands it to me. I take a sip and recall my new earmuffs. "It's pretty good," I lie, not wanting to hurt his feelings. I try handing it back but he won't take it. I can have the rest. He's full. I hold the open bottle at my side.

" . . . twenty-one seventy-four, twenty-one seventy-five, twenty-one seventy-six. There you go, twenty-one dollars and seventy-six cents," the woman says.

The girl behind the register picks up a penny and brings it to the light. What is she going to do, bite it to make sure it's not made of chocolate? Let's move already. "Ma'am, these are Canadian pennies," the girl says. The woman calmly states that she'd like to take this up with the manager if no one minds. Mind? Of course not. This is a perfectly reasonable scenario. She puts the pennies back into their ziplock bag to maximize freshness and waits. The girl phones the manager while ringing us up. When it's our turn to pay William hands her his wallet. He just gives it to her like it's a coupon. Evidently he has yet to figure out American money. This is exactly the kind of thing that leads one to lose coffee cakes. She takes a fifty out of his wallet.

After collecting his change, William picks up the grocery bags and heads for the door. I am about to follow when I hear a "psst." The girl behind the register is attempting to get my attention. "Is that your boyfriend?" she asks. I glance in William's direction to make sure he's out of earshot range. I nod. Why, yes, he is. Her eyes widen. "You are so lucky," she offers. "That's amazing." If she only knew. But she doesn't and there is something gratifying about telling strangers that hot William is my man.

The next friendly face we see is that of a grimy panhandler leaning against a parking meter in front of the store. Hey gorgeous!!!! Im cumin!!!!!!! "Got anything for me?" the bum asks. He gestures obscenely and announces that I'm a great piece. Thank you!

    I hand the man my bottle of Tummy Shockers. He thanks me and immediately tosses the bottle over his shoulder. William tries to kiss my cheek but misses. "That was very nice of you," he says approvingly, trying again. "That man has had a hard life. It's important to help people. You should do volunteer work with a local homeless shelter." That is just my style! How did he ever know? "Can you reach into my wallet and pull out a hundred dollars?" he then asks. Saddled with grocery bags, he can't reach into his back pocket. He turns his ass to me. "It's in the right back pocket." I look at the wallet. It's about to fall out. I explain that no one gives bums a hundred dollars. "I do," he answers. I take out his wallet and pull out a single and hand it to the bum, who immediately takes off down the street screaming with joy. Must have been a slow afternoon. That or he was one buck short on the crack bill. William smiles. "Look how we made his day!" he marvels.

We are crossing the street when William abruptly stops to stare at an anorexic-looking middle-aged woman hiding behind a baseball cap and sunglasses. She is moving briskly and pushing an empty baby carriage. "I can't believe it," he says and continues to stand in the street. A taxicab swerves to avoid us. I pull him to the sidewalk. What is he looking at? I have to go to the bathroom. "I just had my first Hollywood sighting," he says. "I think that was Kelly LeBrock." I motion for William to continue. "Kelly LeBrock, the star of *Weird Science*," he says as if she is a household name. "She played Lisa the seductress." I vaguely recall the actress William is talking about. He doesn't know what a bagel is but he knows Kelly LeBrock? I inform him that the woman we saw was not Kelly LeBrock. "I think it was," he insists. "Maybe you couldn't tell with the hat and glasses but it was definitely her . . . Great!" he marvels. "I just saw Kelly LeBrock! She's done a lot of charity work removing mines in Africa. I should have asked for an autograph." Whose autograph should he have asked Kelly LeBrock for, a real actress's? William again turns around to stare at the "star." I begin tugging on his sleeve. No need to worry, Kelly LeBrock will be here tomorrow and the next day. She's probably married to that bum who threw my Tummy Shockers all over Second Avenue. Now let's go so I can take a leak. And while we're at it, let's have these burgers at Libby's. I don't want to clean up a fire or William's charred remains should anything go wrong.

One block from home William stops again and points at a white limo in the middle of traffic, its tinted black window slowly going up. Whoever is inside just discarded a cigar. It rolls toward the curb then falls into the sewer. "I think that was Manuel's father," he says. "Maybe Manuel is inside. We should see." I look up at him. Who? "Don't you remember Manuel?" he asks, not taking his eyes off the limo. "He was a guest at the lodge when you were in South Africa." I nod. I remember him. No question there. And I'm so sure that was Manuel's father. He's probably looking for Kelly LeBrock. "That was definitely him," William confidently says as the limo pulls away.

* * *

We invite ourselves over to Libby's, where we'll be cooking and eating dinner. She's happy to have us and calls Max. While the layout of Libby's apartment is identical to that of my own, the decor is completely different. Everything in her place came out of the Pottery Barn catalog—except for her creaky futon, which, ironically, is the only thing that should have come out of the Pottery Barn catalog. She could use an actual couch. Instead she has a sagging mattress over a plastic frame that's surrounded by vases and candles and enough extra-large colorful, ruffled throw pillows for an orgy. If ever Hollywood wants to make a movie set in a harem, they should film it at Libby's apartment.

As William finishes preparing our meal, Max walks in. He is dressed in a turban and a long flowing white robe. I close my eyes, count backward from five, and reopen them. Yup, he's still dressed in a turban and a long flowing white robe. Libby doesn't even blink. "I'm beat," he says, stretching out across the futon. He stares up at the ceiling and puts his hands behind his head. "You really learn something when trailing a man all afternoon dressed as a Shiite. There is a lot of prejudice in the world. Richard kept looking over his shoulder but not once did he offer me water."

William turns from the stove with plates of food. "I agree that there is a lot of prejudice in the world," he says to Max. When he notices Max's outfit he asks if he is Muslim.

Max takes off his turban and accepts a plate of food. "I'm Muslim." He nods and bites into the burger. "Praise be to Allah."

We eat and talk. The burgers are delicious. I tell Max and Libby that they are invited to Leona's on Thursday, and William tells them that he saw Kelly LeBrock, then asks if we've ever seen Judd Nelson. Max is shaking his head no when he receives a text message on his cell. He looks down at the phone. "Anyone have scissors I can borrow?" He looks up. I ask what for. He looks back down at the phone. "I need to cut a string," he absently answers and begins texting something. "Forget it. I'll take care of it." I keep staring at him but he won't meet my eye.

As we are finishing up with dinner, the ranger announces that he has something in his pants that we're really going to love. I don't doubt it. He reaches into his pocket and pulls out a deck of cards. "Anyone up for a game of Uno?" he asks, waving the cards in the air. Oh. I thought we were talking about something else. Libby, sitting Indian-style on the floor, pats her stomach. "I'm stuffed," she says and takes several quick breaths, the kind pregnant women in Lamaze classes take. Max tells William that he doesn't remember how to play Uno and suggests that we enjoy a round of spin the bottle instead. I mention that I don't remember how to play Uno, either.

"It's easy!" William says. "I'll teach you."

"I used to love Uno," Libby chimes in. "I think the last time I played I was on a water bed." William, who for whatever reason loves the 1980s, shouts that water beds are great. They are something else, I add. We all agree that water beds are something else.

William makes himself comfortable on the floor and patiently explains the fundamentals of Uno. We are back in South Africa, getting a lesson about plant life. And just like in South Africa, we are not exactly paying attention. When he's done explaining the rules I still don't know how to play. William shuffles the deck and deals. I collect my cards. William tells Max to go first. Max stares at his cards. He begins pulling one out then tucks it back in. William assures him that he can take his time. Max does, repeating the pull and tuck move seven times. The wait is excruciating. I look at the clock. Max is averaging a pull a minute. I wonder if he's related to the Canadian penny lady. I've never known him to move so slowly. I tell him to come on already. "I'm trying," he barks, concentrating hard, "hold your horses. This isn't a competition unless I win." After ten more minutes William cheerily urges Max to just drop any card. Any card will do. Max pulls out a card. Let's play Uno! He hesitates, then tucks it back among the other cards.

"Go, babe!" Libby finally says. "Why are you taking so long?"

He looks at her. "Libby," he calmly responds. "I'm going to have to ask you to leave."

She points at her face: "I live here." She folds her arms over her chest and closes her eyes. Good night, nice knowing you. After another minute of silence, during which Max greedily cups his hand over the cards so we can't see what he's been dealt, a final decision is made. "I'm not playing," he abruptly states and throws down his cards. "This is boring me." I drop my cards on the table. William looks disappointed that we will not be playing. Libby takes in his pitiful display. "William," she asks, "can you tell us the story again about what you were thinking when the buffalo charged at us?" William nods. She begins slowly fanning herself with her cards: "You must have been so scared. Tell us again."

"Well, as you know . . . ," William starts. He recalls the story while collecting our cards; Libby watches him intently. When he's done she lights an after-sex cigarette and whispers thank you. She needed that. "Pleasure," he says and gets up.

He informs us that he's off to bed. He has to be up early to work on the book. Knowing that I'll want to sleep in, I ask how early he'll be getting up. "Not too early," he promises and kisses me on the lips. Max hugs his own knees and asks if he can have a kiss, too. William looks at him like he said something funny. "Since when do men kiss?" William says, looking genuinely amused, like he finally got one of our inside jokes. I wonder if he knows Max is gay. I bet not.

* * *

Max, Libby, and I hang out at her place for the rest of the night. We laugh, we bond, we make fun of Scientology and Tom Cruise's smile, which is as soothing as Jack Nicholson's grin in *The Shining*. We target Maddox Jolie, whom we agree has already hit his prime in terms of looks. We spend a good thirty minutes calling out the celebrities in the latest issue of *Us Weekly*, some of whom are dressed in garish fashions that recall employees at roller rinks. Mostly we ask the important questions: How much money would we have to be paid to sleep with Larry King? And why, come to think of it, is TV journalist Anderson Cooper already gray? He's like forty and a millionaire. Where's the stress, Father Time?

I know the moment to call it a night is upon us when Libby kicks off her heels, yawns wildly, and collapses onto the futon, not having the energy to make it the three feet to her bed. "Will someone brush my teeth?" she groggily asks.

"Oh my God," Max says, turning toward her. "You are completely out of control."

"Babe, I'm exhausted," she whispers and in an instant starts faintly snoring.

He looks at me. "Brush my teeth. Her husband is going to have his hands full."

When I return to my apartment William is asleep. I quickly change and tiptoe across the living room and get into bed. William rolls over and puts his arm around me. He's still asleep when he does this. I lay next to him quietly, feeling the warmth of his body. It's a comforting moment, and I try not to think of the fact that it is happening while he is unconscious. And just like that I happily drift off . . .

* * *

Sundays are usually complicated days at my place. They involve a lot of moping around while resenting the workweek. But this Sunday is different. It's painful, yes, but in a different way, and not just because I have to do deli duty at noon in Brooklyn. William gets up at four thirty in the morning. It's not even the morning—it's still the night before as far as I'm concerned. He is trying to be quiet and not wake me but it's no use, all the paper shuffling and finger drumming—not to mention the sounds emitted from his sapphire-colored parachute pants as his legs rub together—would wake a hibernating bear. Everyone and everything, including the dolphins at the Bronx Zoo, know he's trying to write a book. I get out of bed and walk to the closet.

"You're up!" he says merrily. "Good morning!"

I look at the top of his head. What's he balancing up there? William is wearing some kind of crazy box-shaped dunce's cap with a tassel hanging off it. I don't have the strength to ask what the hell it is. I take my mother's earmuffs out of the closet. I'm going back down, but not without my headgear. I put on the muffs.

"Are you cold?" I hear him ask from the beyond. It's four thirty in the morning. I don't answer. And what would be the use? He's wearing a hat, for God's sake, so why is he asking if I'm cold? Put on a mink, William. I get back in bed and try to fall asleep. My eyeballs are burning.

William's writing project is more like a lab experiment. By 6 a.m. he is pacing back and forth, faster and faster still, across the kitchen, mumbling to himself in frustration. I am not able to fall back asleep. I watch him from the bed while smoking frantically and praying that his eureka moment will strike like lightning. But it does not. Not at six, not at six fifteen, not at seven or at nine twenty-one. I can almost see him holding the lightbulb over his own head. The whole operation looks like it's about to run out of juice. Knowing I won't sleep again I get up and start making the bed. Just as I'm fluffing the pillows William races over to the desk and starts typing. Thank God, no more pacing. But William stops almost immediately. He gets up from the chair and starts the pacing anew. My father was right, I should have the super fix that squeaky floorboard. If William keeps this up he's going to fall through the neighbors' ceiling and land in their kitchen sink. I politely inquire whether he's making progress. I don't need to know what he's writing, just when he'll be done writing it. "I'm working on the acknowledgments page," he admits. "There are so many people to thank. I'm so grateful to everyone who has supported me over the years. I think I might dedicate a whole page to my dead uncle Dale."

William begins to pace again. I repeatedly ask no one in particular to please make him stop the racket. Eventually William stops. I inhale the smoke of my twenty-ninth cigarette and look up. He is in the middle of the kitchen, staring at me, an expression of concern on his face. I ask what's the matter. "You are smoking an awful lot," he says. "Have you ever considered quitting?" I don't blink. "You really should. It's bad for you."

Now let me just say how much I hate—really, truly hate—when people tell me smoking is bad. Michael Jackson's "Thriller" video is "bad." Smoking is good. I don't need to be told it's bad. It's not bad for me. It keeps me alive. Come to think of it, my smoking benefits both of us tremendously. If I stopped smoking right now William would die, just like his dead uncle. I'm not a morning person. I should point this out to the Samaritan before he gets ahead of himself. I like to smoke and will continue to smoke forever and ever. And as long as C. Everett Koop is under my roof, he'll have to put up with it.

I shake my head no. It had not occurred to me to quit. "You should," he says, "and when you do quit we can cleanse the apartment by burning elephant dung, which is a great incense." He walks over to give me a hug and adds that he hopes I live two hundred billion years. "Thank you," I bitterly respond. "You're generous and sweet." William tips his hat like a gentleman. But what is this hat for? Seriously, it looks to me like a dunce's cap slash ice bucket. Did he give himself a time-out or ground himself after a cocktail party? I touch the fabric and ask if it's made of felt.

"I don't know what it's made of," he says, "but it's called a fez, it's my favorite hat. I wear it sometimes when I'm writing. It inspires me."

Here we go again. "I thought the flag inspired you. Because if it's not inspiring you we can take it down right now." William informs me that he is inspired by both the hat and the flag. He adjusts his fez and/or ice bucket and asks if he could watch some TV. He needs a rest. I tell him to go right ahead. My answer "inspires" him to lunge recklessly for the remote, dive onto the couch, and hit the power button. "Great!" he cheers, changing channels. "Maybe *Alf* is on."

I get ready to leave for the deli. As I am walking out William screams, "*Melrose Place*, even better!"

* * *

The Polonia deli is located on the corner of Nassau Avenue and Manhattan Avenue in a predominantly Polish neighborhood. Like a rectangle, the store is long but narrow. Extremely narrow. My parents could afford to move into a bigger space, but my father won't hear of it. He's been in the location for a quarter of a century, and it suits him just fine. Polonia sells every kind of meat imaginable—bacons, loaves, sausages, hams, livers, head cheeses, loins—as well as imported candies, drinks, jams, spreads, and canned vegetables. You can even buy Polish newspapers, magazines, and greeting cards. There are other delis in the area, in fact there is one two storefronts down, but everyone favors Polonia even though most of the meat is overpriced. What Polonia has that the competitors do not is my father, who knows everyone by name, knows what they need even before they know it.

When I open the door I am confronted by a sea of people, four deep, pressed against the counter, all yelling at once. I can barely hear the jingling bell over the glass door. My father does not believe in customers taking a number: It's first shout, first served here. It reminds me of the stock exchange. Hanging from metal hooks over the counter are hundreds of sausages: garlic, smoked, fresh. And behind the counter are four men taking orders. Well, three men and my brother, to whom I nod as I walk in. The three men are wearing white paper hats and white smocks that on the back read POLONIA and bear the Polish nobility crest: a white eagle wearing a crown, its fierce talons ready to grip something. My brother is wearing the smock but has retained possession of his baseball cap, which is pulled low, as always.

I push my way to the stockroom and put on a white smock— I'm not down with the paper hat, either, hair in a bun will have to do. I jump behind the counter and am immediately overwhelmed by the chaos. These folks are hungry. I yell to Henryk, asking if our parents are here. He shakes his head no. A man shouts at me in Polish. Here's the other thing. Everyone who enters Polonia orders in Polish. They have to, or they are ignored. The workers are straight off the boat, in a manner of speaking, so if you don't address them in the native tongue, good luck to you. "Three pounds of liver sausage!" the man says to me, trying to push his way closer. Three pounds of liver sausage. I nod. Where's the liver? I look through the deli case and spot it. I remove what looks like three pounds and weigh it. It's six. I take some off the scale and weigh it again. Still not right. I do this a few more times, have it almost right, give up trying, then move to a machine that prints out the labels. I wrap the meat in white paper and hand it to him. He takes it and moves off. That was not so bad. Next an old woman pushes past people like she owns the place and shouts at me. "Half a pound of pork loin, one baked pâté, six prune pączki, and . . . !" What, wha . . . ? She adds something I don't understand. I look around for a pen to write this down. There is no pen. I ask her to repeat the order and she fires it off again. I locate the pâté and the pączki (Polish doughnuts with filling in the middle) but tell her we are out of prune. She demands strawberry. I get six and in the process forget the rest of the order. "Pork loin!" she yells. I get the pork loin then attempt to use my very bad Polish to collect the rest of the order once more. She says it but I am paralyzed. I find myself standing dumbly behind a counter, listening to an old woman emit unintelligible sounds. Then Henryk rushes over. He speaks to her in Polish that is so far superior to my own that I fall into yet another trance. He leads me to a section of the counter. "Kiszka," he says. "She wants a pound." Kiszka. I nod. It's a sausage-shaped item, filled with barley and beef blood. My father cooks it at home on a skillet and it stinks so much you have to cover your nose. It smells like, well, beef blood. Henryk takes it out of the case and quick as lightning weighs it—perfect on the first try—wraps it and hands it to the old woman, who nods at him approvingly. She asks him who I am. He responds that I am his sister. "Oh," she says. She looks at me carefully. "Tell your father I said hello. He's an old friend." Henryk tells her he will. She leaves. He rushes back to his orders before I have a chance to thank him. And then it starts all over again.

By the end of the day I'm more physically exhausted than I've been in years, and I probably got one out of thirty orders right on the first try. I have never had to provide service with a smile, or service at all, for that matter, and my shitty Polish is a grave obstacle here. I don't know my ass from my elbow. When the store finally closes I begin the process of cleaning up. My back and neck are burning. I am polishing the blade on one of the meat-slicing machines when Henryk walks over and unplugs it. "Unplug the machines before doing that," he advises. "It's safer." I nod.

After cleaning the counters I sweep the floor. One of the workers, Josh (given name Jasua, but everyone calls him Josh), scrutinizes my technique. He removes a large dill pickle from a glass jar on the counter and sucks on it like it's a cigar. Josh lives in Queens, doesn't own a car, and, according to my father, gets picked up from work by a different woman each night. The last time I saw him he was wearing, under his white pants, a leopard-skin-patterned thong that peeked out when he bent down. I'm pretty sure he's wearing it again. My father keeps him around because he'll work seven days a week if asked. He's never turned down extra hours, and he's always asking for more. "So the big city girl is sweeping floors, huh?" he says, wiping pickle juice from his chin. "We never see you here." I tell him that I'm just helping out my father. I squat down and with the broom push some litter into the dust pan. "You missed a spot," he says. Henryk walks past carrying two boxes stacked on top of each other, one marked CANNED BEETS, the other SAUERKRAUT. "Can you give me a hand?" he asks Josh. Josh sets down the pickle and jumps to take the top box. I hastily sweep up the bits of litter I missed to prove I can do it. Throughout the day the other workers— and the customers—eyed me suspiciously, like they knew I was not one of them. I know Josh thinks—and rightly so, based on the evidence—that I'm too delicate for this labor.

Henryk sets down the box in front of a shelf, Josh sets the other box next to it (he's definitely wearing the thong), then walks back to the counter and for a time resumes his pickle sucking while Henryk stocks the shelf. A car horn beeps three times. "That's my ride," Josh says. He walks out, sucking loudly on the pickle, the paper hat still on his head.

* * *

When I return home that evening stinking to high heaven like beef blood and pork, William is on the bed, the phone against his ear. I take off my coat and head for the fridge. "I know," I hear him say into the phone, "but writing is so hard . . ." He must be talking to his mom. He told me yesterday he was planning to call her. I hope he's calling collect. I'll have to bring that up when he gets off. "Uh-huh," he utters repeatedly. "Uh-huh." His mother must talk as much as my mother. This will take a century.

I pull out a loaf of bread and a package of cheese from the fridge. I love cheese. And I love it even more today because I've been staring at meat for hours. I open it. Okay, only two slices left. William eats as much as I do; he polished off this cheese in one day. I could devour these remaining slices right now and they wouldn't make a dent. I have hungry-man hunger. The sandwich will be an appetizer.

I run over to Libby's place and raid her fridge. She has better stuff. I bring back with me an armload of food including chips and homemade cookies. When I return William is on his back, phone still glued to his ear. "The world is such a complicated place," he says. "It's hard to explain. So many people are suffering and I just want to do my part through public service and good deeds. Life on Planet Earth is amazing . . . uh-huh . . . It's hard to explain. Sometimes I want to give all my money away . . ." Jesus, don't do that. "Uh-huh, uh-huh, uh-huh." A pause. "You must be thinking of someplace else. Yeah. The political situation might be bad there, too. I don't know, it's hard to explain. Maybe that will be the subject of my next boo . . . Uh-huh, uh-huh, uh-huh." A longer pause. For a writer, William sure uses the words *it's hard to explain* often. "It's always been my dream. Always. And now I feel like I can finally get it done. If only I could write. It's so hard . . . Uh-huh, uh-huh, uh-huh . . . It's very difficult . . . Uh-huh, uh-huh . . . It's not easy . . . uh-huh . . . I never knew that! That sounds so simple . . . Uh-huh, uh-huh, Nelson Mandela, yeah, uh-huh, uh-huh."

Maybe she's trying to convince him to come back to the farm. Better not interrupt. I take a seat on the couch and start eating my sandwich. "Uh-huh," he says, "no there's no question I have to be here now . . . Uh-huh, the stars are aligned . . ." Great. No question. "Yeah," he continues. "Uh-huh, uh-huh, uh-huh . . ."

I take another bite of my sandwich. I really do like cheese. What a super product. You can eat it plain or on bread, you can cut it into fun shapes or squirt it out of a can. It always tastes great. Especially the smoked kind. Bleu cheese, too. Bleu cheese is good in salads. I also like it as a dipping sauce for Buffalo wings . . . "A Taurus, uh-huh," I hear him say. I turn my head and swallow hard. A Taurus? What's his mother doing, reading his horoscope? "Uh-huh, celestial bodies, uh-huh, uh-huh . . . ambassadors of the universe . . . uh-huh." I massage my throat to get the lump of yeast down. "We are stubborn by nature. When we get something in our heads . . ."

I start coughing. I need water. "Uh-huh, Age of Aquarius, uh-huh, my chakras, uh-huh, uh-huh Mars uh-huh, uh-huh . . ." I get up off the couch and take a step toward him. "Uh-huh, uh-huh, crystals, uh-huh, uh-huh twelve houses uh-huh, uh-huh." I start hitting my chest, giving myself the Heimlich maneuver. "I used to wear a bracelet made from magnets after that rugby injury I told you about . . . uh-huh . . . pyramid scheme? I've never . . . uh-huh positive aura . . ."

"William?" I say and cough again.

"Uh-huh, sun sign descriptions sound fascinating . . . uh-huh, uh-huh, I know," he continues. "You are so right about everything. I feel like I know you . . ."

"William," I say a little louder, trying to clear my throat in the process. William looks up and covers the mouthpiece with his hand: "I'll be off in a minute."

"William, who are you . . ."

"Uh-huh," he continues, "but you see my birthday falls between those two signs so maybe your calculations of my birth chart . . ."

"William!" I scream to get his attention. "Who are you on the phone with?"

William covers the mouthpiece again. "It's Miss Celeste from the psychic hotline. This will only take a minute. She's inspiring me to write my book on the polit—"

I grab the phone out of William's hand. "Good-bye, Miss Celeste!" I scream into the phone and hang up.

William is startled: "What's the matter? Are you stressed out again?"

"William, how long were you on the phone with that woman?" I ask.

He looks at the clock: "Let's see, I was watching *Melrose Place* and then looking for *Alf* . . ."

"You've been on the phone with her that long? I've been gone all day!" I shriek. "Do you know how expensive that call is going to be? Those people are con artists!"

"I'll pay for it," he says sheepishly. "I'm sorry if I upset you. Please don't yell at me."

I take a seat next to him on the bed. "You will have to pay for it," I say more gently. "You have to. I don't have the money to pay. Look, I'm only saying this for your own good. That call probably ate up half your savings . . ."

He sits up: "Are you breaking up with me?" His eyes begin to water, and this gives me pause.

William is definitely not S. Konrad.

"William," I say, "just don't call Miss Celeste again, okay?"

He nods. I give him a peck on the cheek. I do want to like this guy. But he's just so . . .

"Okay," he assures me. "And don't worry about how much it will cost. It was a bargain, less than two dollars per minute. Miss Celeste is a miracle worker, offered me some fantastic advice. She told me I will soon meet a mystery man who will change my life." William puts his arms around my neck. "I want to tell you again how happy I am that you are helping me. I trust you completely. Miss Celeste said I just need to have faith in my vision, as much faith as I had in you when we made love that first time. She said that when Albert Einstein was working on his theories in the 1800s he was rejected for a promotion at work. He was a clerk third class and wanted to become clerk second class but they wouldn't let him . . ." Did William just compare himself to Albert Einstein? ". . . so you see, there is hope for me," he continues. "I'm going to be a great writer with a big career." I nod. This would be so much easier if William would just stop pouring his heart out while telling me how trustworthy I am. He continues after a pause: "I have some questions for you." I light a cigarette as William grabs a pen off the desk. "How do you spell your last name? I'm trying to create a romance compatibility diagram. I'm also going to need your birth sign and . . ."

✳ ✳ ✳

As I make my way past Barbara's desk on Monday morning she strikes me in the pelvis with an empty ink cartridge from her printer. "I'm sorry," she offers distractedly as the cartridge falls into pieces on the floor. "I was aiming at the wastepaper basket."

When I get to my desk there's a Post-it note on my computer screen. I peel it off. "Meeting with S. Konrad next Wednesday at 5. Mark your calendar," the note reads. Before I can mark my calendar my boss is at my desk. Excellent misuse of paper. He points at the note and asks if I got the note. I wave the note. I think I got the note. Yup, it's right here. I ask if he liked the book. He takes a sip of coffee. "I liked the book," he tells me. "I want to take him on as a client."

I smile. That's good news. I shuffle a few manuscripts around in an effort to simulate work. It's the kind of thing I would be doing with my plate of string beans if I were a ten-year-old boy in the 1950s. I next ask why I'm invited to the meeting. Not that I'm opposed to going, but, well, I'm never invited to meetings.

"I told him my assistant read the manuscript first and he asked if you could come along, too, so he could thank you for bringing it to my attention," he responds.

Wow. He wants to meet me. "So he's excited?" I ask.

My boss shrugs: "I can never tell, and we don't even have a deal yet." His cell phone rings. He takes it out of his pocket and looks at the number. It's one of his twins, he has to answer. He turns around and walks off. I stare at the back of his bald head.

I spend the rest of the morning trying to figure out what kind of person S. Konrad is. I am so absorbed in this activity that I barely have time to get pissed off about and delete the twenty-three links to anti-smoking Web sites that William sent. At lunch I meet Max for salads at a coffee shop near my office. When our food arrives he immediately removes all the tomato slices off his plate and throws them on mine. "So slimy," he says. Throughout the meal I can't help but talk about S. Konrad. I want him to be handsome, with a disarming wit and keen sense of style. I want him to own his own tuxedo, not rent from some mall. I want him to look like William (from the neck up, of course) but not be William. I'm confident that at least I'll get the second half of my wish fulfilled. I mean he can't be too disappointing if his book is any indication of his personality, which it inevitably must be.

At the end of the meal Max points out that I'm acting as though S. Konrad and I are being set up on a date. Maybe he has a point. Haven't I learned my lesson yet? No, I haven't. Perhaps hope does spring eternal. Based on that book, which

I loved, S. Konrad is my dream man. I don't care if he is fifty . . . okay, not fifty. I don't care if he is thirty. "What kind of pretentious name is S. Konrad?" Max challenges. "You and your nerd reading. He sounds like a fruit." He places his gym bag on the table and unzips it. He removes a white lab coat and puts it on, followed by a stethoscope, which he hangs around his neck. Then a pair of eyeglasses with large round red frames and a men's black wig, which he haphazardly slaps on his head. Finally he takes out a white lunch bag folded at the top and stapled shut. On the front of the bag is written: PSYCHIATRIC MEDICATION FOR PATIENT RICHARD STEIN. He gives me his hand. "I'm Dr. Leon Devereux," he says in a bad British accent. "I don't believe we've met." He explains that he is going to Richard's office building. He's going to give the bag to the receptionist to give to Richard. He rattles the bag. "It's full of Tic Tacs," he tells me, "but she won't know that." I ask what this is going to accomplish. He shrugs. "It will freak him out. He's obviously going to deny that he is on psychiatric meds and she's going to think he is and so on and so on." He slaps a twenty note on the table and tells me lunch is on him. He slings the duffel bag over his shoulder and heads for the door. "Doctor coming through!" he says loudly while moving past booths lined with diners. "Doctor here!"

On my way home from work I scan the subway platform looking for S. Konrad's face. Is he the guy with the beard? No, S. Konrad can't have a beard. Beards tickle. Is he that businessman with the expensive suit? Of course not, he's a writer. He can't afford suits like that (he spent too much on that cute tuxedo). Maybe it's that guy there . . . wow, I can't believe he managed to wrap his entire head in toilet paper. Impressive but not S. Konrad. Maybe he's that guy, what is that guy reading? I wait for him to lift his book. Maybe that's him. No, that's not him. S. Konrad wouldn't be reading chick lit. Desperate love stories narrated by dizzy girls are so beneath him. Maybe it's that guy with the parrot on his shoulder. The guy with the parrot on his shoulder is reading a big adult book. Literature! The kind of literature that spends chapters describing the nicks in an antique table. Moody stuff, not a lot of dialogue—that's quality! What is he reading? Now I'm curious. I can't make out the title . . . Oh, it's the Old Testament. Maybe the parrot is reading it. Now I'm confused. And why does that guy have a parrot on his shoulder in the first place? That's not S. Konrad. S. Konrad wouldn't let a parrot soil a towel draped across his shoulder. So who's S. Konrad? I decide then not to ask my boss any more questions about the author. The act of wanting can be better than getting the thing you wanted, and I need something to look forward to.

* * *

"Cover your eyes!" William shouts when I get home from work that night. I haven't even closed the door behind me. I stare at him. What? He bum-rushes me. He puts his hand over my eyes as I struggle to break free. I nervously ask what's going on. "I have a surprise!" he says. "It's big!" Big like how? Seriously, the last time this happened he was showing me an elephant in South Africa. William guides me across the apartment, his hand still over my eyes, and starts giving me clues: "Okay, remember the other night at Libby's when we were playing Uno?"

"Yeah," I say. "Do we have to play again?"

William tells me to let him finish. "Remember you said you loved this certain thing and then I said I loved it, too."

"What are you talking about?" I say impatiently. I can't see anything with his hot hand over my damn face. "Did you bake a pie?"

"It's better than that," William says and begins jumping up and down. Nothing is better than pie, don't even joke about that. I tell him to stop jumping up and down. "Oh, sorry," he says and stops jumping. "But do you remember that thing you said you loved?" he repeats. I ask him to please remove his hand because I'm scared of the dark. "No, you're not," he says and laughs. I roll my eyes, which I wish he could see me doing. I'm the man in the Iron Mask. "Do you remember that thing you said you loved," he says a third time.

"No," I truthfully answer. "I have no idea what you are talking about. Can you just please take your hand away so I can see?"

"I'll give you a hint." He pauses. "Water."

"You bought an aquarium?" I ask. William just laughs. "A rowboat?" I offer.

"You're getting warmer," he says.

Warmer than a rowboat? "A steamer, an octopus, a gargoyle, moon boots?"

"No, no, no, and no," he playfully answers. "Open your eyes."

He doesn't take his hand away. I tell him they are open but it's not doing me any good with his hand still over them. "Oh, right," he says and finally takes his hand away.

I look in front of me. "What is this?" I ask accusingly, pointing to where my bed should be. William stands in front of it like a Barker's Beauty from *The Price Is Right*. There it is, the thing he claims I have always wanted. This thing, which is taking up way too much room, is my very own . . .

"I BOUGHT A WATER BED!" he screams. William touches the bed. It begins to jiggle like an unsettled Jell-O mold.

Suddenly everything goes into slow motion. Whaaa-teeer-bbbbbbbbbbbbbbbbbed.

"I bought it for the both of us," he explains. "I've always

wanted a water bed, too! It's like our stars are aligned. We
have so much in common!"

I look around me. My mattress is propped up against the
wall. The dismantled bed frame is beside it on the floor. I
put my hands to my cheeks. I'm getting light-headed. When
I begin to swoon he catches me. "Are you okay?" he asks. It
sounds like he's talking to me under murky water. I mumble
that I need to lie down for a minute. "That's what this is for,"
he says and forcibly pushes me onto the water bed. I fall
backward. Help me! Oh God, I'm stranded at sea. "I bought it
on a whim," he continues while my limp body rides the waves
of shame and confusion. "You were so stressed out yesterday
over Miss Celeste that I thought I'd make it up to you."

I open my mouth and put out my hand. Who are these
people? It's all so surreal. I'm parched, my lips are chapped. Is
that the sun? No, it's the living room light. "You have to . . . ," I
try again but stall. If someone would just dampen my tongue
with a Q-tip soaked in water . . . "you have to . . . return this.
It's . . ."

"Final sale," William says excitedly.

NOOOOOOOOOOO!

"The man told me that ten times," he continues. "I don't
know if he thought I was hard of hearing or what. But the
money isn't an issue, I got a great deal on it. I had to call
almost everyone in the phone book to find it, too." He pats
me on the shoulder: "Don't worry, I used a phone card." I
nod. "Finally, after calling all these places I found a company
in Long Island . . . It's pronounced Long Island, right?" he
asks. I nod again. "Yeah, in Long Island. The man I spoke
with was so excited. He said he hadn't had an order in years.
He was just about to go out of business. He delivered it right
after we got off the phone. Isn't this exciting?" William starts
shaking the bed.

I plead with him to stop it. I'm seasick. "Oh, yeah"—he nods—"I forgot you don't know how to swim. I guess this will be your big introduction! Now you can be a beautiful mermaid." I knit my brow to the best of my ability. Right. That makes a whole lot of sense. William joins me on the water bed and tells me he loves me. That makes a whole lot of sense, too. As much sense as saying that a water bed is the same thing as a swimming lesson. Okay. "Before I forget," he adds, "the man told me it's best to be nude when lying on the bed. They've had a lot of complaints about leaks and stuff."

I don't want to be nude ever again. Not even in the shower. I need a prescription for Dramamine. "Do you want to make love on the water bed?" he shyly inquires. I smell the sea air and catch a whiff of cologne. That same cologne William wore in South Africa. I *hate it*! I tell him I just got my period. I'm going to have it for a very long time. I try to get off the bed but can't because I'm stuck. William gets up in a flash and gives me his hand. He hoists me out like an anchor covered in seaweed. I catch my breath. I still have liquid in my lungs, I have it up my nose, in my ears. Are my clothes raggedy? Am I sunburned? Where are the palm trees? Who goes there? I'm mixing metaphors. I'm delirious. The phone rings. I turn. I pick up. I ask what. "Hey, it's me," Max says. "Do you happen to have a whoopee cushion?" I hang up. No I do not.

I walk stiffly across the apartment to look for my cigarettes. I push a few credit card bills aside. These things will be the end of me, I'm down so much money. During those fifteen days of waiting for Richard to call I conducted some major shopping therapy. On day twelve I bought four pairs of $150 jeans and five $75 T-shirts in an array of colors. Who buys $75 T-shirts? This fool does. Why? No clue. It just made me feel good in the moment. It's a clichéd move for a reason—it works. In my defense, I like very expensive jeans that look cheap and slightly less expensive T-shirts that look even cheaper, jeans and T-shirts are pretty much all I wear (and my mother can't stand it), but buying four pairs of jeans in under fifteen minutes? I think I set the land speed record. I couldn't have done it faster on a luge.

I push many white envelopes aside before finally finding my salvation. William sees me walking toward the door and asks where I'm off to. "I need a cigarette," I say, still trying to catch my breath. "You stay right here and don't play with anything sharp. I'm going on the stoop."

"Did you get my e-mails about that? I really want you to quit."

"I got your e-mails. I do not want any more of those," I mumble and close the door. Call me a romantic but that water bed needs to be taken out back and shot.

* * *

The next day is like a blank piece of white paper, and I walk across it like a zombie with black rotating swirls where the eyeballs should be. I have no idea what happened. When I get home that evening, while taking off my coat, I again see the mouse, the one that first plagued me days before William's arrival. The mouse runs over my foot and I scream, properly waking myself from the daze I was in all day. Like a baseball player stealing home, William dives across the floor in an effort to catch it. But the mouse is too fast. It bolts through the crack underneath the door. I am too shaken to point out that he would not have to throw himself against the floorboards if he would just let me leave some glue traps out. As he volunteers that traps are inhumane, evidently reading my mind (for once), I notice the flashing red light of the answering machine. I press play. "We have to talk. It's urgent." Richard. Shit. I press delete.

* * *

On Thursday night Max, Libby, William, and I head to Leona's in Brooklyn for the combo birthday/twenty-fifth-anniversary dinner. William is disguised as a yahoo. He is wearing a red tracksuit with gold piping and his fez, which he keeps saying is his favorite hat. His outfits make him look ridiculous every day, and now, with a water bed in the apartment, he looks ridiculous every night, too. Purchasing the water bed was an act of war and the sad thing is that he genuinely meant well. He hasn't done one—not one—intentionally malicious thing since he arrived. Only a devil would wish him ill.

"Okay, Libby, listen," I cup my hand and whisper when we are a few blocks from the restaurant. "We have to take him out. I need your cooperation. I can't handle the tracksuit and the fez. I can't handle the kindness or the anti-smoking leaflets." I look over at William, who's listening to Max talking loudly about something. I continue: "When I give the signal you grab him by the ankles so he loses his balance and falls, then I'll chloroform him. It's my only way out and we have to act fast. Are you in?" Libby just laughs. I look over at William. Now he's doing the talking. I hear the word "money." Max nods at him. I ask why she's wasting time. She needs to shimmy under him so he falls. Libby refuses to shimmy under him. "You're so funny," she says. Well, I'm only 10 percent kidding, to be honest. She points out that I should be grateful to have such a nice man in my life. He buys me gifts, he cooks and does dishes, he tells me he loves me, he's great in bed, he's beautiful, kind, honest . . . She needs to stop it. Who needs a man like that? I never asked for a man like that. Did I? Besides, she adds, I'm William's first love. This is a very emotional time for him. I have to be gentle. I nod. Obviously I understand that or he would not still be staying with me.

Max turns around and asks what we are whispering about back there. I smile. Certainly not chloroform, if that's what he's asking. "We're just complaining about bills," I say dismissively. "I'm broke as a joke." (In fact, we had been talking about bills just moments before.) He and William wait for us to catch up. As soon as we do William puts his arm around me. He asks if I am having money problems. When am I not? I admit it's the same as always: Bills pile up; sometimes I don't know how I pay the rent. Typical New York complaint. William gives me a squeeze. "I never knew you were poor," he says sadly. "Poverty is terrible."

I never said I was poor, though I am, relatively speaking. Mostly I'm just an idiot who doesn't know how to manage money. Max laughs dismissively. "Oh, she's poor all right," he says, pointing at my $150 jeans. When William asks how much I pay for rent, Max asks William what he can afford to pay, just out of curiosity. William mentions that he went to an ATM earlier today and opens his wallet. It's bulging with hundreds. William thinks about Max's question and determines that he can afford to give me three thousand dollars in rent for this month. He adds that it's worth it if I'm poor.

"Three thousand dollars!" Max exclaims and grabs him by the arm. "William, you sure you don't want to live with me?" William laughs—he'd rather live with his girlfriend. He turns to me and says that I should never be too proud to accept help. He wants to help me and, financially speaking, he's more than capable. He has a great deal of savings to help advance the dream of writing a book about the political situation in Monaco. This month he wants to pay my entire rent. It's the least he can do.

I start to tell William that I don't pay three thousand dollars, but Max jumps in. "Come along," he urges. "You lovebirds can work out the bills later. I wouldn't want anyone to commit to anything without thinking it through. That mistake was already made once."

"When?" William asks in confusion.

"It's not important anymore," Max answers. "Let's just go to Leona's and have a one-night stand like civilized people. We're already late."

William gives me a hug and repeats that he had no idea I was poor. I remind him that I am not technically poor. He's not listening. As we approach the restaurant he reaches into his pocket and pulls out the necklace of white stones bought on his first day in the city. "You forgot this at home," he says. "I know you said that you only want to wear it on very special occasions, but in my opinion there is no more special occasion than dinner with family." William holds out the necklace. I reluctantly take it.

William gets to the door of the restaurant first. I am right behind him. When he swings it open he somehow manages to elbow me in the nose. AHHHHHHHH. I put my hand over my face as he tips his fez while holding open the door like a hotel doorman. "After you," he says, not realizing what he's done. When my nose begins to sting and my eyes begin to water from the lethal blow he puts his hand on my shoulder. He assures me that everything is going to be okay,

I needn't cry. Poverty is an international epidemic. I wipe my eyes dry.

Every table at Leona's is decorated with a lazy Susan, at the center of which is a bust of a pope. I spot our table (Pope John Paul II graces our lazy Susan) and begin moving toward it, just as a woman walks briskly across the restaurant, stops in front of our group, and stares at Max. "Dr. Devereux?" she asks.

Max looks up. He does not miss a beat. "Why yes!" he says in a bad British accent. "It is indeed." He explains to me that this is the receptionist at Richard's office. He stopped by there the other day to drop off Richard's medication. He gives her his hand. "Debra, right?" he asks. She takes his hand. "Susie," she corrects him.

"Of course," he says. "Susie. How is my patient? Any problems delivering the medicine to him?"

Susie nods. She begins to whisper conspiratorially. "Yes, just like you said there would be, Doctor. He denied it."

"Well, I knew he would," Dr. Devereux responds. He puts his index finger to his temple and makes a stirring motion to indicate that his patients are all cuckoo. "They always do." Susie nods then mentions that the good doctor looks different; she hardly recognized him. Didn't he have black hair and red glasses? "I dyed it and got contacts," he explains. He shakes her hand again and tells her he must run. He's late for dinner.

"Of course, Doctor," she responds and smiles.

When she leaves I give him a shove. "Stop playing pranks on Richard," I tell him. "He left a message at my house and he sounded pissed. I'm not getting in trouble for your bright ideas anymore."

He tilts his head and stares at me like I'm the most boring person in the world. "Get in trouble," he mockingly repeats. "Who is he, your dad? I would love to see him"—he makes air quotes—"get you in trouble. You just remember what he did."

When my mother sees us she stands and immediately comments on the necklace; she's never known me to wear anything so ladylike. Granite is feminine? William proudly informs her that it was a gift from him. "A gift," she repeats. She tries to mask her pleasure but I can see that she approves, this gift taking her one step closer to grandchildren. William just blushes, as he's been known to do.

I greet my father, brother, and paternal grandmother. Her long gray hair is pulled up into a bun, as always. You can depend on few things anymore, but you can always depend on that bun. I kiss her rouged cheek, wish her a happy birthday, and take a seat next to William, whose accent is going to drive her crazy. Good ol' granny—who has a thick Polish accent herself, mind you—has a very hard time understanding people with accents. William pushes the tassel out of his eye and says he's pleased to finally meet her. My grandmother, queen of eccentricity, looks to my father for help. I hear her ask if William is wearing a propeller hat. Here we go.

"This hat inspires me to write my book about the political situation in Monaco!" William boldly shouts across the table. My grandmother turns to my father, who is visibly preoccupied, in an effort to determine what the hell was just said. I wonder what's wrong—he rarely loses his cool, or at least his pleasant disinterest in histrionics—but he looks annoyed. He turns to William and explains my grandmother's issue with accents. William is instructed not to bother talking to her and to please stop shouting. She's not deaf, people often make that mistake. My father looks around: "Where is that waiter? He walked by earlier and completely ignored us."

Uh-oh. My father's biggest pet peeve is bad restaurant service. I hope this joker shows up soon.

My mother looks down at her empty plate and explains that the waiter is likely getting high on cocaine. She read that it happens a lot. She reminds Henryk to watch it: If he keeps getting bad grades he's going to be a busboy. My brother, blue baseball cap pulled low over his eyes, responds by saying nothing. He should learn sign language. "And take off that hat!" she screams at him. "It's not appropriate! How can you see anything?"

When William makes a move to take off his fez, I tell him my mother is talking to Henryk; this is an ongoing battle between them. As I begin playing with my napkin, which is folded on my plate like a swan, my grandmother addresses William: "You're a handsome young man. How tall are you?" William tells her how tall he is because he has short-term memory loss. My grandmother of course has no idea what he is saying, which leads us back to my father, who is called in to translate. When he does my grandmother nods. "A giant," she says mostly to herself.

William smiles: "I'm not as tall as . . ." I cover his mouth.

"Nice teeth, too, just like my husband," she adds, referring to my deceased grandfather. "He reminds me of my husband, the more I see him."

William puffs out his chest. Settle down, I tell him, everyone reminds her of her husband, may he rest in peace. When my grandmother suggests that perhaps William is the waiter my father explains that William is just a friend of mine from South Africa. She seems fascinated: "But he's white"—she squints—"isn't he?"

My mother leans in. "They have both black and white people in South Africa," she says as if she has known this fact all her life.

"Why?" my grandmother asks. I do give her credit for the question. Unfortunately, people major in its answer.

"It's a diverse country!" the South African who majored in nothing shouts. I tell him to cut it out as my grandmother asks what he said.

My father spins the lazy Susan, which makes three rotations before stopping. Pope John Paul II looks at me with knowing eyes as my father whispers to my grandmother that William doesn't know what he's saying: She should read his book and see his limp. I'm not surprised that my father has a cruel opinion on this matter, I'm just surprised he's sharing it now. He is cranky today, boy. I'm going to try to stay out of his way. William taps me on the shoulder and asks what my father just said. I lie: "He said you are a nice person." William smiles and tells me he likes my father, too. I'm glad, everyone cares.

My grandmother points to William: "Is he talking to me?"

William nods. Certainly he's talking to her. He can't shut up. "Where's your husband tonight?" he shouts. "Will he be joining us later?" I squeeze his knee under the table. He looks at me for a second and then squeezes my knee in return. He thinks we are flirting.

I remove his hand as my father begins waving his arms in the air. "Finally!" he exclaims. "Here comes that waiter." He addresses the waiter just as Libby lets out a bloodcurdling scream. My mother jumps out of her chair and asks if Libby saw a cockroach. Everyone looks at Libby, who points to something over my head. I hope there's not a cockroach over my head. I turn around in my chair. I almost didn't recognize him without the silk suit and tie.

"Manuel!" Max, William, and I gasp in unison. Manuel stiffens at the sound of his name. He sets down a stack of menus and tucks his order pad into his white apron. He weakly smiles at Libby: "Are my eyes playing tricks on me? It cannot be."

I snap him out of his trance. "Manuel, what are you doing here?" I ask. Manuel puts a finger to his lips and looks behind him. He leans in and informs me that I must call him Bob from now on. Bob? Why would I want to call him Bob? I look over at Libby. She's speechless; she's turned into my brother. William hears this, too. He hasn't changed; he's himself. He's fine with the code name, no problem. "Hi, Bob!" William says excitedly. Manuel notices him. The expression on his face resembles the one my mother had when she thought there might be a cockroach in the restaurant. William volunteers his latest and greatest news without prompting. "I live here now, Man . . . Bob," he declares. My mother brings the fact that William is only visiting to my attention. I hope he is. And even though she's warming up to the idea of her newly feminized daughter having a tall friend of the male persuasion, she still needs to be assured that the tall friend of the male persuasion isn't having sex with her newly feminized daughter. I understand—it's called morals and family values. It's the closest thing to my heart.

Manuel bows his head in shame: "My name is Bob. I am currently a resident of Brooklyn."

"Since when?" Libby asks. Manuel's Adam's apple begins bobbing up and down like a buoy. He gazes at her longingly as the theme music from *The Godfather* blares through a set of speakers over my grandmother's head. One of us, I can't be sure who, asks what happened to the tube socks. Manuel takes a seat at the table. "It is complicated," he says, screening his eyes with his hand.

My father frowns. "Who is this guy?" he asks in confusion. "He's not the waiter?"

"That's our friend Bob," William offers helpfully. "He's rich."

My grandmother points to William: Maybe he's the waiter. I look at William. Well, he was the waiter, in South Africa. Now he's the guest.

Manuel continues: "I will tell you my entire story," he says. "I do not enjoy discussing private affairs but so be it. Allow me to set the scene." I'm tempted to tell him that while he's at it he should set the table with some food. My father needs service.

Manuel clears his throat while gazing out at an imaginary horizon. William shifts in his seat. "I was in the greenhouse on my family's estate in Mexico City, composing my last will and testament—" he begins.

My grandmother cuts him off. "Is the boy reading the specials? What are the specials today?" she asks. Accent.

My father admits that he doesn't know and reminds her that specials are usually rip-offs. But he asks Manuel for the specials anyway, and when he does Manuel hands him a menu as my grandmother mumbles that Manuel looks, just a little bit, like her husband. My father is temporarily appeased; he puts on his reading glasses and inspects the selections.

"Where was I?" Manuel asks the group. My captivated mother reminds him that he was telling her about his will. Manuel picks up a spoon off the table and examines his reflection. "Of course, yes. I was in the greenhouse on my family's estate in Mexico City, composing my last will and testament. My tenth trip to South Africa left me with much to consider . . ." Manuel nods in Libby's direction and puts down the spoon. ". . . I pondered all that I had and all that I aspired to possess. I began to tabulate all that which would one day be rightfully mine. My will and testament would be a momentous document against which so many middling lives would be measured. What of the butlers, I thought to myself, what shall I leave them, when in truth all they have ever wanted was to ensure my felicity. I thought of the valets who lay out my silk dressing gowns; I thought of my jovial cook whose nourishing breakfasts have fortified me; I thought of the faceless woman who rolls my corn tortillas late into the night; I thought of the shoeshine boy and the chauffeur. These humble, infantile people depend on my magnanimity, I thought, while pouring bordeaux into a priceless goblet, a gift from a venerable bishop who is like a second godfather to me . . ."

My father looks up from his menu and pushes down his glasses: "What is this?" he asks.

". . . I peered through the stained-glass windows of my greenhouse while reflecting upon the critical role I was playing in all their lives. I thought of what I mean to my honorable parents, who have encouraged me . . ."

My mother nods in my direction and softly repeats the words "honorable parents."

". . . I contemplated how much more I would have to give upon inheriting the fortune, and how much would be left—if anything—after I was entombed in the sitting position. With that, I began to consider how I might divide my wealth among the help. There were so many names, most of which I did not know. Perhaps I will give the cobbler my preferred riding crop when I pass from this world, perhaps the stable hand shall receive my lucky rabbit's foot. Shall I bequeath my snuffbox to the footman? My rosary to the steward? I have so many possessions and so many servants—more than there are grains of sand in front of my beach house. Such philanthropic visions of benevolence were preoccupying my mind's eye when, in an instant, I began to smell something . . ."

"Shit?" Max asks.

". . . What is this curious odor? I asked myself. The smell of plastic and yet . . ."

Manuel points to the ceiling. Everyone looks up except for me and my father, who stares at his menu.

". . . I was smelling the air just as my maid burst through the greenhouse doors, nearly knocking over one of my irreplaceable orchids. 'Behold what you almost did!' I shouted as she steadied the clay pot with arthritic, double-jointed fingers. 'What is the meaning of this interruption?' I asked in dismay. 'The tube sock factory!' she wailed. 'What of it?' I said. 'It is . . . ,' she began. 'What?' I demanded. 'Speak, I command it, you insolent rube!' . . ."

Manuel pushes back his chair and stands up dramatically.

". . . 'It is, it is, it is buuuuuuuurning!' she howled, hot tears running down her ragged face. I stood up, letting the pen with which I was composing my last will and testament drop out of my hand. Once as light as a feather from a black swan it was now as heavy as pewter. 'It cannot be!' I screamed and fell to my knees with a thud . . ."

Manuel gets down on his knees. "Where'd he go?" I hear my grandmother ask.

". . . I turned an accusatory eye onto the merciless sky and shook my fist. 'Damn you, Lord,' I cursed and immediately regretted it. I choked back tears and regained my composure for the sake of the maid, who is impressionable. 'Get out of my way!' I said, pushing her aside. 'Get back to your potter's wheel this instant! I must see to the factory.' I ran across the grounds of our compound as fast as my legs would carry me . . ."

Manuel gets to his feet and begins running in place.

". . . In the distance I saw the plumes of black smoke. It was like watching a hideous serpent unfurl itself in front of my naked eyes. 'The tube sock factory!' I shouted. 'Noooooooooo ooooooooooooooooooooooooooooooooooooooooooooo!' I still had a distance to travel but fatigue was consuming my limbs. I looked around out of desperation. The thoroughbreds! I thought. I jumped on the back of one of my trusted colts, a black beauty named after an emissary of the Grimaldi family with whom my father once played billiards, and rode bareback the rest of the way . . ."

Manuel pretends he is riding a horse.

". . . But when I arrived on the scene it was too late . . ."

Manuel drops the imaginary reins.

". . . Everything was ruined. An arsonist is to blame, I immediately concluded, looking around at the guilty faces attempting to extinguish the fire. A jealous rival has reduced my livelihood to smoldering lumber. It was too much for one man to endure. What of the family's gristmill, what of the distillery, what of the gunboats, and what do they all matter now without the tube sock factory? The news was unbearable. 'You will be held accountable, you covetous slime!' I shouted at the charwomen holding empty buckets . . ."

Manuel points a finger at my grandmother. She turns around and looks at the wall.

". . . I abandoned my colt to the flames and returned to the greenhouse on foot. I tore my last will and testament to pieces, letting the scraps cascade around me like ash. I left the greenhouse in a daze as a light rain began to fall. I walked, a hopeless mute, across the grounds—past the marble fountains adorned with Mother's beloved angels, past the citrus trees and the palms, past the armed guards, past the apple orchards, past the frolicking bay mares, past the man-made waterfall, past the fútbol field, past the chapels, past the servants' quarters and the wooden outhouse they all share, past the flower beds, past the heliport, past the hammocks, past the fully stocked fishing pond, past the hummingbird baths, past the peacocks mocking me with their vibrant plumage, past the onyx columns and matching onyx panther statues that lead to the main house, past the prizewinning parrots calling my name. And then, finally . . ."

Manuel catches his breath. He sits back down.

". . . Past the bowling alley erected in 1999 at my request, past the sweets shoppe nestled inside it, past the bulletproof steam room, the weight-lifting center and the three massage booths, past the galleria of family portraits dating back centuries, past the chandeliers, past the black-and-white surveillance photographs of my father's adversaries that are mounted to the refinished walls like hunting trophies, past the Hall of Mirrors, past the solarium, past the terrarium, past the wreaths made of geranium . . ."

William turns to me. "Wow," he says, "Manuel has a big house."

". . . past the exotic-gems room, past the drawing room and the ballroom, past the terraces, past the balconies, past the satellite TV room, past the movie theater, past the mural of Quetzalcoatl, past the bathrooms, twenty in all, not including those under construction. I walked past all of it, over the Oriental divans dappled in midafternoon sun, to my sleeping chamber. I threw open the French doors and looked upon my king-size canopy featherbed set off by velvet ropes whose color, for the first time, resembled an ominous blood-red sky . . ."

"I will have the lasagna with meat sauce," my father announces.

". . . This, I thought, while pulling the drapes shut, had always been my sanctuary, a place of repose, where so many dreams had been fabricated. Now all of it was dashed, like a piece of expensive crystal hurled against a stucco wall . . ."

"I changed my mind, I'll have the spaghetti and meatballs," my father says.

". . . I gazed upon my nightingale. I placed a black kerchief over her gilded cage. 'Sing no more,' I whispered, before collapsing onto the featherbed in despair. I rested my weary head against the silk pillows and fingered the Egyptian cotton sheets whose thread count is higher than the skyscraper I own in Manila. With my tired eyes I followed the swinging pendulum of the imported grandfather clock. What will become of my decadent lifestyle? I thought as a single tear made its way down my cheek. How will I triumph over this insurrection? And then, as I struggled to outrun the barren desert of my mind, as I forged ahead through a labyrinth of horrific questions, as I began to play a hypothetical game of Russian roulette with my own indispensable life, I saw before me an oasis . . ."

Manuel looks at Libby, who, as she leans into the table, is displaying more cleavage than she probably realizes. Not good for Libby, but judging from the renewed zeal with which Manuel tells his tale, very, very good for Manuel.

". . . An angel she was. An angel whose china-white hands deserve to be sculpted by Parisian artisans. Whose countenance gives meaning to the gay science of poetry, whose every perfumed breath inspires minstrels and troubadours, whose heaving, ample breasts, bountiful, bountiful breasts . . ."

Manuel is cupping the air when the manager walks by. He has an expertly groomed black goatee, thick black hair combed back like Elvis, a diamond earring in his left ear, and, last but not least, a nameplate that reads MANAGER. He does a double take when he notices Manuel sitting at our table. He stops to consider our empty plates and grimaces. "Manuel, what are you doing sitting down?" he asks.

Manuel's soap bubble bursts. "I'm in the middle of a conversation," he says distractedly. "And how many times must I tell you to refer to me as Bob? That is my name. Bob. I know of no Manuel."

"Have you taken their order yet?" the manager asks. My

father pipes up that he's most certainly ready to order. The manager apologizes and urges Manuel to please take our orders. Manuel rises from his chair as if it is a throne and asks what we would like for dinner. My father, the most eager, orders first. When it is Libby's turn Manuel can't help but talk over her. "I will have . . . ," she begins.

"Do you remember the enchanted evening we spent in the swimming pool?" he asks. "Those were inspired nights, the world held such promise . . ."

". . . a glass of red wine," she says.

My disapproving mother asks Libby when she shared a swimming pool with the waiter. Let me guess: Abstinence before marriage makes the heart grow fonder? "We were all in the pool," Manuel says to no one in particular. My mother scowls at me. "Were you in the pool, too?" she asks. I shake my head no; he doesn't mean me. I make sure not to look at my father.

William places his order next. It comes in the form of a question: "Was it an arsonist who burned down the factory?" he asks Manuel with concern.

My mother leans in. "Yeah, was it?" she wants to know. As long as we are not talking about premarital sex or bugs she's doing great.

Manuel sighs: "That is yet to be determined, though it has been confirmed that the tube socks were not made of one hundred percent cotton as previously thought. They were a blend, at least fifty percent polyester." He momentarily looks back at the kitchen in disdain. "But that wasn't the worst of the news. As devastated as I was about the tube sock factory, what happened to my father was worse—"

My own father interrupts to say that he thinks he'll have the lasagna after all, but with an order of meatballs on the side. Manuel looks up. He forgot where he was. My mother folds her hands in her lap and praises Manuel for his ability to tell a story. She recommends he write a novel because everyone is doing it. Manuel responds by again pulling out the empty chair. My father warns him that whatever he does he should not sit back down. Manuel sits back down and shakes his head. "I am afraid that would be impossible," he says. "I have discarded every one of my many journals. You see, I am a superstitious man . . ."

"How are you a man again?" Max asks.

"As I was saying," Manuel continues without answering, "I am a superstitious man and have not written a word in my own hand since that fateful day. The last time I tried to write my family's tube sock factory was burned beyond recognition. I do not wish to invite more devastation . . ."

My mother tells him that William is a writer. She asks to see the book. William admits that he didn't bring it because he didn't think he had written enough. Yes, and that's because he's been too busy composing acknowledgments pages—acknowledging events that have yet to happen. It's amazing how little someone with so many inspirations—the fez, the flag, the psychic—could get done. But, as I've come to realize, there are always excuses: The pencils aren't sharp enough, the timing is not right, then of course there's the television set. It glows like the ultimate inspiration, illuminating the brain with static.

Manuel considers my mother's words. He's like a wicked stepsister watching Cinderella try on the glass slipper. "But he's a lowly park ranger," he utters in disbelief.

"Not anymore," Cinderella says. "I'm writing a book."

My mother assures Manuel that William is a writer.

"Is this true, William?" Manuel asks, growing curious. "Are you a writer?"

William squeezes my knee under the table. I wish he wouldn't do that. He smiles at Manuel in confirmation of the fact. My mother puts out her hand as if to say, *I told you so, William has talent.* Talent, I'd like to point out, is not the same thing as good looks. I fell for it, too. Don't be taken in, Mother dear.

When Manuel expresses interest in having someone write his biography, Max suggests placing a call to Tom Clancy. Manuel has never heard of Tom Clancy. He closes his eyes. "Perhaps, and this is just a thought, I will commission William to help commit a book about my life to paper," he says.

"No!" I abruptly protest. My mother immediately scolds me for being rude. The boy lost his factory. Why am I being insensitive? William tips his fez: He'd be more than happy to lend his expertise. Manuel next asks William where he now lives. "With my girlfriend," my boyfriend beams. To Libby's great dismay, William proceeds to reveal that she lives across the hall. I look over at my mother: William is sleeping in the tub and leaving this Sunday, et cetera, et cetera. Please believe me, I would never lie, et cetera, et cetera.

William tells Manuel that he'd be honored to help with the book. I hit his leg to signal that I would not be honored to have him help. No response. I consider trying again with an anvil. Manuel approves. "Of course you would be honored," he tells him. "You would be a fool otherwise."

William readjusts his thinking cap as Manuel announces that he will be arriving at my apartment tomorrow after the lunch shift. As soon as I hear this I make eye contact with Max from across the table and begin frantically tapping my finger against my nose. I don't care if William is a virgin and I don't care about the rent money. William can stay with Max; I can't take both William and Manuel hanging around me.

Max knits his brow and shakes his head no, just as my mother catches a glimpse of me with my finger on my nose. "Don't pick your nose, honey," she says, puckering her lips like she just sucked a few lemons. "That's not nice." I take my hand away. Oh my God.

Max begins talking to me from across the table, he doesn't care who hears him. "No way," he says. "All bets are off now. You're on your own with that guy, sister." He points at Manuel, who continues to stand over the table, looking deep in thought. When my father asks him for bread, he gets no response. We should go in on an anvil.

It is William who finally gets his attention. He asks Manuel why he decided to come to Brooklyn. Manuel explains that he and his mother have taken up temporary residence with his uncle, a failed entertainer turned failed dishwasher turned failed Leona's manager. He elaborates as only he can: "You may have noticed him earlier. He was the hack who forfeited good judgment when he told me what to do." Manuel flippantly gestures toward the manager (now his uncle), who is standing at a nearby table talking with a customer. "He arranged for this job," Manuel continues, "which I am working at my mother's request. It is her impression that we would both benefit from the experience. As you know, I would never go against a parent's wishes."

Max takes the opportunity to ask Manuel where his father is now. Manuel turns up his nose: "That is a crushing story and one that, in light of recent developments, I do not care to reveal. You must wait like everyone else." Max's eyes narrow. He was just told to wait! Ha-ha. Waiting is not his strong suit. If someone dares put him on hold he simply hangs up the phone. Manuel smirks at Max: "I invite you to read the book."

William looks up. "What book?" he asks as if emerging from a heavy brain fog.

"The one I have commissioned you to assist me with," Manuel explains. "We begin tomorrow. I wish I could say that you will be composing a carefree roman-fleuve but it cannot be."

"Great!" William cheers. "I'm so excited!"

I turn to William. I ask how he's going to write two books. William gives me a merciful look. "But don't you understand?" he says. "By helping Bob I am helping myself. It is my duty to help people. If I don't help Bob I will have disappointed everyone." If William helps Manuel he will have disappointed me. "Besides," he continues, "Miss Celeste told me someone new is going to enter my life, a mystery man. I think that somebody is Bob. I have to help him. And it will be good for my writing career. I'll get extra practice. You understand, don't you?"

I don't understand and make sure William knows it. He needs to focus on his own life, and he needs to stop calling Manuel Bob. "I have to do unto others what I would have done unto me," he says, "that's what Miss Celeste said and I think she's right."

I just nod. Jesus, there's no convincing him now. He thinks he's saving the world.

When he asks if I am not the least bit interested in finding out what happened to Manuel's father—maybe he needs help, too, he adds—I inform him that I'm not, even though I am, just a little bit. When he tries to kiss my cheek I jerk away as if from a scalding cinder. Not in front of my mother—I have a virginal persona to maintain. He pats my knee under the table. "I love you," he coos. "You are such an honest person.

I am so glad we met and that I trusted you. Helping Bob with his book is the right thing to do." William again squeezes my knee. "And I meant what I said about the rent. I will pay the whole thing this month. I want to and I won't take no for an answer. My arms and my pockets are open." He spreads his arms, raises them toward the ceiling, and looks up, like he is channeling something from the beyond, or perhaps preparing for his ascension into Heaven.

After an excruciating forty minutes and a great deal of shouting at his fellow staffers, Manuel brings out our food. We are eating our entrées when he returns to the table. My father begs for more bread. Manuel nods but doesn't make a move to get it; he claps his hands to get our attention and announces that he has a special treat.

My father begins to grumble as William looks up from his plate. A piece of spaghetti hangs from his chin. I peel it off for him. He needs a bib. Manuel continues: "As you know, I excel in many arenas, often eclipsing even my own expectations: Archery, fencing, skydiving, calligraphy, martial arts, glassblowing, bullfighting, puppetry, I have bent them all to my will. I pride myself on being a Renaissance Man, someone who bedazzles large groups on a whim with feats of daring. But there is one sphere I have not mastered, one corner of the cultural globe I have yet to successfully navigate . . ." My father raises the empty breadbasket and points inside. He just wants one roll, just one. "Music!" Manuel shouts. My grandmother drops her fork and grabs her heart. "I have yet to master the art of making music. I realize this revelation comes as a shock to some of you." Manuel looks at Libby, who gives him a *Who me?* shrug. "Rest assured that this lapse in my résumé has been accounted for. I have taken it upon myself to learn an instrument with the hope that I may someday play music—

the kind of music that could soothe a savage breast—as freely as I do so many other things, including pleasure a woman." Manuel winks at Libby and pulls a long tube out of his apron. "This, my friends, is a recorder. It is an instrument whose beginnings trace back to antiquity. Thus far I have only taught myself one song. I acquired the sheet music from a beggar woman selling paper flowers near my temporary residence here in Brooklyn. I would like to take this opportunity to play the melody I have been practicing since yesterday. And now, without further ado, a taste of things to come." Manuel takes another look at Libby. He readies his instrument of love and blows.

He is playing the instrument with every part of his body. His hips are swaying like those of a schoolgirl defying logic with a hula hoop. He is moving the recorder up and down and side to side. He is tapping his foot to the beat of a nonexistent drummer. He is playing his amorous jingle loudly, he is play-ing it softly. My father puts down the breadbasket as Manuel continues to play with undiminished vigor, even as Max gives him the finger, even as Libby dozes off, even as a Dean Mar-tin song blares through the restaurant's loudspeakers. Manuel grows more daring. He is just warming up, steadily increasing the volume in order to drown out things like "when the stars make you drool just like pasta fagiole" and "when the moon hits your eye like a big-a pizza pie." Manuel continues to play as a fellow restaurant patron, who had been sitting at the next table with his family, flicks Manuel's shoulder. He is attired in a black Harley-Davidson T-shirt and black pants. A red ban-danna is tied around his head.

"Hey, bandleader," the man says in a heavy Brooklyn accent. "Listen up."

"What did he say?" I hear my grandmother ask.

Manuel lowers his recorder and stares cockily at the man. "Stop the tootin', okay?" the man says. "We're not at a Mardi Gras." The man begins walking back to his table, confident that the waiter will heed this warning, no questions asked. He's a big fella, about three hundred pounds, the kind of dude who gets heard the first time; his stomach is like a hill. Manuel pushes out his neck like a rooster. "Pardon me?" he challenges. Great, just what we need. The man strolls back over. "I'll tell you what," the man says, reaching into his pocket. I peek under the table. There's plenty of room if things get ugly. The man pulls out a coin and puts it in Manuel's hand. He very slowly closes Manuel's fingers around the money, one finger at a time. "Are you hurt?" he continues, now looking Manuel in the eye. "You got problems at home?" Manuel remains silent. The man continues: "I don't know, either, but if it's change you need, you got it. Now go buy yourself an ice cream soda or a jawbreaker. Do anything you'd like, pal, just lose the fricken piccolo. I don't know what kinda parade you're rehearsing for but the show's been canceled, you know what I'm sayin'? Trust me on this one."

"It's a recorder," Manuel corrects him.

"Wha?" the man asks, putting a finger to his ear. "What you say to me?"

"This is not a piccolo," Manuel clarifies. "It is called a recorder and it rivals the best instruments of earlier ages, including the crwth, the shawm, the panpipe, and the portative organ." The man shifts his weight from one large foot to the other. He silently pats his stomach, leaving me to wonder if he's considering eating our waiter. But Manuel remains unaffected, even though he'd need a harpoon to take the guy on. Across the table I hear my grandmother tell my father that her husband was a great man who died too young. He didn't even make it to a hundred. Manuel sighs: "You see, it is exceptionally simple if you know anything about wood-winds, which you obviously do not. Most musical instruments fall into three categories: the strings, the winds, and the percussion. Among the stringed instruments the violin is perhaps the best known; others include the cello and the double bass. The percussion instruments are the least appealing. They include the kettledrum and the cymbals. In fact, you seem like the sort who would play a kettledrum. Moving on, both the piccolo and the recorder are considered wind instruments. The piccolo is a small flute with a hole in the side. It is set an octave higher than—"

"Listen, killjoy," the man interrupts, "it don't matter to me if you're playin' a trumpet or a cowbell or a policemen's whistle or a fricken seashell. Whatever it is reminds me of my mother-in-law's voice. This is no talent showcase. If you got music in your soul become a choreographer. We've been waitin' on you for a good half hour"—the man points to his table, at the center of which is a bust of Pope Pius X—"and I'm gettin' a little bit ticked off . . ."

Manuel's uncle reappears before the patron can rearrange Manuel's face. He nervously appeases the man, who agrees to go back to his designated pope after being promised free dessert. Manuel breathes a sigh of relief. His uncle gently puts an arm on his shoulder. He looks tired. Gee, I wonder why? Manuel, evidently under the impression that the uncle is on his side, again touches the recorder to his lips and begins to play. The instrument is confiscated before Manuel can finish the first note. The screech emitted is something like what you might hear if your friend sat on a cat, (almost) killing it. Manuel stares at his uncle like a defiant school bully called into the principal's office.

"We have hungry customers," the uncle says in a pleading

voice. "Please can you try to be supportive and do the work? I don't want you to lose this job. People are starting to walk out of here. Don't do it for me, son, do it for your mother's sake."

Manuel stuffs the recorder into his apron. The Achilles' heel has been struck. Game over. You can say a lot of things about Manuel but the truth is, the boy loves his mama. What she says goes.

My father tries again. He'd like some bread, and maybe some of that lovely free dessert everyone's enjoying.

"Coming right up," Manuel's uncle promises.

My father calls after him to put some candles on it. My mother gives him a look. "What?" he says. "That way we don't have to get a birthday cake."

The uncle escorts his nephew to the kitchen. "You should be honest about what's happened," I hear him say to Manuel as they walk away. "There is no use hiding it." Hiding what?

When Manuel returns with a full breadbasket he apologizes on his uncle's behalf: "He means well. Unfortunately, he is an idiot of gentle rank whose mind has gone soft from watching too many cartoons." My mother compliments him on his recorder playing and suggests that I take up piano. She asks my father if he still has his old guitar. Are we starting a band or something? I have to pee.

I get up to use the toilet. Max and Libby go, too. We are making our way down a hallway lined with tall potted palm trees that leads to the his and hers, wondering what Manuel is hiding, and marveling at how crazy it is that he is here in the first place, when a man jumps out from behind one of the trees, blocking our passage.

Libby puts her hand to her heart. "Geez, you scared me," she says.

He ignores her and stands in front of Max. "Well, if it isn't my old friend," the man says. "It's nice to see you again." He looks to be in his fifties and has a tuft of silver hair. He is wearing cowboy boots and a flannel shirt tucked into light blue jeans. The outfit looks odd on him. He's too slight for it. He pushes up his Ben Franklin–style wire-rimmed glasses.

"Do I know you?" Max asks.

"I believe you do."

Max shakes his head: "Sorry, I think you have me confused with someone else."

"I really have to tinkle," Libby says. "Excuse me." She continues down the hall. The three of us stand next to the palms.

"I don't have you confused with someone else," the man says. "What is your name?"

"Max."

"Max what?"

"Max Parker," Max responds. He smiles. "You have me confused with someone else." He tries to move past but the man stands in his way.

"Max Parker, you said?" the man asks.

"That's right," Max confirms as the women's bathroom door opens and out walks the receptionist from Richard's office. She sees Max and waves. "Good-bye, Dr. Devereux! Have a good night!"

Max calls after her in the fake British accent: "Good-bye Debra!"

"It's Susie," she corrects him.

"My mistake!" he says and waves back. "Cheerio!"

The man eyes him suspiciously. "I thought you said your name was Max Parker."

Max waves him off. "It's a long story, and not one for your delicate ears. Anyway, ciao, we have to run."

Max again tries to leave, and again he is detained. "When I met you, you told me your name was Richard Stein," the man says. I bite my lip. "Perhaps I should introduce myself again. My name is Phillip. I work at the New York Public Library. Remember me now?" He puts his thumbs through the belt loops of his jeans.

Max shakes his head no, but he's obviously lying. This is the librarian who checked Max out less than an hour before he threw those books into the East River. "You came in recently," the man continues, "but you misrepresented yourself. You're not Richard Stein, and I know this because the real Richard Stein came into the library this week to check out a book, only he didn't have his card. When I checked the name in our computer it showed that Richard Stein, or in this case some-one posing as him, checked out a series of expensive books whose titles I vividly remember. There was a book on Greco-Roman wrestling, a book on gay porn . . ."

"That wasn't me," Max says. "I don't want to embarrass you but you have the wrong guy." He pats the man's shoulder. "Get your glasses checked."

The man grabs Max's wrist. "Don't play me for a fool. I know it was you. It would be hard to forget someone who checked out so much homoerotic material, flirted with me mercilessly, and then didn't leave his number. Besides, I checked the surveillance footage after the real Richard Stein came in. I have proof that it was you. And now"—he gives Max's wrist a squeeze before letting it go—"I have you."

Max puts a finger to his own lips. "Um," he says, "Phil. Philly. You're freaking me out."

"I would like to point out," Phillip continues, "that you have stolen state property, and I'm going to need that prop-erty back."

"I don't have it," Max quickly says.

"What do you mean you don't have it?" Phillip asks.

Max takes out his wallet. "Let me pay you for the books. How much will it cost?"

"This is not about money," Phillip informs him. "This is about stolen state property—government property. This is about false representation and impersonation. This, I'm afraid, is punishable with steep fines and jail time. I can make that happen. The library is not a place for games. The library is *sacred*."

Max tries to regain control of the situation. He uses his best weapon: charm. "Okay, Phillip, I'm going to be honest with you," he says. He explains that Richard Stein is a cheater and two-timer and that he was only trying to get some innocent revenge on the guy to teach him a lesson. Yes, maybe he took it a bit far but then so did Richard. He was just trying to even out the universe. "I mean look at this innocent girl," Max says, pulling me closer. He squeezes my cheeks, exposing my teeth. "Look at her limp hair and the bags under her eyes. She's a mess. She has low self-esteem. She's been beaten down by life. I was just trying to cheer her up. I'm sure we can work this out." Limp hair and bags?

"Are you his beard?" Phillip asks me. I shake my head: I don't know what that means. "Beard," he repeats, "his front." Max gets in there. He says no, he's openly gay.

"And why," asks Phillip, "would you bother getting revenge on a guy you never dated?"

Max shrugs. "I believe in love."

Phillip slowly walks in a circle around him. "I'll tell you what." He stops. "I'm willing to overlook this. I usually like my boys beefier but there's just something about you. I'm willing to forget I ever saw you here, under one condition."

"That we leave quickly and never enter your *sacred* library again?" Max hopefully asks.

"I want a date," Phillip says.

Max cringes. "I don't make passes at men who wear glasses," he tells him. "Can't I just write you a check?"

"Your number," Phillip says. He pulls out his cell phone. Max starts giving him the number. But it's a wrong number. "And may I remind you," Phillip adds, "that if you give me the wrong number we're going to have a problem, Mr. Max Parker. The police will find you and I will help them. I'll press charges myself." He again grabs Max's wrist.

"Let me give you that number from the top," Max hurriedly says. "I think I just gave you my old number." He mumbles "shit" under his breath.

"I'm glad we understand each other," Phillip says. He programs the real number into his phone. "Ever hear of the Lone Star Bar?" he asks.

"Um, yes," Max responds with a trace of mockery and disdain, like he's too good for the place.

"I'm a regular, know what I mean?" Phillip says. He takes a step back. "Wear tight jeans and a cowboy hat next time I see you. I'll be calling." He taps his belt buckle, it has a bucking bronco on it, and leaves.

"Oh my God," Max says with revulsion as Libby exits the bathroom. "I just got blackmailed!" I tell him he asked for it. I add that he also has to show up looking like a ranch hand. What's up with that? Max shudders. "There is a whole gay subculture of men who have a cowboy fetish and Phillip is apparently one of them." He puts his hands in his pockets. "This is brutal. Bru-tal. Those guys genuinely freak me out. Lone Star is their big hangout. They role-play like they are cowboys. And none of them have good bodies. They're like that guy"—he points in Phillip's general vicinity—"or they are fatties with tummies. They just do not take care of themselves." He pauses. "I can't believe that librarian just black-mailed me! A librarian!"

* * *

William, Libby, and I share a cab home that night. When we get to our building's front door I notice that the lock is broken. The door shuts but doesn't lock, meaning that anyone could push it open without first getting buzzed in. I'd better notify the super of the security breach. Pretty soon there will be bums sleeping in the foyer. That happened at the last place I lived. A bum refused to leave until the cops showed up. The whole building smelled like a diaper for months afterward. That dude was awful. His odor could knock down walls—it was like a superpower.

* * *

I stop at a coffee shop for a vanilla latte on my way to work Friday morning because I saw a woman on the train drinking one and it made me salivate. I get to the office thirty minutes late. "You're in trouble," Barbara says as I make my way past her. I tell her there was a line for the coffee. "It's not that," she says. She points at my boss's office door, which is closed. "He told me to tell you he wants to see you as soon as you get in." I stare at his gray office door. He wants to see me in there? He never wants to see me in there. "Go on in," Barbara says and winces. "Good luck. He's mad about something."

I take off my coat and set it on the copy machine, along with my purse and coffee. I knock on the door. "Come in!" is the gruff response.

I tentatively open the door and peek in. "You wanted to see me?" I ask.

"Come in here," he says, "and close the door behind you."

His office is messy. Papers litter the desk; manuscripts sit in boxes on the floor. The ledge of the big window behind him is lined with half-dead plants. A cheap plastic watering canteen in mint green is sitting next to a fern so dry and brown it looks like it was set on fire.

I close the door behind me. The lock clicks. Click. He picks up a piece of paper and hands it to me from across the desk. "Do you mind explaining this to me?" I look down at the paper. It's a printout of an e-mail sent by me on behalf of the agency. It reads: "You are a talentless loser. We feel sorry for you." I blink a few times.

"Please tell me," he says, trying to keep his cool, "why you would send something like this to an author?"

I begin to stutter. "I-I-I . . . I did not mean to send this. Oh my God. I'm so sorry . . ."

I explain that I was sending my weekly polite rejection letters, thanking authors for their submissions, and I just wrote down some things to get them off my chest, but I thought I had deleted them, not sent them. "I know better," I helplessly add.

He puts his hand to his temple then jerks it away. "Obviously you don't know better," he reminds me. "This author phoned me. Five times. He published this letter on his blog this morning and said he would make it his mission to get the word out about our agency. That we are unprofessional, that we don't care about writers . . ." He pauses. I tell him I will clear this up. I'll contact the author and explain myself, that it was a mistake, that I didn't mean . . .

"I already talked to him. He is unwilling to relent, and frankly I don't blame him. This agency does not need the kind of publicity you have generated. It does not."

I apologize again. I would never have . . .

"Get to your desk and check the outbox on your computer," he orders. "If you have sent something like this to any other authors, I want to know about it right away." I nod. He tells me to leave and to shut the door behind me. I get out of there as quickly as possible.

"Everything okay?" Barbara asks as I collect my stuff from the copy machine. She is chewing the end of a pencil, a phone book open before her. I shake my head no. "Do you know the names of any good pet psychologists specializing in emotional distress?" she asks. I shake my head again. "Buddy has sibling rivalry. He's acting up. He chewed a hole in my living room carpet last night." I tell her I'm sorry to hear that. "It's just too much," she adds, "raising these little guys on my own."

Back at my desk I search the outbox for more e-mails. All the other rejection letters I sent turn out to be legit. Small consolation, though. Idiot. How could I do that? Fuck, I'm going to lose my job. That is all I need. Fuck me. I always have to have a clever line. Shit.

* * *

Manuel, in a pin-striped suit, is spread out across half the couch when I get home. He is gesticulating frenetically with a rolled-up newspaper, in the middle of explaining to William the proper way of ironing money. William is occupying a square of the third couch cushion, balancing the laptop on his knees, type type typing like mad. I'm a touch cranky. I light a cigarette and throw the burned match into one of William's I LOVE NEW YORK coffee cups, then lie down on the water bed. When I ask them to keep it down Manuel claps his hands three times. "Let us take our break now, William,"

he says. "I am quite parched. Can you offer me an assort-
ment of beverages?" William tells him that we have beer and
water. Manuel corrects him: Where he hails from guests are
not offered water. Water is for peasants, as is beer. "I believe
I will have a cup of Colombian roast with one sugar cube,"
Manuel decides. William tells him we don't have that. "In that
case," Manuel says. "I will have a small glass of dry aperitif or
cognac." I look over and tell him we don't have that, either.
William jumps up: He'll go to the corner store for cognac, or
coffee, whatever they have. Old habits die hard. William has
reverted to his days on the reserve, serving rich people or, in
this case, formerly rich people.

When William returns with the coffee (surprise! No cognac to
be found at the dinky corner store), Manuel peers at him from
behind his newspaper. All I can see are two dark eyes steadily
narrowing their focus. He slowly lowers the newspaper to
reveal a frown. "I'll need my coffee transferred out of that
unsavory container and into something porcelain," he says,
referring to the foam coffee cup. William pours the coffee
into one of his I LOVE NEW YORK coffee mugs. Its handle could
fit the hands of ten children around it at once. He presents
it to Manuel, who calls the mug a trough, but he takes a sip
from it anyway. He promptly spits the coffee back out into the
cup as if he were a fountain. "This is not Colombian roast,"
he cringes. William explains that it's all they had. "This is too
acidic!" Manuel protests. "It will upset my stomach and I could
get an ulcer. It will never do." He again claps his hands three
times. "Let us continue then," he says. "We may now move on
to my birth. It is the story of a life crowded with lore and sup-
position." William begins slapping the keys. Slap, slap, slap.
"My birth"—Manuel crosses his legs—"was a joyous occasion for every member of my immediate and extended family,

not to mention my servants, who on that day admired the camel riders from an appropriate distance. A masquerade, the most lavish, regal affair imaginable, was hosted in my honor. Every guest was required to arrive dressed as someone else. Gratitude and exuberance mingled with the plate spinners and cancan girls. My father's trusted colleagues, influential men with impeccable pedigrees, arrived to pay their respects with toasts of Veuve Clicquot. I was ushered into a world of relentless living. I was fed my first morsel of caviar off my mother's pinkie. I was presented with the best the world had to offer and I accepted the warm invitation wholeheartedly. But with this life of leisure came unmitigated responsibility. And that night, as my father, still wearing his masquerade mask adorned with gold feathers, cradled me in his arms under the stars, as he lifted my smooth body upward, toward the constellations, I understood what a burden my life would someday be. I was to inherit everything, more treasure than could be looted from a pirate's ship, as much money as there were lighted specks in the heavens, and this realization made me melancholy . . ."

William looks up from the computer: "I'm sorry, Bob, how old did you say you were then? I didn't get the date down."

"One day old," Manuel clarifies. "I remember everything." William keeps typing. He was just checking. He's a fact checker. Good for him.

"As I was saying," Manuel continues, "I was dejected past consoling. I thought to myself, Can I ever live up to the responsibilities that come with my last names? Will I ever measure up to my forbearers, audacious warriors who fought in the Mexican War? Will I ever be good enough? And the answer, of course, was yes, I would. I am. Etiquette, deportment, chivalry, compassion to castoffs and lepers, the essence of my being encompasses . . ."

William is in the middle of telling Manuel to slow down, he's a fast typist but not that fast, when Libby and Max walk in. Max is holding a bottle of wine. "So what did he say about his fa—" Max begins. He goes quiet when he sees Manuel. He and Libby turn back around. They'll be back later. I know Max is curious to learn Manuel's father's whereabouts, not to mention why Manuel has christened himself Bob, but he was hoping, as I was hoping, that Manuel would be gone by now, leaving only gossip behind. I pull my friends by their collars and take the bottle from Max. "Get in here," I order. "Especially you, maxi pad. This is all your fault, if I need to remind you." He takes a seat on the couch and points at William. "Only he's my fault," he says.

While I open the wine, Manuel stands and urges Libby to have a seat next to him. She sits on the floor instead. He grabs his newspaper, removes the want ads, and carefully lines the floor with them. He plops down beside her like a puppy who has yet to be housebroken. "I will sit on the floor as well," he explains. "I agree that it is more quaint."

I ask if anyone wants wine. William shakes his head no. Manuel demands a glass only after hearing that Libby is having one. If she weren't here he'd be throwing it up all over the floor and making William do the mopping. I pour three glasses—one for me, one for Max, and one for Libby—and tell Manuel to get his own, it's on the counter. He gets up, groans about the quality of the wine after reading the label, then pours some and sits back down. He asks how she's doing. "I'm fine, babe," she says with a sigh.

"I feel wonderful myself," Manuel admits. He peers inside the glass and notifies William that there's a stray piece of cork floating inside. When William starts to get up I order him to stay put. Manuel has his own legs. They're short but they'll do. Manuel stands and moves over to the counter, the newspaper he was sitting on still attached to his ass. "I was just about to tell the stenographer about my plans to retire someday with you in Acapulco," he says to Libby over his shoulder. He gets a fresh glass and fills it with wine. Libby takes the opportunity to move to the couch. Manuel turns around. He begins talking to the spot on the floor where Libby should be. "Libby?" he asks. He sees her on the couch. "There you are," he says. He walks to the couch and squeezes in next to her, pushing William the stenographer off the couch. As he falls to the floor, William clumsily grabs, for support, the newspaper stuck to Manuel's ass. It rips in half.

Max asks Manuel to tell us about his father. Manuel recommends that he read the intriguing book where everything will be chronicled. In the meantime he'd like to talk to Libby. "Acapulco," Manuel continues, "is a Shangri-la, an infamous cliff-diving destination. I want to return there with you on my arm." He assures Libby that she will adore it and mentions how much he loves to Jet Ski around Acapulco Bay. "We will spend our days shopping, our nights luxuriating at waterfront cafés, indulging in premium liquors while cheering the bungee jumpers for which Acapulco is renowned."

Max interrupts to ask if Manuel's days of frolicking can continue now that he's a waiter at a Roman Catholic–themed restaurant. Manuel corrects him: Life has just begun and this is merely the second phase of a work in progress. He compares himself to a wet painting by Renoir, then promises Libby that he will teach her to speak Uralic, the language of Russian reindeer herders. When, one hour later, he begins to serenade her with a version of Ave Maria, sung in Latin, Max gets to his feet and heads for the fridge. He removes an armful of beer bottles and sits back down. He opens one and holds the rest in his lap. Manuel, for whatever reason, takes this as a cue to leave. He checks his Rolex and gets up. "Don't forget me," he says to Libby, "I'll be back tomorrow before the dinner shift to continue the tumultuous story of my life." He blows her a kiss and says adieu. Tomorrow, good. At least I won't be here. I'll be at the deli again. I told my parents when we were at Leona's that I would work. The deli is having a sale to commemorate the anniversary. It's the first sale in its history: five dollars off each hundred dollars spent, one day only. William shakes his head. "Tomorrow won't work, Manuel," he says. "I was invited by Mrs. Sienkiewicz to Polonia deli! I'm going to check it out!" He smiles at me. I stare at him. My mother is a piece of work.

As soon as Manuel leaves Max asks what we uncovered about the dad. Well, not much. Manuel was too busy telling us about the day he was born. Max is crestfallen: He wants to know what Manuel is hiding. When his cell phone beeps to signal the arrival of a text, he moans. I ask what's up. "Phillip just gave me a list of items he wants me to wear on our date." Libby turns on the television, then lies down on the floor and starts making snow angels—well, dust angels, actually. Max stares at his phone. "Where the hell am I going to get spurs?" he asks. I point out that it could be at the same place he got his turban and police uniform. What goes around comes around.

William slaps his fez on and turns to face the group. "Do you mind if I do some more work on my book about the political situation in Monaco?" he asks. I tell him to go right ahead. We can move the party over to Libby's place.

Max turns to Libby and tells her he's going to sleep over tonight. "Okay," she says.

"Aren't you going to ask me why?" he asks, putting away his phone.

"No." She examines her nails, then softly says to herself that she needs a manicure.

"Because," he tells her anyway, "I have a paranoid fear that Phillip is going to break into my pad and jump me while I sleep."

"You, paranoid?" I laugh.

"Have you seen the guy?" he rhetorically asks. "Seriously."

"Great, then," William says. "If you're all going next door I can really get some work done. I have a lot to do." More than you know, I think, and turn off the television. "Oh, you can leave it on," he says. "I may put on *MacGyver* just to have some background noise." *MacGyver?* I hand him the remote. I can already tell that tonight's writing session will involve less writing and more channel flipping in search of canceled programming.

* * *

Polonia is already packed when William and I arrive at 10 a.m. There are huge signs on the walls: SALE! ONE DAY ONLY! The mood is celebratory. Among the patrons are two nuns from the local parish, St. Stanisław, heavy crosses on chains around their necks.

"I like this place!" William says. My father makes his way through the crowd on crutches while struggling to hold on to a flask of vodka. Customers pat him on the back as he passes. I give him a kiss and ask what he's doing with the vodka. It's the morning. He reaches into his breast pocket and pulls a shot glass, which he hands to me. A customer brought the vodka as a gift, he says; William and I both have to try it. This is an old-school Polish moment. He dribbles a few drops into the glass and I tip it back. It's like drinking gasoline. I hand the shot glass to William. My father pours way too much. William tips it back reluctantly and coughs. "That's strong," he says.

"It's Polish holy water," my father says, laughing. "Take it like a man."

He seems happy to be in his element. For a while there my mother would not let him come in; she didn't want him to overexert himself. I spot her across the store. She waves and hurries over. She and William hug like they are in love while the female customers eye him indecently. When a few approach my mother introduces him. "This is my daughter's *friend*," she says and lifts an eyebrow.

"Oooooooh," they respond. I almost have to manually lift the corners of my mouth to show how overjoyed I am.

I leave William and my mother to chat. For some reason they have more to talk about than we do. I overhear a woman tell my father that his son's Polish is excellent and that it's nice that he raises his kids to respect their roots. I make a note not to open my mouth in front of her.

In the back room I put on my smock and head behind the counter. I say hi to Henryk, who is fielding three orders at once, and take my place facing the masses. This work does not get easier. Like last time, I am slow on the uptake. When I forget where something is in the deli case, or what something is, I scream to Henryk frantically and he calls out instructions.

At one point my mother drags William behind the counter to give him a feel for deli work. She gives him a smock and a paper hat, which he dons proudly. "Who's next!" he jokes and waves his arms like a cartoon character as my mother stands next to him and smiles.

A hush falls over the store.

And then the place goes wild as every single female customer moves over to his station, including the nuns. They all stand in front of him. "I'm next!" they scream, waving grocery lists and purses and empty shopping baskets, indiscriminately hitting one another in the head. "Sausage!" one screams, giving the others the same idea.

William doesn't last long behind the counter. His mere presence is too distracting. After William takes his first order, my father shoos him out of there—"I'm losing money if he's taking all the orders," he says. "Besides, I'm not paying an extra head." Just in time, too, because Manuel walks through the front door in a fedora as William is removing his paper hat. I ask what Manuel is doing here.

"He didn't want to lose any time working on his book so I told him to meet me here," William explains. I roll my eyes. One-night stands are the devil's work; keep it in your pants, kids. "Should I tell him to come behind the counter? There's not much room for us in the store." I answer that they can go to the stockroom.

While leading them to the back I stop to greet my grandmother, who showed up with a friend who has red lipstick on her teeth. "This is my granddaughter," she tells the friend as I give her my hand. "She's being courted by an African native as tall as a brick house. I had dinner with him recently. He wore all kinds of tribal regalia. Funny hat and everything you'd want." My grandmother doesn't seem to notice—or maybe she doesn't care—that William is standing right there.

Everyone love wooden crates? Hope so. In the stockroom I set William and Manuel up with three of them; two are their chairs and the third is their desk. Manuel wipes down his crate with a white handkerchief before sitting down. William sits opposite him. His legs are so long that his knees are practically touching his nose. Manuel takes off his jacket, loosens his tie, and rolls up his sleeves. "Let us begin with my axioms for living a rewarding life," he says to William, who nods and leans in. "There are two hundred in all. The first . . ." Manuel stops. "How are you writing this down?"

William looks around. "Right," he says. "I don't have the computer." He looks at me. I tell him to hold on. I find a notepad and pen in my father's office and bring it back. I hand it to William. Enjoy.

"Now then," Manuel starts again, "because I expect the book will run to ten volumes, not including the appendix and extensive footnotes, I'm going to need your undivided . . ."

I tiptoe out of there and return to the front to find that Libby and Max have shown up. Max is talking animatedly to one of the nuns as Libby inspects a shelf of imported Polish cookies while Josh, our leopard-print-thong-wearing employee of the month, evidently on his break, and sucking a dill pickle, watches her. As I walk over to say hi I hear Josh ask Libby if she has a car. When she shakes her head no, he takes a generous bite of pickle and wanders off.

For the rest of the day I work, taking occasional time-outs so that my father can introduce me to customers, who lavish praise on him. He passes out candy ("It's the stuff that's about to expire anyway," he whispers in my ear) and gives shots to all takers ("I got a second free bottle of vodka," he crows, "I'm not spending a dime"). As I watch him interact I realize something. He's not cheap. I mean he is, when it comes to paper money. But he makes up for it with generosity of spirit.

In this place, everyone knows his name, and they speak it with pride. "Good man, your father," is the reverberating sentiment.

When business slows to a trickle Max, Libby, and I head to the stockroom to check in on William and Manuel. Max tries to convince Libby to show a little tit and get the dirt on Manuel's father's whereabouts. "Show him yours," Libby responds. He promises he'll give her a massage if she cooperates. This gets her attention. She could live in a day spa.

Manuel stands as soon as Libby walks into the back. He quickly rolls down his shirtsleeves, puts on his jacket, tightens his tie, and claps three times. "Time for our break!" he says to William, who sets down his pen. But Manuel, having just remembered something, addresses him again one second later. "Write down that I need to buy milk."

William picks up the pen, scribbles in the notepad, and looks up. "Anything else?" he asks.

"Bing cherries."

William jots it down and looks back up.

"That will be all," Manuel concludes. He begins to say something to Libby but is upstaged by Max, who addresses William.

"Looking good today, hot pants," Max says. William looks down at his aquamarine-colored tracksuit, which has a pink watermelon slice on the pocket, and which he has paired with his purple high-tops, and says thanks. Maybe he's color-blind? "I meant the face and the bod," Max clarifies.

"Oh," William responds.

"You're doing good, though?" Max asks, like he never sees him.

William nods. "Doing great!"

Max nods back. "Good, good." He sighs and admires him for a second longer than is appropriate, then shakes his head. "Sometimes even I can't believe how hot you are," he whispers. And then more loudly adds: "Do me a favor?"

"Sure!" William responds. "Anything!"

"Say my name."

"Your name?" William asks.

"Say Max."

"Max."

"Say it again. Say it like we're in the dark together."

I hit him. That's enough.

Manuel clears his throat. He grips his lapels and announces that he's been bitten by the acting bug; he will be appearing next Wednesday in a local production of *Fiddler on the Roof.* "Of course I have secured the title role of Fiddler," he brags to Libby. He hands each of us a flyer for the play, then proceeds to summarize the plot of *Fiddler on the Roof,* the story of an honest, hardworking Jewish family living in a farming village in turn-of-the-century Russia. They endure anti-Semitism and, along with the rest of the villagers, are eventually, tragically, made to abandon their homes, leaving their futures gravely uncertain. I refrain from telling him that Libby loves *Fiddler on the Roof.* We both do. Manuel asks if she will do him the honor of attending and tells her she can take all the time she needs to think it over. She informs him that she doesn't need time.

"Wonderful," he says. "I will make the necessary arrangements. William will make a note of it."

William picks up the pen while Libby raises a finger in objection: "Babe, that is not what I meant."

Max hits Libby's shoulder, then begins massaging her neck. He means for her to get down to business.

"Manuel," Libby coyly says, elongating his name to the length of William's penis, "you never told us what happened to your father." Manuel seems touched. Finally she's warming up. He appreciates her concern; it is reassuring. He begins talking in circles about his father's spotless reputation. Max quickly grows impatient. He starts doing push-ups. As Manuel is telling Libby about his father's lucrative investments, Max jumps back up and snaps his fingers. "Quick question for ya, Bobby," he says, "is Daddy involved with drugs by any chance?"

Max turns to Libby. "Sorry," he says, "but I just realized that your way would take longer."

A silence falls over the stockroom as Manuel straightens his back. He's appalled by Max's inappropriateness. Even his black locks seem to flatten. He sits down on the crate then gets back to his feet in an effort to defend his family's honor—if he had a white glove he'd have already used it to slap some cheeks. He sees William writing furiously in the notebook even though no one is speaking. He takes the pen out of his hand. Libby's mouth is slightly open—she appears shocked by the suggestion that Manuel could be mixed up with drugs. Had it never crossed her mind? She leans in: "Was he?"

Manuel puts out his arms as if ready to embrace her. "Libby, not you, too," he says in the tone of a disappointed parent. "I am both startled and dismayed that you would presume such a thing." Max leans up against the wall and points out that Manuel shouldn't look so hurt. He had a heliport, followed by a name change. It was bound to come up.

Manuel begins to pace from one end of the stockroom to the other. It's not that big so it doesn't take very long. If he needed a journey of self-discovery, that wasn't the one to take. "We are wealthy!" he finally exclaims. "Or, we were wealthy. Yes, I had a heliport. Yes, I had Chinese porcelain from the Qianlong period of the Qing dynasty. I was a tube sock magnate! Of course I had such things. Of course I lived resplendently, like a king. I was my father's only son. He cherished me until . . ." He shakes his head. Qianlong period of the Qing dynasty? I bet William is relieved to have gotten out of spelling that. "I cannot stress this enough to people," Manuel continues, "tube socks are big business. Everyone wears tube socks." He hesitates, as if searching for the right expression. He closes the stockroom door and goes on. "And just because they could be made infinitely more profitable if stuffed with cocaine does not mean my father would do such a thing. I resent the very implication of your question. He is not a narcotics and weapons attaché, he is not connected to the mob. He is merely a businessman with a Swiss bank account! A deeply religious tycoon whose life took a grim turn." Manuel pauses. "And as for the name change, well, I longed for anonymity—I longed to recede into the ether after what happened to me . . ."

"So where is he now?" Libby asks Manuel, who begins nervously tugging at his left ear.

"He was required to stay behind in Mexico for the sake of his health," he quietly informs us. Libby encourages him to go on. She should take her top off. Manuel shakes his head: "My father, as you know, is a premier citizen of aristocratic lineage. He was never the same after receiving the news. Where he is is hard to say. Could he be enjoying a mandatory respite in a sanatorium on the outskirts of the silver-mining town of Taxco? Perhaps. Could he be trying at this very moment, nerves frayed, to have a conversation with a chicken? I do not know. Alas, wherever he is, it is for his own good, as well as the good of my mother. She has sacrificed much during this period of transition." Manuel sits down. "Can we please discuss something more pleasant before I get a nosebleed?" he asks. "Do you have any croquettes or canapés? I am rather famished." William asks what canapés are, leaving me to wonder if he knows something I don't about croquettes. An exasperated Manuel clarifies: "Delicate pieces of bread served with a spread as an appetizer." William looks at me. He asks if we have any delicate bread to be served as an appetizer. I'm afraid we don't, no. I'm fresh out of delicate bread. William has a plan: We can go get some. We? Manuel tells him that would be lovely. Of course he will wait right here. He claims there's a chill in the air and tells William to pick up a cashmere sweater while he's out. "Please be sure it is not a blend," he stresses.

I tell William to stay put. Then Max's cell phone rings. He looks at the number but doesn't pick up. Instead he begins texting furiously. Libby gets up. Manuel gets up, too. Where is she going? he asks in alarm. Was it something he said? He takes a tentative step toward her. "Please, sit," Manuel coaxes, "William will procure the canapés."

Max closes his phone. "No one's procuring anything," he says. "Don't be such a bastard."

The comment is a finger in the eye. Manuel sits back down. "I am all but spent," he says. "The discussion of my father's perfectly legal business transactions induced a migraine. I need to recompose myself. William, bring a damp cloth for my forehead." William tells him we don't have that. Manuel removes his handkerchief from his pocket and drapes it across his eyes. "Thank you anyway, Salvador," he groans. I look at Max. *Who's Salvador?* he mouths. I shrug. I probably don't need to know. I bet he was one of the many servants who warmed Manuel's bed before he got into it at night. God forbid Manuel should do anything for himself and ruin his image as a generous sock heir whose father's perfectly legal business transactions induced a migraine.

As Manuel rests, his eyes covered, Max opens his phone and starts furiously texting again. Libby begins walking toward the door, but when someone knocks, she freezes. I open the door and immediately duck as Spanish expletives fly like poisonous arrows. It is the end of the world! It is the one and only señora, followed by Manuel's uncle. Manuel throws off the handkerchief. I can't even imagine what his head feels like now. His mother marches over and grabs him by the ear. She continues to scream without catching her breath. It is like one long word whose definition is anger. "It is time for me to leave," Manuel says to Libby. "My mother suspects that you are an informant. I am in the process of convincing her otherwise."

He leaves with his mother. The uncle, who may just be the only normal person in the family, gives me his hand. "I'm very sorry for the interruption," he says. "Manu . . . Bob snuck out after his mother told him not to leave the house. She made me tell where he went. I had no choi—" Manuel marches back over to the door, his mother still holding on to his ear. He grabs his uncle by the ear and orders him to be quiet: "You're ruining everything," Manuel snaps. The three leave, Manuel's mother squeezing his ear and Manuel squeezing that of his uncle. They're a Mexican chain gang, basically. They leave the stockroom door ajar.

Within seconds my father pushes it open with one of his crutches. He's got the vodka bottle in hand. Henryk is with him, holding a flyer for *Fiddler on the Roof.* My father asks what the Leona's waiter is doing here. I shake my head. Leaving, that's what. He lifts the vodka bottle and asks if anyone wants to try more. I think he's tipsy; he's looking a little wobbly on those crutches. Henryk puts his arm around him for extra support and chuckles. My mother comes in after them. "Put that down," she says and takes the vodka bottle out of my father's hand. She makes a motion for William to come over to her. "I want to introduce you to some nice ladies," she says. "Come to the front, dear."

* * *

There's a message on the machine that night from Manuel informing William that the book is being put on indefinite hold. William is disappointed—probably because he must now continue not writing his own book. Manuel reminds us that he is performing in *Fiddler on the Roof* at Brooklyn Community College. As a way of apologizing for his uncle's intrusion—he points out that his mother is a dignified woman who never would have barged in had it not been for the uncle, who is a fool—he adds that we will all be treated to front-row seats. William is eager to go. I remind him that he should work. "Maybe you're right," he says, "I should work on my book about the political situation in Monaco." He smiles at me lovingly. Tomorrow is Sunday, he reminds me, and he plans to get up early. I nod. Let's hope he's not using a Dictaphone at daybreak. "There's a program on Animal Planet about bush babies that I really want to see," he adds. "I can't wait." Of course he can't, and neither can I. We're certainly on the same channel. I take a seat on the couch and my thoughts immediately drift to S. Konrad, which they've been doing a lot since I read that book. We meet in a few days. I wonder if he's cute . . .

* * *

Barbara is at her wit's end, or so she tells me when I see her on Monday. I would buy this argument if I suspected she had wits, which I don't. Lately Barbara's brain cells have been shooting out of her nose like marbles. She's completely flipped out; wits are not an issue. She and William, who watches more Animal Planet marathons than any human in history, should get together. I try to move past her desk without stopping. She sits right next to my boss's office, and I am desperate to avoid him. I have a sinking feeling about that rejection letter I accidentally sent. Over the weekend he sent me a link to the spurned author's blog on which the guy slammed our agency.

Barbara sees me looking over at his closed office door. "He's not in today," she says with a sigh. "He wanted me to remind you that you are meeting with the Konrad author on Wednesday. And you also need to see this." She hands me a piece a paper. It's a memo. "I was supposed to make you a copy but I've been busy." I read it. "Things are changing here," she adds.

It seems our boss has finally decided to enforce an office dress code. The memo states that we are a professional organization and that our attire must reflect that. Consequently, we are no longer allowed to wear jeans or "sporty gear." No more jeans? Damn. I don't even own business attire. Barbara seems to be taking the news particularly hard. She sighs again. She will no longer be permitted to wear her trademark New York Yankees baseball jerseys. She can't believe it. When I hand the memo back to her, she crumbles it into a ball and throws it. It hits me in the stomach. "Sorry," she gloomily offers. I start to walk away. "Do you want to hear the worst of the news?" she calls after me. I stop. Not really. What could be worse than not being allowed to pair Yankees baseball jerseys with wool skirts five days a week? "I'm in love," Barbara reveals. Oh. I ask how that is a bad thing.

Her eyes begin to water. "He doesn't love me back," she says between deep breaths.

I'm tempted to tell her to take my man, please. He loves everyone. She'll have no trouble.

She wipes tears with her sleeve and hands me a moist business card. It reads:

Fred Stewart, Canine Coach
Specializing in small pet behavior manipulation techniques

Barbara goes on to relay the whole affair, explaining that Fred Stewart was hired to train Buddy the beagle, who's been acting up. Seems he taught himself to open dresser drawers with his teeth and began pulling out Barbara's delicates. She came home the other day to find him wearing a pair of Hanes Her Way on his head. He had torn the elastic waistband and he was angry. He demolished Barbara's favorite chair, pulled a fern out of its soil, tipped over his water dish—on purpose, mind you—broke a watch, and lapped up a bottle of olive oil after knocking it off the dining room table (let's just say this led to an "upset stomach"). Barbara bought renter's insurance and stocked the kitchen with canned soup in case there was more trouble. And then she found Fred Stewart's name in the phone book that Buddy had ripped in half in a jealous rage because, evidently, Barbara has been spending too much time with the cat. She called, he came. Barbara fell head over heels; she'd never met anyone like him. He's wonderful and dear.

Over the weekend Fred Stewart "manipulated and modified" Buddy's behavior using "logs of pepperoni and sedatives." Buddy is already improving, Barbara assures me, but she is desperate. Fred was prepared to exit Barbara's life immediately following Buddy's round of treatment. Knowing this, she asked him out on a date. He accepted; she was thrilled. Yesterday they dined on steak and lobster and afterward Barbara said call me. Fred didn't call but he did FedEx a letter today, which Barbara tore open excitedly the second she realized who it was from. She was expecting a little note thanking her for treating him to dinner, perhaps confessing his longing. Instead Barbara received an invoice. Not only was Fred not prepared to thank her for footing the tab, he was charging her for the date. "He billed me for four hours," she wails, "but we were only together for two."

I tell Barbara that I'm very sorry for her and hand back the card, which she folds in half and throws. It ricochets off my chin before landing on the carpet.

"Should I call him?" she asks.

I shake my head: No. That does not seem like the best idea.

"I'm calling," she says and picks up the phone. "I can't live this way. We had a connection. It was undeniable."

Glad I could help.

*　*　*

That evening, William, looking subdued in an eggplant-colored jumpsuit whose zipper runs from navel to neck, expresses interest in seeing more of New York. I agree to help out. The alternative is listening to him report on the progress he's making with the acknowledgments page of his book. We take a cab downtown and stroll through the streets. The downtown folk are categorically pretty people. While we are out, five different beauties, three blocks apart, give him their telephone numbers. Blindsided by his attractiveness, they don't seem to notice that he resembles an inmate at a futuristic correctional facility, or that he's already walking with a girl. Oh well. A confused William throws the slips of paper in the trash.

When William tells me he wants candy we stop at a bodega, where he examines the flowers displayed in green buckets around the entrance. "These are fantastic," he says, smelling a

bundle of lilies. *"Convallaria majalis."* The con-who-what? I
have to hand it to him: The guy definitely knows his nature.
He considers a few more varieties then walks inside. I light a
cigarette and wait. And then I see Richard walking toward me
with determination. Where did he come from? I turn to flee.
"I have to talk to you!" Richard calls out. He runs up.

"What are you doing here?" I ask. My heart starts racing.

"I'm on my way to get my hair cut," he says. "But I'm glad I
ran into you because we need to talk. You have not returned
my calls," he sternly continues. He seems shaky, nervous. He
looks over his shoulder and back at me. "You—" Richard stops
talking when William walks out of the store with a lollipop
and puts his arm around me. "Who are you?" he asks William
accusingly. He takes in William's gorgeousness and his height.
He seems annoyed by both. Now, why do short men take such
issue with tall men? They do do it and it's so lame. I happen
to like guys who are my height. Come to think of it, I don't
trust anyone I can't look in the eye. But you know what? I'm
not here to comfort Richard. I put my arm around William's
waist and lean my head against his chest. "This," I say, pulling William toward me, "is my boyfriend." I wince when the
word comes out of my own mouth. "He is a wonderful, very
attractive, as you can see, South African who happens to be an
amazing author currently working on an important book. He's
a genius." William beams. I reach into one of the green buckets and pull out a rose. I hold it up. "William," I ask, "what is
the scientific name of this flower?" This will teach Richard.

"Rosa," William answers with a smile.

I put the flower back in the bucket. Okay, let's try something a fly couldn't figure out. I pull out a daisy. "What," I ask
William, "is the scientific name of this flower?"

"Chrysanthemum leucanthemum," he answers. "It's a Eur-
asian plant . . ."

Aha! See that! "See," I tell Richard, "he's a genius. Mind like a sponge."

"I have to talk to you in private," Richard says to me. He begins looking around nervously.

"No can do," I shoot back and pull William by the arm. Come on, let's get out of here. I won't be able to talk myself out of it if Richard accuses me of plotting revenge. I flag down a cab and push William inside it. "We have to go home and have a quickie!" I shout to Richard as the cab pulls away.

William turns to me: "What's a quickie?" he asks.

"It's a nap," I answer without thinking. I tell the cabbie to drop us at Banana Republic so I can buy ugly clothes for work. I think my boss is enforcing that dress code to punish me.

* * *

"He still hasn't called," Barbara offers at work the next day. I am struggling to pull off my jacket, underneath which I'm wearing a white shirt and black "trousers." They call them trousers at Banana Republic. I hate that place. I tell her I'm sorry. "Before I forget," Barbara says, "I have something for you from the boss. He had to step out." She produces a slip of paper. I take it and say thank you. The note is written in Barbara's hand. Why not just tell me what it says, you stinking bureaucrat?

Meet at Clive's Bistro @ noon today instead.

She adds that the author had a conflict. S. Konrad! Today! Shit. I was counting on it being tomorrow after work. I already had an outfit planned out and everything. I was going to wear a pair of less humiliating "trousers," not to mention wash my hair. I wanted to wear it down! I look like greasy crap today; I figured I'd only be seeing Barbara. Damn! What if S. Konrad turns out to be a stud? What kind of impression am I going

to make? Fuck, nothing ever works out right. I should go to
the Gap and at least buy a different shirt. But I don't want a
Gap shirt. Maybe I should buy it, wear it with the tags, and
return it tomorrow. But that would mean going to the Gap
twice. I don't even want to go to the Gap once. Besides, what
if S. Konrad and I begin to make out and he discovers that I'm
wearing a shirt with the tags still attached? Ah, forget it, I'll
have to make do with my fucking brilliant smile. He'll have to
fall for it the way everyone else does.

Once at my desk I check e-mail. I have three forwarded messages from William. Glad to see he's working hard. Every last
sentence is a bunch of nonsense. The first e-mail claims that
if I count backward from ten to one in the next minute and
make a wish, that wish will come true. If I want to make
sure it comes true I must immediately forward the e-mail to
ten friends. The second e-mail is some kind of mind-bender
riddle requiring me to do advanced algebra in order to figure
out who will get to some train station first. The third is a top
ten list: top ten ways to tell if you are a real South African.
How this applies to me is a mystery. I'm pretty sure I'm not
South African. I don't need a list to figure it out. Also I don't
need any mind-benders. Ever.

I spend the rest of the morning in the bathroom, trying to
style my hair. It looks dirty no matter what I do to it. I finally
throw a few bobby pins in and call it quits.

* * *

At five till noon I stand in front of Clive's Bistro and smoke a
cigarette, a way of prolonging the suspense. I read the menu
encased in glass next to the door. I don't know why they
needed to encase it. It's not the Declaration of Independence,
it's a list of overpriced salmon entrées. I extinguish my cigarette

between the words TARTAR and LENTIL and walk in. Whas up, flunkies. The hostess points me in the direction of our table. I see my boss, talking on his cell phone. I sit down as a waiter delivers a bottle of red wine. My boss closes his phone. "The kid will be here soon. He has some kind of play to go to Wednesday so we moved up the day."

"The kid?" I repeat.

"The author," he clarifies.

"He's a kid?" I ask.

My boss nods. "Well, I mean he's young."

"Like my age?" I ask hopefully, brightening up.

"Bit younger," he responds disinterestedly as his cell phone rings. He looks down at the number: "Hold on, it's my twins again," he says. He flips open the phone. "Renee, Chris, Daddy's at work. I can't talk now . . ." He begins to lecture them.

I pour myself a generous glass of wine. Bit younger? I take one of the bobby pins out of my hair and begin chewing on the end of it. And on Wednesday he has a play?

I turn toward the door. The hostess is greeting a party of husky businessmen. I squint. I know the person at the front of that group. That looks like . . .

My boss calls my name. I glance over at him as he puts away his phone. "There's Mr. Konrad," he says and points where I was just looking. I turn back around. Mr. Konrad? I stare at the person he's pointing at. The person he's pointing at is certainly not Mr. Konrad. "Is this a joke?" I demand in bewilderment. My boss asks what I mean as "Mr. Konrad" parks himself in front of me. "Well," I say, shifting in my seat, "this is my brother, for starters." I almost didn't recognize him without his baseball cap. I don't know if I've ever seen him without it . . .

My boss takes a step toward Henryk. "Your brother?" he repeats. Henryk nods: "Hi, Dan." What is this? Mr. Konrad reintroduces himself as Henryk Sienkiewicz. *S. Konrad* was a pseudonym. My boss seems as confused as I. "Did you know you were related?" he asks me. I look at my brother. I dumbly shake my head no. I mean obviously I knew I was related to my brother, but clearly I never knew who my brother really was.

Henryk mischievously asks if I'm surprised. I would have to admit that that's about right. I feel like someone is asking me to walk a straight line after spinning me in a circle. "Henryk," I say, trying to take it all in, "did you really write that book?" He takes a seat and laughingly asks who else would have written it. Well, I don't know. A writer, perhaps? "You didn't plagiarize it, did you?" I press.

I had no idea Henryk could write, that he was even remotely interested in it. I ask if our mother knows and realize immediately that this is a dumb question. If my mother knew, I would know. She tells me everything.

"No one knows," he admits. "What's there to know? I haven't sold the novel or anything."

My boss nods: "I can sell that novel."

"Cool," Henryk says and takes a sip of my wine. My brother drinks wine! That's illegal. What else is he doing behind my back? Underage voting?

My boss's cell phone rings yet again. "Excuse me for a sec," he says and gets up from the table. "Chris, calm down, and if Renee kicks you in the knee one more time . . ." A pause. "Put her on speakerphone . . ."

I look at Henryk. And I keep looking at him. I can't believe I am looking at Henryk. I can't believe Henryk is S. Konrad. I had dirty thoughts about my brother. This is following me to the grave. "Who's S. Konrad?" I ask.

"I am," he grins.

"I know that. I mean where'd you get the name?"

"*S* for Sienkiewicz," he explains, "and *Konrad* is my middle name." God. *Konrad* is his middle name? I don't even think I knew that. "This is really freaking you out, isn't it?" he adds when I don't say anything.

I've never sworn around my brother, thinking it might negatively influence him, but this is as good a time as any. "Well, no shit," I say. "It's a strange thing, Henryk. How could you write a book? No wonder I liked the book so much, those characters were like our family members. They were our family members. Hey, was I the annoying sister who never shuts up?" Henryk tells me not to flatter myself. No problem. "Never mind. I don't want to know," I continue. "You wrote a book. But you never talk."

Henryk shrugs; he's still not much of a talker. "I don't need to talk much to write," he points out.

I stare at him as if for the first time. It's incredibly weird. I've spent a lifetime ignoring this person. What do I do now? Should we pretend we just met? I feel as though we have. We've never had a conversation that went on for more than ten words. We have spent our lives passing each other like guarded strangers in an alleyway. I've had longer discussions with South African porters. I've always rushed him off the phone. Even when working with him side by side at the deli I usually addressed him only when I needed his help.

He's supposed to be the teenage mute. But he's not. How did I ever miss that? Was he trying to communicate with me and I just didn't listen? Was he talking while I was busy cutting him off?

"Henryk, that book is funny," I offer. "I can't believe you wrote such a funny book. I mean I thought I was funny but you're funny funny." I lean in: "Are you funnier than I am? You are funnier, aren't you?" Henryk tells me he might be funnier. That's too bad. But how could I have known that? He never draws attention to himself. I guess he's said amusing things on occasion. I ask if he's sure he's funnier because I'm funny. I know I am.

"Might be funnier," Henryk says, nodding. "At least in print."

That scrappy underdog. What did he just say to me? "You could at least be modest about it, Henryk," I offer. "You're not very modest."

"I'll try to be more modest," he tells me.

"That's all I'm asking."

Our eyes lock again. I like my brother! He's . . . cool.

I compliment Henryk on his ability to keep a secret. Why did he not tell me? Henryk says that he considered it but that he didn't want to compete with William and his book. He asks if William is my boyfriend. My brother and I have never discussed our personal lives. It never occurred to me that he had a personal life to discuss. Not in a million years could I see the two of us at a table debating my love life. I'm not sure I'm ready to start now. "Don't make me explain the whole thing to you, Henryk, it's too ridiculous," I say. "And no, he is not my boyfriend." Henryk asks if William knows that. What kind of question is that? Of course he doesn't. I stare at my linen napkin. "Don't make me explain the whole thing to you, Henryk," I repeat, "it's too ridiculous."

I roll my eyes. My seventeen-year-old brother wrote a book. My live-in South African "boyfriend," meanwhile, snores loudly while pretending to write one. We need a new topic, and I need a new South African.

And then I remember the play. I ask what play he's in. "I'm not in a play," he says, squirming in his seat at the very thought. "I'd have mad stage fright. No, I want to go to your friend Manuel's play in Brooklyn tomorrow. He gave me a flyer when he came to the deli. That guy is pretty entertaining."

I nod. He sure is. I tell him that I recently found out that Manuel is not only "entertaining" but the son of a drug lord. I rehash the story for his amusement. Henryk frowns: "So the tube sock factory is a front for drugs? That seems pat. It plays into every stereotype out there." I laugh and begin to tease him. My brother the author could come up with a million imaginative twists. His head is swollen! I offer that sometimes people are as obvious as they seem, present company excluded, of course. "I don't know about that," he concludes.

While we eat lunch Henryk drinks a full glass of wine and asks that I not rat him out to our mother, who would have a fit. My brother is all grown up—he talks and he lies! I guess I shouldn't be surprised by this, but I am. Seventeen isn't that young. Obviously it's not. But we are a decade apart in age. He never struck me as someone I could have a conversation with. I always dismissed him, treated him like an annoying baby. And so he grew up without me, or without my noticing.

When he announces that he has to get back to school to take a test my boss stands and shakes his hand. "What do you say then," he asks Henryk hopefully. "Do you want to come into the fold, sign with the agency?"

Henryk nods. "Sure. It would be cool to work with my sister. Thanks."

I adjust my gross business trousers as my boss considers me with something approaching—well, at least not approaching hatred and annoyance. "This is some secret weapon," he offers as Henryk smiles sheepishly. I think my boss thinks I planned this. And I certainly did not.

I walk Henryk out of the restaurant and give him a long hug. "I'm really proud of you, man. Really proud," I say. I don't remember ever squeezing him so hard. In fact, I can't remember ever hugging him, though it must have happened. Right? I assume he's going to pull away but he doesn't. He enthusiastically hugs me back, like he's been waiting for me to make this move. I push open the door and ask about the letter he submitted with his manuscript: "I wrote this book to impress a girl." I want to tease my little brother about it. Now that he's met William it's all fair game. I ask who the girl of the letter is. She's a lucky son of a bitch to know someone so thoughtful. Henryk laughs and tells me it's not what I think. He shouldn't be so sure. I've heard it all before. He flags down a cab. "The letter was referring to you," he says, getting in. I cover my mouth with my hand. "You're my favorite only sister and I look up to you. Writing is the only thing I'm good at. It was nothing."

It was nothing. After the cab speeds off I look down at the ground so passersby can't see my eyes well with tears. It was nothing. I begin to sob. When Henryk was about five or six he shadowed me constantly. It was nothing. I was too old and wise to pay him any mind. One day I was typing a research paper for school and he kept asking for permission to push a few of the keys. It was nothing. He wasn't even nagging, he was urging quietly. He was a kid, just a little kid, and I wouldn't let him. It was nothing. I kept impatiently putting him off, trying to get my homework done. I didn't stop until he left the room. It was nothing. This is the kind of sister he looks up to. Me. I didn't even turn my head to check if he was okay. It was nothing, after all. Who cared?

For the last seventeen years my brother Henryk—the only

sibling I will have in the world—has been trying desperately to be my friend. For some reason a moment we recently had at the deli pops into my head. I was cleaning the blade on the meat-slicing machine when he rushed over to unplug it so that I wouldn't accidentally hurt myself. Remembering him standing over me that day makes me cry harder because I don't know if I said thank you.

I really need to open my eyes. I'm so stupid.

part *Three*

That evening after work I find William on the water bed, eyes closed. Talk about a whole lot of nothing. Wake up, meathead, I think to myself as I shake him awake, it's six thirty. The liquid mattress begins to swoosh back and forth. I'm rocking a cradle. I've never made time for my brother, never once gave him a fighting chance, and yet I opened my home to a stranger. It's fucking pathetic, the way I've been behaving. I need to make this up to my brother. William opens his eyes and assures me he wasn't sleeping. Right. He tells me that earlier in the day, while on his way to the store, he thinks he saw Victoria Principal. Right. Okay. I tell him Henryk's news. William's reaction is a little off. I expect him to be ecstatic. He loves everyone and everything, after all, but he looks, well, concerned, if that's the right word, though I suspect it isn't. I study his face. "Are you jealous?" I ask. William avoids the question. He may not be able to tell a lie, but it seems he is quite capable of dishonesty. I did not know that. But then it's been that kind of day.

"I'm just worried about my future," he explains. "Writing is so hard."

He is jealous. Huh. If he were any greener he'd be a field of Astroturf. William begins asking all sorts of questions: How long did it take Henryk to write the book, how long did it take to find an agent? Within five minutes he is pacing across the kitchen deep in thought about his own writing career. He needs to get the book done, there's no time to lose. His fez, his flag, Miss Celeste, his dead uncle, and my brother are his inspirations. Now all he needs is talent.

I dial my parents' number. I wonder if Henryk told them. If he didn't I have to keep mum, which is going to require the assistance of a Zen master. My mother picks up. "Henryk is a novelist," is the first thing she says after I greet her with a hello. I stare at my pack of cigarettes but don't light one: "I know," I say. "Isn't it great."

"It certainly is great," she continues. "He's a child prodigy." Now he's a prodigy? I remind her that just last week he was a bum. She protests the very idea. She never called him a bum. She just wanted him to clean his room once in a while, maybe take out the trash and take off that hat that hides his handsome face.

I ask if she's been calling everybody in the family to spread the news. It's a rhetorical question, of course she has. "Here and there," she answers. "I have to call a few more people. It's so wonderful." My mother sighs. "Where is that phone?" she mumbles. I point out that she's already on the phone. "Oh, right," she says. "Where is my head? I'm looking for the phone and it's in my hand." I tell her to go make her calls. She's obviously distracted. We'll talk again later.

"Hold on, don't go anywhere," she says. "Your father wants to talk."

My father gets on the phone. "My son is a writer," he says. "How do you like that?" I like it, old man, I like it. "The first writer in the family," he adds with pride. My father goes on to say that he will be joining my brother during the negotiation process. I remind him that that's what agents are for. My father doesn't trust agents, they're just after money. I remind him that

that's the point. He tells me we'll figure it out on Wednesday; we're all going to the play *Fiddler on the Roof.*

"*Fiddler on the Roof*?" I ask. "Why do we all have to go?"

"Your brother wants to go so we're going, too. We'll celebrate. It's free."

I suggest that we go out to dinner instead. He tells me we just went out to dinner and reminds me that the play is free. I throw my head back: come on. "Hold on," my father says. "Your mother is tearing the phone away from me."

My mother gets on the phone and tells me that we are all going to see *Fiddler on the Roof* because that is what my brother wants and it's his day. I ask her to put him on. She tries but he refuses to pick up the receiver. "He won't get on the phone," she tells me, then strongly urges him to get on the phone already and talk to his sister for goodness' sake. He relents. Our conversation is familiar in its brevity.

"I want you to see *Fiddler on the Roof* with me," he laughs and gives the phone back to our mother. Brat! I guess I owe him one. I've been such a lousy sibling. I tell my spastic mother to go make her calls. "I'll see you tomorrow night I guess," I add. "I love you."

"I love you, too," she says. I hear my father scream I love you in the background. "Did you hear that?" she says. "He said he loves you." Ditto. I hear another scream in the background. "Your brother says he loves you and that he will see you at the play," she reports. Such a brat!

I hang up the phone and turn around: "William, your dream is coming true. Guess where we are going?"

He looks up from the laptop. "Monaco?" he asks hopefully.

I shake my head. What? "No, keep dreaming," I answer. "We are going to see *Fiddler on the Roof.*" Monaco. I wish. William looks back down at the computer screen. "Sure," he softly says. Envy, envy.

I race over to Libby's and tell her the news. "So exciting!" she squeals and immediately decides to bake him cookies. I then use her phone to call Max. "That's sexy!" he says. "He is going to get majorly laid now." I frown. I don't want to know about that. "Let's take him out," he adds. As Libby begins banging pots and pans and pulling out cookie sheets, I tell Max he can see Henryk tomorrow if he'd like. My family and I are going to Manuel's play in Brooklyn—I emphasize that it's absolutely my brother's idea and I can't say no. Not now. He moans. "I have my date with Phillip tomorrow." Gross. I wish him good luck. "But you know," he carefully adds, "maybe I'll bring him to the play. That's a date, right?" I laugh. Max wants to go to Manuel's play? I never would have suspected that. "Believe me, I don't want to see Manuel," he points out. "But if I take Phillip to the play I won't have to be alone with him. And I totally have to see him tomorrow because I already canceled one date and he's getting impatient. This might be a really good idea." Libby places a hand mixer in a bowl and turns it on. It's loud. Too loud to hear Max talk. I end the call as a fine cloud of flour rises into the air above her.

William is typing furiously when I return to the apartment. The phone rings. I walk over and check the caller ID. Max again? It's Richard. Shit. I stare at the phone, willing it to stop ringing. William stops typing and asks if I want him to answer the phone. I shake my head no. Why is he still calling here? The phone rings two more times then stops. Richard does not leave a message.

✳ ✳ ✳

Thanks to my mother, we arrive at Brooklyn Community College with way too much time to spare.

William, once so eager to see the play, is now express-
ing concern that it will interfere with his writing schedule.
He has brought the binder and laptop and tells me that he'll
work on the book during intermission. He keeps mumbling
that it's almost time to find an agent and hints that he'd like
to be introduced to my boss. I lie that my boss isn't taking on
new clients. No one, as far as I know, is taking on clients like
William. William seems bitter over my brother's success, and
that's not cool with me. Another thing that's not cool: Last
night he was grinding his teeth in his sleep between episodes
of mumbling. "I have to help all the poor people" was all I
could make out. I'd rather have him snoring. The grinding
and mumbling are spooky.

An actor dressed as a rabbi is at the door, serving as both the
ticket collector and the will-call booth. Manuel, he tells us,
has arranged front-row seats and "backstage passes." I ask
him to put three aside—for Libby, Max, and his new buddy
Phillip—when Libby walks in with a huge plate of cookies for
Henryk. She hugs and congratulates him. The cookies smell
divine and when Henryk is not looking I plan to eat them all
in one sitting. That's what sisters are for. Libby tells me that
Max called: He and Phillip are on their way.

Before handing William his ticket the rabbi pauses as though
considering a work of art and tells him he should model.
Now, this is about the fifteenth time someone has suggested
that William should model since he arrived in New York. It
must be some kind of record. William smiles meekly before
delivering his stock response: "I have a higher calling," he
says and shows the rabbi his binder. The sage fake rabbi
twirls his ringlets as William explains that he is writing a
book about the political situation in Monaco. He offers that

people are really suffering over there. "From what?" Henryk and the rabbi ask in unison. "You see, the area has legalized gambling," William explains. "Gambling devastates populations and promotes greed. Nothing good comes of—" I push William past the rabbi. Come on already, the show's about to start, in twenty hours.

As expected, this *Fiddler on the Roof* will be a low-budget affair. The play is taking place in a gymnasium, and there is a basketball net over the stage. We walk to the first row of folding chairs. Ten are marked RESERVED FOR LIBBY. I guess that means us. My father sits down and my mother moves one of the chairs in front of him so he can prop up his leg. She rests his crutches under her seat. I grab the aisle. Manuel runs over with his fiddle before we can get comfortable. He is wearing a tuxedo; a mustachio is glued to his upper lip. William greets him with a distracted "Hi, Bob," and gets to work on his book. He is hacking away, type, type, type, type, type, type, typetypetypetypetypetypetyping, when Manuel asks Libby if she would like to be seated closer to the front. He offers to move her. She tells him she's fine, thanks, but I'm tempted to ask where he means to move her. Closer than the front row? Where, to his pocket?

My father asks Manuel why he is wearing a tuxedo and facial hair. Manuel explains that there was not enough money in the budget for costumes and that each actor was asked to provide his own period clothing. I remind him that *Fiddler on the Roof* is set long before the advent of the tuxedo; he counters that there are no provincial vests and burlap trousers among his belongings. Makes sense. He adds that the tuxedo will lend a measure of authority to the role. Henryk asks what the handlebar mustache is adding. Manuel ignores him, as he must. "It gives the fiddler a more weathered appearance," he says to Libby. The topic of fiddle playing comes up as well. Did Manuel bend the fiddle to his will? Last we spoke the recorder was his instrument of choice. He twirls his mustache and tells us he can't play a note. The soundman has a cassette tape with the appropriate music. He will be fake-playing, it turns out. He stresses that he would have preferred to fake-play a violin but that he's agreed to compromise for the sake of authenticity. After giving the ends of his mustache a few more twists he informs Libby that he must return to his "dressing room" but asks that she come backstage at intermission. My brother assures him that we'll be there. Manuel smiles at Libby and leaves.

As soon as he does I am tapped on the shoulder by a pudgy guy with freckles seated behind me. "Do you know that Bob character?" he asks. The guy strikes me as particularly humorless. I hesitate: Depends, who wants to know? He informs me that his sister Maria, who just moved here from Chicago, is an extra in the play. She thought it would be a good way of meeting people around the neighborhood. "That Bob Apple gave my sister a hard time," he says, sounding like the overprotective older sibling who would accompany her on a first date. "He's lucky he didn't get his behind kicked." Bob Apple? What the hell is Manuel doing? "My sister talked about him every time she came home from rehearsal," he adds, shaking his head. "He had her in tears more than once." The pudgy guy introduces himself as Joe. According to Joe's sister, Manuel got the part in the play after the original fiddler, Ryan, was diagnosed with schizophrenia. Manuel managed to learn every part in the play over the course of six days (I guess he wasn't exaggerating when he told Libby that he has a photographic memory) and threatened to depose the director when things weren't going well during rehearsal. He was particularly dissatisfied with the pair of women playing the mother and the matchmaker, whom he recommended be fired. He suggested that both roles be given to him. (Well, he is a ventriloquist.) When the director reminded Manuel that the scene required the two women to be sitting next to each other while conducting a conversation, Manuel pointed out that he could move from one chair to the other with relative ease while having the conversation with himself. I braid my fingers and suggest that perhaps Manuel thought he was auditioning for *One Flew Over the Cuckoo's Nest.* Humorless Joe doesn't find this funny. He continues: "My sister told me he was real, real bossy. Everyone was annoyed with him. When he did manage to settle down, which wasn't often, she said he wasn't half bad—definitely had a flair for it. The only problem is that no one liked him." That's our Bob Apple. No surprises there. "Well, enjoy the show," humorless Joe tells me. I nod. Many thanks. A child in the row directly behind William bursts into tears. I look over at the author, who's hunched over the laptop, type type type type typing like mad. He begins to mumble that the crying is distracting. I almost point out that he loves children. It's one of his favorite things to discuss with my mother. I turn around to look at the caterwauling gentleman drowning in spittle behind us. He's about four and having a serious tantrum. He begins banging a yellow yo-yo against the back of William's metal chair. William puts his fingers in his ears and concentrates hard on the screen as the boy's mother tries to calm him by lovingly smoothing his blond hair. "There, there, Teddy," she offers. He bares his teeth. The front two are missing in action.

Yo-yo boy calms down and for a moment it is quiet. Then the auditorium doors swing open and slam shut. "Don't grab my ass like that!" someone loudly says. I turn. It's Max, with Phillip.

They are both wearing flannel shirts, ten-gallon cowboy hats, snakeskin boots with spurs, large belt buckles, and black leather chaps over their jeans. I put my hand over my mouth as Phillip tries to grab Max's ass again. Max jumps. It's like a gay episode of *Gunsmoke*. Or just an episode of *Gunsmoke*.

As they mosey over—and really, in all that hindering gear, all you can do is mosey—the sound of clinking metal can be heard. Max was not kidding about Phillip having a fetish. He and Max silently take the remaining seats in the first row, between Libby and William, respectively. I look over at Max. I'm about to say something when he draws a line with his index finger from one end of his lips to the other. "Zip it," he says. "Just shut up about it. I don't want a word."

But immediately my mother engages him as my father stares. "Oh, Max," she says, not sure what to make of the cowboy gear. "Is this your father?" She offers Phillip her hand. I turn away to hide my laughter. She's got a point. They seriously look like they are headed to a father–son dance somewhere in the heart of Texas Hill Country.

The lights flicker to signal the start of the play. Someone asks Max and Phillip to take off the cowboy hats because they are obstructing people's views. I tell William to stop the typing. He sets the laptop on the floor and opens his binder. Booming fiddle music begins to play as dawn breaks over the shtetl. It is not much of a shtetl, which is perhaps why the fiddle music is so loud. There is also no roof because there is no house to put a roof on. Manuel and his tuxedo enter stage left. I can see that he is holding the fiddle's bow a few inches from the strings. He approaches center stage and closes his eyes. He is smiling. He is a happy fake fiddler without a roof. The fiddle music stops; Manuel stops fake-playing. He looks at the audience and wipes his brow for effect, then twirls his mustache. He is an exhausted fake fiddler without a roof who needs a close shave, we get it. The lights dim briefly while Manuel makes a reluctant exit. The play's first scene unfolds. Considering the meager set, the production is entertaining. The actors are talented. The only thing keeping me from a good time is William, who occasionally asks for the spelling of complicated words like *receive*. "Is *countryside* hyphenated?" he asks during a song-and-dance sequence. "That's all I need to know." Is that really all he needs to know? Somehow I doubt it.

Manuel comes back out before the end of the first act to fake-play. One of his diamond cuff links catches the light, emitting a glint that refracts off my cornea and (quite possibly) gives me free laser surgery to correct my astigmatism. If it happens again I may get X-ray vision. "Don't touch me there!" Max loudly whispers to Phillip.

As Manuel enthusiastically falls into his role, I begin swaying my head to the melody.

And then the fiddle music unexpectedly goes into hyperdrive.

Uh-oh.

Where's my babushka? I sit up. Something must be wrong with the cassette tape, I think, while looking on in horror. It sounds like someone hit fast forward on the machine without first pressing stop. It sounds like an Alvin and the Chipmunks version of fiddle playing. Manuel looks to his right, evidently over to where the noise is coming from. I look over at William. He's writing in the dark, unaffected.

The fiddle music is only getting faster and louder. Manuel begins to fake-play faster and faster to keep up. He's got the

bow moving a mile a minute and is kicking his legs and spinning in a circle. I think he's pretending to be delighted, or
ethnic. Whatever it is isn't fooling anyone. "He's going berserk
out there," I hear my father say from a few seats away. After
an excruciating minute, the music stops. Manuel wipes his
brow. I think he means it this time. The curtain falls to signal
the end of act one. It's intermission. The crowd claps politely;
a few people laugh. My brother wolf whistles, which I never
knew he could do. Will this kid's talent never cease? Max
bolts from his chair. William is too busy to look up.

A riot has broken out backstage. The soundman is hunched
over in a chair, holding a mangled cassette and a foot of
exposed black ribbon in the palm of his shaky hand. Manuel
screams in his ear: "I cannot work under these conditions!
Your unprofessionalism has reduced this production to a spec-
tacle. You would not last the length of one eighteen-hour shift
in my father's tube sock factory. You would be hanged by the
ankles and quartered over far less than this!" The soundman
screams back that Manuel needs to shut his mouth. He's trying to concentrate. He looks down at his confetti. It's a party.
"You would first need a brain in order to concentrate!" Manuel points out. The director, your typical New York hipster
with black-framed glasses, runs over and breaks up the fight.
    "Just please let the soundman do his job, Bob," the director
says.
    "If he only knew his job I would let him do it," Manuel
retorts. "But clearly he has no understanding of what is
expected of him." Manuel waves his hand dismissively in the
soundman's direction: "All he is capable of doing is breaking
cassette tapes. At such work he excels beyond measure. His
sophistication is newsworthy."

The soundman protests: "I did not break the tape, chief."

Max whispers in my ear: "Ask Bob for an eight-ball of coke."

I look him up and down. "You're in no position to be making fun of anyone today, Howdy Doody," I remind him.

"Shut up," he says, adjusting his cowboy hat.

The soundman orders the director to get Manuel out of his sight. Manuel folds his arms over his chest: "That is the only intelligent thing you have suggested thus far." He turns to the director: "Bring in my understudy. I am not going back out there in order to be humiliated by bumbling technicians." The director bows his head, the way everyone eventually does around Manuel. His next words are barely audible, his strength depleted: "What understudy, Bob? What understudy are you referring to? This isn't Broadway, it's Brooklyn. We don't have an understudy. You are the understudy. You walked in on the day Ryan was diagnosed."

Manuel tenses up. He looks like he might rip the director's shirt off: "You have no understudy for the lead role?" The director shakes his head: "Bob, how many times must I tell you that yours is not the lead role? It's not even a speaking part. You're just supposed to go out there and pretend to play the fiddle. It's no big deal."

Manuel begins to scream: "No big deal! No big deal! Music is the language of this play! The fiddler begins and ends this production because he is its essence. He represents the undying hope of everyone portrayed here tonight. Nothing is possible without him. The fiddler is indispensable."

The director raises his voice: "Don't bother explaining the fiddler's role to me. It's all you've been talking about. I'm the director and I know what the fiddler represents. I even agreed to add a few more fiddling scenes at your request, remember?"

Manuel looks up at the ceiling. Of course he does. The director continues: "I finally gave in because you spoke so elo-
quently on the fiddler's behalf while following me to my car
every day with books about the Jewish Diaspora. The fiddler
may very well represent the hope of this play but all the hope
in the world isn't going to get that cassette fixed. Stanley is
going to get it fixed. And I'm sorry we had to use a cassette
but this is rarefied music, they don't record this kind of thing
anymore. It's the cassette or nothing. At this moment the play
revolves around Stanley, who has to fix it, not you, so please,
just stop antagonizing him. If he can't get it fixed we're roy-
ally screwed because that means you'll have to actually play
the fiddle."

This final, flippant comment makes Manuel's blood boil.
"How dare you, you bumpkin!" Manuel challenges. "You
would have me play a commoner's instrument? I have my
pride to protect! I cannot play the fiddle and do not intend
to learn. You should have agreed to my request for a violin.
That I would attempt to master in five minutes. But this, no,
never. I was told the fiddle music would be provided. I am an
actor, an artist, perhaps someday a violinist, but certainly not
an agrarian fiddler chasing livestock through a meadow . . ."
Manuel notices Libby and peels off his mustache. There is
white glue stuck to his upper lip. "I am sorry you had to see
this," he says. "I had no recourse. I have been undone, I quit."
He storms off. Somewhere in another room a door slams.
Libby turns to me. "Will you rub right there?" she asks, pointing to her neck. "I have a kink."

At the beginning of act two, when the fiddle music begins to
play at the appropriate tempo, several members of the audience break into spontaneous applause. "They fixed it," my
mother says too loudly. Manuel is relieved, too. He begins to

fake-play with renewed intensity and determination. William, meanwhile, is scribbling happily in his binder.

The second half of the play is as good as the first. Manuel comes out a few more times and fake-plays like a fake expert. After each set he draws attention to his mustachio by smoothing it with the tips of his manicured fingers. By the end of the play, when the shtetl's inhabitants are forced by the Russians to abandon their homes, Libby and I tear up. Never fails.

I sigh deeply when the final scene is upon us. This play gets me every time, perhaps because, more than anything, it's a story about family. Manuel walks onstage and begins fake-playing. I am momentarily distracted by William's elbow, with which he keeps jabbing my hip. "Can you move over?" he whispers. Where does he want me to move, into the aisle? "I need more room," he hastily offers. More room. How's South Africa sound, Hemingway? Lots of room there. I am moving my chair when the fiddle music prematurely stops. Silence follows—the most uncomfortable kind. "Shit! It ate the tape," someone from backstage shouts. I look up. William starts clapping and asks if it's over already. I let the legs of my chair touch the ground.

"Get your hand out of my pocket right now!" a clearly frustrated Max says to Phillip. "I'm not a piece of meat!"

Manuel, not realizing at first that the music has died, continues to fake-play. When it dawns on him what's happened, he lowers the bow but continues to stand in the middle of the stage, bewildered—he might was well have his pants down. He looks to his right but finds no help there. He looks to his left. Same problem. He looks down at the fiddle, probably hoping it will begin the melody of its own accord, like something out of a Grimm Brothers tale. He again touches the bow against the strings, then hesitates. He opens then closes his mouth, he looks up, he looks down, then back up again. His eyes widen. I can see that he doesn't know what to do next. The spotlight is slowly being moved off him—it is a thief who, having robbed Manuel of his dignity, is now creeping away from the scene of the crime. Manuel takes two steps left. At first I think he is going to walk off stage. In fact, he is just following the spotlight. He is not yet done with it. He must know that if he does not make a decision quickly the spotlight will be turned off and the curtain will be pulled, clumsily ending his career as a misunderstood fake fiddler. But what decision is there to make? I have a feeling there will be no more music tonight. Manuel again begins fake-playing, without the benefit of music, and opens his mouth to the size of a pothole. What is he doing now, miming? As the spotlight begins to again sneak away, hoping no one, including the audience, notices, Manuel chases it to stage left, gives Libby a quick look, and starts to sing Ave Maria in Latin while continuing to move the bow inches from the strings. The stoplight has no choice but to surrender. It finds him once more. Oh for the love of God.

As Manuel finishes with Ave Maria the spotlight periodically bobs up and down. Whether this is a sign of anger or amusement on the part of the stoplight operator is unclear. He could be shaking with laughter or trembling with loathing. The curtain falls soundlessly. Even it is speechless. I look behind me at little Teddy, who's managed to stuff the yo-yo into his mouth, like a gag.

* * *

Manuel runs over after the play and informs Libby that he panicked when the music cut out. Max stands up and stretches.

"Yeah you did," he agrees. Manuel breathlessly continues: "It was as though my entire life were passing before my eyes. It was a subconscious response, a primal instinct, a volcanic eruption of the id . . ." My father shakes his head. Singing Ave Maria during a production of *Fiddler on the Roof* is not part of any human instinct he can think of. That wasn't acting, that was overreacting. I sit back down in my chair. Manuel must be so embarrassed. What a faux pas. ". . . What an invigorating moment," he marvels, undeterred. "I feel as though I could fly. To save the production in such a manner, it was an absolute triumph. I am a true improvisator . . ." Well, I guess he doesn't embarrass easily. Now, why am I not surprised?

The director storms past and tells Manuel never to show his face again. "I should have went with the schizo," he barks, "it would have been more predictable." When the director notices Libby he smiles. She, as always, looks great in a skirt and heels. Libby politely waves to the director. When Manuel sees that the director is flirting with Libby he gets jealous. He methodically peels off his mustache and tells Libby to excuse him for one moment. He follows the director and covers his back with curses as if from a spray-paint can. "You are an ungrateful swine," he tells him. "You would have been a laughingstock had it not been for me. I saved your production. And now here you are coveting my dearly beloved . . ."

A man seated across the aisle tells his companion that he appreciated the director's postmodern take on an old classic. He must teach at the community college, part-time. My mother, clutching her purse, gets up to go to the bathroom. My father goes with her. Libby turns to me as soon as they are out of earshot. She needs a cigarette. I'm right behind her. I ask if she has perfume in her purse. I can't stink when we get back. She opens her purse and shows me two bottles. I guess that's a yes. Now all we have to do is hurry up. I inform the boys that we are going to the little girls' room. Max calls us cancer patients; he knows where we are going. Phillip takes Max's hand and places it on his own crotch. Max jerks his hand away. "Whoop, daddy!" he calls out. "Didn't expect that!" William opens the laptop and starts typing. Henryk leans over for a look. I wouldn't do that if I were him. He's liable to turn to stone.

"Well, that was priceless," I say when we get outside. Libby puts a cigarette in her mouth and hands me one. We are making our way to the side of the building when I spot my parents. Shit. I impulsively stuff the cigarette in my pocket. She pees fast. My mother turns around. She is exhaling a stream of cigarette smoke when our eyes lock. My father notices me and smiles as my mother drops the cigarette. He extinguishes it with a crutch. I hurry over and ask what she's doing. My mother shakes her head: Nothing. "What nothing? You smoke?" I ask loudly. The couple standing next to her turns around. I point a finger at my mother: "You do!" She puts her foot over the butt and tells me not to be so silly. My father steps up and advises her to come clean. It's not nice to lie to children. My mother takes her foot off the cigarette. The evidence! I stare in disbelief. "You are such a hypocrite," I say. "You have been tormenting me for years and now here you are smoking. What do you think you're doing, Mom?"

My father answers on her behalf. Obviously she needs a spokesperson, possibly a lawyer. He explains that she didn't want to get me addicted. She meant well. My mother seems frazzled. She bites her lip. "But I was right all along," she says, trying to deflect attention from herself. "You do smoke." I put my hand back in my pocket as Libby smokes her cigarette. I begin to lie. No, I don't smoke. She challenges me: "Then why are you out here in the cold, without a jacket no less, if you don't smoke?" I gesture in Libby's direction: She smokes; I just came outside to keep her company; I'm trying to get her on the patch; I read that it works.

For some reason I can't bring myself to admit to my mother that I smoke. Lying about not smoking is a habit, like smoking, that I can't easily break. Our relationship is built around it. Lying about not smoking is the first thing I think about in the morning. I think about it after a meal, I think about it after I've had a few drinks . . .

"I would never lie to you," I lie to my mother. "I have never even tried a cigarette. But you . . . you are . . ."

She nonchalantly informs me that my father smokes, too. He's the one who got her hooked. She's not going down alone.

I lean into my father: "Now you smoke?" He tells me that that's a bit of an exaggeration. He rarely smokes. I accuse them both of being liars. Why didn't they tell me this sooner? He answers that I never asked, which means it wasn't a lie. It was more of an oversight on my part. I should be more inquisitive.

My mother clears her throat. "Here comes your brother," she says, putting her foot over the butt. "Don't tell him that your father smokes. He would get the wrong idea." She is as good at denying the truth as I. We have so much in common. We are peas in a pod.

My brother pushes open the glass doors, his cap pulled low over his eyes. He isn't wearing a jacket. As soon as he sees us he stuffs something into his pocket and strolls over. Are you kidding me? These people are ridiculous. Do I even know them anymore? He comes up and nervously asks what we are doing outside. Libby takes a drag off her cigarette while I explain that we are getting fresh air and discussing life's coincidences. My brother glances at Libby. "Libby, I didn't know you smoke," he offers. I didn't know you smoke, Henryk, I think to myself.

My brother looks at me.

My parents look at my brother.

I look at my mother.

My entire family came outside to smoke cigarettes but none of us can smoke cigarettes because we are all trying to hide the fact that we smoke. Libby discards her cigarette and asks if we'd like to go back inside. She's a little chilly. My father puts his arm around my mother. "Let's go," he says with a smirk.

Back in the auditorium the fake author is still glued to his computer screen. We collect our coats and the rest of the posse and make our way toward the doors, where an angry Manuel is now standing with his uncle. Unless we crawl through an airshaft there's no avoiding our buddy. Manuel's uncle, who really does look to be a kind man, puts his arm on Manuel's shoulder. Manuel throws it off impatiently. The uncle shakes his head. "Manuel, you must accept that you have been disinherited," he tells him. Manuel shouts that he is to be called Bob Apple from now on. Max perks up. "Disinherited?" he repeats before racing over to them. He puts his hands in his pockets and stands on tiptoes. "Whacha talkin' 'bout?" he asks. A flushed Manuel instructs him to mind his own business. Well, that's not going to happen. My mother and father leave. They'll be in the car, running the heat.

Max pushes on, mentioning that Manuel told us that his father was busted for drugs. Is that related to him getting disinherited? A deep wrinkle forms between the uncle's eyebrows. "He said that?" he asks. He turns to Manuel and begins to lecture him. How could he say such things about drugs? As a Mexican he should be more responsible. Manuel counters that he never said that. In fact, he said the opposite. His father did not stuff socks with cocaine. His father was not a weapons attaché. The uncle grows impatient. "This has to stop," he tells Manuel and begins berating him. He refuses to contribute to the stereotype that Mexicans are criminals or worse, druggies. "For the sake of your mother," he urges, "please make your peace here and now. Stop inventing. It is not healthy. You must move on. Do not be ashamed." Manuel snaps that he is not ashamed, the uncle should be ashamed after what he did. Max pipes up: "What are we ashamed of? Can I know?"

Manuel looks at Libby. I tell William to go work on his book. "I've been working so hard," he complains. "I'm going to need a quickie soon." An old lady walks by. She stares at William, her lower lip trembling from age, and perhaps emotion. William glances at her. He's not sure what the problem is and smiles, then goes to find a seat.

Manuel begins to explain that his father is not involved in drugs—and stresses that he never actually said that, Max did. Tube socks are in fact big business. You don't need to stuff them with anything but feet. When we met him in South Africa he was getting ready to inherit the business—socks, not drugs. He was going to be set up for life: peacocks, heliport, and so on and so on.

"Right," Max says. "And then the factory burned down, we know." Manuel shakes his head. "It didn't?" Max asks.

Manuel clarifies: "It did, and that was certainly devastating. But of course we had insurance. What business doesn't? That is not quite the whole story."

Manuel explains that the day the family returned from South Africa, Manuel's father, already eager to retire, began the process of turning over the business. But there was one formality. A mandatory DNA test. Manuel had his blood drawn then went poolside to count his chickens before they hatched. Three days later the factory burned down, and on the same day the test results came back. The problem was that the test showed that Manuel's father was not really his father, he couldn't be. Learning this, the man who thought he was Manuel's father approached his wife, Manuel's mother, for answers. And that's when the shit hit the fan. After Manuel's mother made her confession her husband sent her and Manuel on a one-way trip out of town. The factory is being rebuilt, bigger and better, rising from ash at this very moment. The only thing that permanently went up in smoke was Manuel's mother's credibility, not to mention her only son's identity. She had had an affair nearly eighteen years ago and never told her husband, who thought the child she delivered was his.

"I received the news about the DNA results just as I was returning from the site of the fire," he says. "That's the part I failed to mention at Leona's."

I glance behind me at William, now sitting on one of the folding chairs in the last row, busy staring at the computer screen. This might be something he'd like to write down; Manuel's biography seems back on track. Libby puts her hands on her curvy hips. She admits she doesn't get it: What's going on? Max poses the next question: "So, then, your father is not your father?" Manuel shakes his head and points at his uncle the failed entertainer failed dishwasher failed restaurant manager. "This," he says, "is my father. He is my uncle's brother." This admission seems to melt the uncle's heart. Finally Manuel is coming around. He puts his arm around his son. When Manuel again pushes it off he tells Manuel that he'll wait outside and reminds him that he needs to accept his fate. "Your mother and I love each other very much. We always have," he adds. "We plan to be together for the rest of our lives now that this is all over." Manuel calls him a ne'er-do-well.

Max pipes up: "So, the bottom line is that you are . . ." Manuel touches the bow tie of his tuxedo. "Yes, that is correct," Manuel says, raising his chin in a dignified manner. "I am a bastard." I look at Henryk and shake my head. He was right, there was more to Manuel's story. Hearing this from Manuel's mouth, Max begins to laugh like I've never seen him laugh before. He can't even stand. He's doubled over. His cowboy hat falls off. "Cheer up, Manuel!" he snorts. "Everyone already knew you were a bastard. This is not even news!" Libby hits Max. She tells him to be nice. "I am being nice," he says. "This actually redeems Manuel as far as I'm concerned." He shakes his head. "A bastard," he repeats to himself.

Libby walks up to Manuel and gives him an unexpected kiss on the forehead, leaving a red lipstick mark. "I'm sorry this happened to you," she says. "But you'll be okay." Evidently she's been moved by the fact that Manuel is now, officially, a poor bastard.

He takes a step back and touches the spot where Libby kissed him. "You kissed me," he says. "Can I have your telephone number?"

Libby dismisses him. "You're too young for me, no."

"I'm eighteen now," Manuel protests. "Allow me to take you flamenco dancing in Saint Tropez. We could—" She cuts him off. She doesn't want to go to St. Tropez. Or Acapulco, or anyplace else. "Then we'll partake in an American activity. I shall purchase cholesterol-ridden foodstuffs from a local take-out emporium. Whatever is your desire. We can dine with plastic utensils and consume unhealthy volumes of condiments. I believe I am allergic to mustard but it is a risk I am willing to take."

When he begins to beg, Libby reaches into her purse, removes pen and paper, and writes down her phone number. She hands it to Manuel. "Babe, you can call me when you turn twenty-one," she says. He takes the paper and kisses it. "Remember," she sternly adds. "Twenty-one, you're too young for me now."

He leaps into the air with joy. "Only one thousand ninety-five nights to go!" he excitedly proclaims. "Expectation whirls me 'round!"

Libby shrugs as he runs off with the digits. "He'll forget about me by then," she reasons. "He's so silly."

I give her a disbelieving look. We'll see if he forgets.

I call to William. We're out of here. Max reaches his hand out to Phillip. "Well," he says, "thank you for the date and good luck at the library and"—he gives him a once-over—"with everything else you have going on."

Phillip does not take the hand. He shakes his head. "This wasn't a date."

"What are you talking about?" Max asks.

Phillip repeats that this was not a date.

"But you groped me like an octopus!" Max protests. "What do you mean?"

"You invited me to see a play," Phillip says. "So I went. But this wasn't a date. Our date is on Friday. We're going to Lone Star Bar for line dancing."

"What!" Max shouts. "We had a deal!"

Phillip grabs Max's wrist. "And the deal was that I could take you out. A play is not a date." Max protests: He's not going; this was supposed to be one date. "Yes, and it's on Friday," Phillip tells him. "And if not then I'm going to get you in some trouble." He lets go of the wrist and gives Max an open-mouth kiss. Max is too stunned to move. "See you Friday at nine. Don't be late." Phillip moseys out. Waaa-Waaa-Waaa.

As Max stands there, looking like he might vomit, yo-yo boy Teddy, who was sitting behind William during the play, wanders over. "Are you in a circus?" he asks Max. Max silently studies him. He's clearly had enough. "No," he answers, bending toward him. "Are you?" The little boy shakes his head and sticks his tongue through the front gap in his teeth. His mother walks over and tugs at his arm. "Mom said you look like a circus rodeo clown." The horrified mother picks the boy up. "That's enough, Teddy," she says, now embarrassed. "Oh," Max says. "She did, huh?" He straightens up and looks at the mother. He covers the boy's ears with his hands. "Let me give you some advice," he tells her. "Before you come knocking on my door with insults, go buy poor junior here a full set of front teeth. You're no winner yourself." He uncovers the boy's ears and walks away, mumbling something about Phillip and books and line dancing.

* * *

We are enthusiastically invited back to my parents' house for drinks and snacks after the play. While my parents are in the kitchen, Max tips back a couple of rum and Cokes to help him forget his woes. His mood improves and before long he calls Henryk over. He reaches into his pocket, pulls out a driver's license, and hands it to my brother. "There it is, friend," he says and pats him on the back. "Your very own fake ID. According to this you're twenty-two." Henryk grins from ear to ear as he takes it. I cover my mouth with my hand. Henryk can't . . . Max tells me that Henryk certainly can. "From what I hear most great writers are alcoholics," he explains. "Henryk is going to need to step up his game."

Henryk continues to beam. "Word," he says. "Thanks so much, dude."

My parents emerge from the kitchen and my mother sets down some food. We gather to toast my brother. Everyone picks up a glass except for William, who can't be bothered to even look up. He's busy in front of the computer, composing his Morse code. Max proceeds to give a convoluted, indulgent speech that recalls all the good times he's shared with the author. He couldn't be more proud of the boy, not if he were gay. Mazel tov. Of course my mother won't let Henryk touch a glass of alcohol during this monologue—More milk? she periodically asks. If she only knew about the fake ID, or caught wind of the fact that he'll be ditching third period tomorrow to come see me at the office.

After the toast my father takes us into the backyard for a tour of his still-barren garden. My mother points to a clump of dirt that represents the bounty. I'm told my father spent a lot of money on seeds, which is saying something considering that he argues over the price of screwdrivers at hardware stores. He patiently explains that there are some things—like his cherished garden—that he is willing to drop cash on, which of course means that when all those delicious vegetables and herbs start growing he'll be charging market rate, no exceptions. He tells my mother with a straight face that she can watch him eat them all if she doesn't have the cash. He won't feel sorry for her even if it breaks up the marriage. She laughs: "What are you saying? I'm going back inside." If I'm not mistaken she seems more carefree in her movements. It's like she's levitating. I guess telling the truth for once will do that to a deceitful mother of two. My father follows close behind: "Keep laughing, Estie, but don't ever say you weren't warned. I'm the best thing that's ever happened to you." He turns and gives me a wink.

Max calls his father's driver to pick us up when it's time to leave. His father is out of town on business and when that happens, he gets use of the car. Beats taking the subway! I'm in. While we wait for George the driver my mother wraps up plates of food for me to take. She comes out of the kitchen with three bags. Some things never change. I hug her and say I love you. She kisses me. "I love you, too," she says. "Don't smoke." I'll take that as a compliment from now on. Max asks where his leftovers are. "Make no mistake," he adds. "I love you most." She responds by messing up his hair. Where did that come from? Smoking does make people cooler! I need to spread the word to grammar schools. Now that my mother smokes she's much more fun and interesting. I want to tell her so but know she'd send me flying across the room. I take the food. "Don't smoke," she repeats as the best thing that's ever happened to her gives me a kiss.

When George shows up Max teasingly tells Libby that she has to ride in the trunk. "That's where you're riding, babe," she responds. My father mentions that he knew a fella once who locked himself in the trunk of his own car. Max laughs: "Is this a Polish joke, Mr. Sienkiewicz? Because Kas refuses to tell me any." I'm pretty sure that if he keeps at it he'll be the one in the trunk.

We say good-bye and head for the door. William is lugging the binder and computer. He has a red pen between his teeth. My mother doesn't bring up the fact that he is still staying with me. I think she really wants those grandchildren. She wishes William luck with the book, which she's eager to read. I take the pen out of his mouth so he can tell her it's coming along—he'll be finished any day now. William then asks Max if we can stop at an ATM on the way home. Max nods. "I need to withdraw a lot of money," William says. I put the red pen back in his mouth before he can add that he needs it to pay rent, not to mention a $672 phone call to Miss Celeste. Before we can make it out of the house my mother throws out a few parting words: "Watch the speed limit because there are a lot of drunk drivers out there and wear the seat belts because they are cracking down on that and giving tickets and . . ."

Chill out, Mom. Smoke a cigarette.

* * *

"How do you declare bankruptcy?" William asks back at the apartment. "Can you just declare it?" I turn around. What is this crazy book about anyway? Does he really need a chapter on . . . "I'm broke," he adds, scratching his head. "They just told me." I feel my face get hot. What? I take off my jacket and throw it across the chair. It lands on the floor. I ask who told him that he's broke; I don't understand what he's talking about. William hands me the ATM slip. He has four dollars in his account. I disbelievingly ask if that's all he has left. He shakes his head no. I breathe a sigh of relief. He pulls a wrinkled five-dollar bill out of his pocket and tells me he has nine. Nine? I ask how this happened. Last week when he was buying water beds and paying me three thousand dollars in rent there was plenty of money. He informs me that he was mixing up rand and dollars and that he hadn't been checking receipts when making withdrawals. "Keeping it all organized is hard," he says.

I tear open a pack of cigarettes and dump the contents onto the coffee table. I light two and hold one in each hand. "You shouldn't smoke so much," he says. I squeeze my eyes shut. Forget about the rent for a second, I need money for the bills.

William has been wasting so much electricity. He thinks the apartment is too dark and keeps all the lights on; he watches television incessantly; he even burned out the motor of my blender making thick protein shakes that he claims help him think. God knows what they help him think about.

William takes a seat on the couch. He assures me that it's going to be okay, everything is going to be okay because tomorrow morning he is going to find an agent for his book. I exhale through my nostrils like a bull. He's sure he'll be able to find one. He's positive. Miss Celeste told him that nine is his lucky number, at least he thinks she said nine. It's going to be okay, at any rate. He's been writing some great stuff over the last two days. The best stuff he's written yet. The people of Monaco are going to be so happy—and relieved! He asks if I want to proofread it. I tell him no thank you. In that case, he informs me, I better get to bed because he has a lot of work to do and will be up all night. "This book is going to be better than your brother's," he says.

I collect my cigarettes and throw them on the water bed I'd like to puncture with a fork. William puts on his fez and starts pacing. I go to the closet and get the red earmuffs. I've never used anything my mother has given me this often. "I love you," he says as I get into bed. I pretend not to hear him. I wish he were walking on quicksand. "I love you," he repeats as I adjust my earmuffs.

When I don't answer William walks into the bathroom. "You know millionaires don't start with much," he calls out. "I watched a television program yesterday about a man who made a terrific amount of money by coining phrases like *All good things come to those who wait*. I was thinking maybe I could coin others, like *Don't wait twice for the same thing* or *Don't wait for things that you don't know aren't coming*. Maybe I can think up some tonight. And maybe after I sell my book I can build up my credit and buy rental property and open a store. Do you realize how much money I could give to charity if . . ." I put a pillow over my eyes but can still see the living room and kitchen lights beyond it. I hear the toilet flush and a crash, followed by a moan. William calls my name. What now? "I just accidentally flushed the contents of your makeup bag down the toilet," he yells from the bathroom. "The bag fell from the shelf into the bowl. I'm very sorry about that." Pleasure. Don't mention it. I sit up and stare at the clock as the countdown to work begins. This is going to be the longest night of . . .

I hear another moan. "The toilet is overflowing!" William shouts. "Can you help me?"

* * *

"Good morning! Isn't it a wonderful day?" Barbara bellows when I pass her desk the next morning. I'm taken aback. I've never seen her smile like this. She looks like she borrowed ten sets of extra teeth from a morgue. All I can see is bone and enamel. It's the opposite of dazzling. "Spring is in the air," she enthusiastically offers. "Isn't it beautiful outside?" I yawn. It hurts to open my mouth. My head feels like it's being knocked around with a sledgehammer. Everything is blurry. My contacts are hardening, ready to pop out and shatter. William, if it needs to be said, kept his promise of staying up all night. When he wasn't typing he was pacing, and when he wasn't doing that he was sharpening pencils. Have you ever had someone sharpen a pencil next to your ear at 3 a.m. while you're trying to sleep? Try it sometime. It's not a nice sound.

"Wake up, sleepyhead! You need a pick-me-up. Do you want me to get you coffee? I can't have any myself because I've started bleaching my teeth but I can get you some, just say the word." I shake my head. Am I having a nightmare? I can't tell but this isn't right. I feel around for the water bed. I have never heard Barbara say the things she's saying right now. Calling me sleepyhead? Offering to bring coffee? Labeling the outdoors beautiful? Bleaching her teeth? Maybe she's on Prozac. Remind me never to get on Prozac. "I went shopping yesterday," she says, smoothing her black-and-white-checkered blouse. "I absolutely splurged. I figured I deserve it." Why isn't she crying about the dress code? She's not mad about the jerseys? I've been standing here, an open target, for a good minute and yet she has not thrown one shoe or stapler or ceramic figurine. I look down at my nails. They're all chewed and haggard. I've been neglecting my appearance and it's starting to show. I should spend the ten dollars on a manicure. I'm not going to be able to pay my bills anyway, may as well look presentable for debtors' prison . . . "I'm in love!!!" Barbara yells out of nowhere. "And it feels so good all over."

I look up in alarm as she runs her hands through her hair in a seductive fashion. I certainly could have lived out my days without seeing that. This is grounds for a civil suit. "Love, love, love," she sings while whipping a pen through the air like an orchestra conductor. I ask Barbara to please explain to me what is happening to her. She bites the end of the pen. She has a glazed look on her face. "Well, I guess there's no point keeping it a secret," she offers. No, I guess not, megaphone mouth. She asks if I remember Fred Stewart, Buddy's behavior manipulation coach. How could I forget him? I was assaulted with his business card. I still have the paper cut on my upper lip. I answer in one word: yeah. "Well," she says, "he called me back! It turns out the invoice was a big misunderstanding." He wanted more money? "Really?" I rhetorically ask. "Yes, really, silly!" she responds. Willy-nilly, frilly filly. Dillydally. Speak it, Sally. What the hell? Let's get this over with so I can fall asleep underneath my desk. I urge her to go on.

Barbara undoes the top button of her blouse and smiles again. Does she think she's being coy? "Freddie called to say that he meant to mail the invoice to another customer who had sought out his behavior manipulation skills," she explains. "It wasn't even meant for me!"

I'm about to collapse. I yawn again. I try to keep Barbara in focus but all I can see is a white light. I've died, haven't I? I'm dead now. "Right. Okay," I answer.

Barbara sighs: "He told me he'd be honored to let me treat him to dinner again. He would be absolutely honored."

"You don't say."

Barbara squeals: "He's coming to the office this evening to pick me up. I'm on cloud nine. He's so sensitive and romantic."

I give Barbara a thumbs-up as she informs me that Freddie is a gentleman sweetheart and a keeper and that she can't wait for me to meet him. I tell her that meeting Freddie sounds great even though it sounds terrible. "Love is wonderful," she offers. "It finds you when you least expect it."

Later that morning I get an e-mail from William that should be donated to science.

Subject: mo!!!!!!!!!!!!!!!!!!!!!!!!!!!!!!!!!!

no tim 2 loos. Iam goig 2 find an agant 2day--I think I cane seel mi bok on mo 2day!!!!!!! wish mi luk. Iwill now news when u get hom 2nite. I am goin 2B an publihsd auto r. Ilov u buterful !!willy//-can i borow 100dolarz 2 help wth/ expensis????

Can he borow 100dolarz? No, he fucking can't borrow . . . "Hey," I hear someone say. I press delete and look up. Henryk. He asks if everything is okay. He observes that I look like I'm about to start crying. I close my mouth. Don't ever have sex with people, Henryk, don't ever do it, I want to tell him. I pick up a stack of manuscript pages and pull a pack of cigarettes out from underneath. I throw the pack at my brother, who extends his arm and stops it in midair. He's a toad catching a fly. I stand up and tell him we're going out for a smoke and some lunch.

"But I don't . . . ," he starts to protest.

"Don't give me that," I tell him. "I was just starting to like you."

Henryk takes a pack of cigarettes out of his jacket. "I don't smoke your brand, that's all I was going to say."

It's an unseasonably warm day and Henryk and I decide to dine alfresco. After grabbing sandwiches we take a seat on a park bench near a guy wearing reindeer horns. "Lovely weather we're having," he says to himself. As the sun warms my cheeks, rather like an interrogation lamp at the police station, I tell Henryk everything. I recall the graphic circumstances under which I met William and explain how he came to live with and mooch off me. I spare none of the gore. I tell him that I accidentally blurted "I love you" after my one-night stand, that I enjoyed the feeling of power that came with being associated with a hot specimen. I tell him that William has been buying me gifts I don't want and declaring his love, which I don't want, either, and that he thinks I'm helping him turn dreams into reality while he deprives me of life, liberty, and the pursuit of happiness. Basically I feel sorry for him: He has this dead uncle he's always trying to impress, he has all this devotion to causes that mean nothing to me, he was a virgin when we met. But now that he's broke he has to leave. I have to kick the altruist to the curb.

Henryk rewraps the uneaten portion of his sandwich. He tells me that if William wants honesty than I should be honest with him. If I don't love him I should say so, and if I don't think he has a writing career ahead of him, I should say so, too. He shrugs: "Just tell the truth." The innocence of youth! Henryk is right about one thing, though: William will never sell that book. He looks at me. "I mean there's no way, right?" he asks. I nod. Right. Henryk gets up. "You'd think he'd want to write about South Africa. Maybe apartheid . . ." I give him a good-bye hug. Enough already. I don't care. Before he has time to run off I ask what classes he missed today. He chuckles: "English and geography." Ah. How very American. I toss my sandwich wrapper into the garbage. I'm not going back to work just yet. I'm going to get some coffee and think.

* * *

"You are so bad," I hear Barbara laugh when I finally return to the office to collect my things. "I've never met anyone like you." As I approach her desk I see that there's a pasty man with a comb-over sitting atop her desk like a wilted Thanksgiving centerpiece. Barbara, who certainly is re-imagining that dress code, has changed out of the black-and-white-checkered number and is now wearing a tight, cleavage-baring white top. I can see her nipples. Why me, Lord? Barbara's boobs need their own rented storage space. Avoiding them proves surprisingly difficult. I attempt to focus all my energy on her right earring as a way of coping. It doesn't work. There, I peeked again. Fuck! I would like to go in the corner now and rock myself gently until the voices in my head grow quiet.

I am introduced to Fred Freddie Stewart, who tells me I'm as young as a schoolgirl. I don't answer. Barbara proudly explains that Freddie is always flirting with everyone because he's "a ladies' man." Is that what he is? Really? He reaches over and squeezes Barbara's breast. I feel like I've been sexually harassed from two feet away. "I don't have to flirt," he says. Barbara tells him to behave. Maybe he should take his own behavior manipulation course. Freddie picks Barbara's purse off her desk. "Let's get a move on, Barbie," he offers, "we've got a lot on our plates." Barbara applies an entire tube of lip gloss and turns off her computer. I accidentally glance at her big sagging boobs again. This is a shameful day. Freddie tells her he knows the perfect dinner spot. She asks what it is. She can't wait. "It's called my apartment"—he squeezes the other breast like he's milking her—"it's got great atmosphere."

As they lock arms Barbara imparts a bit of sage advice: "When you find a good man, hold on to him." I'll remember that, yes. Go get your groove, Barbara.

As I watch them walk out it dawns on me that this is the first day in the office that Barbara has not been hostile to me. Maybe Freddie ain't so bad. If he gives her an orgasm she might bake me a cake.

* * *

I stand in the hallway of my apartment building and light a cigarette. The nasty reality of what I am about to do sinks in. I push open the door and see William on the floor. My first thought is that he's too weak to move, having been verbally violated by every literary agent in the business. He's wasted a day aimlessly roaming around town trying to sell his book idea and it is now my job to console him as he uses the thin pages of his opus as a hankie.

I survey the heaps of tracksuits crowding the floor. It looks like a piñata exploded in my face. Why has he pulled all his Desert Sand, Carnation Pink, Fuzzy Wuzzy Brown, Cadet Blue, and Vivid Tangerine–colored belongings out of the closet? Oh God, he's so out of it he's decided to sell his clothes to make rent. This is awful. Now I have to tell him he's a bad dresser, too. Even Goodwill would reject him. When I ask what he's doing he jumps up and gives me a hug. "I have wonderful news about my book about the political situation in Monaco!" he shouts. My lit cigarette accidentally touches his arm, burning a hole in his sweatshirt. He looks down and mumbles, "My hoodie." Is it possible he found someone interested in his book? Who would buy his writing—who could decipher it? A fellow park ranger? A lonesome divorcée? I can't imagine any agent would be interested. Or would she? His physical prowess already made a fool of me. Who's next? As he takes off the hoodie I ask for an explanation. "I'm going to Monaco!" he exuberantly exclaims. "I'm finally going to fulfill my dreams! Everyone believes in me and wants me to succeed." I take his beloved hoodie, toss it on the couch, and invite him to explain. I am waiting for the words *self-publish* and the question *Can I borrow ten thousand dollars?* but they never come.

Apparently that morning, when walking out of the apartment building, his musings on Monaco's political situation tucked under arm like a weapon of mass destruction, William was stopped by a scout from a modeling agency. The man was captivated. He asked William if he's ever considered a career in modeling; William, of course, shook his head no. Modeling isn't part of the dream. He elaborates: "I told him I wasn't interested in being a model. The man looked very disappointed that I wouldn't even consider modeling.

He said I would be making a lot of money. He said I was a natural player. I told him that I couldn't model because I was writing my book, which is my dream. I explained to him about my book on the political situation in Monaco. He said, 'Monaco? We send models to Monaco on photo shoots all the time. If you're going to write about Monaco you should go there to see it for yourself. If you become a model you can go for free. Think of it this way, the agency will be paying you to write your book!' We talked about Monaco for three hours! He was so concerned! The owner of the modeling agency even has a house there, so it's like fate! I'm going to become a high-paid supermodel so that I can become an award-winning writer. And I'll get my big advance after all! The book is really moving along, too. The acknowledgments page is almost finished!"

If I had a penny for every time I've heard Paul Auster say that.

William hands me the scout's business card. I look at the name. For some reason I recognize the name of the modeling agency. I watch too much bad entertainment television. I need help. "I have to go to Monaco," William continues. "Remember how Miss Celeste told me a new person would come into my life?" I nod. "Well, that person was not Bob, it was Randy Sexton from the modeling agency! He's such a nice man, and so interested in Monaco!" I return the card. Randy Sexton and Willy Johnson, together at long last. "Are you upset?" he asks, touching my cheek. I shake my head no: I respect your dreams, Martin Luther King Jr. hyphen Jesus Christ, even if you are becoming a model, doing the very thing you said you would not do.

We embrace. "You're definitely going to see your name on the acknowledgments page," he tells me. "Though it's only right that I dedicate the book to my dead uncle Dale." I pat him on the back. I am tempted to admit I'd rather not be acknowledged. "Say good-bye to Libby and Max. I can't acknowledge them because all those names just won't fit, but I'm sure if you explain it they will understand what it's like to be a writer . . ." I ask when he plans to move out. "Oh, today," he answers. "I have to go to the agency right now. They are going to put me up in an apartment with some other male models. But it's only a matter of time before I get to Monaco. Maybe next week." He takes a moment of silence to consider his achievement. "I am officially a writer! This is so fantastic! I'm going to change the world!" He sits back down on the floor and continues packing. Good-bye high-tops, good-bye nylon parachute pants and Giants pendants. Good-bye pumpkin-colored hoodie. "I can't wait to interview and help the citizens of Monaco," he gushes. "It's going to be great! It's what I need for inspiration—to be there. You know? I can't believe I didn't think of it before. It seems so simple now."

William closes his suitcase. I stand up. He tenderly strokes my cheek before hugging me again. He then picks up his suitcase—"It is time," he says—and carries it to the kitchen, which is when I notice the hamster cage on my kitchen table. I give it a second look. What is in there? Something gray darts across the cage. I let out a scream as gallons of blood begin pounding in my head. I run for the door. "What is that?" I scream while jumping in place. "What is that, William?"

"The mouse," he whispers, slapping his forehead. "I almost forgot. I trapped the mouse." He puts down his suitcase and walks over to the cage. "Earlier today while I was on the couch he just came up to me and started nibbling on my shoelace." William explains that he tried to release the mouse outside but that it followed him back into the apartment, which is when he carried it to the pet store in his pocket and bought a cage. He adds that he paid for the cage with forty dollars he found in a drawer. Great, my emergency money. "This mouse is meant to be here," he tells me. "It has a very unique aura." I peek at the mouse from a safe distance. It stares back at me with tiny black eyes. That's some unique aura, for sure. Why don't we find out its sign and maybe do its romance compatibility diagram. "I think it will have a wonderful home here," he says with a nod. I open the door. We'll see about that.

William and I walk outside and I immediately hail a cab. William gets in and waves to me through the window. I stand at the curb momentarily overwhelmed by the brightness of his blue eyes. He is so pretty—so much prettier than I. For old times' sake I run over and put my hand through the open window, palm-side up. William touches it with two fingers. "You have an artist's hand," he observes and smiles, a tear in his eye. My eyes are as dry as the Sahara Desert. "I will write to you as soon as I get to Monaco," he promises. "And someday, when I am as big as Tom Clancy, I will be back in New York. I am going to try to be as good a writer as your brother. I may be better. I know I can do it because I have so much faith in the goodness of the world!" I blow a kiss. Anything is possible. And I mean that in the most abstract sense.

The cab pulls away then stops at a red light some twenty feet away. I move back to the curb and stare at William, who sticks his head and arms out the window. He puts on his fez. "Monaco, here I come!" he exclaims just as a car comes racing down the street and smashes into the back of the cab, whose trunk folds like an accordion. Hubcaps pop off like buttons off a fat man's coat while gray clouds of smoke rise into the air. The cab's curved tailpipe dangles from the wreckage before falling off. It rests on the ground like a comma, as if to signal that the day is not yet done—we are merely transitioning.

But the last thing I need now is a *but . . .*

"I'm hurt!" William shouts from inside the cab. Hurt? Oh no. I run to him as both drivers, cell phones at the ready, stand in the middle of the street screaming at each other. A dazed William stumbles out of the cab. His shoelaces are untied, his fez is missing its tassel. "Help me," he moans as a crowd begins to form, "I think I broke my arm. It stings." Broke his arm? Oh my God, he's going to have to stay with me longer! I'm never going to get rid of him. He is worse than herpes. "Can we go back inside?" he asks. "I need to apply a compress." I shake my head frantically as he tells me he loves me. No, you don't. You don't need to love me and you don't need a compress. Another cab pulls up behind the accident. I wave my arms. When it stops I reach into William's cab, pull out his suitcase without assistance using superhuman strength miraculously mustered for the occasion, and throw it in the back of the other cab. Now I need a compress. I hold my back as William holds his wrist and asks where we are going. We? We're not going anywhere. "You'll be late for your scheduled appointment with Randy Sexton," I say, acting like it matters. I push him into the cab. Godspeed! He looks at me pleadingly through the window. "But my whole arm is . . . ," he starts to protest. I see that there is a bit of blood running down his forehead. Stigmata? It's no big deal! The rugged look is in this season. He's at an advantage. I smile at him. I've turned from Florence Nightingale to Doctor Death. William's kindness has brought out the very worst in me. "No pain no gain!" I yell as the cab slowly maneuvers around the accident. "This is Monaco we're talking about after all! Turn the other cheek!" William nods in confusion as the cab speeds off. I needn't say more and for once I don't bother. Who the hell goes bankrupt after two weeks, by the way? Ask William.

I am walking back to my apartment building, feeling rather drained, when someone bumps into me. "Sorry," I mumble, trying to get out of the way. "Oh, wow," he marvels. I look up and he smiles, flashing dimples that give his face a certain wholesomeness. Huh. He's okay. The guy has brown tussled hair, greenish blue eyes, and a toothy, goofy grin. He's about two inches taller than me—not too short, not too tall. I offer an "excuse me" and try again to pass. He continues to stare at me. "You don't remember me, do you?" he asks. I tell him that of course I remember him. I didn't get amnesia when we ran into each other just now. He tells me that we met on Valentine's Day. I don't say anything. "I was the bartender," he adds. "I served you two whiskeys. One on the rocks, one neat, and later, after mashing a cup into some dude's face, you told me you didn't like my joke. You remember that?"

I nod. He's talking about the day I clobbered Richard. "Yeah, I remember you," I say.

"You know, I thought about you a few times after that night," he admits. "I don't know why but I did." He pauses. "I guess you could say you made an impression." I dismissively offer that I'm sure he couldn't stop thinking of me because he's never met anyone like me. "I don't know you well enough to say I've never met anyone like you," he points out. "Give me a few days."

He offers his hand. Newland is the name. When he tells me he was just about to grab some food and asks if I'd like to come I shake my head no. "I just ate," I lie, "but thanks."

"Not hungry," he says mostly to himself and nods. "How about dinner sometime?" I give him a disbelieving look. Is he actually trying to pick me up? "What, you don't like dinner, or just don't like dinner with me? If it's the latter I can seat you at a separate table."

I take in his attire. He is wearing a black coat over what look like hospital scrubs. Not a good sign. "Are you an inmate at an insane asylum?" I ask, pointing at his light blue wrinkled cotton pants. "Just curious before this goes any further."

He explains that he's in residency at St. Vincent's hospital. Internal medicine. I look at him suspiciously. "And you moonlight as a bartender?" I challenge. "I find that hard to believe."

He tells me that he was working that night as a favor to the owner, who is a friend. "He was in a bind," he says. When I continue to stare he pulls out his cell phone. "If you don't believe me you can call him." I put out my hand. "Let me see your hospital badge," I demand.

He wrinkles up his nose. "What?" he asks in disbelief. I extend my hand a bit farther toward him: "You heard me." He pulls a hospital ID out of his pocket. I examine it. Looks real enough. "Good picture," I officiously offer with a nod. "Thank you, ma'am," he says before returning it to his pocket.

Newland takes a seat on the bottom step of the stairs leading to my apartment building, leaving me no choice but to sit down next to him. We talk for an hour while watching the cleanup of William's car accident. Two squad cars pull up, followed by two tow trucks; drivers exchange information; officers issue tickets. Talking to Newland turns out to be as easy as talking to my friends. No effort required, no awkward pauses. As we sit there I notice that he laughs a lot, and that when he does, his shoulders shake, like he's really enjoying himself. Before he leaves I give him my number. But only because he asked. Three times. While ascending the stairs I offer that he shouldn't get his hopes up. I'm taking a long break from men.

The only man in my life at the moment is my brother. We have seventeen years' worth of catching up to do. Before I can make it to the door he calls to me. I turn around. "Why did the lettuce blush?" he asks. I frown. "What, you heard that one before?" he asks and immediately bursts out laughing. Fucking Newland, he thinks he's funny. Stupid cute drink-making doctor who has a sense of humor. I'm definitely not answering when he calls. "I have other jokes, you know," he adds and again bursts out laughing. "But they might be too funny." I playfully roll my eyes. "Don't look so bored," he says and puts a hand to his heart, "you're hurting my feelings."

I unlock the front door of the building, push it open with my foot, and tell Newland that he needs to stop flirting with me. It's shameless. He takes a step back onto the sidewalk and waves good-bye. "See you soon, I hope," he says. "I'm going back to the bar now." I whip around. He told me . . . He waves a hand: "It's a joke." I watch Newland walk away. Nothing I said bewildered him. He caught everything I threw *and* he teased back. I turn back to the door, which is when I remember the mouse. I whip around. I scream his name. He stops and turns. "You have a second?" I shout. "I need help with something!"

I lead Newland upstairs. "This relationship is moving faster than expected," he says. "You should know that I like to sleep on the left side of the bed and that I'm a cuddler." I assure him he'll be coming in for only a minute. I don't want to deal with the mouse alone. He can dispose of it, pretty please. If he's a doctor in training he can't be too squeamish. We stand in my kitchen and stare at the mouse in the cage. I know it's the same mouse I saw weeks ago because of its distinctive marking—a patch of white on the rump, right above the tail.

As I contemplate what we should do with it I notice that the mouse is trembling. It's scared of me and I'm scared of it. I lean over the cage. Its gray fuzzy mouse ears are kind of sweet. It looks helpless, and it's kind of pudgy. Its little face is . . .

"Cute," Newland says with a chuckle. "Look at those little ears."

"Yeah, I guess they are," I answer. "Even if they are on a rodent."

"I mean your ears," he says. "They are cute."

"Stop looking at my ears," I say, starting to smile.

"Yes, ma'am. I'll only look at your ass from now on."

I turn toward him. "Will you stop?"

"I'm finding it hard, but yes," he says and grins. "So do you have any cheese?"

For the next few minutes Newland and I attempt to feed tiny pieces of American cheese to the mouse. When it realizes we are not going to hurt it, the mouse waddles over to the silver bars. I'm pretty sure it doesn't need any rich cheese, being chunky and all, but that's okay. I never liked diets anyway. It cleans itself like a cat after it finishes eating, rubbing its paws on it furry ears and tiny mouse face. The mouse stops cleaning itself and looks up at me. Awwwwwww. When Newland leaves, he leaves alone. Max is going to kill me.

That evening I get an e-mail message from William.

Subject: hey gorgeous!!im gong---me arm is beter
         Amstil in nyc//goin 2 mo, son---hopfuly/idontknw. Mi new apt is excelent//the other mail modals are nice//we hav a fooze ball table. I won!!!!!!!!!!!! My bunkmate is oliver.he will

b sleping ontop of me. He promise 2 take me 2 the turkish
bath hous 2.U now I luv u &this is hard 2 sy but I hav 2, we
hav to break up. Sory. We canot conitnnue know that im goin
2 mo!!!!!!!!!!!I wil be very buszy. I luv you. mayb sum day!!!/
1!!your willy
    PS $%%^&*%$## -u r gorgeous//I will sent u money--3000.
will be there son! Pss--Me arm is beter!!!!!!!!!!!!!!

I shake my head. Wow. I write a response saying that I understand everything, which I don't, and wish him the best on his
convoluted journey to Mo (let's just hope "Oliver the bunkmate"
turns him into a mo before he gets to Mo. It's likely if they visit
that Turkish bathhouse together). As for the money? I tell him
he doesn't have to send it and turn off the computer.

* * *

At work on Friday, Barbara—or Barbie, as Freddie would
say—is all sunshine and light. And, on an even better note,
so is my boss. He calls me into his office. It seems that a
major Internet media news site known for its cruelty and
general fuck-you attitude, The Daily, picked up a link to the
blog published by the disgruntled author whom I rejected.
They thought it was the funniest thing ever, that we would
be so mean. They wrote a flattering article about the agency,
recommending us to all writers looking for representation. I
spend the day opening mail and reading e-mail submissions.
Some of the new submissions reference The Daily's article in
the cover letter, one is even addressed directly to me. Writers
are lunatics. But good for them.

* * *

That evening Libby and I are watching TV at my place when
Max bursts through the door, again wearing his cowboy duds.

Tonight is his date. "I have a serious situation. Do you have
Benadryl or anything like it?" He begins to scratch his neck,
then his leg. His face is red.

"What's the matter with you, babe?" Libby asks. "You're all
red."

He throws off his ten-gallon hat and begins manically
scratching his head. "Okay," he says, still standing in the
kitchen. "So remember how I sent Richard itching powder
inside a greeting card awhile back?" We nod. "Well, I still
had a lot of it left over. Like a huge bottle of it." He begins
pacing back and forth. "So I was getting ready to leave my
house tonight for this stupid date and I was reaching into the
cabinet and I accidentally knocked it off the shelf, and I guess
the cap was loose. The bottle tipped over and all the powder
dumped out on top of my head and got all over me. I took a
shower"—he begins wildly scratching at his chest and talking
even faster—"but I had to put this stupid outfit back on and
it's like all over the clothes I guess and I can't stop itching.
And I'm late. I have to be there now and I have no time to
get new clothes because I have to wear this stupid cowboy
getup. And I can't cancel because if I do he will turn me in, I
know he will, I can see it in his eyes . . ."

He just keeps talking and itching, and I remain strangely
calm. I've done my share of frantic pacing lately. Now it's
someone else's turn.

". . . So I'm wondering if you have Benadryl because I'm
freaking out here."

"You should have stopped while you were ahead," Libby
says, shaking her head.

"I'm always ahead," he snaps. "How should I know when
to stop?"

He walks over and asks us to scratch his back. Libby and I
pull away. We don't want to get the powder on us. He walks

back into the kitchen and notices the mouse cage. "What is that?" He frowns. I tell him I have a pet mouse. He raises an open palm. "Okay, we'll talk about that later." He jerks open a drawer and pulls out a wooden spoon. He puts it down the back of his shirt and starts scratching himself, his eyes rolling to the back of his head. "Oh my God that feels gooooood," he says. He takes out the spoon and stares at it. "I have to psych myself out. I have to will this away and power through. Just have to get this over with." He looks down at his watch, scratches himself one more time with the spoon, then tries to hand it to me. I tell him to keep it. I'm pretty sure I'm done with that spoon. He puts it in his back pocket. "All right, I'm going. I have to go." He scratches his neck. "I feel like it's spreading, not going away. It's like ants crawling on my body . . ." He opens the door and walks out, mumbling to himself.

Libby puts her feet up on the coffee table. "What do you want to do tonight, babe?" she asks and yawns.

I look at her disbelievingly. What does she think?

* * *

The bouncer at Lone Star Bar tells us that the cover to get in is fifty dollars. "Fifty!" I shout.

"That's what they tell me," he responds. He's tall and built, with light eyes and blond hair. We open our wallets. We have twenty-three bucks between us, and twenty-two of that is mine. I ask if he'll just take the twenty-three dollars; we only want to be in there a little while. "Sorry, cowgirl," he says as two men in chaps approach. "Five dollars," he tells them.

"Hi, Felix," they say in unison. Like Phillip, they must be regulars. The bouncer nods. They hand over five bucks each and he opens the steel door. A very loud Billy Ray Cyrus song attacks my ears before the door closes once more.

"Wait a minute," I protest. "You told us it was fifty dollars to get in. And just because we're not gay?"

"I don't make the rules," he says. "They're not friendly to ladies here. You'd be better off somewhere else."

I start to walk away. Fifty dollars? Yeah, right. I turn to say something to Libby but she is still standing next to the bouncer. I walk back over as she puts her hands on her hips. "Hey, Felix," she says, tilting her head, "you're straight though." He nods: "I know I am."

"Then why are you working at a gay bar?" she asks.

He tells her plenty of straight bouncers work at gay bars; they pay better. "And gay dudes never fight," he adds. "I don't know what it is. Gay dudes just don't fight. It's easy work."

Libby tells him we came to see about a friend. She explains the situation. He nods. "I saw that dude, he's in there. He's in bad shape."

"Can you cut us a break?" Libby asks. This guy is totally her type. She likes that built, vaguely meathead-ish but sweet sort.

He shakes his head. Can't do it without collecting the cover; strict policy. Libby gives him puppy-dog eyes. "There's nothing you can do?" she says in a baby voice. She opens her wallet and shows him the measly one-dollar bill. "Pleeeeeeeeeesh."

Obviously it doesn't take much to convince bouncer Felix. He's a meathead. It's his job to get hosed. Score one for puppy-dog eyes—and probably boobs, who's kidding who?

The bar serves food in addition to drinks, and the bouncer sneaks us into the kitchen through the back. The cooks are straight (of Latin flavor, incidentally), and don't mind that we're there, as long as we agree to stay in the kitchen. In the center of the door leading from the kitchen to the bar is a round window. We pull up chairs and look through. It's a clear view of the dance floor. I've never seen a place like this. There are bales of hay decorating the floor and a big neon bronco over the main door. There are four dartboards and an ATM machine. On the walls pinups of naked and half-naked men in cowboy hats have been plastered. A Shania Twain song is blaring. In one corner is a mechanical bull. The place is filled with couples. All men in Western wear. One guy has a lasso strapped to his black jeans. Most of the men are line dancing. A few are sitting in the corners, watching, tapping their feet. "Man, I feel like a woman!" Shania sings.

Out of a shadowy corner come Max and Phillip. Max scratches his neck and then, after a few words are exchanged, Phillip scratches Max's neck. They begin to line dance. Step one, step two. Max bends down to scratch his leg and bumps into the guy next to him. He then itches his wrist and continues. But not for long. Midsong he raises his finger to Phillip, like he's telling him to hold on a sec, then runs over to a chair, leans his back against its back, and begins moving up and down, bending at the knees. He has a look of great relief on his face. His back must really itch. He pulls his arms behind him, grips the chair, and begins to slide it up and down his back. Finding this ultimately unsatisfying, he runs to the bar, barks an order, and is soon downing three shots of something in a row. Phillip walks over and pulls him back onto the dance floor.

The men in the kitchen, by the way, are definitely straight. They flirt with us and give us free food. We sit down for a while and eat thick burgers and potato wedges with ketchup. Afterward we get back up on our chairs. Max and Phillip are no longer on the dance floor. I scan the bar and almost fall off my chair when I see Max atop the mechanical bull, waving one arm in the air as a pack of men cheer him on. When he goes to scratch himself he loses his balance and is thrown from the bull onto the edge of the blue mat underneath it. He gets up and is momentarily consumed by a fit of itching. He scratches at himself wildly. I see him ask Phillip to help him out. This time Phillip just stares at him.

Libby and I leave. Before heading home we walk to the front entrance and say good-bye to the bouncer. "Can I have your number?" he immediately says to Libby, already holding his phone.

"Sure thing, babe," she tells him. There's a twinkle in her eye. He's definitely her type.

＊ ＊ ＊

By Sunday the dust settles and the cigarette smoke triumphantly rises again. Max, Libby, and I come together at my place and have champagne in the afternoon. Max is a little worn—he has a few self-inflicted scratch marks on his arms and one on his cheek—but in good spirits, the itching having stopped. Phillip gave him the cowboy boot soon after he fell off that mechanical bull. He became highly suspicious of the itching and was convinced that Max had crabs or some other venereal disease that he didn't want to catch. Not only is Max off the hook, he was told by Phillip never to call him again. Max's only problem now is the scratch mark on the cheek. He keeps slathering glistening Neosporin gel over it. If he asks me one more time if the mark is noticeable, I'm going to punch him in the mouth. Vanity. I'm glad I don't suffer from it.

Libby, meanwhile, received a letter from Manuel. It is written in calligraphy. In it Manuel reveals that he is moving to

Los Angeles to pursue an acting career. He adds that he and his father (formerly his uncle) are starting to see eye-to-eye, thanks in large part to the wine-tasting class Manuel signed him up for. He closes by telling Libby how much he is looking forward to his twenty-first birthday. He calls her the most beautiful girl in the world. "He is so weird!" Libby says with a giggle. "He's counting down the days!" That this genuinely surprises her, surprises me.

Max, as expected, mocks me for keeping the mouse. "How can you keep that cage on the kitchen table?" he asks with a frown. "I would not be able to eat." I jump to the mouse's defense. It's cute. I don't know. I can't explain it. It's not something I'm known for, saving animals. Maybe William did have a positive effect on me. Regardless, the mouse seems to like me. I even opened the cage to give it an opportunity to escape, and it just stayed put. After that I was trying to think of ways to make it comfortable in its new home, which is when I remembered what William said about first noticing the mouse when it was chewing on his shoelace. So I bought a pair of black shoelaces. I put one in the cage to see what the mouse would do. And what do you know? This mouse likes shoelaces. It grabbed it and started chewing on it. I think it thinks it's a toy.

Max stands up and walks to the kitchen. He leans over the cage. "You're disgusting," he says to the mouse. "And fat."

"Hey," I protest. "Don't say that."

He walks back into the living room holding the cage. "You think it understands what I'm saying, Dr. Dolittle?" I chuckle. I tell him to bring the cage here, I want to see Butterball. He sets it on the coffee table and sits back down. "You named it Butterball?" Max says. "Good, encourage its obesity." He pours himself another flute of champagne and tells us he has a secret to share. I inform him that I can handle any type of news that doesn't involve William's disgraceful return. Although the guy did send me a thousand dollars in cash fastened with a rubber band. I got it in the mail yesterday.

"So what do you want to tell us?" I ask as my pet mouse drags its shoelace across the cage.

"I paid for our trip to South Africa," Max confesses. "I didn't get it from my dad."

Libby sits up. "Babe, you did that?" she asks in disbelief. "Why?"

He nods: "I wanted to take a trip with my girls. And you two never have money. I thought we'd have fun." He explains that he was going to tell us when we got back but then William happened. He rubs his temples. "The hysterics over that compelled me to wait. I hope you'll forgive me." I give him a hug. We forgive him, we love him. Always have, always will.

As we sit around sipping bubbly Max grows reflective. He points out that it's been an active several weeks. "We've changed for the better, haven't we?" he asks. He looks at Libby and asks how she's changed. Libby sighs. "Well," she answers, "when I tried to file for unemployment last night I was told that it was my last week." She lets out a whimper. "I have to get a job."

I give her a merciful look. That sucks. Max volunteers to do her résumé. "I'm telling you," he says, "list skills you don't have. By the time they figure it out it will be too inconvenient to fire you." She objects, which is when he offers to get her a temp gig at his gym, answering phones.

"Do I have to lift anything?" she asks with concern.

"Um, the phone?" he answers.

"We'll talk about it later," she responds. It's great how lazy people get when they're unemployed. Even the phone—as an idea—starts to feel heavy.

Max next asks how I've changed. I take a sip of champagne and begin to muse aloud. I'm pretty sure we have not changed in the least as friends. In fact, we've come full circle: We are the same assholes, and that's nice. We like it that way. But a lot has happened in a short amount of time, and my reality has shifted. I discovered that my mother, when not behaving like an android programmed to remind me to marry before thirty, is like any other human being—with vices to match! Most importantly, I was introduced to a new man by the name of Henryk. He's like no one I have ever met, in a manner of speaking . . . and guess what? He's my fucking brother. I couldn't be more excited to get to know him better. His brain is like an encyclopedia. The other day he told me that he's already at work on a second novel. He's so impressive.

Max pats my knee. "That's precious." He opens the Neosporin tube and rubs more ointment on the scratch on his cheek. "Do you know what I learned?" he asks. "I learned two things. One, don't mess with the library system. And two, always tighten the cap on your itching powder. Always."

I lift an eyebrow. "That's all you learned?"

He takes a drink from the flute and, while he thinks, rinses his mouth with champagne like it's mouthwash. He swallows hard. "I'll admit there's a lesson in all this about Karma. And it might be good for me not to always demand a hand in everything that happens. But who's to say?"

I get up to open another bottle of champagne at the kitchen counter. If I have learned anything it's that friends and family are where it's at. You can run the globe, you can go to South

Africa, but the most important people you'll ever meet are those you already know.

"Hey, Kas," Max tentatively says.

I turn around. Their faces are pressed against Butterball's cage. Libby has her mouth covered.

"Yeah," I cheerily answer. "What's up?"

"Remember, oh, five seconds ago when Butterball was fat?" Max asks.

I look at Max like he's crazy: "What are you talking about?" Just then Libby pulls her hand from her mouth and squeals with delight.

Max looks up at me. "Butterball just gave birth to six babies in her cage," he reports with a laugh. "I hope you like roommates because this apartment is about to get seriously crowded." His cell phone rings as I approach the cage. He doesn't answer it. I look inside the cage. Oh dear. Butterball is a mama. Max begins rapidly texting. He's pounding the buttons. When he receives a text back he heads for the door. "Okay then, this ended better than expected," he says. "I'll be on my way now. Enjoy your mice." As he opens the door I ask where he is going. He answers that he has an appointment. I tell him to come back later for dinner. I'll invite Henryk, too. He nods, begins texting again, and closes the door. I look back at the cage. I am living with a single mother of six.

* * *

I don't hear from Max for the rest of the day. I call him but he doesn't pick up, which is strange because he always takes my calls. He once answered during sex. I leave him a message. I call Henryk a few times, too, but each time my mother informs me that he's not home. Where the hell is everybody? I wait half an hour, then yell to Libby to find out if she wants to go in on a pizza. I hear her through the wall: "Totally! But no olives, babe!"

I order a large. No olives. While waiting for the pizza I watch Butterball and her six kids in the cage. The babies already look to have personalities. One is off in the corner alone, another is climbing over its mother like a mountaineer at the South Pole. When there's a loud knock on the door I reach for my purse and pull out my wallet. The knock is followed almost immediately by several more, louder knocks. I close my wallet. The knocking starts again. But even louder this time. Take it easy, I'm coming. The persistent knocking continues. Knock Knock Knock Knock Knock Knock Knock. Go knock yourself out, idiot, because you just knocked your way out of a tip. I throw open the door. I look at the person standing in front of me. It's definitely not my pizza man. "I have to talk to you," Richard says. I panic and slam the door in his face. Shit. I don't need a confrontation with Richard. I light a cigarette. I barely escaped the last time.

I walk into the bathroom and study my reflection in the mirror. I rest my palms against the sink and take a breath. My left eye begins twitching. There's another knock on the door. "I'll be right there," I call out, pulling at the skin under my eye, "just give me a minute."

I'd better get over there and have it out with him. I'll just play dumb. I'll tell him I have no idea who's been making doctor's appointments and ordering pounds of takeout in his name. And I certainly don't know who left a banana peel in front of his door. I come out of the bathroom; Richard knocks loudly. I throw open the door. I'm right here, shut your pie hole already.

"I have to talk to you," he sternly repeats.

I step out into the hall and close the door behind me. He's not getting into my apartment. Richard takes a step away from me. I can see that he is holding something behind his back. He's got a gun, I just know it. He seemed nervous and jumpy the last time I saw him, and he does not look better now. I should give him Max's address. That's who he should be spraying with bullets. I'm not the one who threw a carton of eggs at his windows at 4 a.m. Okay, so maybe I watched and laughed. That's still not the same thing. "Listen . . . ," he begins to say. How can I listen? I TALK TOO MUCH.

"What is that behind your back?" I interrupt. "I don't need any trouble. What's done is done, Richard."

I grab the doorknob. It feels cold.

"We broke off the engagement," he says. "Noreen and I would never have worked out. She's not the woman I want. I realized that when I saw you that night at the concert."

"You did?" I ask. I let go of the door handle.

He nods. "She's not even the person I thought she was," he says. "She's been crank-calling my apartment, soaking my doormat in water. She even sent me an envelope full of itching powder. I thought it was anthrax and reported it. They quarantined my apartment for three days. And don't even get me started on the pigeons. When it dawned on me that she still had keys to my apartment I changed the locks. But it was too late for some of the damage. I know she was letting herself in. She stole all my forks, rearranged furniture, filled my shampoo bottle with vinegar. I nearly went blind. I should sue her. I just can't prove any of it." He pauses. "I mean what kind of immature person would stoop to that level? This woman spray-painted a penis and balls on my door." Richard looks to me for an answer. I shrug: "How should I know?"

Richard shakes his head: "It's been a horrible few weeks. So many things have gone wrong and it's not just Noreen. I'm starting to feel like I'm going crazy. I think people are spying on me from the bushes, I'm being shadowed by strange bearded men, my neighbors are giving me dirty looks, no one will talk to me. Not too long ago a cop showed up at my door. He said someone complained about my loud music. He said, 'Turn down that U2 album.' I don't even own a U2 album. I looked at him and asked, 'What music, Officer? I'm not playing music.' And then he eyed me suspiciously and said, 'You can't hear that music, sir? It's coming from your apartment.' And I couldn't hear it because there was no music and he looked at me sternly and said if it happens again he's going to issue me a ticket. And then after he left I thought, maybe I am playing music and I just can't hear it. It was very disturbing. I had to go see a psychiatrist after that." He pauses. "I want to get my life back on track, I want to make it work with you this time."

Richard pulls a gorgeous bouquet of flowers tied with a yellow ribbon from behind his back. It's the first bouquet he's ever brought me. He once told me flowers remind him of funerals. "These are for you," he says, holding out the bouquet. I remind him that he doesn't "do" flowers. "I made an exception," he tells me. "They were expensive but you're worth it. Say we can work things out. I never meant the things I said that night at the club . . ."

Richard goes on to explain that he loves everything about me. Noreen, whom he was marrying out of obligation, as a result of family pressures, is boring.

I take the bouquet. Roses, lilies, tulips, freesias . . . I close my eyes and inhale deeply. They smell so nice, so fresh. How did he know I love freesias? I reluctantly open my eyes. Richard smiles. Oh, Richard. I tell him that I'm touched. Richard winks: "Is that a yes?" I nod. It's a yes. Why not? Yes! I tell Richard to come closer so we can kiss. I haven't felt this energized in weeks. I'm so glad he showed up here. This is what I've been missing. I'm sorry I ran from him the last time.

"This is good," he says, leaning in.

"This is great," I admit. I smell the flowers one last time then start beating him over the head with them. "You idiot," I hiss, whipping him with all my strength, "what do you take me for, huh? What do you take me for?" I say, whacking him across the face. "Get your stinking ass out of here and never come back. Bringing me weeds like I give a shit about your tired life and your itching powder. You should be embarrassed, you malformed menace!" I whip him like a dying mule a few more times. I swat him on the back, on the shoulder, near his eyes. And then I start hitting him over the head. Richard is wearing a stupid beret on his head and I give that a few licks as well. What's with everyone wearing dumb hats? First William and his fez and now this. I'm sick of dumb hats! I continue beating him relentlessly. "This one is for Noreen, I know for a fact she broke it off with you," I say. "And this is for the other girls . . ."

Richard is shielding his head with his hands. I whip him across the forehead and his beret falls off. I stop and stare at him in horror. "What happened to your hair?" I ask in disgust. There is a shaved patch running from his forehead to the crown of his head. It's like a reverse Mohawk. The sides have been dyed red and yellow.

Richard picks the beret off the floor and puts it back on his head. "Don't look at it," he grumbles. "I had a misunderstanding at the place where I get my haircut. Some new guy came in, didn't speak English. I hate the French. Now I can't get the dye out. Don't look at it."

I tell him that he should do himself a huge favor and get out of here. Richard mumbles something and starts to walk away. "I hope you enjoy the flowers," he bitterly says and reminds me that they were expensive. He continues down the stairs. It's lonely at the bottom. He points an accusatory finger: "You're a big bitch, you know that?" Bitch, huh? I stand on tiptoes and cup my hand over my mouth. "Fuck you," I call after him. "Nice hair, assbag!" I slam the door.

I am walking toward the couch when, not two minutes later, my front door flies open with a bang. I turn with a start. Richard? A figure with a short white beard, dressed in a blue sailor's suit, like a maritime captain or the Gorton's Fisherman, runs in holding a clear bag full of deflated balloons. It takes me a minute to process it. I lean in. "Max?" I ask. The bearded one pulls down the white beard, which was held in place by a black elastic band. "It's me, Noreen!" Noreen says in her mousy voice. Noreen? Just then another identically dressed maritime captain runs in. He's tall, like William, and thin. Who? The captain pulls down his beard. "Kas!" Henryk says. "Heard about Richard. No one does that to my sister!" My mouth falls open when a third captain comes flying in. I can tell by the way this one is running who he is. "We need to use your sink!" Max says, grabbing the bag from Noreen's hands. He turns on my kitchen faucet and starts filling up balloons. When they swell to the size of volleyballs, he hands them off to Noreen, who collects them in her arms. Henryk pulls a small plastic orange water pistol out of his pocket and fills that up, too. Max looks over his shoulder. "We'll be out of here in a sec!" he says. I ask what they are doing. "We followed Richard here from his house!" he says, filling up more balloons. "We're going to whip water balloons at him right now! We're in a rush!" Well, I should have known he wouldn't stop. And now he's got my brother involved.

In a flash, Max gathers up an armful of balloons and heads for the door. "Love you!" he calls out. "Bye!"

Captain Noreen trails behind with her own booty. "Your friend is so cool!" she gushes. "This was the best breakup I've ever had!" Oh man, she totally wants to be his fag hag.

Henryk waves the pistol in the air and fires off a round of water. "Come join us!" he says. I nod. "By the way," he adds with a little smile, "I'm nearly done with the second novel. It's written from the perspective of a girl, about your age, who gets a surprise visit from a one-night stand. I'm calling it *I'm with Stupid*." I grin. Max hears this and turns. "Go with a female pen name this time," he tells Henryk. "I'm seeing you as an Eileen, or an Elaine. I'll work on it. If you widen your readership I expect a kickback." Henryk fires more water. This is the weirdest group of vigilantes in history, I think as they file out.

I race into the hallway and shout to Max, who is sliding down the banister. Henryk and Noreen are thundering down the stairs two at a time. "Do I even need to ask if you had anything to do with Richard's haircut?"

"Whee whee! Of course I did!" Max answers, jumping off the railing. "This is my last hurrah and then I'm done!"

"I thought you learned your lesson?" I shout.

"I'll learn it tomorrow!" he shouts back. "Today I'm in it to win it!"

The downstairs door slams shut. Libby opens her door. She has green clay smeared on her forehead, cheeks, chin, and nose. Someone's giving herself a facial. She stares at me blankly. "Babe, was that the pizza man?" she asks. "Was he cute? I didn't want to show my face." I shake my head no, not the pizza man. I quickly explain what is happening. She pats her cheeks, hesitates, then says the hell with it. "Let's go see!" she exclaims. Then the phone rings. I tell Libby to hold on and run inside and check the caller ID. It's Newland. I pick up.

"Mouse ears, do you want to have dinner with me tomorrow night?"

I say sure. ButIhavenotimetochatnowsorrygottarun. I slam down the phone and point at the cage. "Don't break anything while I'm gone," I tell the mice.

Libby and I race out of the building. She does pretty well considering she is in four-inch heels the width of pins. We look left, then right. In the middle of the block three maritime captains have Richard up against a building. Each is holding a water balloon. "Apologize for the way you treated me!" Noreen screams. She's in the midst of a bra-burning moment. Richard responds that he has nothing to be sorry for. "Wrong answer!" Max shouts back. The water balloons go flying and Richard gets down on his knees and covers his head. Come to think of it, I've never heard Richard apologize for anything; not even when he canceled plans with me at the last minute (presumably to meet up with his fiancée or some other victim) did he say sorry.

"I want my engagement ring back," I hear Richard say to Noreen. "Don't think you're keeping it after everything you've done to me."

Everything she's done to him?

Libby and I arrive on the scene. The captains stop throwing balloons. Sopping-wet Richard looks up. His beret has again come off. His hair is truly repulsive. That cut and color job should curb his misogyny for at least a while. "Hi Libby!" Noreen says. "Thanks for all the makeup tips. I feel great!" Libby waves. She can't smile because of the clay, which has hardened into a mask. Richard looks confused. He asks if we all know each other. I nod. We do. I tell Henryk to give me that orange water gun. He puts it in my hand. It's a cheap little thing, worth about twenty-five cents. I turn it over and take a step toward Richard.

I slowly raise the gun and take aim between his eyes. "You people are crazy," he moans. Everything around me goes still. I curl my finger around the trigger. Richard cheats, then uses me, then comes to my house and calls me a "big bitch"? I don't think so, pal. Women aren't bitches. An unnecessarily elaborate revenge scheme, however? Now that's one badass bitch.

I snarl at him then pull the trigger, just as he mumbles the word "Sorry." Too late. I fire four times. Squirt Squirt. Squirt Squirt. The water rolls down Richard's nose. A single drop hangs off the tip like snot. Noreen storms over. "And I have your ring right here," she says, pulling it out of her pocket. "I planned to give it back. I'm not a jerk like you." She sticks the ring up Richard's nose, sideways. It expands his nostril to the size of a quarter. Pretty. Richard gets up off his knees and pushes out the ring. He begins walking away. He looks nervously over his shoulder then picks up the pace. Noreen cheers. She gives Max a hug and words of thanks and admits she's never felt better. We wave down a cab for her and she gets in, still talking excitedly.

The cab pulls away and I raise the plastic water gun to my lips. I blow on the barrel to cool it. Better get out of here. I turn, tuck the gun into my jeans, and walk silently back to the apartment. Dating is hard. It really is. Most people are not a fit (see my time with William Johnson for more info), but you try, if only to experience that single flicker out of the darkness, that possibility of a flame. In the event that it burns out fast, well, at least you felt heat. And you know you want to feel heat, so stop showing off like you don't. In the meantime,

there are friends. They got your back. I know mine do. I don't
have to turn to know that right now my friends and brother
are, in various states of disarray, marching close behind.

And then I see a water balloon sail over my head. And then
I feel one hit me. It explodes between my shoulder blades.
Pop! I stop. Fuck that's cold. I whip around.

   Max raises his arms and laughs. "It totally slipped! I'm
sorry!"

   I stand there shaking my head, which is when the three
begin walking toward me. Yup, these are my people. There's
no doubt.

about the author

I'm with Stupid is my first book, and it was written thanks to booze: I began it after returning from a press junket in South Africa sponsored by an alcohol company. I can hear certain members of my family now: *Why tell the people that? Don't talk about booze! It's not nice! Talk about where you came from! Talk about your schooling and career! And make sure to stress that the book is fiction so no one thinks you're loose or that your mother is pushy like the mother in the book!* All right, I'll try not to mention booze again, though what I said is technically true.

I was born in Kraków, Poland, and immigrated to Chicago, Illinois, with my parents, Maria and Stanisław, three months before the country was placed under martial law by the communist government. (Not a good time to be a Polish writer, to understate a point.) I graduated from the University of Illinois at Urbana-Champaign and began my writing career at the *Financial Times*, as an assistant, and currently serve as editor of *Kirkus Reviews*, a book review journal. *I'm with Stupid* is a work of fiction; I am not loose; my own mother is not pushy. She's delicious. And so is my father, and my brother, Robert. But more about that press junket . . .

My friend Patty, at the time working for a men's magazine, had been invited, along with a few other writers, and mentioned that the company was looking for one more person. I called the public relations department at her suggestion, not at all convinced anything would come of it, and the next day stood in my apartment holding round-trip business-class tickets to Africa and an itinerary. I was going to Johannesburg, Cape Town, and on safari—all for free. I had three days to pack.

When the news sank in I began to laugh maniacally like a black-gloved villain who got away with bank robbery, which is how I felt. That evening, while buying travel-size toiletries, I volunteered to clerks and shoppers, in a casual, slightly bored tone like this happens all the time, that I was "off to Africa." I even told a guy at the video store. I might have sighed.

The weeklong trip found Patty and me bonding with two other journalists (conveniently named Elizabeth and Elizabeth, and now my close friends) and exploring the land. There was some official business but mostly we hung out and had fun, giving me ample time to consider scenarios, both real and imagined, that would inform the writing of *I'm with Stupid*, a book in part inspired by South Africa, where I never would have traveled had it not been for booze.

5 items to pick up at a *Polish Deli*

1. Oszczypek

Shaped like a football, oszczypek is a hard, smoked cheese traditionally made from unpasteurized ewes' milk by highlanders living in the Tatra Mountains. At Polish get-togethers, it's usually found next to the vodka bottle.

2. Pączki

Doughnutlike pastries—minus the hole—pączki are filled with marmalade or jam (flavors include plum, raspberry, and strawberry) and topped with icing. They are offered year-round but are especially popular on Fat Thursday (*tłusty czwartek*), before the start of Lent.

3. Kabanos

A long (about one to two feet), finger-thin hunter's sausage that resembles beef jerky, kabanos is made from pork and seasoned with spices, then smoked and air-dried. It's eaten alone or with rye bread.

4. Barszcz

A sweet vegetable soup made from beets and beet root, barszcz, prepared hot or cold, is sometimes served with croquettes or dumplings called *uszka* (the word literally means "little ears"). It's my favorite Polish soup, not that you asked.

5. Opłatek

Part of a centuries-old Roman Catholic Christmas tradition, opłatek is a delicate, rectangular wafer embossed with religious images. Before the start of Christmas dinner, families share pieces of opłatek, offering good wishes for the coming year. (My dad's tidings generally include the words "make a lot of money.")